OVERKILL

NOVELS BY SANDRA BROWN

OVERKILL

SANDRA BROWN

HODDER

First published in the United States of America in 2022 by
Grand Central Publishing
A division of Hachette Book Group, Inc
First published in Great Britain in 2022 by Hodder & Stoughton
An Hachette UK company

This paperback edition published in 2023

1

A CIP catalogue record for this title is
available from the British Library

Paperback ISBN 978 1 529 34178 2
eBook ISBN 978 1 529 34177 5

Printed and bound in Great Britain by Clays Ltd, Elcograf S.p.A.

Hodder & Stoughton policy is to use papers that are natural, renewable
and recyclable products and made from wood grown in sustainable
forests. The logging and manufacturing processes are expected to
conform to the environmental regulations of the country of origin.

Hodder & Stoughton Ltd
Carmelite House
50 Victoria Embankment
London EC4Y 0DZ

www.hodder.co.uk

OVERKILL

Prologue

The blowout was in full swing.

It had gotten off to a comparably moderate start at around ten o'clock. By midnight, boundaries of behavior had begun to wobble under the influence of liquor, controlled substances, and carnality.

By now, in the wee hours, any semblance of civilization had been abandoned. More guests than not had discarded articles of clothing. All had thrown off their inhibitions. Rap pounded from speakers discreetly hidden throughout the stately home, making it seem as though the walls themselves were secreting the cacophony. It thumped through the otherwise decorous Buckhead neighborhood. For hours, that precinct of the Atlanta P.D. had been kept busy taking noise complaint calls.

The host of the bacchanal had issued a blanket invitation. The majority of revelers overflowing his house were strangers to him, including the young woman who'd offered her inner thigh as the surface from which he was snorting a line of cocaine.

For a while now, the two of them had been lounging on a sofa in a relatively private corner, sharing not only a vial of the white powder but also a bottle of vodka. The latter had been the source of numerous phallic innuendos.

If she'd ever told him her name, he was too stoned to remember. When he'd asked her what she did, as in a vocation, she'd replied, "This."

"This?"

"I party."

Perfect. She was here to have a good time, and that happened to be his specialty.

She was a looker. She had dark eyes, which were heavily lined like Cleopatra's. Her hair was black and sleek, worn perfectly straight and long enough to almost reach her oh-so-smokin' ass. Plush breasts were on display above the low, loose neckline of her slinky dress. The fabric was gold and shimmery and so gossamer-sheer that her areolae showed through.

When he'd complimented her on the dress, she'd told him she'd worn it "on the red carpet," but he didn't know which red carpet, and didn't care. From his vantage point as he sniffed the remaining cocaine, he enjoyed the view beneath her short skirt all the way up.

This girl had a spirit of adventure and no modesty.

He inhaled deeply, then sat up, flung his head back, and shouted an obscenity toward the ceiling to express his ecstasy.

She giggled and took a drink from the bottle of vodka as she slid her bare foot up his thigh, stopping just short of her toes touching his crotch. "While you were down there, did you peek?"

"What do you think?" He grinned. "I'm a naughty boy."

"Naughty boys are just my thing."

"Are they?"

She raised her pair of perfectly shaped brows.

He laughed. "Then you're going to love us."

He looked around for his two best friends and spotted them across the room at the food buffet, which looked like it had been plundered by a wolf pack. A naked girl was curled up asleep on a bed of lettuce where chilled shrimp had been earlier. His friends were garnishing her slumbering form with leftover slices of citrus.

"Come with me," he said, taking Cleopatra's hand.

She resisted. Reclining against the sofa cushions, she raised one knee and swayed it back and forth as she whined, "What's wrong with right here?"

"Too public." He hauled her up and caught her around the waist when she swayed against him.

As they walked toward the buffet table, she looked over her shoulder. "I left my sandals."

"They'll be fine. I want you to meet my friends." When they reached the table, he said, "Boys, we're going upstairs for some grown-up fun and games. Wanna come?" He laughed. "No pun intended."

With glazed eyes, the two looked Cleopatra over. The tall blond, who had a drowsy smile that women found irresistible, drawled, "Sure."

The other looked down at the girl sleeping among the lettuce. "What about her?"

"You can come back for her later," the host said. "If you have the energy."

"You won't," Cleopatra purred, tiptoeing her fingers up his sleeve. "I can go all night."

"My kind of girl," said the handsome blond.

She gave him the look most women did, like she wanted to lick him all over. "We're gonna have fun."

The host felt a pang of jealousy, but another line of coke and a swig of vodka would take care of it. He would be the one Cleopatra remembered from tonight, not his irresistible buddy.

"I left the coke on the table over there. Go get it and her sandals," he said to the third man. "We'll take the elevator. I don't trust any of us trying to climb the stairs."

The cocaine and gold sandals were retrieved. The quartet threaded their way through other guests who were either already passed out or engaged in their own debauchery.

The elevator was situated beneath the sweeping staircase and was for the private use of the homeowner. It was built seamlessly and invisibly into the paneling. It was small. The four of them crowded in, which required sandwiching Cleopatra's curvy body between the host and the blond. The third wrapped them in a group hug.

The ride to the second floor was brief. They piled out of the elevator and staggered their way down the wide hallway to the bedroom. The host went in first, then bowed at the waist and gestured them all in with a wide sweep of his arm. He shut the door and locked it.

He turned Cleopatra to face him and, smiling, said, "Our games have only one rule. I call the shots."

She slid the skinny straps of her dress off her shoulders and let it slither down her body to the floor, then walked naked across the room and stretched out on the bed, arms extended above her head. "Fire away."

Chapter 1

———◦◉◦———

Zach Bridger's life was upended while in the Cayman Islands, sitting at the pool bar, sipping a cold beer, and chillin' to Buffett's "Cheeseburger in Paradise."

It was only eight-thirty in the morning, but his date-of-the-week had wanted to claim an ideal spot for sunbathing the day away, so she'd dragged him out of bed early. Other guests at the swanky resort must've been of the same mind. A line had formed for the breakfast buffet at the open-air restaurant, and the bar itself was doing a lively business.

"Isn't that your ex?"

Zach, who'd been enjoying the array of lubricated female flesh around the swimming pool, turned toward the bartender, who hitched his goatee up toward the TV, where a photo of Rebecca dominated the upper right-hand corner of the screen behind the anchorwoman's shoulder.

An indifferent grunt was Zach's response to both the

bartender's question and the picture. He couldn't attach the word "wife" to the woman beguiling the camera with her sloe eyes. It escaped him how he could have pledged his everlasting love, honor, and fidelity to her. Neither of them had kept the vows. He had, however, endowed Rebecca with a helluva lot of his worldly goods.

He said, "Best years of my life have been the five since our divorce."

"Hear ya." The bartender gave him a kindred grin. "It's been three since mine." He reached for Zach's plastic glass and topped it off from the beer tap, then glanced over his shoulder at the TV, which now featured another picture of Rebecca. "Recently she's been hanging with a hockey player. One of those without any vowels in his name."

"Pity the poor bastard," Zach said.

The bartender chuckled. "I think they've split."

"I don't keep up."

Zach hadn't seen Rebecca in the flesh since she'd flounced out of the divorce court. She'd left through the front entrance to endear herself to the paparazzi waiting there, while his lawyer had sneaked him out through a rear exit to avoid them.

Occasionally, by accident, he'd catch a mention of her on one of those hyperactive, celeb-tracking shows. She was usually featured as a gorgeous accessory draped over the arm of a guy who was trending on social media.

The bartender wiped up a spill. "You must've whetted her appetite for professional athletes."

Zach saluted the bartender with his fresh beer.

"We're supposed to be cool with celebrity guests. Not

make a big deal, you know. But I have to tell you, I'm a huge fan."

"Gotta pen?"

"Uh, yeah, sure." The bartender produced a ballpoint. Zach pulled a cocktail napkin from the holder on the bar and scrawled his autograph on it.

With sleight of hand, the bartender pocketed the signed napkin. "Thanks, man."

"No problem.

Zach was tipping the glass of beer toward his mouth when he saw that the images on the TV had changed. Now live video was being transmitted from either a drone or a helicopter as it circled above what appeared to be a sprawling private estate, currently encircled by police cars and emergency vehicles. Rebecca's name still appeared in the bulletin scrolling across the bottom of the screen.

Zach set down his beer and slid his sunglasses onto the top of his head. "Turn up the sound, please."

The bartender did as requested, upping the volume enough for the anchorwoman to be heard above "Good Vibrations."

She was saying, "Authorities have told us that the nine-one-one call came in at three-oh-eight this morning, but the caller has yet to be identified."

Zach and the bartender exchanged a look. Zach got up from his barstool and moved around behind the bar in order to better see and hear.

"First responders arrived at the Clarke mansion within thirteen minutes of the nine-one-one and found Rebecca Pratt in an upstairs guest bedroom. We don't have details yet, but her condition has been described as unresponsive. She was taken to Emory University Hospital, but there's been no word on either the cause or seriousness of her condition.

"Investigators are at the scene, questioning everyone who was attending the party at the lavish home. It's estimated there were between forty and sixty guests. Police report that illegal drugs and drug paraphernalia were found in various rooms of the mansion. Foul play has not been ruled out.

"Rebecca Pratt, often seen on red carpets with high-profile personalities, has remained single since her bitter divorce in 2017 from Super Bowl MVP quarterback Zach Bridger, who as yet has been unavailable for comment. We'll bring you updates on this breaking story as we get them. Now, we'll turn to the political brouhaha being raised in Washington over comments made by—"

Zach took the remote from the bartender and clicked off the audio. The Beach Boys had given way to Lionel Richie's "All Night Long," but nearby activity had been suspended and conversations had ceased.

Zach became aware that he had the undivided attention of everyone in the immediate area.

He came out from behind the bar, replaced his sunglasses on the bridge of his nose, and avoided making direct eye contact with anyone. He and Rebecca had walked away from their brief but tumultuous marriage without looking back. But it seemed that nobody else was willing to let it go.

She'd reverted to using her maiden name, but their names were still linked, and rarely was one of them mentioned in the media without a reference being made to the other, like it or not. He didn't like it. In fact, he hated it like hell because her current reputation was an ongoing embarrassment to him. But there it was: the price of fame.

Even though he had to dig deep to find any emotion beyond indifference toward her, he had never wished her ill. "Unresponsive" didn't sound good at all. He wandered back toward the pool, trying to remember where he'd deposited his date-of-the-week, trying to remember her name.

He finally spotted her chatting up a slender, hairless Euro type in a Speedo, who was half reclined on the chaise next to hers, which Zach had vacated not twenty minutes earlier.

As he wended his way around other sunbathers toward them, his cell phone rang. He was often razzed about never being without it. It was an extension of his hand.

Recognizing an Atlanta area code, he figured it was a news outlet who'd bribed his number out of somebody. Likely they would want a sound bite from him regarding Rebecca and what was certain to be today's lead story.

In his mind, he formed something appropriate to say, something to which no one could take exception, something conveying concern but disconnection. He thumbed on his phone.

"This is Zach."

Within thirty seconds, he wished he'd never answered that call.

It took him almost twelve hours to get from the hotel swimming pool on Grand Cayman to the hospital in Atlanta.

He didn't feel too bad about abandoning his date; she and the Speedo seemed to be hitting it off. He told her to enjoy the rest of her stay and to charge everything to his credit card the hotel had on file. He tipped the concierge three hundred bucks to get him a seat on the next flight to the States and to book ground transportation at both ends.

The car that had been arranged to meet him at ATL was an innocuous black sedan. After the mandatory greeting, the driver, who'd already been told which building of the medical complex where Zach was to be dropped, sensed his passenger's disinclination to chat during the drive from the airport.

Zach had braced himself for a chaotic scene, but there was even more pandemonium than he'd anticipated. It was escalated by his arrival. As soon as he was seen getting out of the car, the media throng waiting outside the main entrance converged on him with the impetus of a tidal wave, or more like a school of sharks that had smelled fresh blood.

"Zach, when did you hear?"

"Was it a drug overdose?"

"Was she depressed over her recent breakup with—"

The female reporter shouted a name that sounded foreign and like it didn't have any vowels. Zach kept his head down and didn't even deign to say "no comment" to the barrage of questions. He plowed through the reporters and videographers until, through the glass doors of the entrance, he spotted Bing.

Ned "Bing" Bingham had coached him at Clemson. The bond they'd forged there had grown even stronger when

Zach went pro. Now retired, Bing was still his go-to person whenever the shit hit the fan.

He saw Bing bark an order to the uniformed men guarding the door. Like most people did when Bing barked an order, the officers hopped to. They opened the door for Zach and he squeezed through, leaving the news throng outside disappointed, but all the more frenzied.

His showing up here had added considerable spice to the story, catapulted it into the stratosphere of the sensational. Ordinarily he took the media's insatiable appetite for buzz in stride. But these circumstances weren't ordinary, and he resented like hell the intrusion, not only into his privacy, but into that of Rebecca and her parents.

He thanked the officers who'd allowed him in, then went over to his friend and mentor. "You're a welcome sight, Bing."

"Not you. You look like hell."

"Feel like it. An administrator of something or other here at the hospital called, said I had to get here ASAP."

Bing nodded glumly. "Fourth floor."

He motioned Zach toward the bank of elevators. As they strode across the lobby, Zach was aware of people blatantly holding up their phones, cameras trained on him. Every move, every expression, anything he said or did would be orbiting in cyberspace within seconds.

He and Bing got into the elevator alone. When the doors closed, he said, "Thanks for coming."

Bing frowned, although his face was so leathered and creased, it was hard to distinguish one expression from another. "I texted you to expect me."

"I saw, but my phone was blowing up, so I stopped even looking. I'm damn glad you're here."

"You're in a shit show. Where else would I be?"

His familiar gruffness was comforting. "Do you know what happened?"

Bing shook his head. "Either nobody knows yet, or they aren't saying."

"Who's Clarke?"

"Eban, son of Sid. Bigwig locally. Big rich on anybody's list. Eban was with Rebecca in that bedroom when she lost consciousness."

"News labeled her unresponsive."

Bing shot him a bleak look. "While waiting on you to get here, I got those cops guarding the door to talking. Some of them had talked to the EMTs who brought her in. What they said was, her heart's still beating."

Zach said nothing, waiting in dread of hearing the rest.

Bing sighed. "But it looked to them like all the lights upstairs had gone out for good."

Zach covered his mouth with his hand. "Jesus."

"Yeah."

Zach looked at the lighted panel beside the elevator door. They were passing the third floor, so he spoke with urgency. "The administrator who called me referred to a document."

"Medical Power of Attorney."

"Rebecca and I divorced five years ago. That should have automatically canceled it. How's it still valid?"

"I don't know, Zach, but her daddy has a copy of it, and he's waving it around and frothing at the mouth."

The elevator began to slow. Zach said quickly, "Boil it down for me."

Bing looked at him with pity. "Boiled down, the decision of whether or not to take Rebecca off life support falls to you."

Chapter 2

———◦◉◦———

Four years later . . .

This morning, Zach's view of the waterfall was spectacular.

After one of the wettest North Carolinian summers on record, the falls were gushing an enormous amount of water down the rocky mountainside into the river two hundred fifty feet below. Sunlight shining through the overspray created a rainbow.

He stood on the very edge of the cliff, staring out across the wide chasm between him and the falls. Overnight, a storm had brought with it heavy rain. The ground beneath the multilayered, multicolored carpet of recently fallen leaves was so saturated it squished beneath the soles of his hiking boots.

But the weather front had moved on east, leaving the sky a crystal-clear blue. The air was crisp and chilly. He smelled woodsmoke and spotted a wisp of it curling up out of a chimney on the opposite side of the gorge. A dense forest of dark evergreens blanketed the mountainside. Hardwoods at their autumn peak added vibrant splashes of color.

Sensory overload.

Cruelly reminding him that it was football season.

His decline as a player had started four years ago with that fateful telephone call about Rebecca. Two years later, he'd hit rock bottom and had gotten booted from the sport entirely. The bite of regret was still sharp.

He cursed into the coffee mug he raised to his mouth. Steam rising from it momentarily blurred his view, but the distant roar of the waterfall didn't drown out the sound of an approaching vehicle.

An SUV pulled to a stop just beyond the stacked river rock pillars flanking his front walkway. For the curving, climbing roads in this mountainous region, nearly every-body who lived around here owned some model of utility vehicle.

But this one wasn't standard issue. It was new and sported an optional matte black grille and matching wheels. They screamed *Watch out. I'm a badass.*

Zach gave a snuffle of disdain for such an obvious attempt to intimidate him. He'd spent three-quarters of his life averting defensive players who had one steely purpose: to put the quarterback out of commission. He hadn't been easy to sack. He still wasn't. Whoever this hustler was, no matter how glib the sales pitch, his answer would still be no.

She got out. *She.*

The first three envoys dispatched by GreenRidge Incor-porated had been good-ol'-boy, favorite uncle types who'd waxed nostalgic about Zach's glory days on the gridiron.

When the folksy approach failed, they'd sent a cool dude in a sports car and aviator sunglasses, oozing expensive fragrance and bullshit in equal portions.

The next had been a fifty-something, maternal type who offered to make him pot roast on Sunday. Then an attractive divorcée who was trying to make it on her own with two kids to put through college and an ex always late on child support checks. Her blatant appeal to Zach's softer side failed.

She'd been followed by a babe. He suspected she was being paid by the hour rather than working on commission, because her none too subtle body language had telegraphed *Sign on the dotted line and I'm yours for the asking*. He'd turned down both the contract and her favors.

And now here came the babe's successor. Her arrival was spoiling his peaceful morning, but he was curious to see what tack this one would take. He set his coffee mug on the tree stump he'd created for just that purpose and folded his arms across his chest.

She came around the hood of her SUV and smiled at him. "Mr. Bridger? Zachary Bridger? Good morning."

"It's not for sale."

Even now with the rock pillars, she drew up short between them and shook her head slightly. "Pardon me?"

"It's not for sale. So you'd just as well leave before you get permanently stuck." He gestured toward her feet where the heels of her stilettos had sunk into the waterlogged strip of ground between the paving stones.

She didn't seem particularly troubled by her predicament. Nor was she deterred. She pulled first one heel out of the mud, then the other, and proceeded on tiptoe, which had to have been difficult, considering the height of the heels.

They didn't contribute all that much to her stature, however. When she reached him, she had to tilt her head far back in order to look into his face. People usually did. But she had to tip her head back at a steeper angle than most.

"Mr. Bridger, my name is Kate Lennon."

She handed him a business card. He took it from her but didn't bother to look at it before slipping it into the pocket of his flannel shirt. He also ignored the right hand she extended for him to shake.

"When are you people going to give up?" He gestured broadly at the vista. "Why would I want to leave this?"

She pulled her hand back and took in the panorama, spending several seconds on the waterfall alone before coming back to him. "I can't imagine that you would. It's breathtaking."

"Right. More importantly, it's mine, and it will stay mine till the day I die. Got that?"

If her recoil was any indication, she had. Good. Point made.

But her reaction also made him feel like he'd slapped a fairy. The pixie haircut, heart-shaped face, and all. And the constant whoosh of the waterfall was no excuse for his raised voice. Not entirely anyway. "Look, I don't want to be rude, but—"

"But you are. Being rude, that is." She plucked a sealed gray envelope from her oversize shoulder bag. "Personally, I take no offense, but, under the circumstances, your rudeness is grossly misplaced."

She pushed the envelope at him with the snapping precision of a Pro Bowl center. He caught it against his chest to prevent a fumble.

She said, "The envelope contains several documents, but of particular importance is—"

"I've seen them."

"Yes, but it's been a while."

"I've got a good memory."

"Excellent. It will serve—"

He ripped the envelope in two, documents and all, and dropped the halves to the ground.

Slowly she lowered her head and looked down at them, and then with the same lack of haste raised her head and met his unyielding gaze with her own.

And he'd thought the sky was crystal clear blue.

She said, "Tomorrow morning at ten o'clock."

He shifted his feet into a wider, more assertive stance, which was wasted because she'd already turned her back on him. "Tomorrow at ten, *what?*"

"We'll meet. The location is handwritten on the back of my business card. Room two-oh-three."

"Don't hold your breath."

He wanted to add one more line, something with a bit more of a sting, but he was distracted by her calf muscles, which were well defined and strong enough to keep her balanced as she covered the distance back to her SUV on tiptoe.

And he looked at her butt. PC or no PC, he still had a pair, and they worked.

He waited until she'd made a sharp U-turn and headed

out of his cul-de-sac before picking up the halves of the envelope and taking them with him as he returned to the house.

Curiosity kept him from immediately trashing them. Instead, he tossed them onto the kitchen island, poured himself a refill of coffee, and sat down on the counter stool he always sat in. No one except Bing had ever sat in any of the other three.

He took a sip of his fresh coffee, then pulled the contents from the two pieces of the envelope. The official-looking pages had been stapled together, but the cover letter was separate. He lined up the two ripped edges of it. Without first reading the text, he glanced down at the signature. *Kate Lennon* had been signed in black ink below a typed *Sincerely, Kathryn Cartwright Lennon.*

"Well, Kate Lennon, what terms are you hawking?"

That's when he noticed the letterhead.

The courthouse in the city square was old-school and imposing for a mostly rural, sparsely populated county in western North Carolina in the shadow of the Blue Ridge. The edifice was constructed of red brick and had four white columns supporting a pediment above the entrance.

However, that wasn't where Kathryn Lennon had instructed him to meet with her. The address she'd handwritten was directly across the street from the courthouse. It was as ugly a building as Zach had ever seen.

Its two floors seemed to have been squashed to fit between its flat roof and the sidewalk. There was no facade to speak of, only a row of windows extending from either side of a glass door with gold letters designating it as the Office of the District Attorney.

Inside, it smelled like all old government buildings: musty, metallic, and moldy. Zach took the stairs two at a time. The long hallway leading off the landing was floored with worn carpet that silenced his footfalls as he approached room 203. The door stood ajar. He rolled his shoulders, popped his neck, and knocked.

"Come in."

He pushed open the door but remained on the threshold. The office was small and as unattractive as the rest of the building, but it smelled better. A fragrance candle flickered on the windowsill behind the desk setup.

Kate Lennon turned away from the computer on the ell and swiveled her chair around to face the main desk. And him.

She looked much the same as she had yesterday. Short, platinum hair that was feathered on the crown of her head, smooth by the time it reached her cheeks. Small stud earrings. A no-nonsense watch on her left wrist, one slender bracelet on her right. Tailored suit jacket, navy blue, near military in cut, with a double row of brass buttons marching down the front.

He couldn't see below the level of her desk, but he'd bet the bottom half of her suit hugged like yesterday's pencil skirt, and that she'd be wearing another pair of high heels that made a statement as bold as the grille on her SUV.

New today was a pair of eyeglasses with red frames, which she removed and placed on her desk as she said coolly, "Good morning, Mr. Bridger. Thank you for being punctual."

"Not a problem. I couldn't wait to get here."

"Please close the door and have a seat."

He went in, pushed the door shut with more emphasis than necessary, and sat down in the chair facing her desk. In the process, he loudly bumped his knee on the modesty panel. Embarrassed, but not wanting her to know it, he feigned annoyance and made a big deal of scooting his chair back several inches to accommodate his long legs.

In case she hadn't guessed by now, he was pissed.

She said, "I would offer you coffee, but the sludge they brew in the snack room is dreadful and—"

"No thanks."

"Water? I have—"

"No thanks."

She clasped her hands on the desktop and bowed her head as though praying for patience or counting to ten. When she looked up, she said, "Did you review the document?"

"Yes, ma'am. I found a roll of tape in a junk drawer, pieced it back together. It wasn't what I expected."

"What did you expect?"

"Land survey, property plat, topographical chart. Like that."

"I don't understand."

"You wouldn't. We can skip that part. It has no bearing."

"All right," she said. "I highlighted specific sections, which—"

"Neon yellow. Couldn't miss 'em."

"—I need to discuss with you. Did you reacquaint your-self with them?"

"I already knew what they said." He reached into the

front pocket of his blazer and took out the torn sheets that he'd reattached with tape. He set them on her desk and pushed them toward her in a gesture of dismissal. "I can't think of a single reason why you'd come to my house and shove this in my face."

"That's a copy of an advance directive, Mr. Bridger. Signed by the principal and two witnesses."

"I don't care if it's etched in stone, it's no longer important."

"I assure you it is."

"I assure you it isn't. It hasn't been for years. Four to be exact."

"I wouldn't have contacted you if it wasn't still valid and very important. The points of the document—"

"No need to remind me what they are. Doug Pratt already did. He announced the points of the document to everybody in the whole freakin' universe. It was quite a scene, played out right there in the hospital corridor. A dozen people captured it with their cell phone cameras and sold them to the highest bidder. I'm sure you saw those videos."

She didn't respond, but he could tell by her almost guilty expression that she was well aware of his confrontations with Rebecca's father. All were blistering, but the first was fiery enough.

Doug must have been notified of his arrival at the hospital, because he was waiting on the fourth floor at the elevator. Before the door was fully opened, he launched, wrathful and emphatic, accusatory and argumentative, even before Zach had learned the gruesome particulars of the situation or Rebecca's condition.

The videos taken by bystanders had been televised and circulated countless times on every platform of media. They continued to live on and could last for-fucking-ever.

Now, rocking slightly in his seat in an effort to curb his anger, he said, "I left Rebecca's fate with her parents, where to my mind it belonged in the first place. Whatever it is that makes this your business, Ms. Lennon, you need to be taking it up with Pratt."

She hesitated, then slid the pages of the document back across the desk and placed her hand palm down to anchor them there directly in front of him.

"The original document is in order and the specifications in it remain in effect, Mr. Bridger. It was instated in November—"

"November of nine years ago, going on ten." Feeling claustrophobic in the cramped space, he pushed his chair back and stood up. "Months—you could almost count it in days—after that..." He pointed down at the sheets. "What did you call it?"

"An advance directive. In this case, a Medical Power of Attorney."

"Right. Practically before the ink had dried on it, Rebecca and I split. We *divorced*. We were no longer married. No longer anything."

"That doesn't matter, Mr. Bridger. In the state in which it was drawn, your divorce would have automatically revoked this, your will, and all other advance directives unless *otherwise specified*." She paused for emphasis.

"Rebecca Pratt Bridger wrote a proviso, as the MPOA allows, stating that she wished you to remain her primary agent even if you should divorce. She didn't name an alternate agent. She entrusted you, solely, with control over her health care and end-of-life decisions in the event that she became incapable of making those decisions for herself."

He dismissed that with a sound of disgust. "Don't be misled. Trust had nothing to do with it. Or sentiment. Or affection. Rebecca didn't do anything that wasn't self-serving. By writing that proviso, as you call it, *she* was seizing control over *me*, not the other way around."

He walked a tight circle and wound up facing the wall. He raked his fingers through his hair, then placed his hands on his hips and, head bent low, took several deep, stabilizing breaths.

He'd thought he was done with this, thought that it had been resolved with him more or less at peace with Rebecca's parents and with himself. But every now and then, a reminder of it would crop up, and it never failed to affect him as gut-wrenchingly as he'd been affected four years ago when confronted with a choice that would have bedeviled Solomon.

Ms. Kate Lennon earned points for allowing him the time he needed to grapple with the fact that the worst, most pivotal days of his life had been conjured.

Memories of them lurked in a deep, dark rabbit hole of his subconscious. He tried to avoid it, because whenever he went down into it too far, it was a struggle for him to climb out. He'd spent every day of the past four years trying. He would make headway, then something, or someone like this angel-faced herald of Hell, would pull him back into the abyss. He had to make her see reason.

He turned around to face her. "Ms. Lennon, what you don't seem to understand is that Rebecca and I had a bitter breakup. Before all was said and done, we couldn't stand the sight of each other. We wanted nothing to do with each other. Nothing. Especially not…" He indicated the POA again. "Neither of us would have entrusted such important decisions to the other."

"Then you should have had superseding documents instated."

"I did. Immediately after filing for divorce."

"But Rebecca didn't."

"Through our attorneys, I kept reminding her to."

"To no avail, it seems."

"She signed the divorce papers quick enough, though. She had a boyfriend waiting in the wings. Not that I cared. I just wanted out, so I paid what her dragon of a divorce lawyer demanded. Not over time, either. I didn't want to drag the thing out, so I paid her in one lump sum, and was done with it.

"After that, we had zero contact. Zero. Zilch." He paused and looked aside briefly before coming back to her. "Not until five years later when I was on vacation in the Caymans and was suddenly summoned to Atlanta and confronted with a dire responsibility that I didn't want, and knew damn well that Rebecca wouldn't want me to have, regardless of what she'd *specified otherwise*, which, at the time she did it, was out of sheer spite.

"You know what happened when I arrived at the hospital. Her father's very public rebuke of me said it all, don't you think? 'God, and only God, will call Rebecca home when it's her time, not you.'"

He stopped and took a breath. "Her prognosis was as bad as it could be. Tragic. Despite the recommendations of every doctor who examined and analyzed her, I went by that," he said, again indicating the document, "as her parents insisted that I do. Then I gladly left the rest of the decisions up to them."

Kate Lennon inhaled deeply and held her breath for several seconds before exhaling. She patted the document. "This can't be revoked verbally, Mr. Bridger. If you were willing to relinquish your responsibility and resign as Rebecca's agent of record, you and her parents should have filed a petition with the court that would have legally transferred her guardianship to them."

"I wouldn't have contested it, but things were crazy, nuts, and going to court, all that, was unnecessary because I didn't buck her family's wishes."

"Then this document remains in effect."

"Okay, but I just told you that the Pratts and I came to an understanding. So what's the problem?"

She stood up behind her desk, as though about to make a pronouncement. "There's been a development, of which Mr. Pratt has been made aware. I wanted to tell you in person."

"Why?"

"Because you may wish to reverse the decision you made four years ago. You may decide that taking Rebecca off life support is in her best interest after all."

Chapter 3

———◦◉◦———

At her suggestion they walked across the square to a cutesy coffee shop called Wholly Ground. Zach had noticed it, but it wasn't his kind of place, so he'd never been inside. She ordered something with decaf, skim milk, and vanilla flavoring. He, regular black coffee.

Other customers included a pair of seniors who were working a crossword puzzle together, a trio of women in workout clothes, and a scattering of young people with earbuds and laptops who were probably students at the community college.

Kate Lennon fit right in, but he felt conspicuous in the small-scale environs. Though thank God he wasn't recognized. He was in no mood to sign an autograph, or pose with a stranger taking a selfie, or answer questions about what he was up to these days.

At the moment, he wanted to know what Kate Lennon was up to.

She insisted on paying, and he let her. As she passed him his lidded cup, she asked if he minded sitting outside. He nodded and motioned for her to lead the way. They went through a door that opened onto a patio paved with mossy bricks and enclosed by ivy-covered walls. No one else was out there.

"We won't be overheard out here," she said as they seated themselves at a wrought-iron table smaller than most pizzas.

As he sat down, his spindly chair rocked on the uneven bricks. "We wouldn't have been overheard in your office."

She set her shoulder bag down beside her chair, near her feet, which were shod, as expected, in high-heeled pumps. The bottom half of her suit wasn't another slim skirt, but a pair of narrow slacks that fit her compact figure just as well.

"I thought you might appreciate some fresh air." She took the plastic lid off her coffee drink, blew on it, and took a sip, leaving a mustache of foam on her upper lip. Unselfconsciously, she licked it off.

That drew his attention, but the distraction lasted for only a few seconds. "The air feels good all right," he said, "but what I want is for you to get that power of attorney nullified once and for all. We'll file that petition you talked about. I'm sure you'll get no objection from Doug and Mary, who'll be happy to make their guardianship of Rebecca official."

She tilted her head and looked at him with puzzlement. "You don't know? Mary Pratt passed away."

That was like taking a clip on the chin. "Mary died? When?"

"Just a few months ago. April."

"Nobody told me. What was the cause?"

"Her obituary reads 'after an extended illness,' but doesn't specify what the illness was or how extended."

He turned his head aside and processed that, his regret over not being told surprising him.

Sensing his thoughts, she said, "Mr. Pratt should have notified you as a courtesy."

"I guess he figured he didn't owe me the courtesy. So he's on his own now, seeing to things?" Seeing to Rebecca was what he meant.

"I gather so, yes."

He picked up his coffee and removed the lid, but set it back down without drinking from it. "Four years is a long time for a loved one to be in the shape Rebecca is. Has Doug rethought his stance?"

"When I spoke to him, he gave me no indication that he'd had a change of heart."

Zach breathed a little easier. As long as Doug maintained his adamant position, Zach wasn't obligated to make the ultimate decision.

But he still didn't have an explanation for this meeting. "If things are status quo, why'd you bother me with this? What's it got to do with the DA's office?"

"I'm getting to that."

"Please." Hoping the unstable chair would hold him, he leaned against its slatted back and assumed an aspect of listening.

"Before coming to see you," she said, "I searched for anything that would have revoked that MPOA. You never received a notification of its revocation?"

"No."

"Rebecca instated a new will after your divorce, naming her parents as her beneficiaries."

"Oh, I know about the new will. Doug threw it up at me during one of his public tirades. He said he and Mary wouldn't cut Rebecca's life short just so they could 'cash in.'"

"Rebecca changed only her will and nothing else. I find that odd."

"Not me," he said. "She would have made damn sure I never got back a red cent of her hefty divorce settlement."

Realizing how harsh that sounded, he sighed. "Look, I don't want to talk bad about her. What kind of shit would that make me? I'm just being up front with you, putting things into context so you'll better understand where I'm coming from."

"I do understand, and I appreciate your candor."

"It was no picnic for her being married to me, either. Believe me."

"I'm not here to make judgments about either of you or your marriage."

"Marriage is a very loose term for what we had. We were only married for ten months before filing for divorce, and the final three months was one battle royal after another."

He took his first sip of coffee, now cold. "Why'd you come to me? Why now? You must have thought something was off kilter with that damn document, or else why were you looking for something that had revoked it?"

"I thought that perhaps you were either unaware of its permanence, or had forgotten it, but that whatever the case, having to address the issue again would be upsetting to you."

"Yeah, no shit. It didn't help that your approach was to shock and awe."

Storm clouds formed in the clear blue eyes. "My *planned* approach was to be considerate, even sympathetic, toward you. But you acted like a complete ass. I had hoped that by this morning you would have reined in the bad attitude. You haven't.

"So here we are, Mr. Bridger, undeclared adversaries, when what I had intended was for us to help each other navigate our way through a provocative, controversial, combustible, and emotionally fraught situation."

He'd been a challenge to some of the best tacklers in football history, but she'd left him nowhere to scramble. He'd been taken to the turf by a sprite.

He held her vexed stare, and when she didn't back down, he said, "Where'd the Cartwright come from?" At her surprised look, he said, "Your full name was on your cover letter. Maiden name?"

"Middle."

"Middle?"

"As it appears on my birth certificate."

"What's wrong with Sue, or Beth, or Jane?"

She gave a half smile. "Nothing at all. They're perfectly lovely names."

"For girl babies. Cartwright, on the other hand..."

"I was named after my maternal grandfather."

'Huh. Was he a lawyer, too?"

"Judge."

"Huh." He took another sip of his coffee, then set down his cup with exaggerated care. "In my defense, yesterday when I acted like a complete ass, I didn't know what was in that envelope you pushed on me. I mistook you for fresh bait."

"Fresh bait?"

He waved that off. "It doesn't relate to this."

"The property plats and topographical charts?"

Seeing no reason not to explain, he shrugged. "The company that's developing the other side of the mountain is after my side, too."

"It has a coveted view."

"They won't take no for an answer."

"They're thinking that every man has his price."

He placed the pads of his fingers around the rim of his coffee cup and gave it a few quarter turns. "We're talking about something else to avoid the subject, aren't we?"

"Yes. We are." She arched her back slightly as she took a breath, then relaxed it.

The motion called his attention to the two brass buttons that formed the third row on her jacket. The topographical charting that instantly sprang to mind wasn't that of his mountain.

"Under the circumstances," she said, "you get a pass for your rudeness."

"Thanks." He made out like he hadn't been looking at her chest. "From here on, I'll try not to act like a complete ass, and confine myself to acting like a regular ass."

Giving another half smile, she tipped her head down and fiddled with the stud in her ear, a small gold sphere. With any other woman, one could read coyness in the action. But with her, it was just a moment taken to pull her thoughts back on track. When she looked over at him again, she was all business.

"Let's start with the provenance of the MPOA. What prompted it?"

"Is it important?"

"It could be."

"For this thing we're going to get to? At some point. In the not too distant future. I hope."

"That sounded like a complete ass."

He gave a short laugh then stacked his forearms on the table and leaned on it, hoping the thing wouldn't tip over. "You know I played pro football?"

She gave him a look.

"Okay. We were playing an away game in Detroit. In the second quarter, our safety, Chadwick, hell of a guy, hell of a talent, collided with a running back on the other team. Both were going full throttle, because the back was charging toward the end zone, and Chadwick was our last hope of preventing a TD. Anyway, when they hit, Chadwick's spine snapped. You could hear it from the sidelines. He's living out his days as a paraplegic."

She murmured an unintelligible word that conveyed remorse.

"Flight home seemed to take forever. When I got to the house, I woke Rebecca up, told her we had to talk. She was sleeping off half a bottle of vodka. Pills, too, I suspect. She was cranky, said she didn't want to talk, couldn't it wait till morning. I said no.

"I told her we were going to see an attorney without delay, 'Tomorrow,' I said. She asked why. I told her we needed to get advance directives in place. I didn't know the term then, but that's what I meant."

He looked into his coffee. "Football is a contact sport. You zig when you should have zagged, and it's kaput for you. End of career, end of life as you know it, or end of life, period. With every snap of the ball, the risk is there.

"But you're taking a much greater risk when you get in your car to make a milk run. Or, hell, when you step into your shower." He paused, expecting her to take issue with his rationalization. When she didn't, he continued.

"I'll admit that what happened to Chadwick shook me. It happened quicker than a blink, but it was a life-changing blink, and no going back. It didn't change my mind about playing, but it made me think of what I would want to happen if I suffered a head injury that left me totally incapacitated. Or unresponsive.

"I wanted those directives in place, but I sure as hell wasn't going to leave the decisions up to Rebecca, who had a hard time deciding what color to paint her toenails. I asked my old coach Bing Bingham to be my primary agent. And my sports agent to be the alternate."

"Rebecca didn't take offense at your choices?"

"She didn't know. She didn't care. Our marriage was already shaky."

Kate Lennon raised an eyebrow. "Earthquakes are shaky."

He gave a wry laugh. "True. Ours was the Big Bang of breakups." He squinted one eye and looked her over. "Are you even old enough to remember?"

"I was in college when you won the Super Bowl. Law books didn't hold a candle against the latest issue of *People*."

Groaning, he dragged his hands down his face.

"Sexiest Man Alive," she said and clicked her tongue.

"I was way down on the list of contenders. Number forty-two, I think."

"Actually you were fifth runner-up, and the competition was fierce that year."

He gave a huff and a half grin, but actually found little humor in it. For all the razzle-dazzle that had enveloped him during that period, his personal life had been a public train wreck, at which everybody rubbernecked. It was hard to smile about any aspect of that short-term but extremely volatile time with Rebecca.

"Back to the directives," he said. "As it turned out, Rebecca skipped the attorney meeting. I went through with it, had all my directives signed, notarized, the whole business. The attorney sent me home with a standard form for her to fill out. I went over it with her, explained the basics, then talked her through each point and stressed their importance."

"Why were all the sections pertaining to life-sustaining measures crossed out?"

"She called it the 'sad stuff' and refused to discuss it. I kept after her to reconsider, but ultimately I let it go. Dumb, I know, but I was more worried about something traumatic happening to me, not her.

"She said she wanted to appoint me her agent, and I said fine. Only later did I learn that she'd added the 'otherwise' provision, appointing me her agent forever and ever. She had two of her airheaded friends witness it. I can envision them having a good laugh over her enslaving me."

Kate Lennon didn't laugh. In a most serious voice, she said, "Rebecca might have taken it more seriously if she'd known that Eban Clarke was in her future."

Chapter 4

—◈—

As though the mention of his name had created an ill wind, the breeze picked up and swirled around them. It rustled the enclosing wall's clinging ivy, tinged now with the russet color of the season. Kate Lennon reached down into her bag and came up with a scarf, which she artfully knotted around her neck.

Zach said, "If you're cold, we can go inside."

"Thank you, but I'm fine." She made a steeple of her fingers and held them against her chin. "Tell me how you felt when you heard about Rebecca."

"Jesus. Bad. I saw it on TV while sitting at a poolside bar. It had been years since our divorce. I hadn't seen her except in the media when one of her exploits made the tabloids, but that news flash hit me like a two-by-four.

"I didn't love her anymore, couldn't remember why I ever thought I did, and looked back on our time together as a disaster I'd somehow survived. But still. She'd been my wife. Her life was hanging in the balance. So yeah, it came as an awful shock. I was trying to wrap my mind around it, thinking what a horrible fucking thing to have happened to her. Then, within a few minutes of hearing about it, I got the call."

"Who called?"

"Someone at Emory. She introduced herself and said... Well, I don't remember exactly what she said, but I got the message, and I remembered that fucking POA, and it felt like a dump truck–load of shit had landed on me." He met her gaze. "It still feels like that."

She didn't comment.

He picked up the lid of his coffee cup and began fiddling with it. "Pardon my language."

"I'm not that prissy."

He bent the plastic cap, then dropped it onto the table. "No, I don't think you're prissy at all."

His snide undertone caused her to frown. "I'm on your side, Mr. Bridger."

"Really? Be sure to give me a high sign when we get to that part."

She ignored that. "Doug Pratt brought a copy of Rebecca's medical POA with him to the hospital."

"With all those clauses about life support marked out. I remember thinking that Rebecca was never happier than when causing an uproar, and that she was still at it. Sounds horrible, I know."

Kate Lennon made a forgiving gesture.

"They put her in a drug-induced coma, to let her brain rest, they said. They hooked her up to a machine to assist in her heart and lung function. They said they'd wait a few days to take her off the machines and bring her out of the coma, then reassess the damage.

"During those days, Doug and Mary and the Right to Lifers, who were picketing outside the hospital, cited that the reason Rebecca had marked through those clauses was obvious, and that I was obligated to abide by her wishes and take whatever measures were necessary to prolong her life. But the doctors brought up what they called 'substituted judgment.' That's what—"

"What in your best judgment Rebecca would have really wanted, despite her leaving no directives."

"Right. They described to me what life would be like for her if she survived at all, but, in the same breath, stressed keeping her on life support long enough for the organ banks to determine who on their lists got what before they let her die. Every time that was mentioned, Mary went into hysterics and resorted to begging me not to 'kill her daughter.' Chaplains came around periodically to pray over Rebecca's soul and my decision. And then—"

He broke off, looked down at the bent lid, and scooted it a few inches away from where he'd dropped it.

"And then ... what?"

He dug his thumb and middle finger into his eye sockets and shook his head slightly.

"Then what?"

He lowered his hand from his eyes. "The media. You wouldn't believe how vicious it got. Not a grain of respect or sensitivity or conscience. An ongoing mad clamor for the goriest information, the tastiest tidbit of gossip.

"Despite Doug's animosity toward me, I felt bad for Mary and him. They had to have heard all the malicious things being said about Rebecca, about her partying lifestyle, her reputed drug and alcohol abuse, her promiscuity. They had unbendable religious convictions. Hearing all the trash talked about their only child had to have been hell for them."

"What kind of relationship had you had with them before?"

"Contentious." He scoffed. "Hell, why mince words? They hated me from the day they met me, and from the day they met me, I didn't give a shit. But in light of what had happened, you would think that all that crap could be put aside, that there would be some compassion extended on both sides, that it would draw us closer, not—"

He placed his elbow on the table and rubbed his forehead. "I mean, I get it. They were shredded. So, in the end, I told them that I respected their position, that by taking no action at all, I was, in fact, following Rebecca's wishes, and that I wouldn't intrude unless asked by them. And I split."

"Soon after, they had Rebecca moved from Atlanta to a special care facility in New Orleans."

"You've done your homework."

"I have a copy of your letter granting them permission."

He raised a shoulder. "The move only made sense. Rebecca was born and raised in New Orleans, and the Pratts still lived down there."

Quietly, she said, "I also know that the facility declined to take her. Initially."

"The doctor in charge had a dim outlook on Rebecca's 'viability.'"

"Until you guaranteed to cover the expense of her care in perpetuity."

He shifted his weight on the unstable chair and focused on a bird feeder hanging from a tree branch beyond Kate Lennon's shoulder. The feeder was running low on seeds. Shifting his gaze back to hers, he said, "It's an automatic draw on a separate account. I don't have any personal involvement."

She let a moment go by, then, "Earlier, I mentioned a development."

"Oh, yes. The development. I hope it's something good. Tell me one positive thing, please. I'm not greedy. Just one."

"I truly am sorry to have to lay all this on you at once."

"Yeah, me too." He glanced at his watch. "In fact, I have a time limit for hearing bad news, and we're way past it." The chair legs scraped against the bricks as he pushed away from the table. But he hadn't yet stood when she reached across and came an inch shy of placing her hand on his arm.

"Please," she said. "I need to finish."

"Finish telling me what this lovely stroll down memory lane has been for?"

"Yes."

"Finally." He spread his arms wide and, sounding like an ass again, said, "Let me have it."

This time she let it slide and went straight to the point. "Did you know Eban Clarke before the incident?"

"No. I'd never heard of him or his family until the breaking news story referred to their mansion."

"Why didn't you attend his trial?"

"Were you involved?"

"No. I came to the case only recently. But while gathering

background information, I read that you didn't appear at his trial. Why not?"

"In his sordid universe, Eban Clarke was a celebrity. I was a bigger one in mine. I knew his trial would be a media event, which it turned out to be even without me there. My attendance would have added more sensationalism. 'The ex-husband and the current boyfriend battle it out in court.' I didn't want to inflict that on myself or the Pratts.

"But I closely followed the proceedings. In my opinion the son of a bitch got off way too light. And then, I couldn't believe it when I got notification a few months ago about a sentence reduction hearing."

She said, "I did the research for the prosecutor who argued on behalf of the state and Rebecca. You had the right to be present and heard at the hearing, but you declined."

"I declined to be present, but I sent my opinion to the judge."

"Yes, your statement was read in court. In essence, you urged the judge to keep Clarke in prison and to throw away the key."

"Little good it did," he said.

"Your argument might have carried more weight if you'd delivered it in person."

"I doubt it. The upshot is that Clarke got his sentence reduced. Last I heard the judge was deliberating by how much."

"Well, he's made that determination. Taking into account the two years Clarke has already served, and the allowance given for good behavior, he's being released."

"On parole?"

"Without any provision."

"You've got to be fucking kidding."

"I wish I were, Mr. Bridger."

"You mean he'll be let go, free as a bird?"

"I'm afraid so."

"When?"

"Today."

Chapter 5

⟞⟝

It might not have been the best idea to give him a quarter-million-dollar Porsche as an early release gift."

Sid Clarke smiled as he poured two bourbons, one for himself, one for the family attorney. "It's a Turbo. Top of the line."

"Silver, red interior. I saw it parked out front. A splash of water in mine, please." Because they always drank their whiskeys neat, Sid gave his friend a puzzled look. "It cuts the calories," Upton said.

"That's self-deluding."

"I'm very good at that."

Sid laughed as he added the requested splash of water, then carried the drinks over and they clinked glasses. "Here's to."

"Here's to."

They drank. Sid sank into the matching leather chair

beside the one occupied by Upton Franklin, who, in addition to being Sid's highly paid legal counselor, was also his sounding board, tennis partner, golfing buddy, poker rival, and best friend since they'd met during their first semester at Georgia's most elite prep school.

Their friendship had been forged by bullying classmates they disfavored for one reason or another and playing pranks on humorless faculty members who insisted on gentlemanly conduct and strict adherence to school rules. By their senior year, Sid and Up practically ran the academy, having cowed even the austere headmaster with their genial terrorism.

Once out in the business world, their bullying had continued, but they'd refined their methods. Sid was the brain behind their schemes to steal companies out from under unsuspecting CEOs. Upton was the legal mind that maneuvered them around the laws and regulations of commerce. Today, the international conglomerate they'd assembled was worth billions and included numerous industries.

They were two of a kind, each possessing ruthless ambition and a blatant sense of entitlement. Which was why Sid was surprised by Upton's chastening remark about Eban's new car.

"Why the frown, Up?"

Upton swirled his watered-down whiskey. "If you'd asked for my advice before buying the car, I would have suggested that you give him something less costly and conspicuous. A wristwatch. Carved marble chess set. Rare breed of dog."

Sid chuckled. "So I splurged. What of it? He's been in prison."

Forehead furrowed, the attorney said, "Exactly my point, Sid."

"Which is escaping me."

"Some might think giving Eban a flashy car to mark the occasion of his early release to be in bad taste."

"I don't give a damn what some might think."

"Obviously not," Up said, "but perhaps you should. I advise a little discretion. Restraint. Eban should avoid drawing attention to himself. The early out notwithstanding—"

"Whenever you say 'notwithstanding,' I know you've lapsed into lawyer mode."

"I'm speaking as your lawyer and friend. The early out notwithstanding, Eban was still convicted. The girl—"

"Was not a *victim*. It was a tragic accident, and as much her fault as Eban's."

"The jury didn't think so."

Sid sneered. "Everybody but that twelve knew better. That was not Rebecca Pratt's first rodeo."

Upton looked at Sid from beneath his shelf of eyebrows. "But it was her last."

Sid didn't concede the point except to curse before taking a drink of his bourbon. When he lowered his glass, he said, "She was drunk, and high, and she went into a bedroom with three men who admitted to being equally drunk and high."

"Because admitting to being stoned mitigated their responsibility for the catastrophic outcome," Up said.

"Remember the DNA evidence? She'd had sex with all three of them."

"Yes, Eban's defense lawyer was emphatic about that in his closing arguments. He described in some detail the sex acts they had engaged in."

"He described a nymphomaniacal contortionist," Sid said and chuckled.

"Sid. Please."

"All right, that was uncalled for. But suffice to say that prior to that night, she was a well-documented party animal, and those are the least offensive words I could use to characterize her. At Eban's trial, Theo and Cal testified under oath that all the fun and games were *her* idea."

"But it was in their best interest to testify to that, wasn't it?" Up argued. "Their lawyer was negotiating a deal for probation with no jail time."

"Which Eban served."

"Because he's the one who took the experimentation too far."

"Don't sound so goddamn self-righteous, Up. You and I had ménages on occasion."

"We did, yes. But none of the women wound up in a vegetative state. Rebecca Pratt did, and even though Eban is now a free man, people aren't going to forget that. He needs to be aware that he'll be closely scrutinized. To be seen blazing around in a new sports car—"

"Blazing around is precisely what I had in mind."

The subject of their discussion strode into the study, wearing a broad smile and the best casual chic Sid's black Amex card could buy. Eban was only a few months away from turning thirty, and it made Sid proud when people said that the older he got, the more they favored each other. They had the same slender build, wide forehead, and cleft chin. Their eye colors differed. Eban's were a cool gray-green, and all his own.

Halfway across the room, he stopped and looked from one to the other.

"Obviously I've walked into the wrong party. I was invited to join you for *happy* hour. This is your idea of happy? You look positively glum."

Sid motioned him toward the bar. "Pour yourself a drink."

"Oh, I intend to." Eban vigorously rubbed his hands together as he went over to the built-in wet bar, a component of the elegant floor-to-ceiling cabinetry that enwrapped the room except for the wall of windows.

He clunked ice cubes into a glass and reached for a decanter of vodka. "Why the sour face, Up? And, by the way, I was joshing. I don't plan to blaze around. I'll break in my new car like it was a baby stroller. Scout's honor."

He carried his drink over to the sitting area and tapped glasses with both men before flopping onto the sofa. He drank from his late mother's finest cut crystal, then gave a long *ah* of appreciation for the vodka as he rested his head on the tufted sofa back.

"Thinking of moments like this was what kept me sane during my incarceration." He gave an exaggerated shudder. "God, am I ever glad that my debt to society has been paid."

"I'll drink to that." Sid raised his glass in a toast. He noticed that Upton was slower to raise his. After they'd all taken a drink, Sid said to Eban, "Frida cooked a prime rib for dinner. Your homecoming gift from her."

"Sounds delicious. She can make me sandwiches with it tomorrow. Tonight, I'm going out."

Sid felt the glance Up sent his way, but he pretended not

to notice it. "I thought you would want to have dinner here with us."

"Sorry. I'm sure you two will do justice to the prime rib, but I've made other plans."

Casually, Sid asked, "Big plans?"

"Cal and Theo wanted to take me to dinner. God, it seems ages since the three of us have been together." He shook an ice cube into his mouth and crunched it.

Upton cleared his throat. "Maybe this fresh start should include cultivating new friendships, Eban."

"We'll see." He shot them a smile, then, after a beat, said, "Look at your glasses. Nearly empty. We can't let that happen." He got to his feet, picked up their tumblers, and carried them to the bar for a refill.

Over that round, Eban was brought up to date on the goings-on of business associates and social acquaintances.

At one point, he quipped, "The good, the bad, and the ugly."

They spent a convivial hour. The only wet blanket among them was Upton, who maintained an uncharacteristic reserve. Eban seemed not to notice, but it annoyed Sid, who couldn't account for it.

After polishing off his second drink, Eban stood. "I'm meeting the guys at one of our haunts. I think they may have secretly scared up some of the old crowd, so if this is to be a surprise party, I don't want to be late."

He went around Upton's chair. From behind, he gripped him by both shoulders and gave them an affectionate squeeze. "See you later, Uncle Up. Thanks for celebrating with me."

Upton reached up and patted the back of Eban's hand. "Be careful in that snazzy car."

"Play your cards right, and I'll take you for a spin. I may even give you a turn at the wheel." As he approached Sid, Sid stood up and shook hands with him. When they broke, Eban looked down to find that Sid had slipped him a money clip containing several hundred-dollar bills.

He whistled. "Thanks, Dad."

"Enjoy yourself, but do as Up said and be careful."

Eban pocketed the money, then headed for the door. There he paused and turned to blow them a kiss. "Don't you boys stay up too late." His laughter followed him down the hallway.

Sid sat back down and smiled when he heard the sports car growl to life out in the drive. He looked across at Upton, who was frowning into his second drink, which he'd barely touched.

Sid said, "All right, I'm spoiling him. You've made your disapproval obvious. But he deserves—"

"Sid." Upton raised his hand palm out. "I don't believe you want to get into a discussion about what Eban deserves. Or what any of us deserve."

"What's with this mood? Cheer up for godsake. Finish your drink."

"No, I've had enough." Up placed his glass on the small table at his elbow.

Sid gave him a lingering look. They'd known each other since adolescence. Upton wasn't being pompous or cranky. He wasn't sulking. He was genuinely bothered about something.

"Tell me what's the matter."

After having avoided direct eye contact for the last half hour, Upton looked straight at him now. "You think Eban's early release is cause for celebration."

"It's not?"

"It is. But I don't believe it's occurred to either you or him what ramifications it may have."

"Such as?"

"Does the name Kathryn Lennon mean anything to you?"

"No, should it? Who is she?"

"A smart, savvy, ambitious state prosecutor, handpicked by the attorney general himself."

"A politician in the making?"

"No. She's much more interested in criminal cases, and she's not afraid to tackle tough ones. In other words, Sid, she's Eban's worst nightmare."

Chapter 6

⟫⟪

Zach scaled the challenging incline. It was the steepest, the hardest, the home stretch of his punishing workout. His leg muscles were burning, heart was drumming, lungs working doubly hard to draw in air. At this altitude, it was thin.

Several times a week, moving at a rapid but safe clip, he made the trek from his house down to the river and back up. He pushed himself through the last hundred yards, cutting himself no slack.

Following his inglorious exit from the NFL, he'd packed on an extra twenty pounds. After his day of reckoning with the sports network that had forced him into an early retirement, he'd awoken one morning with the mother of all hangovers. He'd puked and dry-heaved for five minutes, after which he gave himself a good, hard look in his bathroom's full-length mirror. The damn thing was merciless.

Who the hell was that bloated, spongy, sorry excuse for a man staring back at him through bloodshot eyes?

Zach was disgusted by him. He despised him. He decided he must go.

Then and there his naked self had resolved that he would not continue down the road he was on. For one thing, he didn't want to give those who'd predicted he would self-destruct the satisfaction of smugly watching from the sidelines as he inexorably degenerated.

He'd retained just enough fortitude to make a vow to himself to get his shit together. He might be ridiculed and scorned for past failures and bad behavior. That censure he deserved. But he would never let them say Zach Bridger had fallen from grace and then gone to seed.

That morning of his epiphany, he'd poured out every bottle of booze he had in the house, made a shopping list of healthy foodstuffs to replace the crap his pantry and fridge were stocked with, and had outlined a rigid and rigorous exercise program for himself that even Bing would have approved. Bing might even had said it was excessive.

The first workout, which in previous years would have amounted to a warm-up, had nearly killed him.

But within eight weeks, he'd dropped the extra twenty pounds, then over the course of the next couple of months, he lost another ten. That had brought him down to his pre-NFL weight, and it was all muscle. He was leaner, and, if not meaner, then sure as hell harder, his soul as well as his body.

Now, quads on fire, he covered the last arduous yards to reach the rocky ledge that marked his stopping point. He slowed to a normal walking pace and moved in a circle as he used the app on his wristwatch to check the pedometer, his time, his vitals, all the things he kept track of. He flipped his ball cap around backward and lifted the hem of his t-shirt to wipe sweat off his face. After drinking from the water thermos clipped to his waistband, he leaned against the rough trunk of a pine tree, closed his eyes, and waited for his respiration to regulate.

He tried to empty his mind and let his thoughts simply drift. Instead, they channeled straight back to Kate Lennon. "You can call me Kate," she'd said. But from there forward he hadn't called her anything, because after she'd dropped that H-bomb piece of information about Eban Clarke on him, he'd considered their meeting concluded.

He'd stood up so fast, he nearly knocked over his mini-chair. As it was, his thigh had caught the edge of that teeny table and sent it to rocking. "I'm outta here," he said. "I've got to go before the market closes."

"It's open till seven p.m."

And he'd said, "The stock market."

And she'd said, "Oh," and checked her wristwatch. "Time has gotten away from me, too. I have a Zoom meeting in fifteen minutes." She'd shouldered the bag that he could have packed for a weekend. "But you and I have more to talk about."

"No, Ms. Lennon, we don't."

That's when she'd invited him to call her Kate.

But he hadn't. All he'd said was, "Goodbye. Thanks for the coffee."

Not wanting to scare her or any of the other customers in Wholly Ground, he'd gotten the hell out of there. Because he was about to explode. Like he had that time against Green Bay's right guard who'd taken an extra potshot at him that had been ferocious enough to knock his helmet off.

Before he even realized what he was going to do, he had laid into the guy. It had felt like attacking a mattress, but his teammates practically had to peel him off the asshole. The officials went nuts with their whistles; both coaches were apoplectic. The Packer had been ejected from the game. But still, Zach had never been that angry. Not until this morning when he learned that they'd let that son of a bitch Eban Clarke out of prison.

He wanted to attack the whole damn legal system for allowing that.

It must have been obvious to Kate—what the hell, why not call her Kate?—that the miscarriage of justice had lit a short fuse in him, because she had let him go without protest, saying in his wake something about contacting him soon.

He didn't stop to tell her not to bother, that he saw no point in talking about it further. Rebecca was still locked in a vegetative state. Clarke was free. Thinking about it, talking about it, rehashing all of it was pointless.

Dwelling on it only served one purpose, and that was to make him miserable. It had taken him all this time to extricate himself from that darkness, and it was still dusky. He didn't want to be drawn back into it, not by anybody, but especially not by Kate Lennon, who was bad news personified.

Although she did have that cute butt, and he'd enjoyed watching her lick the vanilla-flavored foam off her upper lip.

So, while he never wanted to lay eyes on the woman again, lying down with her was an enticing fantasy.

He muttered a stream of swear words, pushed away from the tree, and continued along the forest trail that had been charted over time by his own footsteps. He knew the landmarks along it like the back of his hand, and, by now, avoided them almost by instinct.

As he approached his house, he heard something that made him slow down, and then stop altogether to listen. It hadn't been a natural sound. Not leaves stirred by the wind, or a squirrel's scolding chatter, not a bird's flit from one branch to another, nor the incessant white noise created by the waterfall.

The sound had been manmade.

He flipped his cap back around and pulled the bill down to just above his eyebrows, then continued along the familiar path, being careful not to step on a twig or loose rock or anything that could signal his approach.

As he crept through the trees, his house gradually came into view. First, the clearing, an apron of hearty grass that surrounded the house itself. Next, the north-facing exterior wall dominated by the stacked stone chimney. Then the porch that ran along the entire length of the south side.

Zach stopped.

The oversize front door marked the center of the porch. The door was flanked by large windows, two on each side of it...one of which was being peered through by a man in a law officer's uniform. His cupped hands formed blinders that were pressed up against the windowpane.

OVERKILL

59

His Smokey the Bear hat was occupying the seat of Zach's rocking chair, and that pissed him off more than anything.

Still unmoving, Zach looked several degrees to the left. A Bronco was parked in the cul-de-sac. Its all-business tires were caked with mud. It had a serious light bar on the roof, a heavy duty grille guard, and an official insignia on the door.

Zach's porch had one plank that squeaked when stepped on in a certain spot. He realized now that was what he'd heard, not the vehicle's engine as it had come up his drive, indicating to him that the cop had been poking around his property while he was ascending the mountainside.

Zach emerged from the cover of the trees. "See anything interesting in there?"

The man spun around. His expression gave away his embarrassment at having been caught, then he gave a shrug and a grin. "Mr. Bridger? Zach Bridger? Your truck's here." He thumbed over his shoulder toward Zach's pickup. "I figured you were at home but hadn't heard my knock."

Bullshit. Zach walked toward the porch, but he didn't say anything. He wanted to hear first what this guy sporting a shiny badge had to say.

As he came down the steps, Zach sized him up. He was shorter and stockier than Zach, and spent a lot of time lifting weights. His buzz haircut suggested former military. He had a tattoo on the side of his neck, some kind of symbol, but Zach couldn't tell what it was. He had a swagger just a shade off belligerence.

He'd been looking Zach over, too. "Been out hiking?"

"Um-huh." Zach glanced beyond the guy at the window through which he'd been peering. "What have you been doing?"

The officer closed the distance between them and extended his right hand. "Deputy Sheriff Dave Morris."

Zach shook his hand.

The deputy grinned. "Of course I already know who you are."

Zach acknowledged that with a curt hitch of his chin.

"You've lived here for a while now."

"Three years."

"Funny that our paths have never crossed."

"Not so funny," Zach said. "I don't go down into town that often."

"Yeah, but I don't stick to town. I'm out and about, all over the place," he said, making an expansive gesture. "But I heard you keep to yourself. Don't like company."

"Who'd you hear that from?"

He didn't answer. Instead, he looked westward at the sun that had just sunk below the crest of the mountain across the river, casting Zach's property in shadow.

When Morris came back around, he hiked up his belt, which seemed to have the entire inventory of a police department's arsenal attached to it. Zach supposed the move was made to signal that he was getting to the purpose of his visit.

"Mr. Bridger, the folks over on the eastern face—"

"Over on the eastern face there aren't any folks left. GreenRidge Incorporated has run them all off."

"I was referring to the folks of GreenRidge Incorporated."

Zach had known that, of course, but he said, "Oh, pardon."

"Well, they've been experiencing some, uh, vandalism to their property."

"Vandalism."

"Nothing real serious so far, but it's a nuisance, and, added up, it's costly to repair, replace, and clean up the damage done."

"What damage?"

"They've had their signs removed or defaced. Windows of buildings under construction have been broken out. Last night a backhoe had some rather crude messages spray painted on it."

Zach just looked at him and said nothing.

"So they asked me to come over here and check on you, see if you'd experienced anything like that, had any intruders."

"Not until five minutes ago."

Morris dropped the friendly manner. "I'm not an intruder."

"A window peeper then."

"I represent the sheriff's office."

"You're official."

"Damn straight."

"Then the next time you want to look inside my house, bring a search warrant. But you won't find a can of spray paint because I don't own one. And if I wanted to deface a sign or a backhoe I wouldn't leave a message for those GreenRidge folks that was 'rather crude,' it would be down-right obscene."

"Everybody's said you're a jerk."

Zack placed his hand over his heart. "That really hurts

my feelings." He stepped around the deputy, mounted the porch steps, and picked up the hat lying in the seat of his rocking chair. "Don't forget this." He sailed it toward Morris like a Frisbee.

Just as he did, a familiar vehicle pulled up behind the deputy's.

Inwardly Zach groaned. This day would go down in the record books as being majorly shitty.

Chapter 7

Kate couldn't fathom what a sheriff's unit was doing here. Friendly call or official business? She got out of her car and passed between the rock columns into the yard.

No, not friendly. At all. The tension between the two men was palpable. Forcing herself to smile, she said, "Hello, gentlemen. You two know each other? Am I interrupting?"

Zach stood on the porch in the deepening shadows, a mute and antagonistic presence. But the deputy was smiling as he ambled toward her. "Hi, Kate."

"Hello, Dave."

"What brings you up here?"

"I have business with Mr. Bridger."

"Is that so?"

"That's so."

Since it became apparent that she wasn't going to elaborate on the nature of their business, he said, "How was the trout?"

"Great! Grilled to perfection, just as you promised."

"Glad to hear it."

"Thank you for the recommendation."

"Anytime."

Zach still hadn't spoken a word, which was unnerving and provoking, but unsurprising considering their previous encounters. She continued smiling at the deputy. They'd been introduced shortly after her arrival in town. Since then they'd seen each other often enough in and around the DA's office to put them on a first-name basis.

He said, "Have you tried the zip line yet?"

"I haven't worked up enough courage."

"Nothing to it. I could show you the ropes. So to speak."

She gave the expected laugh.

"But we need to do it soon," he said. "They shut down at Halloween and don't reopen till Easter or so. Check your schedule. Let me know what day is good for you."

Her eyes flicked toward the porch. "I will, thanks."

He put on his hat and brushed the brim. "See you soon then. Be careful on these roads. They can be tricky for anyone not familiar with them. Don't get caught up here in fog."

"I'll keep that in mind."

He glanced over his shoulder. "See ya, Bridger."

"You bet." He made the two words sound like *Not if I can help it.*

Kate called up to him, "I'll be right with you. I need to get some paperwork out of my car."

She and the deputy walked together toward their parked vehicles. He said, "Isn't it after your office hours?"

"I had a full schedule today. Business spilled over."

"What business have you got with Bridger?"

She kept her smile in place, but stated firmly, "Confidential."

He took her answer with grace, but said, "Watch yourself with him. He's not a pleasant person."

"He's suffered some very unpleasant experiences."

The deputy gave a snort of disdain. "Hard to work up a bleeding heart for the MVP of the Super Bowl." He looked down at her as though expecting a response. When he didn't get one, he said, "Well, anyway. Bye now, Kate."

"Bye."

He walked to his truck and climbed in, giving her a little wave as he drove away. Kate opened the passenger door of her car, but it wasn't paperwork she retrieved.

Flat rocks imbedded in the grass formed a pathway to the porch. She made use of it and, reaching the bottom step, hefted a bottle of wine by the neck. "I brought this."

"What for?"

"To drink?"

"Haven't you heard? I'm a drunk."

"Okay then, I'll drink the wine and you can be broody and bellicose. But whatever, we've got to talk."

"We finished talking."

"We just got started."

"Whatever it is can keep till—"

"No, it can't. In fact, time is running out."

"On what?"

"Eban Clarke is a flight risk." Which was the truth, just not the whole truth.

"He's out. No provisions. He can fly wherever the hell he takes a mind to go."

"That's right."

"Then what—"

"The sun's gone down and it's getting cold out here." She lifted the bottle again. "Are you going to invite me inside?"

He kept her waiting for about ten seconds, then mumbled something that had the word bellicose in it, and turned to face the front door. He punched a code into the keypad on the jamb, the lock clicked, and he pushed open the massive door and motioned her inside.

There were no lights on, but when he depressed a wall switch, lamps from various points around the vast room came on. "Oh my," she exclaimed. "This is gorgeous."

"Thanks."

She walked forward several steps, then stopped and made a slow three-sixty. The walls of the room were comprised of split logs held together with cream-colored mortar. It had a massive fireplace on the wall to her right, and a wide, open staircase attached to the wall on her left.

In between, area rugs created islands of color and pattern against the hardwood floor. Directly in front of her was a two-story wall of windows that provided a view of the gorge and the waterfall in all their glory. A second-story gallery encompassed the room on three sides.

When her pivot brought her back to him, she said, "I confess that I'm flabbergasted and impressed."

"What did you expect?"

"Nice, but not something out of *Architectural Digest*. Did you design it?"

"I had the basic concept in mind. An architect took it from there."

"It was beautifully executed. And the best thing about it is that it fits you so well."

He raised his eyebrows. "How's that?"

"Well, I mean..."

What she meant was where else would a man like him look more at home? His hair was long enough to curl from beneath a baseball cap that must be a favorite because it looked like it had seen decades of wear. Or war. His t-shirt was also vintage. He wore a flannel shirt tied around his waist by the sleeves. His army green cargo shorts were faded from repeated washings. His hiking boots had red laces; thick socks were cuffed above them. And he smelled of the woods, and resin, and healthy sweat.

He was waiting for her to reply. She groped, then said, "Well, I mean the scale of it, and all."

"Oh," he said, giving a nod. "Most things aren't built for six-four plus."

She laughed. "I wouldn't know how that feels."

He looked her up and down. "No, if you went wandering off in here, you could get lost." A beat, then, "And I'd have to come looking for you."

He didn't say it as a tease. He didn't add a wink. Without a jest behind it, the statement took on weight. Unintended, no doubt.

They looked away from each other at the same time. An awkward silence followed, then both began speaking at once.

"Are you still—"

"What did—"

He motioned for her to go first. She said, "I was going to ask what you and Deputy Morris were talking about."

"You mean *Dave*?"

This time, he did sound as though he was poking fun, but she didn't rise to the bait. Instead, she asked what he'd been about to say.

"I was going to ask if you're still cold. I could start a fire."

She glanced toward the fireplace. "That would be nice, if it's not too much trouble."

"No trouble. It's already laid. All I have to do is start it. Bar's over there. Corkscrew is in the drawer."

On his way over to the fireplace, he took off his cap, tossed it onto an end table, and ruffled his hair. He also untied the flannel shirt from around his waist and put it on but left it unbuttoned. He set aside the fire screen, then knelt and used a lighter to ignite kindling beneath logs that had been expertly stacked.

She went over to the bar, which was recessed into the wall. It had a small fridge and ice maker. Above the granite counter, drinking glasses were lined up on subtly lighted glass shelves. Four highball glasses, four wineglasses. On a shelf all its own was a single bottle of bourbon, looking very mellow with the soft lighting shining through it.

Hearing him coming toward her, she quickly opened the drawer and got out the corkscrew.

"Let me," he said, moving up beside her.

"I can do it."

"I'm sure you can." He took the bottle and corkscrew from her anyway, deftly handled both, and pulled out the cork. He took down one of the wineglasses and poured a goodly measure of Pinot Noir into it. As he passed it to her, he said, "I would've figured you for white wine."

"Why?"

"I don't know. Just would. Maybe because your hair is so light."

Their gazes held for a second or two, then hers moved to the bottle of bourbon. "For a drunk you certainly stock expensive whiskey."

One side of his mouth tilted up. "I gave up being drunk and disorderly, but not good sipping whiskey." He reached for one of the highball glasses and poured two fingers of the bourbon. "I allow myself a drink on special occasions."

"What's the occasion?"

"First fire of the season."

"Ah."

They made their way over to the fireplace. The young fire was casting flickering light. He indicated that she take the sofa facing it, while he sat—more like sprawled—in an adjacent chair positioned at an angle to the hearth.

She said, "I'm guessing that's your favorite chair."

"In the fall and winter."

"What about spring and summer?"

"The rocker on the porch."

"No Barcalounger?"

"Oh, hell yes. In the TV room upstairs."

They smiled across at each other and drank from their glasses. She said, "You never answered my question about you and Deputy Morris. Do you two have a history?"

"Nope. Just met. We didn't exactly take to each other."

"I gathered. What happened?"

Rather than answer, he asked a question of his own. "He recommended the trout? Why does that not surprise me?"

"What's wrong with trout?"

"It swims."

She laughed. "We bumped into each other at a local restaurant. He was coming out as I was going in."

"You two seemed chummy."

"Not chummy exactly."

"More than chummy? Y'all have a thing going?"

She sputtered into her wine. "Good lord, no."

"Not for his lack of trying, I think."

The truth was that Dave Morris had shown more interest than she'd invited or welcomed. His flirtation had put her off, not enticed her. But she wasn't going to go into that with a man who'd yet to address her by her first name.

He said, "Morris did the same thing you did yesterday."

"What did I do yesterday?"

"When you got here, you said, 'Mr. Bridger? Zachary Bridger?' Like you didn't already know who I was. If you didn't know, why would you be coming to my house?"

"You're right. I apologize. Honestly, I do. Of course I knew you."

"Then why'd you pretend not to?"

"I was nervous."

"Nervous? You?" He snuffled a laugh. "I'd have never guessed that."

"Well, good. I pulled off a confident air."

"Why were you nervous?"

"Come on. You're Zach Bridger."

"No." Appearing regretful, he said, "I used to be."

"People still get starstruck."

He raised one shoulder in a negligent shrug. "Some people."

She took a sip of wine, looking at him over the rim of her glass. "My roommate had a poster of you above her bed."

He groaned. "That thing. It was for charity. The league sold the poster to raise money for cancer research awareness."

"It raised awareness, all right," she said around a laugh. He'd been featured shirtless, wearing low-slung jeans and a come-hither-if-you-dare smile that every female fantasized was just for her. "It was killer."

He winced. "Can we change the subject, please? I can't believe I'm saying this, but I'd rather talk about Morris, the trusty deputy."

"When I got here, you two seemed on the verge of pawing the ground."

"I returned from my hike to find him on my porch, hands cupped around his eyes, peering through that front window." He motioned toward it with his glass.

"What for?"

"That's what I wanted to know." He explained the reason for the deputy's visit.

"I don't suppose you . . . ?"

He shot her a look. "Painted a nasty message on a backhoe? No, wasn't me. I'm not the only person pissed off at those people who're carving a golf course out of the forest and stacking up condos on the mountainside."

"They want to do that on your mountainside, too?"

"Hell will freeze over first."

He set his glass on the coffee table and got up to attend to the fire, which by now was crackling pleasantly. He used a poker to readjust the logs. Sparks chased up the chimney. The new flames picked up strands of copper and gold in his brown hair, reminding Kate of the yummy trail that had been a much-admired feature of that poster.

She took a sip of wine, then another, then cleared her throat. "How did the stock market do today?"

"Up and down, closed okay." He returned to his chair, settling back into the plush cushion as he fixed a shrewd look on her. "Is that what you came all the way up here after hours to ask me? You can find out how the market did on your phone."

"Busted." She leaned forward and set her wineglass next to his glass on the coffee table. She shouldn't have drunk it without eating something first. It was burning her empty stomach. But the wine alone wasn't responsible for the mild upset.

She dreaded the next few minutes. Although she'd deliberated on how best to approach the subject, she'd determined that there was no easy way. Nevertheless, she would wade in cautiously, not take a plunge.

She said, "Have you ever heard the phrase 'a year and a day'?"

"No."

"Well, it was a common law, a judicial standard that had stood for centuries, but which, over time, has been abandoned, although it does have limited applications in some places, depending—"

"Cut to the chase."

"All right." She had an illustration prepared. "Say you had a bank robbery back in the 1880s. To frighten people, the robber fired his pistol randomly, but one of the bullets struck the teller. He was critically injured, but he survived."

"I think I saw that movie."

She pressed on. "The robber was charged with aggravated assault, convicted, and sentenced to serve five years."

"With you so far."

"The teller never fully recovered from the near-fatal gunshot. He suffered repeated infections and complications. Affected organs became dysfunctional. His incapacitation became more severe."

Slowly, Zach sat up straighter and leaned forward toward her. "Where's this story going? I'm not liking the sound of it."

"Bear with me. I'm laying groundwork. Similar to what you did this morning when you described your marriage to Rebecca. For context, you said."

He frowned, but said, "Fair enough. Continue."

"If the bank teller continued to deteriorate and died within a year of the robbery, the robber could be charged with manslaughter or even murder. But if the teller lived *a year and a day* after the event, the robber could not be held responsible for his death, and couldn't be charged with it."

"That extra day makes a difference? That's bullshit justice."

"Which is why that common law no longer applies. Medical advancements have enabled people to survive injuries that otherwise would have been fatal. There have been cases where the victims of violent crimes remained alive for years before they succumbed.

"The assailant, who might or might not have been convicted of a lesser crime, could, upon the victim's death, be charged with murder or manslaughter if it's proved that the injuries sustained during the commission of the crime ultimately cost him his life. Many of these cases have gone as far as the Supreme Court. They've been precedent-setting."

He assimilated all that, then said, "What's this got to do with Eban Clarke?"

"He committed an act that placed Rebecca's life in danger. He used his hands, but hands can cause bodily harm or death. Therefore, they're a weapon. He was charged, tried, and convicted of aggravated assault, a felony.

"But the judge who reviewed the case has determined that since Clarke's 'intent' was not to harm Rebecca, he should have been charged with simple battery, which is a misdemeanor. Misdemeanors are punishable by less than one year's incarceration. He's served twenty-six months. Therefore . . ." She raised her shoulders.

"What kind of fucked-up judicial system would allow him to walk the streets?"

"Well, it might be effed up," she said, "but we do *have* a judicial system, and it could be used to see that Eban Clarke receives the punishment he deserves, which I believe should be life imprisonment."

"I wish. But retrying him for the same crime would be double jeopardy."

She took a deep breath and in a quiet voice said, "Not if he's now charged and tried for murder."

"He can't be charged with murder as long as Rebecca is still—"

He broke off. It was plain to her that understanding had struck him like a bolt of lightning.

She hoped he sensed the compassion she felt for him at this moment, hoped her voice would convey it. "Eban Clarke can't be brought to justice as long as Rebecca is still alive."

Chapter 8

———◆———

Eban had endured the obligatory happy hour with his father and Upton, but he'd been itching with impatience to make his escape as soon as possible.

He'd fibbed. His friends hadn't planned this dinner out. He had. And he'd insisted that Cal and Theo join him. "No excuses," he'd said.

For the occasion, he'd chosen a restaurant that had been one of their favorites. In the heart of Buckhead, it was exclusive, expensive, and hip, a spot in which to see and be seen.

When he pulled up in his new car, the awestruck parking valets motioned him into the VIP space near the canopied entrance. God, he loved being kowtowed to. How he'd missed it! Since the so-called "victim" of his "crime" had been Zach Bridger's ex-wife, he'd been afforded no deferential treatment from fans of Bridger's in Reidsville, which had amounted to just about everybody, guards and cons alike.

But Eban Clarke was free and ready to party, and he wanted to blare it to the entire world.

However, upon entering the restaurant, he experienced a crushing letdown. While he'd been away, the place had undergone a metamorphosis. He couldn't quite put his finger on why the vibe felt different.

Well, actually he could. It no longer had a *vibe*. It barely had a pulse.

The hostess was a brunette knockout wearing a short, tight, black dress that showed a good two inches of cleavage. But her eyes didn't light up with recognition when he sauntered toward her. Instead she asked for his name and put it on a list. A *list*!

The previous bartender, who'd made a perfect dirty martini and told great dirty jokes, had been replaced by an indifferent automaton. He had little to say, and his martini lacked a pleasurable sting.

Eban was becoming depressed.

Then Cal and Theo walked in. The hostess indolently pointed them toward the bar. Eban came off his stool and spread his arms. "Finally! What took you so long?"

He grabbed Theo first and pulled him into a man-hug, thumped him on the back several times, then pushed him away to arm's length. "Where's your hair gone?"

"Screw you."

Eban laughed and turned to Cal. "Come here, you son of a gun." He gave Cal a similar hug. When he set him away, he said, "Tell me it isn't so. You got married? *Married?*"

"That's right."

"On purpose?"

"I was afraid she'd never say yes."

"How is married life?"

"I'm happier than I've ever been."

Eban turned to Theo and spoke out of the corner of his mouth. "What else is he going to say?"

Theo chuckled, Cal smiled, but the quip didn't elicit a swap of good-natured putdowns that Eban had expected it to.

The hostess approached and said, "Your table is ready, sir."

Sir? How old did she think he was?

She seated them in a semicircular booth, Eban in the middle. They toasted his early release with a round of drinks. But by the time they'd finished their shared platter of raw oysters, Eban was wondering where his playmates had gone and was asking himself who these two stodgy substitutes were.

He blamed most of the buzzkill on Cal. If ever there was an argument against matrimony and monogamy, one only had to compare the old Cal with this humorless and uptight incarnation. Marriage had drained him of all vivacity and humor.

The old Cal Parsons had never turned down a dare; he'd been game to try anything and everything. Tall, blond, rangy in build, he only had to give a woman his sultry smile and off came her panties. His success with women had been the envy of fraternity row at the University of Georgia.

The envy of Eban Clarke in particular.

His wife, whatever her name was, had ruined him. She'd made him dull as dirt.

By nature, Theo Simpson was self-effacing and studious. He'd never possessed Eban's and Cal's derring-do, and only their corrupting influence had saved him from being a hopeless bookworm. Under their guidance and goading, he'd shed some of his reserve, but Eban wondered now if he'd relapsed into his former, circumspect self.

Wearing his characteristic lopsided grin, he listened attentively to Eban's exaggerated stories about his time in the "zoo" and the "still-evolving species" he'd encountered there.

Theo laughed in all the right places, but underlying his laughter was his annoying inbred caution. He frequently glanced at Cal as though seeking approval for his levity. That began to grate on Eban, because since they'd founded their friendship during rush week at UGA, he'd been the ringleader of the trio.

Of course, he'd always footed the bill, too, making his leadership role undisputed.

They finished their steak and lobster combos and ordered dessert. "How about a round of Louis XIII to wash down the chocolate mousse?"

"None for me," Cal said.

"Come on. My treat."

Cal shook his head. "Thanks, Eban, but I've got to drive home."

Eban guffawed. "You drive better drunk than you do sober."

Cal smiled, but it was strained. "I'm out of practice."

Eban rolled his eyes. "Jesus." He turned to Theo. "You won't turn it down, I know."

"I'm gonna pass, too, but you have one."

Just because he could, and because he wanted to establish himself as a big spender with the robotic barman, Eban ordered the cognac.

Ceremoniously, the hostess brought it to their table on a silver tray. "For you, Mr. Clarke?"

"Yes. But call me Eban."

She smiled as she set the snifter in front of him. "Enjoy."

As she walked away, he said, "What I'd enjoy is getting her on her knees. What do you think, boys? Would a hundred-dollar bill buy me a blow job?"

"Shh, Eban. Please."

That from Theo as he looked around anxiously. Cal said nothing, just stared down at the tablecloth as he traced the weave of the fabric with the tip of his finger.

Eban pressed himself against the back of the booth. "What is it with you two?" For an answer, he looked first to Theo, whose leg was jiggling beneath the table. "*Well?*"

Theo said, "After what happened, it would look bad, sound bad for anyone to overhear you saying things like that."

"Oh, for chrissake."

Cal raised his head from his study of the tablecloth and glared at him. "No, Eban, for our sakes. Mine and Theo's. You're out. But we have another year of probation left."

Eban divided a look between them. "Oh, I get it. You're jealous that I beat the system."

Cal sat perfectly still for an extended time, then calmly took his napkin from his lap and laid it on the table. "You didn't beat the system, Eban. You *bought* it." He pushed back and stood up. "Thanks for dinner."

And just like that, he left them.

Eban felt flushed, not from the embarrassment of having a guest walk out on him, but from rage. He shot the cognac like it was rotgut rye.

As he returned the snifter to the table with a hard thump, he said, "I didn't hear him complaining when I was shelling out money for weeklong parties in Cancún. I *bought* the dope he did, the booze he guzzled, the girls he fucked."

"He didn't mean—"

"Hell he didn't. And stop that goddamn jiggling. It's driving me to distraction."

Under the table, Theo's leg went still. He gnawed on his lower lip, fiddled with the stem of the strawberry that had garnished his chocolate mousse, and eventually worked up his courage, something he'd always had to do before engaging in even the mildest of disagreements, like whether or not hot dogs were better with slaw or chili.

"Here's the thing, Eban."

Eban raised his hands from his sides and appealed to the ceiling. "Glory hallelujah! Let me hear the *thing*."

Theo deliberated for so long, Eban wanted to slap him to see if he was still conscious. At long last, he said, "The thing is, we can't pick back up where we left off. We had some wild times, but they got out of hand, and then...then they caught up with us. Big time. That business, what happened, was a wake-up call."

"It was a time-out."

Theo shook his head. "It changed things forever."

"It didn't change me."

"Well, it did Cal and me. Especially him, because I

never did party as hard as you two. He has a lot more to live down." He glanced toward the hostess stand, where the young woman had returned to her post. "He's not looking to score."

Eban formed a heart with his hands. "Because he's a married man."

"Yeah, he is, and he's all in. He loves Melinda, and she adores him."

"Can you name a woman who didn't?"

"No," Theo said with a wry grin. "But when he met Melinda, and things got serious, he made sure she knew about his past. He owned up to all that wild shit we did, and she loves him in spite of it." Quietly, he added, "She loves him in spite of Rebecca Pratt. That would be a damn hard thing for a woman to accept and forgive."

Theo picked up the stem of the strawberry again, looked at it as though puzzled as to how it had come to be in his hand, then dropped it back into the dish. "Even if Cal wasn't devoted to his wife, he's got to stay on the straight and narrow for another year, Eban, or he'll be slapped in prison. That goes for me, too."

Eban stabbed his index finger into the table as though driving a nail. "Don't forget that I'm the one who actually went to prison."

With rare boldness, Theo said, "Which was only fair. You're the one who actually did the deed."

Chapter 9

———◆———

Eban Clarke can't be brought to justice as long as Rebecca is still alive.

The sound waves of Kate's statement seemed palpable. Though softly spoken, it had substantial impact, and the odious implication of it wasn't lost on Zach.

His declaration of refusal was equally hard-hitting. "I won't do it." He left his chair, went over to his front door, and pulled it open.

"Zach—"

"You could have saved yourself the drive up here."

"Please just—"

"Take your wine with you."

He left the door standing open and headed for the staircase. He didn't look back as he climbed up to the second level and walked along the gallery until he reached his bedroom. He went in and shut the door behind him.

Then he stood with his back to it, rhythmically tapping his head against the wood, the heels of his hands pressed hard into his eye sockets. "Jesus Christ."

He remained like that while a chant ran through his mind. "As long as Rebecca is alive." Kate Lennon hadn't said those words as a taunt, but the imps inside his head did. They repeated them in a diabolical singsong.

After minutes, he pushed himself away from the door and went into the bathroom, where he stripped off his hiking clothes and got into the shower. He turned the water on full blast, stood directly beneath the rainfall shower head, and turned his face up to it.

It had taken him four years to get his life to the point where it was at least comfortable. He had his home, he was financially secure, he was in the best physical condition ever. He could go into a coffee shop and not be hounded by either devotees or detractors. He would never have total anonymity, but he was close.

Primarily, he had what he'd most coveted: distance from the tragedy of Rebecca.

Now this.

But suddenly it occurred to him that this unexpected development didn't have to change anything. He could leave things exactly as they were and let the future play out as it would without any participation from him. He didn't have to do a goddamn thing. He wouldn't. He'd told Kate Lennon *I won't do it* and he'd meant it.

He would take a knee.

Having resolved that and feeling marginally better, he scrubbed himself from head to toe. He pulled on a pair of sweatpants and a t-shirt, and left his bedroom. From the vantage point of the gallery, the silvery crown of Kate's head shone like a beacon. She was still seated on the sofa, gazing into the fire, although the front door was no longer standing open, so at some point she'd gotten up to close it.

Even though he was barefoot, she heard him coming downstairs and turned her head. He said, "It won't do you any good."

"What?"

"Whatever it is you're going to say. I want you to leave."

"I know how difficult this must be for you."

He gave a bitter laugh. "You have no fucking clue."

"Then enlighten me, Zach. Talk to me."

"I'm through talking. Bye." He motioned toward the front door, then headed for the kitchen.

He flipped on lights and went into the pantry, where he ripped open a box of energy bars and took out two. When he came out of the pantry, she was standing in the kitchen doorway, which actually came as no surprise because he'd heard her heels tapping against the floor as she approached the kitchen.

But he noticed that she'd swapped this morning's heels for a pair of flats. No wonder she'd looked so diminutive while taking in his house, sitting on his sofa, standing close to him while he poured her wine. He wished he hadn't noticed.

He held up one of the bars. "Want one?"

"No thank you."

He tossed the extra onto the island, peeled the wrapper from the other, and put the end of it between his teeth, where he held it as he moved to the fridge and took out a bottle of orange juice. He got a glass from the cabinet and filled it with the juice.

When he turned around, she was seated on one of the previously unused counter stools, back straight, knees primly together even though she was still wearing the pants outfit she'd had on that morning.

He sat down on his stool, facing her, and indicated the power bar. "If you change your mind."

She ignored the offer and went straight to the point. "It's the only way to put Eban Clarke back in prison and keep him there."

He noshed a bite of his bar. "When I was playing football, I had to memorize playbooks this thick." He held his hands roughly six inches apart. "I have good retention. But let me make sure I've got this straight." He looked at her hard. "In order to get that Clarke creep put away for murder, I'm the one who has to kill Rebecca."

Looking distressed, she said, "That's a harsh summation."

"You're goddamn right it's harsh."

"And unfair."

"I couldn't agree more." He folded his arms on the granite and leaned across the island toward her. "What's your stake in this?"

"Did you even look at my business card? The embossed part, not the address I handwrote on the back."

"An Atlanta address and area code. What are you doing in the DA's office here?"

"As a courtesy, I was loaned a vacant office to work out of temporarily. I work for the Georgia attorney general. I'm a state prosecutor."

"This isn't Georgia. What work are you doing up here?"

She gave him a pointed look.

He began to chuckle. "Well, you've got your work cut out for you. No, actually your work is done. You can pack up and go home."

"I know it bothers you that Clarke is out."

"Of course it bothers me. I meant it when I said they should have thrown away the key."

"Then why weren't you at the release hearing, waving a banner to that effect?"

"You want to know why I didn't come? I'll tell you why. Because if I'd been there that hearing would have turned into a carnival. Admit it, Ms. Lennon. That hearing came and went without any folderol. It was conducted under the radar. Nobody noticed."

"There was media."

"Really? I didn't see it on TV. It didn't make all those tabloid shows whose lifeblood are scandals and tragedies. It wasn't the cover story of the *National Enquirer*."

She tugged on one of the strands of hair that brushed her cheek. "All right. There was some local coverage because the Clarkes have a high public profile in Atlanta. But you've made your point."

"Thank you." He resettled in his seat and finished his power bar, which allowed time for the air to clear before he resumed. "It was better for Doug, for everybody, if I stayed away and voiced my opinion of Clarke's early release in writing. In any case, nothing I wrote or Doug said mattered, did it? Clarke still got out."

She sighed. "I think the outcome was decided even before

the hearing was convened. I'm guessing, although it will be difficult to prove, that Sid Clarke either bribed or black-mailed the judge, probably a combination of both."

Zach drained his glass of juice and carried it over to the sink. "It sucks," he said, keeping his back to her as he rinsed out the glass. "It truly does. But I won't do it."

He dried his hands before turning back around. "You know, Rebecca wouldn't leave the house, not even to go to a spin class, without being photo-op ready. Hair, makeup, jewelry, the whole shebang. When she crossed out all the 'sad stuff' in that directive, if she had foreseen the indignity of her current condition, I believe she would have said, 'I would rather die.'

"But even if I based my decision on what I *think* would be her wish, I would have to engage in another battle with Doug. I don't want to put him through that, especially since he recently lost Mary.

"And I don't want to put myself through it, either. Apart from the personal agony of having to actually say *when*, the blowback would be more than I'm willing to endure. For a second time."

He ran his hand over his mouth and chin as he gazed down at the hems of his sweatpants that pooled over his bare feet. "I'm sorry." He raised his head and looked across at her. "I understand your agenda. It's sound. It's just. I would like nothing better than for that rich prick to live out the rest of his days in misery. I hope you succeed."

"Eventually, perhaps, I will."

"When Rebecca dies on her own," he said.

"Yes. But what I fear is that 'eventually' will come too late."

"Why the time crunch?"

"The court returned Eban Clarke's passport. If he were tipped of a pending murder charge, he could hop his father's private jet to anywhere. He could be long gone by tomorrow. By tonight. As we speak." She paused and reined in the urgency in her voice. "That's why I came to you, hoping you would at least consider taking this alternative measure."

"Sorry," he said again. "If nailing him is dependent on me ending Rebecca's life, it's not gonna happen. I went through that hell once. I won't put myself through it again."

Elbow on the island, she propped her chin on her fist. Her gaze was nonjudgmental, gently prodding, compelling. And, damn her, it worked. He began to talk.

"As you know, I abdicated to Doug and Mary and cleared out. I thought that would be the end of it for me. Far from it. Rebecca and I, our stormy marriage and divorce, were headlines again.

"Of course the media never let up. That was to be expected. But fans would approach me, too. I couldn't go anywhere, do anything, without being hounded. Even friends too sensitive to bring it up were dying to get the skinny. I could *feel* their curiosity."

Kate hadn't moved or said anything, but had continued to watch him with intensity. Now she said, "Could you have been just a tad paranoid?"

"Possibly. Probably. But at the crux of it, Rebecca's circumstances came to define *me*, not *her*."

"I see that. I'm sorry."

"It was a disservice to her, too. Anyhow, I couldn't wait for training camp to start. At least that would restore my focus, discipline, routine. I counted on the upcoming season to be a diversion, not only for me but for everybody else. But the locker room smack began the first day of camp and soon became intolerable. You know how it is."

She gave a faint smile. "Actually I don't."

"Nothing's sacred. Barbs. Insults. Innuendo. Everything's fair game. But I'd hear things like, 'Give me a chance to pull the plug on my ex. I'd do it in a heartbeat. Oops. No pun intended.'"

"God, how awful."

"And that was from my teammates, guys who liked me, who were joking. Opposing players were ruthless. I'd hear junk like that on the playing field. They did it to distract me, of course, and it did. Best mind-fuck ever. Sorry, but that's what it was."

"It's all right."

"You're not prissy."

She gave that half smile again. "I guess not."

"My game began to slip. I threw two interceptions in one game. First time in my career for that to happen. After the game I got into it with the intended receivers, blamed them for the turnovers. Another first in my career, and something I'm ashamed of to this day.

"Mid-season, I got a back sprain that kept me on the injured list for the next four games. Any other time that would have infuriated me, but I secretly looked on that injury as a welcome reprieve. Backup guy did his best, but we had our first losing season since the team had signed me. Fans got angry, sportswriters got snarky. Word came down from the head office for me to get my shit together before next season. But no pressure, right?"

She laughed softly. "I predicted you'd say that at some point."

"Now you can stop waiting for it." He turned his head and glanced out the window above the sink. "It's getting foggy."

"I'll be fine."

"Deputy Dave warned you about driving in fog."

"I'll take it slow."

He turned back and looked at her. "Or you could bunk here tonight."

Chapter 10

—◦◦◦◦—

Kate lifted her chin off the prop of her fist and lowered her gaze to the surface of the island.

Zach said, "No strings."

She kept her head lowered and didn't say anything. Maybe she had a prissy streak after all, he thought. Or maybe she had a significant other, and he'd been wrong about her feeling the tug of attraction that he was. In either case, he'd plopped the baited line into the water. He waited her out, curious to see if she would bite.

She didn't. When at last she spoke, she returned them to the subject. "The next season, you were no longer the team's starting quarterback."

He wondered how she knew that. It didn't mean she'd followed the team, only that she'd done her homework before making the trip across the state line to inform him that she had the authority and intention of crapping up his life again.

He returned to his counter stool and sat down. "Yeah, they picked up a guy from Bama in the draft. That was the beginning of the end of my career. I warmed the bench most of that season. At the end of it, the team let me go. Nobody else was interested. By then, I was thirty-three years old and had had two bad seasons back-to-back."

"That's when the network hired you."

"Yeah, to talk about a game I could no longer play. It became increasingly harder to do commentary without the chip I was carrying on my shoulder coming through my voice."

"You entered the drunk-and-disorderly phase."

"Which was exposed to the world during a Sunday night playoff game. Rival teams, the Super Bowl at stake, huge viewing audience. I showed up to the set drunk. I insulted the makeup artist who tried her best to conceal the dark circles under my eyes. I verbally abused the sound guy who was trying to adjust my mike level so my slurring wouldn't be so obvious. All this before the first commercial break."

He gave a rueful huff. "They pitched me off the set during the halftime break. That was the end of that. I couldn't even talk about the game anymore."

"Do you miss it?"

It surprised him that she asked. "Playing, you mean? Yes. I started in grade school, so I've spent more years of my life playing than not. Yeah, I miss the game a lot."

"The fame?"

"Not at all."

"Honestly?" She gave him a punch on his arm. "How bad could it have been to be worshiped and adored by thousands?"

"It definitely had its perks." He gave her a grin, but it was short-lived. Serious again, he said, "Honestly, it was absolutely fantastic. But then fame turned to infamy. I don't want either back, thank you."

"You've made that abundantly clear," she said softly.

It was on the tip of his tongue to tell her he was sorry for curtailing her purpose. She was seeking justice, and his decision was preventing her from pursuing it. But an apology would be disingenuous, and she would know that, and probably would resent it. Instead, he asked, "What will you do now?"

"As you said, pack up and go home."

"Dave will be sick he won't be getting you on that zip line."

"He wouldn't be getting me on that zip line in a million years. I have a fear of heights."

"Yet you drove up the mountain road to see me. Twice."

"Risks worth taking."

"They didn't pay off for you, though."

"No. I accept that you're not going to change your mind, and I'm out of arguments." Then her expression changed, as though she'd just been struck with a breakthrough thought. "But maybe not. What's your email address?"

"Why?"

"Why does anyone ask for an email address? I want to send you something. I promise not to share or publicize the address. Okay? You can put it in my phone. It's in my bag on the sofa." She slid off the stool. "I need to be going anyway."

"Before it gets foggier."

"Fog doesn't scare me."

They returned to the living area, where the fire had burned down to a heap of red embers. She took her cell phone from her bag and handed it to him. He pecked his email address into it and gave it back.

"When can I expect the email?"

"Soon."

"Give me a hint?"

"Tonight."

"No, I mean give me a hint of what the email is about."

"It'll be self-evident. Once you've read it, give me a call. My cell number is on my business card."

"Don't hold out hope that I'll change my mind. I won't."

"I respect your conflict, Zach. I do. It's important to me that you believe that." She stuck out her right hand.

"I believe it." He clasped her hand and shook it. "Kate."

She gave him a close-lipped smile, which he returned, then pulled her hand from his. He walked her to the door, opened it, and stepped out onto the porch to check the weather conditions.

"The fog isn't too heavy. You should be all right if you take it slow on the curves."

She went down the porch steps. When she reached the bottom, she halted and looked at him over her shoulder. "I lied to you earlier."

"Fog does scare you?"

"It wasn't my roommate who had your poster above her bed."

Kathryn Cartwright Lennon played dirty pool. The intention of that exit line had been to leave him with something to think about. But if she thought he was going to follow up on it, boy, was she wrong.

Did she think flirting would bend his will? She'd have to do better than that. Team groupies used to throw him their thong underwear. They had his name tattooed around their nipples. They were sexting him before the word had been coined.

Wearing him down by appealing to his ego wouldn't work, either. His had been ground to dust years ago.

Besides, he was probably reading too much into her teenage crush on that damn poster. They were both way beyond that.

Scrounging in his fridge for something for supper, he found a package of deli-sliced roast beef. He built a thick sandwich with plenty of horseradish and took it and his laptop to his favorite chair in front of the hearth. He added logs to the fire and stirred the embers beneath them to get them going, then sat down to eat.

He booted up his laptop and opened his email. The one from her was already there. She'd said soon, but she hadn't even had time to get back to town. She'd stopped alongside the road to send it. What could be so damned important?

Then he read the email's subject line. Cursing, he angrily closed his laptop.

Her half-empty wineglass was where she'd left it on the coffee table. It had a lip gloss imprint of her lower lip on the rim. To look at it fired his imagination and inflated his cock with hope. Vain hope. He tore at his rare roast beef with all the etiquette of a caveman.

Once he'd demolished the sandwich and dusted his hands

of bread crumbs, he reopened his laptop. The one line in the body of the email said that he needed to read only the highlighted sections of the attachment.

With dread, he opened it.

The fire had burned down to embers again by the time he'd read through the specified sections. Twice. He didn't send a reply, but he stared at the screen until it went dark.

Damn her.

Taking his laptop with him, he killed the lights on the first floor, set the alarm, and climbed the stairs. He went into his bathroom and rummaged through the pile of dirty clothes he'd left in the floor when he'd showered. He fished his cell phone from the pocket of his cargo shorts. There was a time when he'd never been without his phone. He'd taken it into the shower, the hot tub, bed, everywhere. That had been before he'd answered it in the Caymans. Now, he carried it only when he thought it might be essential.

He held it in his palm and reconsidered, but then thumbed it on, went into his contacts, and placed the call. He was put through a tiresome menu of options, all of which he skipped until he finally connected with a male human being, who said, "How can I help you?"

"I need to book a flight."

"You can do that online, sir."

"I'm aware of that, but I don't want to book online. I want you to book it for me. Please."

Grudgingly, "Your name?"

"Zach Bridger."

A sustained silence was followed by a guttural laugh. "Are you kidding?"

"No."

"*The* Zach Bridger?"

"I have a VIP code." Zach rattled it off. "I'm not sure it's still valid." Miracle of miracles, it was.

The agent said, "With or without the VIP status, it's my pleasure to help you, Mr. Bridger. Your destination?"

He swallowed, swore, and said a prayer in the same breath. "New Orleans."

Chapter 11

———◆———

Eban was awakened by a persistent knocking on his bedroom door. "Jesus!" He rolled onto his side and opened one
eye halfway. "Later, Frida. I don't want anything."

His father opened the door and popped his head around.
"Not Frida." Without invitation, he strolled into the spacious room. "She told me you two arrived at the house at
the same time this morning. She to report for work. You to
crawl into bed. I understand she assisted you upstairs and
saw you safely tucked in. Apparently Cal and Theo threw
you quite a homecoming bash."

Eban rolled onto his back, stretched, and bunched his
pillow under his head. The clock on the bedside table read
12:04 p.m. His mouth was so dry, his tongue was stuck to the
roof of his mouth. As though reading his mind, Sid poured
him a glass of water from a carafe and passed it to him. He
gulped it down. "Thanks, Dad. God bless Frida."

That she'd stripped him naked when she put him to bed didn't surprise him. She'd been his parents' housekeeper since before Eban was born. God knew how old she was, but she still chugged around like a small locomotive. He had her wrapped around his finger. She often addressed him as "Baby."

Sid sat down on the end of the bed and crossed one long leg over the other. He picked at a nonexistent speck of lint on his trousers. Eban recognized the gesture as his father's most often used delaying tactic. He asked, "So how are they?"

Who? Eban thought. Oh, Cal and Theo. Eban had tried to erase that dinner with them from his mind. It had gotten off to a rocky start and had been capped off by Theo's remark about Eban's prison sentence being fair since he'd actually done the deed. They'd parted with a handshake, but there'd been no authentic comradery behind it.

From the restaurant Eban had gone to the home of his favorite drug dealer. He didn't know his last name. "Simply Simon" was how he'd been introduced to Eban before Eban had been old enough to shave. He'd been a regular customer ever since.

Besides his father, Simply Simon seemed to be the only person in Atlanta who was genuinely glad to see him. He'd unctuously welcomed him into his palatial home where gold leaf had been troweled onto almost every surface. Throughout the house, lounging about in various stages of sublimity, were dopeheads of every stripe, from corporate CEOs to gangbangers. The recreational use of illegal substances was the only common denominator of the demographic.

Eban partook of Simon's smorgasbord, even though Simon cautioned him to exercise moderation until he'd been reconditioned to his pre-prison tolerance level.

He brought Eban two women for his consideration. One had skin the color of cream, the other's was as rich as a dark roast blend. Rather than choosing, Eban had told Simon he'd have café au lait.

The young ladies had been equally beautiful, talented, uninhibited, and, it appeared, expensive. Because when Eban left, the money clip his father had given him was empty.

"What are they doing with themselves these days?"

Eban pulled himself out of the recollection of last night's ménage and realized that Sid wasn't asking after the two whores. He was stuck on Cal and Theo.

What *were* they doing these days? Had he asked? Had they told him? Hell, if he could remember. "Cal's married," he said. "Can you believe it? All the pussy he got without even trying, and the dumb schmuck gets married. Do you think I could weasel a Bloody Mary out of Frida?"

"In a minute. There's something we need to discuss."

Eban had sensed that, but he whined, "Can it wait?"

"No, it can't. It's important."

"All right." Eban tossed back the covers. "Hold the thought. I gotta piss."

He went into his bathroom and used the toilet, chugged a mini bottle of vodka, then squeezed a dab of toothpaste on his tongue.

"Ah, better," he said as he reentered his bedroom. He took a pair of briefs from his bureau and pulled them on, then sat down on the end of his bed and faced Sid, who had claimed a chair near the window.

The early afternoon sun found a crack in the blinds, skewered Eban's eyeball, and pierced straight through his skull. With the sun-filled window behind his old man, his face was in silhouette, a calculated juxtaposition that gave him the upper hand during this "important" chat. Eban knew that tactic, too.

He smiled. "So, Dad? I'm all ears."

"Last night after you left, Up brought up something rather—"

"What's happened to him?"

"To Up? What do you mean?"

"He's all, I don't know. Jowly. Scowly." He made a face imitating Upton's frown.

"He's got a lot on his mind."

"He's always had a lot on his mind. He's different." He leaned back and propped himself on his elbows. "You know what I think? I think he resents me."

"That's ridiculous, Eban. He loves you. You're his godson."

"Yeah, yeah, but when the 'incident'—as he refers to my being maliciously accused of a crime—happened and I was put on trial, he resented being upstaged by my defense attorney."

"We retained him on Up's recommendation."

"Yes, but he ran the show. I took his advice, not Up's. Up played second fiddle."

"Because he isn't a trial lawyer. He doesn't practice criminal law."

Eban chuckled. "No, but he practices law criminally."

Sid wasn't amused. "Nothing came of that bar association

investigation. Let's get back to the subject, which Up brought to my attention."

Eban shrugged and motioned for Sid to proceed.

For the next few minutes, Eban listened as Sid explained Up's warning about the possibility of future legal entanglements.

When he paused for breath, Eban said, "See? He's the prophet of doom and gloom. Hasn't he heard of double jeopardy? I have, and I didn't even go to law school."

Sid picked at another imaginary speck of lint. "He didn't predict that you would be charged for the same crime, Eban. What he said was, this prosecutor could come after you for another."

"Another crime?"

"The same incident. A different charge."

"Like what?"

Sid cleared his throat. "At best, manslaughter. At worst, murder."

Eban went perfectly still, then bolted off the bed. "I didn't murder anybody. Nobody fuckin' died! Why are you bothering me with this? I've already gone to prison for something that wasn't my fault."

"I know, son. But Up is of the opinion—"

"I don't give a shit about Up's opinion. He peaked a long time ago. He's old and tired and he looks it. He's—"

"Sit down."

"—making life difficult, making up—"

"*Sit down!*"

"Don't yell at me!"

But his father did yell, louder than before. *"Sit down and listen to me!"*

Resentfully, Eban plopped back down on the end of the bed.

Sid collected himself before resuming in an even voice. "Your godfather, our trusted advisor, has, for the entirety of your life, sought only our family's best interest in all matters. He has suggested that you keep a low profile, that you remain above reproach and do nothing that incites censure. Your behavior should demonstrate—"

"Demonstrate to who?"

"Anybody. Everybody. You should demonstrate that you've learned a hard lesson about putting yourself in situations that can . . . go awry."

"She didn't die."

"She didn't live, either," Sid snapped. He took another steadying breath. "Up cautioned me, and now I'm cautioning you, that your early release might motivate the prosecutor to attempt to persuade the family to take that girl off life support."

"Her old man won't do it. Remember him at the hearing? Not three months ago he swore that he would never pull the plug on her. Tears streaming down his face." He dragged his fingers down his cheeks. "Boo hoo. As long as my daughter has a heartbeat—"

"I well remember that emotional scene, Eban. You don't need to remind me."

"Then what's got your drawers in such a wad?"

"It's not her father's decision. It's her ex-husband's."

"Oh, right. Bridger. But he adiosed. Washed his hands of it. Didn't come to either my trial or the hearing. Couldn't care less. Besides, I hear that he crashed and burned."

"Up's afraid—"

"Up. Up. I've had it up to here with Up."

"There's a new prosecutor on the case. Up is afraid she'll make a run at Zach Bridger."

"And talk him into changing his mind?"

"That's Up's concern, yes. If Bridger is persuaded, and if he chooses to override Doug Pratt's wishes . . ." He raised his hands.

"The machines are turned off, she dies." Eban flattened his hand against his bare chest. "They can't blame me for that."

His father picked at that damn invisible lint again. In a voice Eban could barely hear, he said, "A case could be made, Eban. It's not without precedent."

His father explained the legal ins and outs as they'd been laid out for him by Upton. As he listened, Eban lapsed into a simmering silence. When his father finished, he got up and walked over to Eban, laid a hand on his shoulder, and pressed.

"There are many hurdles to jump, a thousand ifs, endless debates, moral and legal. Probably nothing will ever come of it, but you needed to know of the threat so you could take care to avoid unwanted attention. A little circumspection would go a long way toward removing the, uh, taint of Rebecca Pratt."

"Sure. I understand."

"Good. Please behave accordingly." Sid patted his shoulder. "You'll be here for dinner?"

"Yeah, I'd counted on it." Eban smiled up at him. "Let's shoot some stick after."

"You're on."

Sid had almost reached the door when Eban halted him. "You said she?"

Sid turned. "Pardon?"

"The prosecutor. You said she?"

"Yes. A rising star in the AG's office named Kathryn Lennon."

Chapter 12

———◆———

Zach was shown into Rebecca's room by a nurse who said, "You have a few minutes before she's scheduled to be turned."

Anxiety had created a lump in his throat that prevented him from speaking. He merely nodded at the nurse and then was left alone.

He had expected the room to be dim and hushed, a deathbed scene. But the window shade was all the way up, letting in sunlight to which his eyes had to adjust. The ceiling lights were on full. Heavy metal rock music was coming from a wireless speaker sitting beside a snow globe of Paris on a wall-mounted shelf.

The brightness and the music could be thought to be inappropriate.

But this was Rebecca's room. She loved the limelight, spotlights, and hard rock.

With reluctance, Zach advanced into the room. To his right was a sink. On the counter next to it were several plastic basins of various sizes, a stack of folded towels and wash cloths, containers of liquid soap, shampoo, body lotion. Nail clippers. Lip salve. A hairbrush. A box of adult diapers.

Quickly looking away, he took in all the medical apparatus: the monitoring machines with their blinking lights, the IV pole, the seeming miles of tubing that snaked around the bed and up underneath the light blue blanket…on top of which a pair of hands rested.

He didn't recognize them as Rebecca's hands. They were curled downward at a severe angle, fingertips almost touching the inside of her wrists. The nails were short, blunt, unvarnished.

After seeing the distortion of her hands, he took several deep breaths before he could bring himself to look at Rebecca herself.

He gasped.

───

"Please have a seat, Mr. Bridger."

The doctor's name was Anna Gilbreath. It was printed on the brass placard at the edge of her desk. The number of letters following her name attested to her qualifications to be the administrator of the special care facility.

She reminded Zach of his tenth-grade English teacher, who'd made the class wade through *Beowulf*: cardigan sweater, reading glasses hanging from a chain around her neck, and, despite her benign features, an authoritative bearing.

She began with a subtle admonishment. "I've been here for two years, but up till now I haven't had the pleasure of meeting you."

He propped his ankle on his opposite knee, then awkwardly lowered his foot to the floor again. "My first time here."

"Welcome," she said. "May I ask why now?"

"First, I want to thank you for seeing me without an appointment. I came straight from the airport."

"Fortunately for both of us I had a clear schedule this afternoon. Where did you travel from?"

"Western North Carolina via Atlanta."

"You came quite a distance. What prompted your visit?"

"I wanted to check things out, talk to whoever is in charge of Rebecca's care."

"Then you're in the right office. What's your impression so far?"

He shifted in his seat, propped his elbows on the chair's armrests, then removed them. "Everything's top-notch. The place, the staff. I'd give it high ratings in every category."

"Thank you. Our staff is committed to providing our patients excellent medical care, as well as treating them with the respect and dignity they deserve."

"That commitment shows."

"I'm glad to hear it." After a brief stall, she said, "I'm told you spent some time in Rebecca's room before asking to meet with me."

He put his fist to his mouth and gave a dry cough. "I didn't really come down here to check up on you, Dr. Gilbreath. The facility has a flawless reputation, which is why the Pratts chose it. I came to get a clearer understanding of Rebecca's condition. I mean, after seeing her, it's obvious that she... Uh. Want I want is to understand...Hell." Dropping his head forward, he expelled a long whoosh of air.

Softly she asked, "Would you like some water?"

He nodded.

She got up, took a bottle of water from a small refrigerator, and brought it to him. He wanted to roll the cold bottle across his damp forehead, but he uncapped it and took a swallow. "Thank you."

"You're welcome." She touched his shoulder very lightly, very briefly, before resuming her seat behind the desk. "Don't be embarrassed by your distress, Mr. Bridger. The Rebecca you knew was a vibrant young woman. You wouldn't be human if you weren't deeply affected by her present condition."

"Which is what, exactly? I've been told she isn't brain dead. Clinically speaking."

"That's right. Her brain stem function is minimal, but enough that she breathes on her own. She's in what we call a PVS. Persistent vegetative state. Rebecca suffered a traumatic brain injury. She was deprived of oxygen for a length of time more than sufficient to cause severe cerebral damage and render her unaware and unresponsive. From a medical standpoint, the qualifier that makes her condition 'persistent' is that it's lasted for longer than twelve months."

"It's been four *years*." Zach plowed his fingers up through his hair and kept them around his head. His scalp was damp from the sweat he'd broken while in Rebecca's room. "I didn't expect her eyes to be open."

"She has sleep-wake cycles. But even while awake, she has no awareness of, or reaction to, her surroundings. She has no cognitive function. She doesn't think or respond to any stimuli."

"Nothing?"

"No." She hesitated. "Family members often cling to the hope, the belief, that their voice or touch is somehow getting through to their loved one, that they're communicating on some level."

Zach lowered his hand from his head and looked at her directly. "Her father."

"He comes every day. He and Mrs. Pratt used to alternate, but since she passed, he's missed very few days. He usually comes early in the morning and stays for an hour or so. You missed him today."

"That's a good thing."

She rolled her lips inward, then said, "Mr. Bridger, I'm not going to pretend that I don't know the circumstances of how Rebecca came to be here."

"They were well publicized."

"I didn't follow the story as it was unfolding, but when I took over Rebecca's care, my predecessor informed me of the contention that exists between you and Mr. Pratt. And, just so you know, the staff is aflutter because you're in our midst. Within minutes of your arrival, it had spread throughout the building that you had darkened our door."

"I'd hoped to sneak in and out with only you knowing."

"I believe that would have been impossible."

"Yeah, me too. Can you keep a lid on it?"

"I already have. Everyone on staff received a text

reminder from me about our privacy policy, which is strictly enforced."

"Thank you. On behalf of Doug and Rebecca, too."

"For you to have risked exposure of your visit, there must be a compelling reason for it."

"There is, but I'm not at liberty to discuss it. I will tell you that it's not a financial problem. The tabloid stories are fiction. I haven't gone broke, I'm not living on the street. You don't need to be concerned about any interruption of the payment schedule. "

"I wasn't." She moved closer to her desk, narrowing the distance between them. Speaking more softly, she said, "Why did you come, Mr. Bridger? What is it you want to know?"

He spread his knees and clasped his hands between them. Head down, he stared at the carpeted space between his shoes. "When your predecessor filled you in on Rebecca's history, did he give you all of it, or just hit the high points?"

"He hit the high points, but I took it from there. I read all the reports, all the doctors' notes and recommendations, examined every chart."

Although he didn't raise his head, he nodded. "So you know about Rebecca's drug and alcohol abuse, all that?"

"Yes, I know about everything."

He did look up at her then.

Her expression remained impassive, but she pointed to a file cabinet. "Rebecca's medical records, the ones previous to her being admitted here, are locked away. They're for my eyes only. You can depend on my discretion."

"That's good. Thank you. If things get crazy again, and

they might, I wouldn't want all that exposed and scrutinized," he said, glancing at the file cabinet.

"Why do you think things might get crazy again? Are you second-guessing the decision you made four years ago?"

"No. Maybe. I don't know."

She must have sensed his impatience with himself. "Take your time."

When he felt ready to put his ambiguities into words, he said, "When this happened to Rebecca, I would have hated it like hell for anybody, for a total stranger. There was no love lost between us, believe me. Neither of us left the marriage with a broken heart. But I guess that vow about in sickness and in health subconsciously factored into my decision to take no action. Now, though, I've been given a reason, a crucial reason, to reevaluate.

"First thing I want to ask is how long can Rebecca remain like this? And, please, no bullshit about the brain being a mysterious organ, or stranger things have happened, or you're not God.

"Based on all those letters," he said, chinning toward the name plate, "and your history with similar patients, you're qualified to give me your best guess. How long?"

She indicated that she understood his request and would give it to him straight. "Rebecca hasn't experienced any organ failure. She hasn't contracted pneumonia, and we do all we can to prevent that and other infections, any of which could be fatal. In every regard, she's well cared for. Her bodily functions are closely monitored and seen to. She's exercised daily. She gets adequate fluids and nutrition."

"Through tubes."

"Yes."

He rubbed his forehead. "What you're saying is, she could stay like this indefinitely, that nothing will ever change."

"On the contrary. She could decline. It could be sudden and steep, or gradual. Any of the things that I just told you hadn't happened yet could occur at any time. For instance, the brain stem could cease function, requiring that she be put on a ventilator."

"I thought she was. What's that tube for?" He touched his Adam's apple.

"She can't swallow. The tracheotomy tube prevents obstruction and eases her breathing."

He assimilated everything she'd told him. "What you're saying is that things could get worse, but she'll never improve."

"Patients who recover from a TBI usually begin showing improvement within a matter of days. After this length of time..." She shook her head. "In the highly unlikely event that Rebecca became even minimally conscious, her mental capacity would be nil. Her most recent EEG and PET scan show virtually no electrical activity or cerebral function." She gave him a kind smile. "But stranger things have happened, and I'm not God."

His throat had grown tight, making it difficult to swallow. "Say you were called upon to play God, Dr. Gilbreath. What would you do?"

Chapter 13

—————◆◆◆—————

Zach had to press Bing's doorbell three times before he heard the bolt clack. His former coach opened the door. "Where'd you come from?"

"Louisiana."

"What the hell were you doing down there?"

"It's raining out here."

Bing moved out of the way and motioned him inside. He took off his jacket and shook rainwater off it, then hung it on the hall tree. "Why didn't you answer your doorbell?"

"Why didn't you warn me that you were coming? If you were on your way home from Louisiana, wasn't coming through South Carolina a little out of your way?" After retiring from his coaching job at Clemson, Bing had moved back to nearby Greenville where he'd begun his career at a local high school. "Now you're here..." He turned and waved his hand for Zach to follow him.

They filed down the dim hallway whose walls served as a gallery for pictures of football teams, players, and high-light game moments captured on film. The images covered the decades of Bing's coaching career. Zach was featured in many of the photos, but he didn't pause to gaze upon them with nostalgia.

Bing led him into his den, a room that defined the word. It had darkly paneled walls, a low acoustical tile ceiling, two small windows with shades that Zach had never seen open, and furniture that was at least thirty years old. But a large, late model, high-tech TV was attached to the wall opposite Bing's vintage leather recliner.

"It was just getting to the good part," he grumbled. On the screen a man and woman, both buck naked, were copulating with vigor in a bed draped in embellished velvet.

Zach said, "Don't let me interrupt."

"Aw, I've seen it." Bing reached for the remote and muted the lusty grunts and groans. "It's one of those historical series. There's a bloody war with horses and swords and castles, and knights shouting, 'Open the gate.'"

"Who's winning?"

"The war? I don't know. I don't think the warriors know, either. They fornicate more than they fight." He claimed his recliner. "Sit down. Want something to drink? You know where the fridge is."

There was a can of beer on the TV tray at Bing's right hand.

"No thanks." Zach sat down on the sofa and leaned his head back against the sagging cushion.

"You gonna make me ask again?"

"I'm not thirsty. I'll get something later."

"Not about that. What were you doing in Louisiana? *Where* in Louisiana?"

"New Orleans."

"Huh." They exchanged a long look, communicating silently what his trip had pertained to. Bing took a sip of his beer, then returned the can to the tray, saying, "Well, you've got the right to know where things stand with her."

"The right." Zach laid his forearm across his eyes. "I'd happily give up that right. I tried to."

"Not hard enough."

"I did what I thought was right at the time."

"You caved under pressure is what you did. Like a rookie."

"Jesus. You're making me sorry I came."

"Why didn't you insist on resigning, Zach? You would have been free of this years ago."

"That was then, this is now. Let's focus on now, okay?"

Bing was scowling, but he eased off. "Did you see Rebecca?"

"Yes."

"Bad, I guess."

"You guess right."

"Was her dad around?"

"No."

"Any particular reason why you chose now to pay a visit?"

"Yes." Zach lowered his arm and looked over at Bing, who had his rough hands linked and resting on his middle. He'd settled in to listen.

"Yesterday morning, I was outside having coffee and enjoying my view of the waterfall. This slick SUV pulls up." Zach began at the beginning and told him everything.

When he finished, having talked for almost half an hour uninterrupted, he kept his eyes closed and waited to hear what Bing would say about it all.

"So this Lennon woman gave you the transcript of Eban Clarke's trial."

"Last night." Last night? God, it seemed like a thousand years ago, and he'd covered at least that many miles since then. "She sent it to me in an email."

"And you read the parts she'd highlighted."

"Twice."

"When did you last sleep?"

Zach opened his eyes. "What?"

"You heard me."

"She left my house about, uh...I don't know. After reading the transcript, I booked my flight, packed, and drove to Atlanta. Left my car in a remote lot at the airport and slept for a few hours at one of the hotels there."

Bing said, "Then took an early flight to New Orleans, went to the hospital and had your meeting, then back to the airport for a return flight to Atlanta."

"Picked up my car and drove here," Zach said testily. "Which I'm beginning to regret. I came to you for advice, and you're talking like a damn travel agent. What am I supposed to do, Bing?"

Unfazed, Bing said, "Well, first thing I advise is that you get some rest. You're too exhausted to think through a dilemma like this. Have you eaten?"

He waved that off. "Ms. Lennon is afraid that Clarke will get word of what she's after and take off to parts unknown. In which case, she'll have lost her shot."

"How determined is she?"

"I think she's made it a mission, but she hasn't told me why."

"It's her job."

"Yeah, but I get the sense there's a personal slant." He only realized as he spoke the words that he had sensed that about Kate. Her packaging was petite, but she had a crusader's persistence.

"Is she a man-hater?" Bing said. "Blames us all for the sins of a few?"

"No, she's not like that."

"What is she like?"

He had hoped Bing wouldn't ask, but now that he had, he hedged. "All business, articulate, smart. She's doing this covertly. Says her success depends on secrecy. First wind of it, and Clarke would take to the skies, which is why she wants my decision sooner rather than later."

"Then tell her later. For crissake, Zach, this is a decision nobody should ever have to make. Tell this Lennon woman to back off. Give yourself a day or two."

"I would. But in a day or two, the dilemma I'm faced with could be the hot topic on every TV talk show. Dr. Gilbreath said her staff was all aflutter over me being there. She reminded them of the strict privacy policy, but I was relieved as I left the building not to see news vans parked outside.

"I'm certain Doug will learn that I was there. He'll go apeshit." He lowered his head and rubbed his gritty eyes. "I admire the guy, Bing. I was in that room for five minutes at the most. When I came out, I was weak in the knees. Came close to losing it in Dr. Gilbreath's office. I expected it to be awful. But it was worse than awful. Much worse.

"Doug lives with it, day in, day out. He's hands on. Rebecca's fate should lie with him, not me. We could have guardianship switched over to him, but could we do it secretly? I doubt it. That's the hitch. The gossip-mongers would be clamoring to know *why now*? That might get Clarke's antenna up and blow any chance Ms. Lennon has of getting another indictment.

"Besides that, I wouldn't want the publicity for Doug or me. The rumors and speculation circulating all over again? No thank you. What if someone at the facility was low enough to leak pictures of Rebecca to the media? God, I can't bear the thought. Dr. Gilbreath has faith in her staff's commitment to the patients and their privacy, but I'm afraid it would go right out the window if enough money was offered."

Zach noticed that Bing hadn't chimed in for a while. He was tugging on his lower lip, seemingly deep in thought.

"Are you listening?" Zach asked.

"Yes, and I'm paying attention. I'm just thinking about all the lives that continue to be wrecked because of that Clarke shithead. I'd love to see that Lennon woman come through."

Zach hadn't yet forgiven Kate for sending him the trial transcript, although he'd learned a lot from reading it. She had highlighted the prosecutor's opening statement and closing argument. She'd highlighted the defense attorney's fiery rebuttal. Also highlighted were the testimonies of Calvin Parsons and Theo Simpson, who'd steadfastly denied that Rebecca had been a victim.

She'd also highlighted the testimonies of the doctors who

saw Rebecca when she arrived at Emory's ER, as well as the testimonies of specialists who assessed her condition after they brought her out of the coma.

He said to Bing now, "The trial transcript didn't make for light reading."

"I'm sure it didn't. But it spurred you to drop everything, come down from your mountain hideaway, and go see for yourself the damage that degenerate did to Rebecca."

"What are you getting at?"

"Like the Lennon woman says, Clarke will remain free unless you—"

"Bing, I *can't*. Whenever I heard of taking someone off life support, I thought of turning off a ventilator. It's horrendous even to think about flipping that switch, but at least it's over in a matter of minutes. Less.

"Rebecca isn't on a ventilator. Do you know what I would have to authorize? Removal of the feeding tube. No more fluids." Zach leaned forward, propped his elbows on his knees, and covered his face with both hands. "It could take days. Is it any wonder that Doug is so opposed to it? Who could bring themself to do that? I just can't."

Bing sat quietly, then picked up the remote and turned off the TV where medieval war was still raging. He lowered the footrest and came out of his recliner. "There hasn't been anyone in the extra bedroom since you were last here. Sheets probably smell mildewy."

The thought of a bed was alluring, but Zach was so exhausted he couldn't bring himself to move from his spot on the sofa. He pulled an ugly knitted afghan from the back of it and grabbed a throw pillow. "I'll do fine right here."

"Suit yourself."

At the door, Bing stopped and turned back. "Maybe you ought to flip your thinking."

"What do you mean?"

"Well, it occurs to me that you've given a lot of thought to how your decision, whichever way it goes, will affect Ms. Lennon and her cause, that Clarke deviant, Doug Pratt, and yourself. But have you given any thought to the person most affected by your decision? Rebecca."

Chapter 14

———◆———

Zach was up before Bing, up before he wanted to be, but he'd awakened early and knew he wouldn't go back to sleep. He wrote Bing a note of thanks for his wise counsel and for putting him up for the night, and promised to be in touch soon.

He left the note on the kitchen table under the salt shaker and sneaked out before daylight. Although there was no sunrise to see. The sky was overcast and glowering.

The drive from Bing's house in Greenville, South Carolina, to Zach's place took five hours. He drove it as the crow flies, keeping to the narrow state highways. Even then it wasn't a straight shot. The roads were twisty and, today, kept slick by intermittent rain.

When he finally pulled into his cul-de-sac, his body was stiff from sitting for so long, and his mind ached from thinking. To work the kinks out of both, he spent half an hour in his home gym, showered, then crawled into bed and took a nap.

When his alarm went off, he dressed and drove into town. He was relieved to see the familiar SUV parked parallel in front of the ugly office building. He pulled his pickup into a metered slot facing the courthouse.

When Kate exited the DA's office at twenty past six, he got out of his truck, jogged across the street, and reached the driver's side of her car ahead of her by a margin of five seconds.

She drew up to her full height and said with accusatory pique, "I called you several times yesterday."

"I know. I ignored the calls because I hadn't decided yet if I was still speaking to you."

"Since you're here, I guess you are." She hoisted her weighted bag more securely onto her shoulder like a soldier preparing for an uphill charge. "What did you come to say?"

"That place that grills trout to perfection?"

Obviously that hadn't been what she'd expected, and it took her a moment to respond. "The Lodge."

"They grill a good steak, too. Are you hungry?"

She kept him waiting while she mulled it over, then said, "I suppose I could eat. After a glass of wine."

"That kind of day?"

"And then some."

"I'll meet you there."

He left her standing beside her car and walked back to his pickup. He didn't want it to appear that this was a date. He hadn't shaved his scruff, hadn't dressed for a date. He was in his favorite worn jeans, an old pair of boots, and a leather jacket over a lightweight sweater.

He got spattered with raindrops as he made his way from his truck to the entrance of the restaurant, where he waited for Kate, watching as she got out of her car and popped open an umbrella. She was the type who'd have one at the ready.

He held the door open and ushered her inside. The hostess greeted them with a down-home smile. "Hi, Zach." And to Kate she said, "You were here last week. I like your hair. Welcome back. I didn't know y'all knew each other. Want a window table or one near the fireplace?"

Zach deferred to Kate, who gave a little shiver. "Fireplace, please."

When they were seated in a cozy booth adjacent to the hearth, the hostess took their drink orders, then left them with menus. Kate, busy with placing her napkin in her lap, said, "You must come here often."

"When I run out of things I know how to cook."

"I thought you might have someone who cooks for you."

"Why would you think that?"

She slapped her menu onto the table. "I don't know, Zach. Actually I never gave a thought as to whether or not you had a personal chef. It was just something to say to end an awkward silence."

"Was it awkward for you?"

She glared at him and was on the verge of saying something when the hostess arrived with their drinks. Zach told her they'd signal when they were ready to order. Kate waited until she was out of earshot. "I guess you were too miffed to speak to me because of what I'd emailed you."

"You blindsided me. A blind side hit is always the hardest."

"Did you read any of it?"

"Yes."

"And?"

"We'll get to that." He clinked his glass of bourbon against her wine balloon. "Cheers."

"Not really." Nevertheless, she took a drink of her wine.

"What made your day rotten?"

"A culmination of things. I had to walk to and from the courthouse a dozen times and—"

"Why?"

"Because the internet connection is better there. According to the lady at the cable office who took my complaint call, the internet service is especially dicey when it's wet outside."

"It is."

"How was I supposed to know that? I don't live up here in the mountains. I should have been cautioned about the internet's unreliability before they stuck me in the horrible office.

"Anyway, I spent all day traipsing back and forth across the street. And now I look and feel like a drowned rat, while you show up looking like a Ralph Lauren ad, which amounts to sabotage, and is very unfair. I'm just saying." She took another slug of wine.

Zach wanted to laugh, but he wasn't that stupid. "You could have saved yourself all this hassle by going back to Atlanta."

"I didn't want to drive through the mountains in the rain.

Besides, I thought I'd stay until I got your reaction to the transcript of Eban Clarke's trial."

He wanted her simmered down before they talked about that. "What else got you riled?"

She hesitated, stared into the low flames in the nearby grate, then brought her gaze back to him. "I have an investigator keeping tabs on him, on Clarke. The AG approved it only this morning. I'm trusting you with that information. It's not for public knowledge."

"Natch."

"I spoke to the investigator just before leaving the office. He reported that Eban is zipping around the city in a spanking new, quarter-million-dollar car. He's buying designer clothes, designer shoes, living the life of royalty." She placed her fingertips in the center of her forehead and rubbed them up and down. "I have a real problem with that."

After his visit to the special care facility, Zach had a real problem with it, too.

He took a look around the dining room, relieved to see that it wasn't crowded. Locals had become accustomed to seeing him in and around, so they rarely approached him anymore. The tall back of the booth behind Kate provided seclusion and would keep them from being overheard.

He said, "We can order whenever you're ready."

His tone must have signaled her that he wasn't yet ready, because she told him she could wait.

He nodded. "I want to ask you a question."

"All right."

"Are you a star prosecutor?" She opened her mouth to speak, but he headed her off. "Don't be modest."

"Well, I'm not a novice. I paid my dues in a county DA's office, much like the one here. The area was rife with meth labs and opioid supply chains. I went after them and got convictions. My win–loss record helped me jump the line of lawyers hoping for a position in the attorney general's office."

"Figured that," he said. "What I want to know is if the AG assigned you this case, or if you took it upon yourself?"

"As I told you, I did background and research for Clarke's early release hearing. The arguments against any reduction of his sentence were so compelling, the judge's ruling floored me. I went to the big boss himself and made a case for pursuing a more serious charge against Clarke once he was out."

"And Rebecca officially deceased."

"Yes," she said, looking rueful. "The AG actually winced. He reeled off a long list of the difficulties and delicate issues involved. He used adjectives like 'polarizing' and 'incendiary.' All of which, he stressed, are trapdoors for a prosecutor.

"And then there's Eban's distinguished bloodline. Never mind that he robbed Rebecca of her life that night, even if she didn't die. Bottom line, the AG would rather avoid the matter until *after* the November election.

"I argued that if we wait, Eban will fly the coop. So I stuck to my guns and cited the precedent-setting cases that made headlines and were debated on national programs like *Face the Nation*. He has an ego, so he liked the sound of that, and, after exhaustive discussion, gave me leave to approach you."

"To test the temperature of the water," Zach said.

"Yes. But it was conditional. He reminded me of all the moral and ethical implications, and advised that I approach you with caution. Not with shock and awe."

She reached for her glass, but rolled the stem between her fingers without picking it up. "He also stipulated that if you declined even to consider a change of course for Rebecca, I was to let it go and apply no pressure to you whatsoever." Having made the admission, she met his gaze head-on.

Studying her, he rubbed his index finger back and forth across his lips. His thoughtful scrutiny made her squirm. "What?"

"I don't think you're going to let it go. I know you're beating the drum for law and order and all that, but there are a thousand criminals you could target to bring to justice without all the trapdoors. Why are you fixated on Eban Clarke?"

"I'm not fixated, I—"

"Why, Kate?"

She tilted her chin up. "I'm an officer of the court. I want justice for Rebecca. That's all the explanation you need."

He knew there was more to it than that, but he'd pushed her as far as he could. For the moment. He took a sip of bourbon then said in a low tone, "I went to see Rebecca yesterday."

To Kate's credit, she didn't begin peppering him with questions. Rather, she looked at him with a mix of compassion and expectation.

"It was a quick trip," he said. "I didn't have to be there long to fully grasp the quality of her life, which amounts to no quality." He took another sip of his whiskey. "I think I mentioned Bing to you?"

Kate dipped her chin in acknowledgment.

"On my way back, I went to see him. He can be as ornery as hell, but I haven't listened to him and heeded his advice for all these years because he talks nonsense." He gave a dry laugh and scratched his eyebrow with his thumbnail. "I didn't ask his advice before marrying Rebecca. Look how that turned out.

"Anyway, last night I laid it all out for him, starting with your coming out of nowhere and dropping this bomb on me. For half an hour, I talked nonstop. But Bing was more concise. After I'd gone off on all these tangents, he honed things down to this." He raised his index finger. "He said that the person most affected by my decision is the person I've given the least consideration."

She spoke the name on a soft breath. "Rebecca."

"Yeah. When it happened, many said she'd gotten no better than she deserved for going into a bedroom, while stoned, with three men. She lived wildly, recklessly, and paid the price." He paused, picked up his glass, and looked down into the bourbon. "Those harsh judges should have to spend time—only a brief time—in that hospital room with her. Nobody deserves having to exist like that."

He shot the whiskey and set down his glass. "I'm giving you no guarantee, Kate. It's gotta be my decision, and I won't be browbeaten or rushed into making it. But I've come around to thinking that maybe Rebecca has been victimized long enough. And not only by Eban Clarke, but by her father. And me."

———

They ordered. During their meal, they didn't talk about anything relating to Rebecca. Kate, and she assumed Zach also, needed a breather.

As she stirred a dollop of cream into her after-dinner coffee, she said, "Bing seems to be an important and trusted person in your life."

"The most trusted. He sort of filled in for my parents when they were killed in a car wreck."

"I read about that in an article I found online. I'm sorry."

"Me too. They were driving home from a game my freshman year at Clemson. Nobody's fault, just a dreadful accident. Four fatalities in all. A number to everybody else. To me, a monumental loss."

"You were close."

He smiled. "Very. Dad was my best buddy and biggest fan. Mom was beautiful, gracious. Exceptional people, really. Both of them."

"What's your favorite memory?"

"Jeez, there are so many, but a standout is the day I signed my letter of intent with Clemson. Full athletic scholarship. Mom and Dad were so proud. They celebrated big, had all their friends over for a cookout. A few months later, they were gone." He snapped his fingers.

"No siblings?"

"No, just me. That's when Bing took over the parental role, although he never came right out and said it, and I probably would have decked him if he had. Nobody could have replaced my mom and dad. But in his own grouchy way, he nursed me through that year, kept me in line, focused. Thanks to him, I came out strong my sophomore and junior years."

"And thanks to you, the Tigers won the national championship your senior year." At his arch look, she added, "I did my homework."

"Of course you did." He smiled before turning reflective again. "It was tough, losing my parents so suddenly like that. But later I looked on it as a blessing of sorts. They didn't have to go through that scandalous mess with me, and they weren't around to watch my fall from grace."

"Maybe if they had been around, things wouldn't have turned out as they did."

"Maybe." He gave a dry laugh. "Rebecca sure as hell wouldn't have been their pick for a daughter-in-law."

Kate hesitated then asked something she'd been wanting to ask. "How'd you two meet?"

"She hung out in the clubs known to be gathering places for team members. There were always these girls, all dolled up and available. You know."

"Looking for action with a hot jock."

"Or the man with the 'it' factor of the moment. That was her job."

"Her job? What do you mean?"

"She'd gone to cosmetology school. Something like that. But she made a career of looking great and showing up at happenings. Events. PGA tournaments, movie premiers, like that. Anywhere she'd be seen rubbing elbows with the glitterati."

"How did she support herself?"

He gave a dry chuckle. "She didn't have to. Her catch-of-the-day would put her up in his hotel suite, take her shopping, indulge her until she moved on to the next guy."

"Which ultimately wound up being you."

"Yeah. That season there was a lot of buzz about my throwing arm and the team going all the way to the Super

Bowl." With bitterness, he added, "And then, following that win, there was a lot of chatter about my new contract.

"After the amount of it was reported, Rebecca came on strong. She made herself noticed among the other groupies. Every time I turned around, there she was. One night, I went home with her. Six weeks later, we were saying boozy 'I dos' in a wedding chapel in Vegas. I'm a little vague on exactly how we got there. I don't recall actually proposing."

He shook his head with self-deprecation. "Jesus, I was so full of myself. I felt invincible. The only serious rift Bing and I ever had was when I skipped two days of spring training. He came storming to our house, dragged me out of bed, backed me into the wall, and told me I had to be the most arrogant, obnoxious blankety-blank on the planet, and he wanted nothing to do with my big-headed self."

"But he took you back."

"Yeah, when I came crawling to him after three months of wedded bliss. I'd found out that Rebecca was in the throes of her first fling."

"Ouch."

"Oh, don't feel sorry for me. When I heard about her affair, I started having fun on the side, too. Women were easy to come by. What escaped me were concepts like humility, gratitude, common sense, responsibility, vital stuff like that."

"How old were you, Zach? Twenty-six, twenty-seven? Fame like that is a lot to handle when one is that young."

"Young, yes. But mostly stupid and self-congratulatory." He folded his arms on the table. "Enough. I've spilled my guts. Tell me one of your deep dark secrets."

She laughed. "I'm boring."

"You're a rock star in your field."

"Not yet. But I'm giving it the good ol' college try."

"What about your parents?"

"Bob and Jenny. Married forty-something years and still in love. I, too, was an only child."

"A brain child, I'll bet."

"I have a healthy IQ. A genetic favor. Both my parents were physicians. They're now retired and living on Hilton Head. They play golf every day, preach the merits of sunscreen and fiber, and complain that I don't call often enough. See? Boring."

"I wasn't bored, but you told me about them, not you. Come on. One secret. I promise not to tell."

She hunched her shoulders and took a deep breath, lowering her shoulders as she released it. "My hair turned white when I was twenty years old."

"Heredity?"

"Neither parent had one gray strand yet. No one could account for it, not even specialists, and we consulted them all. As you can imagine, I was hysterical. I colored it for a while, but that got tedious and expensive. When I considered cancer patients who lose their hair, people with alopecia, I stopped obsessing. So." She framed her head between her hands. "People assume that I bleach it, but this is natural."

"What color was it?"

"Brownish."

"This suits you better."

"Thank you. There. Now you own a deep dark secret of mine."

"I have another one to share."

She grinned. "Oooh. Do tell."

"I've been sitting here for ninety-something minutes, through the drinks, the salads, the steaks, and the coffee, all the time wanting to put my mouth against yours."

Chapter 15

Kate lowered her head and fiddled with the spoon she'd used to stir cream into her coffee. "That can't happen, Zach."

"I know."

"It would be a very bad idea."

"I know." He motioned to her left hand, the one still fiddling with the spoon. "You don't wear a ring. Is there a Mr. Lennon?"

"My dad."

"Besides him."

She shook her head. "I've never married. I've been in a couple of relationships that eventually fizzled for one reason or another, but mostly from apathy."

"I've never been in a relationship."

She looked at him quizzically.

"It's true," he said. "One-night stands, short-term amusements, but never a relationship. Not even my marriage could be called that. Especially my marriage."

"That's very sad."

"Tell me."

"But nothing can happen between us."

"I know."

She gave him a tepid smile, and he gave her one back, then looked around and realized that only a handful of other diners remained. "Now that we've settled that, you ready?"

Even though it wasn't a date, he kept his hand at the small of her back as they walked to the entrance. They thanked the hostess. He pushed open the door and followed Kate out. The rain was really coming down now.

She opened her umbrella. "Do you want me to walk you to your truck so you don't get wet?"

"I've played four quarters in worse than this. I won't melt."

"Thank you for dinner and for talking me into ordering the filet."

"You bet. I'll walk with—" He broke off when, out of the corner of his eye, he saw motion near his pickup. Someone was walking along the bed of it on the driver's side. As he watched, whoever it was rounded the rear end and disappeared behind it. "Hey!"

Mindless of the downpour, he took off in a sprint, splashing through the puddles that had formed in the parking lot. He rounded the rear end of his truck and nearly collided with a hulk draped in black rain gear who was peering into the bed of his pickup.

Zach saw red. "What the fuck are you doing?" Reaching for a shoulder, he spun the guy around.

It was Deputy Dave Morris.

Kate lit out after Zach, battling her umbrella until she gave up and collapsed it. She ran to the rear of the truck where Zach and the deputy were once again in a face-off.

Seeing her, Morris smiled in the insidious way that grew more repugnant each time she saw it. "Hi, Kate."

Before she could respond, Zach sidestepped to put his shoulder between her and the deputy. "What the hell are you doing snooping around my truck?"

Rainwater was dripping off the wide brim of Morris's hat, which had a fitted plastic cover. "There was another incident of vandalism at GreenRidge last night."

Zach's jaw clenched. "Not my problem. Again, *what are you doing around my truck?*"

"I was just wondering if those folks had gotten back at you for perceived offenses against their valuable property."

"What are you talking about?"

"Over here." Morris turned and went around the rear bumper to the passenger side. Kate and Zach followed. From the folds of his slicker, Morris produced a large flashlight and shone it onto the truck, following a jagged furrow that had been dug into it from bumper to bumper.

"Someone's keyed it," Morris said. "I'm guessing in revenge for the vandalism."

"Which I didn't do."

"Well, holes were punched in newly installed Sheetrock last night. Looked like with a ball peen hammer, something of that sort."

Huddled close to Zach, Kate could feel the wrath emanating from him. She said, "Are there any security cameras at the construction site?"

"They're looking into installing some."

"In the meantime," she said, "perhaps they should hire guards to protect their valuable property."

"That's exactly what I advised, Kate." The deputy winked at her as though he and she were a two-person alliance.

Presumptuous ass.

Zach said, "You were just driving past the restaurant and happened to spot that gash in the side of my truck? In the dark? Through the rain?"

Morris took umbrage. "No, I'd called in an order for pickup. I pulled in over there." He tipped his head toward his vehicle, which looked to Kate like a deliberate move to dump rainwater from the brim of his hat onto Zach. "My headlights caught it. I didn't remember seeing it when I was up at your place the other day, so I came to investigate, see if the perp left any clues. I didn't find anything."

"No, I'm sure you didn't," Zach said.

"Somebody was sending you a message." Morris again shone his flashlight along the gouge and made a sound of regret. "I hope your deductible isn't too high."

Fearing that Zach was about to launch himself at the deputy, Kate said, "You don't want your food order to get cold, Dave."

"No." The deputy's eyes sawed back and forth between

the two of them, then he said good night, switched off his flashlight, and started across the parking lot toward the restaurant's entrance.

"I'm sorry," she murmured to Zach. She opened the umbrella and held it above the two of them. Or tried. She couldn't reach high enough to cover him.

His angry expression relaxed. "It's a little late for that to be any good, but here."

He took the umbrella from her, held it over her, and started walking in the direction of her car. She unlocked it with her fob and opened the door. He gave her a hand up, then collapsed the umbrella and passed it to her. "Where are you staying?"

She gave him the name of a popular bed-and-breakfast.

"Main house?"

"One of the cottages."

"I'll follow to see that you get safely inside."

"That isn't necessary."

"I'll follow you." He closed her car door.

He stayed close on her bumper as they drove through the picturesque town center. Tonight, it was locked up tight; the streets were dark. Arriving at the B and B, she parked in the designated space in front of the cottage, gathered her things, and made a dash for the door, where she turned to wave Zach goodbye.

But he had pulled his truck in beside her car and was getting out. He joined her beneath the narrow overhang. "Open the door," he said. "Take a look."

Shaking her head over the absurdity of his precaution, she used the old-fashioned key to unlock the door. Reaching in, she flipped on the light switch. They peered inside. "See? All's well. No bogeyman."

"Okay, laugh. But I don't like that guy. I don't trust him. He has a lech for you. He didn't like seeing both our cars in the parking lot of the restaurant, so he stopped and keyed my truck out of spite."

"Maybe he didn't." Her voice lacked the oomph to convince even herself of that.

"That gash is deeper than a key would make. His utility belt has everything except a chainsaw on it. But the real giveaway to his guilt was his shit-eating grin."

"He is smarmy," she said. "I did envy him his slicker, though. I'm afraid your leather jacket may be ruined."

"No, the more abuse it takes, the better it looks."

Correctly reading his telltale smile, she flipped open one side of his jacket and saw the familiar label. She started laughing and, abashed, bumped the crown of her head against his sternum. "So I was spot on."

"You were."

He cupped the back of her head and held it there against his chest, which was broad and warm and smelled wonderful. His touch was light and undemanding, but all the more captivating because of his restraint. Everything felt far too right, and therefore was very wrong.

"Zach."

"Hmm?"

"We can't."

"I know."

"You keep saying that, but I don't think you understand how unethical, how compromising—"

"Hell, Kate, you don't have to explain how this would complicate a problem that's already so damned complicated. I get it, okay?"

"Okay." She looked up and gave him a soft, weak smile. "Then, let's say good night."

"Good night."

But neither of them moved. She didn't even realize how incrementally they'd been inclining toward each other until his left hand joined his right to cradle the back of her head, and his face was lowering closer to hers.

She closed her eyes. Against her cheek she felt his breath, warm and fragrant with whiskey. Then felt its tickle on the corner of her mouth. His lips made glancing passes across her lower one, whispering, "Feel free to apply all the pressure on me you like."

Chapter 16

The chiming of Upton's doorbell echoed through his house. Because it wasn't often utilized, it startled him. Since his wife's death, he didn't entertain. Neither did friends visit, except possibly Sid, and those rare occasions were scheduled.

He set aside the dense biography he was reading, slid his bare feet into leather slippers, and made his way to his front door. He was not pleased to see Eban on his doorstep, reaching out to ring the bell again.

"I'm here," Upton called through the glass panel. He disengaged his alarm, unlocked the door, and opened it.

"Hi, Up." Eban took in his pajamas and robe. "A little early for bedtime, isn't it?"

"I wasn't in bed. Just relaxing." Upton looked beyond Eban, hoping that Sid was with him, but the only thing in his semicircular driveway was the shiny sports car. "Is anything wrong?"

"What a coincidence! That's exactly the question I came to ask you. Why don't you invite me in and let's chew the fat?"

With reluctance, Up said, "Of course, come in. I was in the study."

He motioned for Eban to precede him down the wide central hallway, which he did in a jaunty stride, having a thorough look around as he went. "Not a thing's changed since the last time I was here, and that's been, gosh, how many years?"

"I'm a creature of habit," Upton said. "Since Alice died, the girls have been encouraging me to downsize. But I can't bring myself to leave this house. It's familiar. I know where everything is and how to operate it."

The "girls" were his two adult daughters. Both were busy juggling careers and families. They called frequently to check on him, but he sensed their monitoring sprang more from obligation than affection.

Alice had been the parent in the trenches, the loving, soft-spoken, levelheaded, well-oiled motor that had kept the family running smoothly through decades. Since she was gone, he and his daughters were like congenial strangers in search of common ground and things to talk about. It shamed him to acknowledge how little he knew of them as individuals, as persons with interests and ideas and quirks.

Much more of his time, his life, had been devoted to Sid and his business dealings, which were extensive, encompassing a grab bag of industries. Up had had far more interaction with Eban than with his own children. If he had it to do over again, he would amend many of the choices he'd made and rearrange his priorities. But unfortunately, the time for making those adjustments had long since passed.

He and Eban entered the study and soon were sitting in facing chairs, a cocktail table between them. Eban had poured himself a vodka; Upton declined. He didn't welcome this intrusion and wished to keep it brief.

"What's on your mind, Eban?"

He was slouched in his chair, legs outstretched and ankles crossed, but Upton recognized posturing when he saw it. Eban wouldn't be here if he weren't stewing over something. Upton had an idea of what that something was, but he wanted to hear it from Eban himself.

He began by saying, "Dad told me something rather astonishing this morning."

Upton didn't ask what. He waited.

"He told me that you had alerted him to a potential..." He drew a lazy spiral in the air. "...ripple in the pond of my future." He slurped some vodka. "No, let me rephrase with more accuracy. Dad warned me of a potential fucking tsunami." With sudden ferocity, he said, "Why aren't you doing something to stop it?"

Upton raised his hands. "At this point, there's nothing I can do. The key word is *potential*. My responsibility was to inform Sid and you that there's a possibility of such an occurrence."

"Wait a minute, wait a minute." Eban slammed his glass down on the table. "All you're going to do is sit twiddling your thumbs until that girl finally gives up the ghost, and then when she does, you'll let this prosecutor pounce on my ass with an arrest warrant for murder? That's the plan?"

"Her name is Rebecca Pratt."

"I know her name! Christ! How could I forget it? She ruined my life."

Upton bit his tongue. *The gall of the little prick!* Speaking quietly in contrast to Eban's shout and his own inner outrage, he said, "Others would say just the opposite."

While Eban sat there glowering at him, Upton took a moment to get his temper under better control. "If Rebecca Pratt had recovered sufficiently to testify at your trial, she could have made a dynamic impact on the jury, and the outcome might not have gone so well for you in terms of sentencing.

"If she had died, even worse. You would be in Reidsville tonight serving a sentence for manslaughter at best, instead of being free to whiz around in your new Porsche. Either way, she did you a huge favor by becoming suspended in the dreadful state she's in."

Sulking, Eban carried his glass over to the bar and splashed more vodka into it. "Where is she?"

"In a special care facility in New Orleans."

"What's her status? Do you know?"

"I have an informant on staff who gives me periodic reports. Rebecca remains much the same as she was when she was first admitted."

Eban swiped his hand in front of his face from forehead to chin and back up. "Nothing there?"

Upton replied with a brusque no.

"How is she otherwise?"

Upton shared what he knew of Rebecca's general health.

Eban assimilated the information as he took several belts of vodka. "And she could stay that way indefinitely? I mean until old age, right? And die of natural causes?"

"In theory. But I'm told that someone in her condition typically doesn't have a long life expectancy."

"Great. Just great," he muttered into his glass before taking a drink. "I've got a sword on the back of my neck."

"That's if nature takes its course."

That caused Eban to start. "And if someone should decide to speed up nature's course? How long would she last?"

"Days at most."

"*Fucking* great."

"My advice?"

"Well, Uncle Up, I don't want to put you out any, but as long as I'm here."

His sarcasm warranted a pop on the mouth, but Upton tamped down the impulse. "Leave the country, Eban."

"What?"

"Pick a spot on the globe that appeals to you and hunker down there."

"Hunkering doesn't sound like something I would enjoy. For how long?" Upton just looked at him, and when Eban caught his godfather's meaning, he chuffed. "You can't mean forever. Are you crazy?"

Again, Upton struggled to keep a lid on his temper. "Listen to me, Eban. The challenges of prosecuting a case like this are as intimidating as walking a tightrope across the Grand Canyon. Crosswinds coming at you from all sides. One misstep would spell disaster.

"Extradition from another country would compound the challenges tenfold for even the most intrepid prosecutor and greatly reduce the chances of the case ever going to trial."

Eban thought it over, then said in the intractable tone of

a child told to eat his broccoli, "No. I don't want to leave the country. I just got home. Besides, running off, disappearing, or even keeping that low profile that you and Dad are so keen on my doing would look like an admission of guilt."

He planted his hand flat against his chest. "I didn't do anything she didn't ask for. She knew what she was getting into when she joined Theo, Cal, and me in that bedroom. Nobody had to talk her into a fucking thing." He paused and then broke into a laugh. "A fitting choice of words."

Having had all of his godson he could stomach, Upton pulled himself out of his chair. "It's getting late, Eban, and I have an early morning meeting with Sid tomorrow."

"Hold on. Are her parents still Bible-thumpers?"

"Her mother has since died. I'm told her father continues to see her daily. I assume his religious convictions remain rock solid."

"So," Eban said, giving an exaggerated shrug, "no problem with Holy Joe. Unless I'm mistaken, he was the hold-out on pulling the plug. And her ex-husband isn't a concern. When his career went from sugar to shit, he became a drunk and went on the skids."

Upton hesitated. He was disinclined to share too much information, but, at the same time, reminded himself that Eban was his client by extension through Sid. He was entitled to be told.

And, as distasteful a human being as Eban had turned out to be, he remained his godson, to whom he had sworn an oath to treat him as his own child.

With reluctance, he said, "He went to New Orleans."

"Who? Bridger? When?"

"Recently."

"How recent?"

"Yesterday morning. He saw Rebecca, then had a closed-door meeting with the facility's administrator."

Eban paled a bit and shot the remainder of his vodka. "That doesn't mean anything. How often does he visit her?"

"Never, Eban. This is a first, and I view it as significant."

"Well, no shit, Sherlock. When the fuck were you going to get around to telling me about this *significant* visit?"

"My source down there wasn't on duty yesterday, so she didn't learn about Mr. Bridger's visit until today. She caught the scuttlebutt among the staff. She wasn't free to share the information with me until late this afternoon when her shift ended."

Eban was breathing hard, nostrils flaring. "What do you think his visit signifies?"

"Maybe nothing."

"*Or?*"

"Or it might be a reaction to your early release and a prompting from a prosecutor."

"Dad told me about this prosecutor. A woman. Kathryn something."

"Lennon."

"What do you know about her?"

"Only that she's been in the AG's office a little over a year and has a reputation for being sharp and aggressive."

"That's it?"

"Isn't that enough?"

"Nowhere near enough."

His hardened features and the coldness of his tone were

discomfiting and a bit alarming to Upton. "Eban, please do yourself a service. Don't blow off our advice about keeping a low profile. It was my duty to make you and Sid aware of what *could* come about, but I doubt very seriously that it *will*."

Eban continued to glower at nothing for several seconds, then blinked Upton back into focus. His handsome features relaxed. He smiled and clapped Upton on the shoulder. "I've kept you up too long. You look tired, so I'm going to let you go night-night. Thanks for the drink."

He quickly walked out and didn't wait for Upton to see him off. He was already revving his car's engine by the time Upton reached the front door. He watched until the taillights turned out of his drive. The car was symbolic of Eban's excesses, to all of which he felt entitled.

Up felt abject remorse for having had a hand in the shaping of Eban's character. He bore as much blame as Eban's indulgent parents: He had approved and negotiated all the bribes that had swept the boy's lifetime of misdeeds under the rug.

As he climbed the stairs to his bedroom, he submitted to the guilt, worry, and weariness that mantled him like chains.

———

Theo still resided in the townhouse village where he'd lived when Eban had left for prison. His unit was sandwiched between two others that were identical to his except for the color of their front doors.

Eban tapped the brass knocker on the cobalt blue door. Theo answered and, seeing Eban there, looked at him with puzzlement. "Eban?"

"Were you expecting someone else?"

"I wasn't expecting you." He hesitated, then said, "But come on in."

"I believe I will."

Eban walked into the main room, which had undergone a facelift during his absence. "I like the makeover. New?"

"Last year."

Eban strolled over to the island that separated the living area from the kitchen, ran his hand along the marbled surface, and made a *tsk*ing sound. "Faux. I hope you weren't rooked into paying for the real thing."

Theo hadn't moved far from the door where he stood, hands on hips. "You're stoned."

Eban grinned. "Stoned but not stingy." He pulled a plastic pill bottle from his front pants pocket. "Mollies. Catch."

He tossed the bottle to Theo, who caught it, then pitched it overhanded back to him. "No thanks."

"I saw our friend Simply Simon the other night. He said he hadn't seen you in a long, long time. Did you switch dealers, or what?"

"It's late, Eban. I was on my way to bed. Let's pick a night next week and meet for dinner. How 'bout it?"

Eban tapped his chin with his index finger. "You know what that sounded like? It sounded like a brush-off. A classic brush-off."

Theo dropped his head forward and stared down at his bare feet—really ugly, bony feet. When he raised his head, he said, "Look, Eban, I'm glad you're out. It's good to see you. But I don't do that shit anymore." He indicated the plastic bottle that Eban was bouncing in his palm, rattling the tablets.

"Seriously? Did you have a bad experience with mind-altering drugs?"

Theo had always reminded Eban of Forrest Gump: endearingly naive and easily swayed. But right now, his scowl better resembled Cal's disapproving expression at their recent dinner. "A bad experience?" he said. "Yes, wouldn't you say we all had a *bad experience*?"

"Ohhh," Eban drawled. "You're referring to..." He rapidly snapped his fingers. "The Pratt chick. The Cleopatra look-alike. I'm glad you brought her up. She's the reason I came to see you tonight. Well, indirectly. Roundaboutly. Do you have anything to drink?"

"No."

He sighed. "Okay, I can tell you're pissy. You were on your way to bed. I showed up stoned."

"I don't mean to be—"

"No, no, I get it." He patted the air with both hands. "I'll hurry this along. Have a seat."

Theo hesitated, then moved to a chair and sat down on the edge of the seat as though he didn't intend to be there for long. Eban threw himself into the most comfortable chair in the room. Once he got settled, he told Theo what he'd learned from his dad. "I thought he'd gone senile on me, but Up confirmed it."

Theo looked worried. "That's double jeopardy."

"See? That's what I thought, but apparently not. Up says

probably nothing will come of it. Any further due process will fall by the wayside because Rebecca Pratt still lives. But, you know..."

He shrugged. "If there *was* to be a reopening of the case, you, Cal, and I might recollect things about that night a little differently than we did at the first trial. Shit," he chortled, "we were so wasted, even the following morning at the police station when we were being questioned, I couldn't clearly recall how it went down.

"After all this time, who could accurately remember who said this, who said that, or who did what to whom?" He pinned Theo to his chair with a knowing stare. "It would be better all around if our memories stayed foggy, don't you agree?"

He let the question settle. Then he sighed again. "This prosecutor obviously has a bee up her butt. I can just see her, can't you? Saggy tits, thick ankles, mannish hands. Probably an unsightly wart somewhere.

"I'd like to look her up on Google or something, but I'm rusty as hell on the computer. I don't want to ask anybody in the company to research her because my curiosity would inevitably get back to my old man and Up, and they're already overwrought. So I thought of you. You're a librarian! Libraries are chock-full of information, right? You could dig where nobody else could."

It was obvious to Eban that Theo had read between the lines of everything he'd said. His brow was furrowed. His leg was jiggling. He was gnawing the inside of his cheek. "What kind of information do you want on her?"

"That's my man!" Eban slapped his thigh. "I knew I

could count on you. I want to know every fucking thing, even the location of that unsightly wart."

Theo swallowed. Nodded. "Okay. In my spare time, I could—"

Eban made the quiz show buzzer sound. "No good. Give it top priority."

Theo's grin was lopsided, visibly forced and uneasy, but, as expected, acquiescent. "What's her name?"

Chapter 17

———◦◦◦◦———

Zach woke up and cursed himself even before opening his eyes.

He'd just had to go and do it, hadn't he? He'd kissed her, which, in their situation, had been a violation of ethics, plus piling on another complication that this situation did not need.

Fool that he was, he'd thought that a little experimentation would satisfy his curiosity and that would be the end of it. But her willing response to his feeler had shot that hypothesis all to hell.

Swearing under his breath, he threw back the covers and got up. He pulled on his hiking gear in stages while scrambling a couple of eggs and brewing strong coffee, which he consumed quickly. He was eager to get on the trail, burn off some pent-up frustration, and clear his head.

But even as he watched for the familiar landmarks along

his path, his mind continued to rewind to the thrill of that first—and technically *only*—kiss. The tentative lips-to-lips touch had led to a tempered exploration of tongues, which had rapidly escalated into a deeper, wetter, hungrier merging of mouths.

She'd come up on her tiptoes and curled one arm around his neck. He'd bracketed her hips between his hands and had drawn her up higher and closer. Then against him. Then right *there*.

But the perfect match-up had lasted for only for a few fragmented heartbeats before she'd moaned as she'd slid her arm from around his neck, stood flat-footed again, and planted her hand in the center of his chest. "Zach, we can't."

"We've established that." But even as he'd said it, he'd moved in for more.

"We can't." She'd applied more pressure to his chest.

They'd held like that for a moment, then he'd given a curt nod, released her, and stepped away. "Get inside. Lock your door."

"On the matter of Rebecca, I'll wait to hear from you."

He'd bobbed his head.

"Good night, Zach."

"Night."

He hadn't had the wherewithal to say anything more. Once Kate was safely inside the cottage, he'd plunged into the downpour, clambered into his truck, and driven home. His windshield wipers had labored at top speed, but they were ineffectual against the hard rainfall, which drummed against the roof of the cab. Hardly a soothing sound, it set his teeth on edge.

He'd arrived home wearing sodden clothes, his skin fever-ish with lust, his cock iron-hard, and mad as hell.

Had Bing known about his condition, he would have had a field day, railing at him for being out of line, out of his mind, and out of luck. "Because," Bing would've said, "this Kathryn Cartwright Lennon sounds like a gal with an unshakable sense of purpose and uncompromising integrity." And Bing would've been right.

Which is why, when Bing had asked him what the state prosecutor was like, Zach had kept his answer factual, but had said nothing that would lead Bing to suspect that Zach would sacrifice his sound judgment, much less his pride, for one kiss.

One kiss straight out of a wet dream, but still.

During his descent, he'd been so preoccupied with rec-ollections of that consequential kiss, that now, when he reached the rocky riverbed at the foot of the mountain, it came almost as a surprise that he'd arrived.

This spot beneath the falls represented to him healing springs. At his lowest, he would venture down here seeking validation and rejuvenation, and somehow had always gar-nered the will to make the more difficult hike back up.

The falls were roaring. The boulders beneath the cascade created furious white water. Zach took a minute to admire the raw and unbridled energy of the churning waters. He then turned to look downstream, where the current's feroc-ity abated. Yet for miles it continued its inexorable tumble over rocks worn smooth by millennia of aquatic polishing.

He'd stood in this spot hundreds of times before, admir-ing the beauty of it all, marveling over nature's endurance, its permanence in defiance of cataclysmic upheavals. It never failed to awe him. Today, it also cemented his resolve.

He began his arduous uphill trek and cut one full minute off his time.

———

GreenRidge Incorporated had carved out a half moon of forested acreage on which to situate its regional headquarters. The sales office was the only completed structure. Home models were in various stages of construction; workers were on site. Temporary buildings and portable restrooms were lined up along the arced perimeter of the clearing.

Zach parked in front of the office. As he entered, he had to admit it was classy. On his left was an elaborate coffee bar. On his right, a counter stocked with soft drinks, bottled water, and bowls of fresh fruit. In dead center was a reception desk, which no one was attending. The mountain face was on display through a wall of windows, but he noticed that the unsightly grouping of portable toilets wasn't in view.

A young woman appeared through an open doorway on the coffee bar side. "Oh, I'm sorry. I didn't know anyone had come in."

"Just now."

She walked over to him and formed a perfect southern-girl-with-grandma's-pearls-and-manners smile. "I'm Penelope."

"Zach Bridger."

Her scarlet lips formed a perfect *O*, and she became flustered. "Oh. Uh, Mr. Bridger. Welcome. How can I help you?"

"Penelope, I'll take it from here." Zach turned toward the voice. A man stood in the doorway through which Penelope had emerged.

Looking like she'd just been thrown a life preserver, she said, "Mr. Parks is our GM. He'll help you."

"Thank you." Zach approached the man, who held out his right hand to him.

"Mackey Parks," he said as they shook hands. "No introduction to you is necessary. Come on back."

He was fiftyish, with ruddy cheeks and thinning hair, paunchy in the way of men who toil for long hours at a desk but never break a sweat. He led Zach into an office furnished much like Zach's home: mountain chic, perfectly suited to the mountain setting without taking on corniness.

Zach sat in the tartan plaid chair he was motioned into. It was one that formed a circular grouping in front of the window. Parks sat and gave Zach a lengthy and unabashed appraisal. Zach was about to ask if he'd passed inspection when Parks said, "I've hoped that someday I'd have the pleasure of meeting you. I confess to having been a huge fan."

" 'Having been.' Not so much a fan now."

Parks chuckled. "You've been a pain in the ass."

"I wouldn't be if you'd leave me alone and stop sending people to my house."

"We covet your side of the mountain and want to buy it."

"It's not for sale."

"Money is no object."

"Money is *irrelevant*. I won't sell for any amount. Period. End of that discussion." Zach leaned forward in his chair to mark a shift in topic.

"As much as I object to what you're doing over here, I would never destroy or damage your property. I haven't sneaked over here in the middle of the night with a can of spray paint. I haven't broken any windows or torn down signs, none of that."

Parks tilted his head and looked at him curiously. "I don't understand."

"Stop siccing Dave Morris on me."

"The deputy sheriff?"

"Yeah, him. The one with the hat. We've had two encounters, both antagonistic. I told him the first time he came snooping that I had nothing to do with the vandalism going on over here."

Parks seemed both stunned and defensive. "Well, I'm glad to know that, but your denial is unnecessary, Mr. Bridger. Nobody in this organization has suspected you of such."

Kate was used to the sound of other lodgers' cars coming and going past her cottage, so she thought nothing of hearing one arrive until there was a knock on her door. She went to the window and pulled aside the curtain. Zach saw her and chinned a greeting.

Trying to ignore the spike in her heart rate, she let the curtain drop back into place then unlocked the door and opened it.

He said, "Good morning."

"Good morning."

"Too early to come calling?"

"No. I've been up."

"Am I disturbing?"

"I'm packing."

"Heading back to Atlanta?"

"Last night you told me you didn't want to be rushed while making a decision about Rebecca. I can't stay here indefinitely, so I'm going home to await further word from you."

"Makes sense, I guess." He rubbed his scruffy chin with the back of his hand. "I don't want to hold you up, but I've got something I'd like to run past you. I'll make it quick. Could mean something, could mean nothing."

"You've at least piqued my interest. The room's a mess. Let me grab a jacket."

She left the door standing ajar while pulling on the jacket. For good measure, she retrieved a scarf she'd already placed in her suitcase and looped it round her neck. Glancing in the mirror, she fluffed up the hair on the crown of her head. He really should break his bad habit of showing up without notice.

As she went out, she said, "There's a trail." She pointed to a signpost. "It makes a circuit."

"Lead on."

They entered the trailhead single file, then he moved up beside her. The path was strewn with fallen leaves and dotted with puddles from last night's rain. As they maneuvered around them, their hips bumped, hands brushed, reminding her of their kiss, replays of which had kept her awake and restless for most of the night.

What had she been thinking? Certainly not about the

jeopardy in which she was placing her career. Or the chink it could create in her resolve to get justice, which depended solely on his heart-wrenching decision.

She hadn't been thinking about any of the wrongness of that embrace. What she'd been thinking is that she wanted to climb him and cling to that marvelous physique like a vine while feasting on his mouth.

She still wanted to.

"You look different this morning," he said.

"Different how?"

"I've never seen you in anything other than a business suit."

"I have other garments in my wardrobe."

He grinned. "You sure as hell do justice to those jeans."

Her cheeks warmed, but she kept her response light-hearted. "Thanks. Is that what 'could mean something, could mean nothing'?"

"No. That definitely meant something." Their gazes locked for a couple of seconds, then both returned to looking down at the path. He kicked at a muddy stone and pushed his hands into the pockets of his leather jacket. "I came straight here from a conversation with the general manager of GreenRidge. A guy named Mackey Parks. We had an interesting chat."

She gave a soft laugh. "I don't doubt that."

"Not interesting in the way you're thinking, Kate."

Before he could elaborate, a woman came around a bend in the pathway. She was being dragged by two leashed golden retrievers. While Kate exchanged greetings with the woman, Zach bent down to scratch each of the exuberant dogs behind the ears, then waited for them to move past before he resumed.

"I went to GreenRidge this morning to make it clear that I wasn't selling my property. Ever. And then to make it even clearer that I wasn't vandalizing their development. I told Parks to stop siccing Deputy Morris on me."

"What was his response?"

When he halted, so did she, and turned to face him. "He said nobody over there has ever associated me with the vandalism. They suspect some kids, a group of pothead punks from one town over, who have prior arrests for that kind of destructive mischief.

"He said my name has never come up in regards to that, only that I'm a pain in the ass for holding out and not selling. He didn't dispatch Morris to check me out, and had no explanation for why Morris had taken that upon himself."

"Do you believe him?"

"Parks? Yeah, I do. I don't like him scarring up the mountainside, but he seemed like a straight shooter."

"I don't understand. Why would Dave Morris pick on you?"

"Because of you?"

She thought it over, then shook her head. "The timing doesn't fit. When I arrived at your house to find him there, he seemed genuinely surprised to see me. I don't think he knew until then that we were acquainted. He does resent the Super Bowl MVP, though. He remarked on it."

They fell into step again. "I could be reading too much into it," he said. "He looks like an ex-jock. Maybe he's jealous of my glory days. Maybe his curiosity got the better of him. He wanted to check out the has-been, and the vandalism gave him a plausible excuse. I've made it no secret that I'm opposed to the development." They walked on a bit, and then he elbowed her in the side. "He'll hate seeing you go."

Again they laughed quietly, although there was no one around to hear them. They hadn't met anyone on the trail except for the lady with the dogs. The woods were supernaturally still. The only sound was that of their footfalls sifting through the fallen leaves. Those, too, fell silent when they stopped simultaneously and faced each other.

She said, "I need to turn back and get on the road. I notified my office that I would be there by midafternoon."

"How much longer is this circuit?"

"You'll do it in twenty minutes."

"I'm going to continue on, then. I've got a lot to think about."

She smiled with empathy. "Zach, whatever you decide will be the right decision. Either way, make it a choice you can live with without regret or self-reproach. Make it right for you."

"I want to make it right for Rebecca."

That choked her up. She had all the compassion in the world for Rebecca Pratt, but she'd been incredibly stupid not to value this man while she had him. "I'll be waiting to hear from you."

"Rain is still in the forecast. Drive safely."

"I will."

He took a step closer. "Goodbye kiss?"

"Zach—"

"I know, I know. I hate it like hell, but I know."

She relented, saying softly, "On the cheek."

He took an end of her scarf in each hand and wound them around a couple of turns, then pulled her up and forward. He pressed his lips to her cheek, held there, and exhaled a warm breath. Then he stepped back and unwound the scarf from his hands.

Without another word, he started off down the trail.

Chapter 18

Even as a child, if he was ever caught doing what other people considered to be wrong, Eban would use a passive-aggressive tactic: behave as though he had every right to be where he was, doing whatever he was doing.

He hadn't known the psychological term for this method of escaping punishment; he knew only that it was effective. Much more so than stealth, which was indicative of shame, and shame was an alien concept to him. His specialness exempted him from censure and correction.

Tonight, his undertaking wasn't without risks. The odds of getting caught were greater than those of getting away with it, but he wasn't too worried about it. If ever put on the spot, he was cracking good at worming his way out with a glib explanation. In the unlikely event that failed, his dad's name and checkbook were reliable fallbacks.

Because of an overflowing commode in one of the

library's bathrooms, Theo hadn't come through with information on Kathryn Lennon. He had spent most of his workday mopping up, but had promised to try again tomorrow.

Rather than be bested by the soiled Pamper that had clogged the toilet, Eban had decided to screw the delay and see for himself what this Lennon bitch was about.

He'd arm-twisted her home address out of Theo, which he'd sent to Eban in a text. What an idiot. If Theo had been to prison, he would know to avoid texting anything you didn't want announced to the world. A single text could be one's undoing.

He'd borrowed Frida's car for the venture. "Because it looks like rain, and I don't want to expose my new baby to the elements."

Not wanting to drive the Porsche in bad weather was a credible reason. But his primary one was that Frida's mid-priced Chevy would blend into traffic and be much harder to tail.

Did they—whoever they were—really think he wouldn't spot the surveillance? Hysterical. Last night as he'd left Theo's townhouse, he'd had to curb the impulse to wave at the guy in the nondescript sedan parked two doors down.

Frida had handed over her car key without a quibble, asking only that he be back no later than ten o'clock. He gave her a couple hundred dollars for the overtime and timed his departure with when she usually left for the day. The sedan didn't follow as he drove out of the gate at dusk and set out for Kathryn Lennon's neighborhood.

Her address was on a street lined with charming houses with shutters and flower beds and the Stars and Stripes hanging from their eaves. He drove past her house, then rounded the block and parked in front of a vacant house that was for sale. In a casual, strolling pace, he walked around the corner, halfway along her block, then straight up the brick walkway to her front door.

He didn't look around to see if any of her neighbors were observing him. In under thirty seconds, he'd picked the lock with tools and skills he'd been taught in prison. It was like performing a magic trick, and he'd always been fascinated by sleight of hand.

He let himself in and fully expected a home alarm to go off. But nothing happened, so, unless it was a silent alarm, which was a possibility, his intrusion had gone undetected. Nevertheless, he gave himself only ten minutes to explore. That was the average time for alarm monitors to respond and dispatch the police.

Prison was more educational than Harvard or Princeton.

During the allotted ten minutes, he wanted to learn as much as he could about the state prosecutor who was operating under the delusion that she would keep him locked behind bars for the rest of his natural life.

"Guess again," he whispered as he paused in the small foyer to slip off his shoes. The glow of a streetlight coming through the windows provided enough illumination for him to see his way around.

In stocking feet, he entered the living room. It was furnished in a style more contemporary than the exterior of the house would indicate. He'd expected chintz and bric-a-brac, but from what he could tell in the semi-darkness, the tones were neutral, the decor tasteful and understated.

Theo would approve. She had an expansive bookcase, the shelves loaded with reading material that ranged from dull-looking literary novels to steamy romances. Hmm. Eban wondered which she read most often.

He moved from that room into the kitchen and was a bit surprised by it as well. She had state-of-the-art appliances, but none of the clutter characteristic of an industrious cook. The sink was empty, a dish towel folded over the edge of it. A ceramic bowl of blooming orchids occupied the center of the island. He pinched off one of the white blooms, sniffed it, then put it in his pocket.

"You're very neat, Kathryn. But not a chef."

He backtracked and passed through the living room again, then followed his nose down a hallway, past a guest room, past a home office, to the hall's dead end at a bedroom that had to be hers. Like all the other rooms, it was tidy, but it had a more lived-in feel. There was a king bed, plus a chaise lounge. Both had an abundance of decorative pillows.

A throw had been left draping the foot of the bed. He ran his hand over its luxuriant pile. Sleek surfaces in the kitchen, plushness in the bedroom. This was where she curled up to read the naughty fiction.

When he opened the closet door, the light automatically came on. Since the blinds were drawn, he felt it was safe to leave it on. The walk-in was well organized. Three open shelves were devoted to high-heeled shoes. Stilettos mostly.

No thick ankles on Kathryn, then.

He glanced at his watch. He had a little over two minutes before he had to clear out.

He went to the built-in chest of drawers. Being careful to cover his hand with his sleeve to avoid leaving fingerprints, he opened the top drawer. Underwear. Not the underwear of a woman with saggy tits and an unsightly wart.

The bras were lacy and sheer, not of a size that would ordinarily attract him, but he became aroused while rubbing his index finger over the moderate cup of one where a nipple would fit.

Her panties also elicited a delightful stirring behind his fly. Some were thongs, some more practical, but none were maiden-like. He took a black lace thong and tucked it into his pocket along with the orchid blossom.

He looked at his watch. Ninety seconds left. Time to go. He didn't want to. He wanted to get to know Kathryn Lennon better. Much better.

He closed the closet door; the light went out. As he was about to slip from the room, he noticed a framed photograph on a side table next to the chaise. There were three people in the picture, but he couldn't see them clearly, so he risked turning on his phone's flashlight.

The picture had been taken on a beach. The trio stood with their arms around one another's waists. Sandy feet, swimwear, all smiles. A man and a woman, who looked to be about his dad's age, were standing on either side of a woman with short, platinum hair. She was wearing a bikini that matched the size of the undies in the chest of drawers.

Her wide smile and the sun's glare had caused her gamine face to scrunch, but she looked cheeky and adorable. He cooed, "Hellooo, Kathryn."

Zach had felt like shit all day.

By the time he'd come full circle of the trail at the B and B, Kate's SUV was no longer parked in front of the cottage. Which was what he'd expected, and it was just as well. A second goodbye would have been more difficult than the first, but it didn't improve his mood to know that she had left.

He'd gotten home in time to check the stock market before it closed. He'd been pleased to see that it had taken a bump in the right direction today. He'd spent an hour analyzing the data and had shot emails to those he knew would be interested, but he'd been restless and unable to concentrate. He whiled away most of the afternoon gazing out the window.

The pending decision he must make about Rebecca's life had been as haunting as a ghostly cold breath on the back of his neck, and as burdensome as leg irons. He had told Kate he wouldn't be rushed, but in addition to his struggle with the moral and emotional ambiguities, time was a factor.

If Eban took off to someplace that was soft on extradition, keeping the miscreant permanently out of reach, would he ever forgive himself? He didn't think so. But the alternative was—

Unthinkable.

The sun had gone down. Dinnertime had rolled around. He hadn't found anything in his kitchen that appealed to him, so he'd decided to drive into town for barbecue. The place was a block off the square, and he was known there.

He'd ordered his regular combo plate and took it to a picnic table on the outdoor deck that overlooked a rippling creek. Heaters had been turned on to ward off the chill, but no one else had come outside, and he'd welcomed the solitude. As soon as he'd finished his meal, he headed for home, his frame of mind still in the dumps.

Now, he was almost to his turnoff when a car shot out from a side road directly in front of his pickup. His tires skidded over the damp pavement as he stomped the brake pedal and swerved to avoid T-boning the other vehicle and the damned fool who was driving it.

His truck shuddered to a stop, his back tires coming a mere foot short of the cliff. Caught by his seat belt, he had to wait until it released, then engaged the emergency brake, flung open the door and jumped out, angry and anxious at the same time.

"Are you all right?" he called as he approached the sedan.

Dave Morris squeezed himself out of the driver's seat. He wasn't in uniform. "Far from all right, you son of a bitch."

He came lumbering toward Zach, who took a stance and squared off. "You were waiting on me to come along. How'd you know I'd be on the road?"

"Saw your truck parked at the barbecue joint. Knew you'd be driving home sooner or later."

"So you laid an ambush. Where's your badge?"

"Temporarily suspended. On account of you. After you talked to Mackey Parks, he called Sheriff Meekes and lodged a complaint against me."

"Ah, gee, that's too bad."

Baring his teeth, Morris lunged and took a swing at him,

but Zach saw it coming and dodged the deputy's meaty fist. He landed what he thought would be a good blow to Morris's belly, but it was like he'd hit a sack of cement.

Morris definitely had the advantage of weight, muscle bulk, and a lower center of gravity, but Zach was more agile. He scrambled backward, and when Morris came charging, Zach sidestepped at the last possible second. Rather than slamming into Zach, Morris rammed into the grille of Zach's truck with such impetus, he bounced back from it and dropped to his knees. Zach planted his large hand over the back of Morris's head and shoved his face into the unyielding metal.

Morris cried out and slumped forward. That's when Zach saw the holster clipped to his belt at the small of his back. He wrangled the pistol from it and used his famous throwing arm to rocket the handgun into the dense woods bordering the road.

Before Morris could regain his senses and balance, Zach wrapped his arm around his thick, tattooed neck, and pulled his head back until they were glaring at each other upside down.

"You knew I wasn't involved in that vandalism over at GreenRidge. You only used that as an excuse to hassle me. I want to know why."

"Fuck you."

Zach pulled Morris's head farther back and dug a knee into his kidney. "Aren't you a little old to be playing back-at-you pranks? Keying my truck? What the hell, man? What's your problem with me? Kate Lennon?"

Morris ground out, "Let me go."

"Not a chance."

"Piss on you, Bridger."

"Why are you harassing me? You're jealous because of Kate, right?"

"Jealous of you? Of *you*? Fuck no."

Zach pulled back his knee and then drilled it into soft tissue. Having had his share of kidney jabs on the playing field, he knew they hurt like bloody hell.

Morris yelped, then whimpered, then gasped, "Okay, okay, yes."

"You're jealous of me and Kate?"

"No."

"Which is it, Morris?"

"Lemme go. I . . . I'll tell you."

He'd given in sooner and more easily than Zach would have expected. Fearing his surrender might be a ruse, he relaxed his hold on Morris gradually, then backed away.

The deputy used handholds on the grille to pull himself upright. Once on his feet, he turned around unsteadily and propped himself at a slant against the hood, favoring the side Zach had jabbed. His lip was split. His nose and eyes were already becoming swollen and discolored.

Zach felt no sympathy whatsoever for wreaking the damage. If he hadn't stopped his pickup in time, it would have gone over the cliff, taking him with it. Without his having had years of experience out-finessing rampaging linebackers, this asshole would have pounded him to a pulp. Or shot him. So, no tenderheartedness for Dave Morris.

"Talk to me," Zach demanded.

"Where's my pistol?"

"Thirty or forty yards that way," Zach said, tipping his

head. "Search to your heart's content. What's behind the harassment?"

Morris raised his hand to his lip and blotted at slobbery blood. "I was asked to keep an eye on you."

Zach hadn't expected that. "Keep an eye on me? Spy, you mean?"

Morris raised a shoulder in admission.

"What for?"

"That's for you to find out, cocksucker," he sneered. "You may have cost me my job."

"No, that'll be your fault, Morris, not mine. I didn't cook up false allegations just so I could go window peeping into your house. Who asked you to keep an eye on me?"

"You're such a hotshot. You figure it out."

With an effort, Morris pushed away from the support and started stumbling away, but Zach grabbed him by the arm and slung him back against the hood of the pickup. "Who's behind this?"

Morris glared with belligerence and remained stubbornly silent.

"Did you take money to spy on me?"

Morris added malice to his glare.

"So you did. Corruption is a lot more serious than keying my truck," Zach said. "You tell me now who retained your services, or you'll tell me in front of the sheriff. I'm sure he'll be interested to hear that you took a bribe."

His jaw working, Morris mulled it over. "Okay," he said, "I'll tell you. But you gotta clear me with my boss."

"Wrong. I don't gotta do shit."

"Then you'll die wondering."

Zach began to chuckle. "No I won't. I don't need you to tell me. I already know who it was."

Through his fattening nose the deputy snorted with scorn. "I'm not falling for that old bluff."

Zach said, "Eban Clarke."

———

Kate didn't remember ever being as weary as she was when she arrived home. It was almost eleven o'clock. After the drive back to Atlanta, she'd gone to her office as planned. What was intended to be a brief stop had turned into a seven-hour stint.

She'd spent that time with her assistant replying to backed-up correspondence and being brought up speed on other cases she was working on in one capacity or another.

Uppermost in her mind, however, was Eban Clarke. Before leaving for home, she'd emailed the AG, writing, "I've had several meetings with Zach Bridger. After some initial reluctance, he became more open to discussing the situation with Eban Clarke, and now understands that our moving forward hinges on his decision regarding Rebecca Pratt. He requested time to think on it.

"In the meantime, I suggest the surveillance on Clarke be continued indefinitely. He has the means, cunning, and backing of his influential father to pull up stakes and flee at any time."

It was a coin toss as to whether or not the boss would approve that request. Eban Clarke was a free man. At this point, there was no probable cause to justify keeping him under surveillance. He was living like a prince but doing nothing illegal.

She entered her house from the garage door that opened into the kitchen.

She flipped on the light, went over to the island, and, with relief, let her heavy bag slide off her shoulder onto the countertop.

Noticing that several sprigs of Spanish moss had shaken loose from the container of orchids, she swept them into her hand and patted them back into place.

In the fridge was a bottle of Chardonnay already opened. She poured herself a glass, smiling ruefully and saying softly, "Sometimes I drink white."

She slipped her phone from the outside pocket of her bag. Taking it and the wine with her, she turned off the kitchen light and made her way through the living room, using only the ambient light coming through the front windows.

But as she moved into the hallway that led to her bedroom, for some inexplicable reason, she paused and looked back into the living room. Everything was as she'd left it, nothing was amiss, but something compelled her to go into the foyer and make certain the front door was locked. It was.

She'd never been a 'fraidy cat, and couldn't account for the odd feeling, almost a shiver, that had come over her, but she attributed it to fatigue and continued down the hall.

In the bedroom, she flipped the switch that turned on the bedside lamps. Setting her wineglass and phone on the table next to the chaise, she started toward her closet.

Chapter 19

———◆———

Just as Kate reached for the door handle, her phone rang.

Thinking—hoping—it might be Zach, she hurried back to the table. In her haste to grab the phone, she knocked over the picture of her with her parents on the beach. The gold frame clattered loudly against the glass tabletop.

She righted the frame, then, after four rings, and without checking the caller ID, she answered rather breathlessly. "Hello?"

"Ms. Lennon?"

Not Zach. She squashed her adolescent disappointment. "This is she."

The man at the other end gave her his name and told her he was with the company that monitored her alarm system. "What's your password, please?"

She hesitated, then gave him an erroneous one.

"I'm sorry, that's not the password on record."

"I'm glad you know that. I was testing *you*."

After giving him the correct password, he said, "Your silent alarm was triggered this evening at nine eighteen. When you didn't answer our call, we left you a voice mail and dispatched the police."

Her phone had rung while she was plowing through the work piled up on her desk. Not recognizing the number and believing it to be a spam call, she'd let it go unanswered and had ignored the voice mail notification.

"Two patrolmen checked your house and yard," he was saying. "They reported there was no sign of a break-in. Your alarm was disengaged a few minutes ago, then immediately reset."

"That was me. I just came in."

"When we got the all-clear from the police, we reset your alarm from here. Sometimes a low battery can set it off. I'm just following up to make sure everything is okay."

Maybe animal instinct had caused the uneasiness that had crept over her minutes earlier. She darted a glance toward the closet door, the foot of the bed, the bathroom door standing ajar, the open bedroom door, and the dark hallway beyond. "Can you please hold on while I check the house?"

"Yes, of course."

She kept her phone in her hand as she looked first into the bathroom. No one there, nothing displaced. She knelt to check beneath the bed then crossed to the closet. Heart in her throat, she twisted the horizontal handle on the door and yanked it open. The light flashed on. Nothing.

Turning quickly, she moved to the door and looked down

the hallway. Empty. Starting down it, she came first to her home office, where she turned on the light, and checked the closet. She did the same in the guest bedroom and bath. Unlike her own glass shower door, this one had a curtain, which she fearfully flung aside, then felt silly for being fearful.

There was no place for an intruder to be hiding in the living room. If anyone had been lying in wait in the garage, she would have been attacked when she got out of her car.

That left only the kitchen. She thought of the disturbed Spanish moss.

Trying to keep the fear from her voice, she said, "Are you still there?"

"Yes, ma'am."

"Thank you."

With one switch, she turned on every light in the kitchen and blinked against the sudden glare. The only place for concealment was the walk-in pantry. She gathered her courage and opened the door. Nothing.

She slumped against the doorjamb, realizing only then how shaky her knees were. Inside her clothes, her skin had turned clammy. "Everything appears to be in order."

"You're all right?"

"Yes."

"Your duress code word, please?"

Her brain scrambled to come up with it, but she did.

"All right, Ms. Lennon. Have a good night."

"Thank you."

She was hesitant to disconnect, but there was nowhere for someone to be hiding that she hadn't checked. Just as she clicked off to end the call, her doorbell pealed.

The first words out of Zach's mouth were, "What's the matter?"

"Nothing."

"Liar. Your face is as white as your hair. What's the matter?"

"How did you know where I live? Did you follow me here?"

"No, I left hours after you did, but made record time and came straight here."

"What's so urgent?"

"Something's come to light."

"You couldn't tell me over the phone?"

"Not this."

"Why?"

He could tell by looking at her that, despite her protests, she wasn't all that opposed to his being here. Something of consequence had happened to both of them during the intervening hours since he'd kissed her on the cheek and told her goodbye. "Let's swap stories."

Looking wan and uncharacteristically skittish, she stood aside. He heard locks being clicked behind him as he left her at the front door and went into a living area where every light source was on full. As she entered behind him, she cut the overhead light.

He turned to her. "What's up?"

"You first."

"Nope. You're shook. Now, for the third time, *what's the matter?*"

She hitched up her chin in defiance, but he stared her down, and she wilted into an easy chair. He shrugged out of his jacket and sat down on the sofa facing her, elbows on his knees, leaning forward. With frequent starts and stops, she told him about the disturbing telephone call from the monitoring service. He listened with a growing sense of dread and apprehension.

She finished with, "I'd just hung up when you rang the doorbell. I nearly came out of my skin."

He stood up.

"Where are you going?"

"To take a look around."

"I told you. I searched."

He pointed his finger at her. "Stay put."

Her house wasn't that large, and he easily found his way through it. He looked into every room and every closet including a large storage area in the garage. After satisfying himself that they were the only two people there, he returned to the living area. Her boots were lying on the floor in front of the chair where she was curled up, a throw covering her legs and feet. She was hugging a decorative pillow against her chest like a teddy bear.

He passed her the glass of wine he'd found on a table in the bedroom.

"Thank you," she said. "Can I offer you anything?"

He declined and resumed his spot on the sofa. "Do you think it was a break-in?"

"I haven't had time to conduct an inventory, but the only thing that seems to have been disturbed is the moss in the planter on the kitchen island, and that could have happened when the furnace kicked on."

"Do you think a faulty battery set off the alarm?"

"It happens."

He just looked at her.

She took a sip of wine. "When I came in, I had this creepy sensation."

"Like someone had been in your house while you were gone."

She took another sip of wine. "I don't know."

"I think you do, Kate. I trust your instincts even if you don't."

He leaned against the back cushion of the sofa and stacked his hands on the top of his head. "My turn?" After she nodded for him to go ahead, he told her about his run-in with Dave Morris. The more descriptive he got, the wider her eyes grew.

"You didn't file the complaint on him," she exclaimed. "The GreenRidge man did."

"But whipping his ass wouldn't have given Morris bragging rights. Whipping mine would have."

"He could have killed you."

"He was no pushover. I was lucky to come away intact. But he's a bully, not a killer."

"As for his moonlighting," she said, "do you really believe Eban Clarke hired him to spy on you?"

"I tossed out his name as a bluff. Morris said he wouldn't fall for it." He lowered his hands from his head and leaned into the space separating them. "But he *did*," he said with satisfaction. "Like a ton of bricks. When I mentioned Eban Clarke, he looked at me like I was too stupid to live.

"He said, 'The rich guy? Your ex's party boy? He's in prison.' And then to prove to me that I was the dumbest dumbass ever, Morris gave up the name. It was Doug Pratt."

With the statement reverberating between them, he sat back and said, "My barbecue supper has worn off."

She admitted that she'd had nothing since a quick salad lunch on her drive back to Atlanta. For the time being they tabled their discussion and relocated to the kitchen. They built ham-and-cheese sandwiches to their individual preferences. She suggested they eat at the dining nook built into a corner.

"Dibs on the side with the couch," Zach said as he carried his plate over to the rectangular table.

"Banquette."

"Pardon?"

"That's what it's called."

"Huh." He slid in, settled into the corner, and stretched his legs along the length of the padded bench. "A bed in the kitchen. What a great idea."

He crunched a potato chip, and his mischievous, poster-boy grin just might have been the sexiest thing she'd ever seen.

They made small talk between noshes. She said, "When you were telling me about your day leading up to your encounter with Morris, you mentioned checking the stock market. That's twice you've referred to it. Is it a pastime, hobby, or something more?"

He pushed aside his empty plate, wiped his mouth with the paper napkin, sat up straight, and drew his legs beneath the table. "How good are you at keeping a secret?"

"I'm an attorney."

"Oh, right. Well, one of the few smart things I did while playing in the NFL was not to blow my salary on cars, boats, condos in Cabo and Aspen. Like that.

"My folks were the salt-of-the-earth kind with a strong work ethic. I guess it rubbed off. Don't get me wrong, I lived well, but I didn't go nuts with the money I was making." He gave a wry smile. "My most expensive extravagance was Rebecca."

Speaking her name momentarily clouded the natural glint in his eyes.

"Anyway, I had sense enough to invest while I had the means, and I seemed to have a good eye for spotting opportunities."

"Just how good an eye?"

The glint returned. "I've done okay. I was able to buy my property and build the house without dipping into my savings."

She raised her eyebrows. "I'd say you've done better than okay. Is that the secret? People think you're washed up and destitute while in reality you're a reclusive millionaire?"

"That's part of the secret."

"Are you willing to share the other part?"

"I have clients," he whispered. "Yeah," he said when he saw her surprise. "Once I was off the grid, I started watching young jocks who'd soared to stardom in their sport but were on the path to self-destruction. I homed in on one in particular. He had all the God-given talent an athlete could dream of. But he was going hog wild with his excesses. He was about to flame out. I contacted him. At first he was flattered that he was talking to Zach Bridger.

"But when I started advising that he give moderation a try, he got defensive and cocky. 'You're just jealous 'cause I'm here and you're not.' Fine, I said, and told him not to call me on his way down, which was coming soon if he didn't get his shit together and his head on straight. I hung up.

"Two days later, he called me. I guess he figured that my advice, coming from one who'd sunk as low as one can go, was worth taking. While dishing out words to live by, I also gave him some tips on money management. He was clueless. Didn't know his ass from an asset. I suggested he give me a trial run, turn over an amount for me to play with. If I lost it, or reduced it, I would guarantee a full refund out of my own pocket."

She laughed. "Let me guess."

"He was my first client, and he's still with me. Last Christmas he sent me a set of golf clubs. *And* a golf cart."

"You're kidding."

"No. I kept the clubs but donated the cart to a college with a golf program."

"That's a great story. Too bad I'm sworn to secrecy. Is there more?"

"I got my brokerage license. The hobby evolved into a business. I can work out of my mountain house."

"Be a recluse."

"For me, privacy is the most valuable commodity. I've got a great setup, and I'm grateful."

"Obviously so are your clients. You probably have to turn down many."

He leaned forward and whispered. "I handpick them. They don't pick me. And each has to sign a nondisclosure agreement not to tell who handles their investments. That's the deal I make with them. That's the secret. And now, I guess I'll have to kill you."

She wanted to lean across the table and kiss him. She wanted to badly. But the specter of Rebecca loomed large.

She pushed back her chair and cleared the table. He slid off the banquette and asked if he could make a cup of coffee. She showed him where everything was. She steeped a cup of tea for herself, and when they were resettled back in the living room, she said, "How did Doug Pratt contact Morris?"

"I asked. Apparently Doug subscribes to the biweekly county newspaper online."

"His way of keeping tabs on you."

"I guess he wanted to see if my name ever cropped up in the local news. It did. I'd signed a petition against Green-Ridge's development. When stories about the vandalism started appearing, and mentioned Deputy Morris as one of the investigators, Doug contacted him.

"Actually, according to Morris, Doug laid it on thick. How I was dead-set against anyone encroaching on what I perceived to be my mountain, how I was a tree hugger, anti this, pro that.

"Morris bought it. He admitted that when he first came snooping, he actually considered me a suspect. But then you showed up at my place, after hours, and that gave him a reason to dislike me." He grinned. "His face is kinda messed up. I hope I didn't ruin the good thing you two have going."

"Please," she moaned. They smiled across at each other. She wished the lighthearted, flirty banter could continue but knew it couldn't. "You believe someone was in my house, don't you?"

"Don't you?"

"I'm reluctant to," she said softly, "but yes. Who?"

"I'm afraid that if I speculate, I'll be right."

"Eban Clarke."

He made a motion with his shoulder. "Or he sent someone."

She crossed her arms over her chest and rubbed her upper arms. "It makes my skin crawl."

"Mine, too."

"But I don't see how it could've been him. The investigator—"

"I'm sure your guy is good. But Eban is sly. He'd have figured out a way to give him the slip."

She shook her head. "I checked with him late this evening before I left the office. He said Eban returned from a racquetball workout at four o'clock and hadn't left the house since."

Zach raised his hands in a gesture of helplessness. "As I said, maybe he sent a toady. But how would he have gotten your name? It hasn't been publicized that you or anyone is considering another charge against him."

"It hasn't been publicized, no. But his father, Sid, has a lawyer on retainer. They've been cheek-to-jowl for ages. Upton Franklin is his name. He's shrewd and he's corrupt.

He's probably got a dozen or more snitches in the AG's office. Any red flag that appears next to a Clarke's name, he hears of it within minutes. If it's nothing but a scratch, he starts immediately stanching the bleed."

Zach took a look around the room before coming back to her. "I don't think it's safe for you to stay here."

"I'm not afraid."

"First of all, you're lying. Secondly, I'm scared shitless."

"What do you suggest I do?"

"Go to New Orleans with me tomorrow."

Chapter 20

———◆———

Kate didn't say anything immediately. Then, "For what purpose?"

"To see Doug."

"Again, for what purpose?"

"You told me you had notified him of Clarke's release."

"He reacted with anger, disgust, all the justifiable emotions. He asked if I had notified you. At that point I hadn't."

"But now you have, and Morris has told Doug that you've been to see me. I'm certain that unhinged him. I need to talk to him, Kate. Face-to-face. When I do, I'd like for you to be there."

"To serve as a buffer?"

"More than that. You represent the attorney general. That makes the discussion official, not personal. Otherwise, Doug will just bang heads with me. It also may influence his thinking if you impress on him what a threat Eban Clarke is."

"A flight risk, yes. But a threat?"

"I doubt he changed his spots or came to Jesus while in prison. If he remains free, other women could fall victim."

She looked at him thoughtfully. "Last night you referred to Rebecca as having been 'victimized' by Eban Clarke. Not everyone shares that opinion."

"Don't you?"

"Well, Parsons and Simpson testified that she went into that room with them of her own volition. She knew what they were going in there for, and she participated. 'Enthusiastically,' to quote Cal Parsons."

"In all probability that much is true," Zach said. "But Rebecca loved life. Loved living. If at any point she'd felt that her life was in danger, she would have called a halt. In fact, I believe she would have fought like hell."

"All three men had scratch marks on their arms and faces," Kate said. "Their tissue was found under her fingernails. Clarke's defense attorney couldn't refute the DNA evidence, but he reminded the jury of the sex toys found in that room. He said that scratching was part of their rough sex play. He raised a reasonable doubt."

"That's what the Clarkes paid him to do. Hell, you could create reasonable doubt about damn near anything. The sky is blue. No, it's gray. Actually it can be either. Reasonably speaking, it's blue, but—"

"All right, you've made your point."

"This is my point, and I'd stake my own life on it. Either

Rebecca was incapable of saying the safe word, or she said it, and they ignored it. But even if she didn't fight, or couldn't, at any time past signaling *No. Enough*, she became a victim."

Kate had been listening, her expression intent, her body tense. Now, her shoulders visibly relaxed. "I believe so, too."

"Then why'd you put up an argument?"

"Because that's what I'm paid to do. By the state."

"Clever. You wound me up."

"I needed to hear just how passionately you felt about it."

"Now that you know, what about New Orleans?" When she hesitated, he said, "I took the liberty of booking a departure flight tomorrow morning for you and me."

"Returning when?"

"That depends on Doug and the outcome of the meeting. I may be coming back by tomorrow evening, or I may be required to stay for several days. You could return directly after meeting with him. In all honesty, Kate, I can't predict what he'll say or do. But I believe it would be helpful to have you there. Will you come with me?"

She thought on it, then said, "You put up a good argument yourself. Mr. Pratt and I met while preparing for Clarke's release hearing. If he still considers me an advocate, that could be beneficial. Yes, I'll go."

"Can you clear it with the AG?"

"I'll send him an email tonight so he'll see it first thing in the morning. I'll phrase it to sound like a breakthrough I need to seize on. Which it is."

Zach stood up, reached for his jacket, and folded it over his arm. "I reserved a room for myself at one of the airport hotels. But that was before I knew you'd had an uninvited visitor tonight. So, here are your choices."

"Who are you to give me choices?"

Ignoring that, he said, "I wait while you pack and you come with me to the hotel."

"Or?"

"I sleep here."

She looked aside, considering the options. "What time is the flight?"

"Eight-thirty."

"Early, then."

"Earlyish, but we'd already be at the airport."

Again, she thought on it, then said, "I'm truly exhausted. To pack, drive out there tonight sounds awful. Let's sleep here." Then meeting his gaze, she added, "The guest room is ready for occupancy."

"*Damn!*" He said it under his breath and with emphasis, but also humor.

She snuffled a laugh.

He went to stand near her but didn't touch her. If he put his hands on her, he knew it would lead to kissing her, and if he kissed her, he'd start pawing her and tearing at her clothes. So he kept his hands and his longing in check. "Go send your email. I'll get my bag out of my truck and lock up."

"All right. If you get up before I do, you know where the coffee makings are. Help yourself."

"Thanks."

"Good night." She turned and disappeared down the hallway.

He went to the front door, undid all the locks she'd secured, then went to his pickup and got his duffel bag out of the front seat. After checking all the door locks one last time, he retreated to the guest room. Like the rest of her house, it was unfussy, unfrilly and, thank God, had a king bed.

He set an alarm on his watch and undressed. As he pulled back the covers and stretched out, he realized that parts of him were sore from his skirmish with Morris. He'd probably feel it more tomorrow.

Through the wall, he could hear a shower running. "Don't think about it."

But of course he thought about it. Kate naked. He'd already spent hours contemplating that. Envisioning Kate wet and sudsy and naked made him tent her floral-scented sheets.

For several minutes after the shower went off he heard her moving around, then on the other side of the wall things went still and silent. With spite, he hoped that for all the misery this sleeping arrangement was inflicting on him, she was suffering at least a little restlessness.

Swearing, he reached up and clicked off the lamp.

———

Kathryn Lennon's house went dark. Down the street, Eban sat hunched in the driver's seat of Frida's car. "Off to beddy-bye," he groused.

He stayed for another minute or so, then started the car and pulled away from the curb. As he drove past Bridger's monstrous pickup, he gave it the finger.

He hadn't believed his eyes when Bridger showed up at her house. *What the fuck!?* He'd actually shouted the words and struck the steering wheel with the heel of his hand when the tall, strapping, familiar form climbed out of the pickup and strode up to her door.

Although, he told himself now as he navigated his way back home, if the prosecutor and Rebecca's ex were planning a sneak attack on him, he was better off knowing than not. Right? Right. Looked at that way, it seemed that fortune was still favoring him.

Earlier, he had made it out of Lennon's house and back to his car on foot just before seeing the patrol car turn onto her street. Note to self: She did have a silent alarm.

He'd driven past her house while two cops were still prowling around it, shining their flashlights at doors and windows. He'd been smart enough to relock the lock he'd picked earlier.

After the policemen left, he'd continued his surveillance. By then, it was approaching ten o'clock, but he'd wanted to stick around for a while longer on the outside chance that he'd get a Kathryn Lennon sighting. In the flesh. In the delectable flesh revealed by her scanty bikini.

He'd called Frida and told her he'd gotten stuck with some old friends who were insisting on treating him to another round. "No problem, sweetheart," she said. "I'll use Uber. In the morning, too. Have fun with your friends."

He'd wondered if his watchdog would follow the Uber car when it left with Frida, but he hadn't worried about it overmuch. If confronted, Frida would cover for him.

Why couldn't everyone be as adoring and accommodating

as Frida? Like Upton, for instance. That grumpy old fart. And his dad, who had spoiled him rotten, was now all of a sudden cracking down.

He'd been about to give up on Kathryn Lennon when a car had approached from the opposite direction and pulled into her driveway, then into her garage, the door of which had lowered immediately. He hadn't gotten a look at her. Lights had come on inside the house.

Not long after, the has-been quarterback had made his appearance and ruined Eban's lurid fantasy of catching the prosecutor unawares, unprotected, and unclothed except for a thong like the one in his pocket.

Mouthing invectives aimed at Bridger, he turned onto his street, noting that his watchdog had either been called off or had followed the Uber car. In any case, he wasn't there.

He opened the gate at the end of his drive with a remote and drove through. The landscape's artificial moonlight and strategically placed security spotlights were all that were on.

His father's bedroom windows were dark. Good. He wouldn't be grilled—in the artful manner that only his father was capable of—on how he'd spent his evening.

He drove around back and parked Frida's car in its place, but didn't immediately get out. He sat staring at nothing through the windshield, deep in thought.

The gloating satisfaction he'd felt for having successfully violated Kathryn Lennon's home, and underwear drawer, had been squelched by seeing Bridger. That bastard was turning up every-fucking-where. First, an unprecedented visit to Rebecca, now a sleepover at Kathryn Lennon's house.

The state prosecutor and the ex-husband, whose finger was on the button of Rebecca's fate, were cozied up and plotting the ruin of Eban Clarke.

It was funny when you thought about it. He actually laughed out loud.

Chapter 21

———◆———

New Orleans was a city ravaged by corrosive elements, Mother Nature's foul temper, and political corruption. Yet it retained its unique charm, and a good part of its enchantment was due to decadence and decay. Under different circumstances, Kate would have been delighted to explore its eccentricities with Zach.

But neither of them had any enthusiasm for this trip and they had said little to each other after their good morning greeting when they'd met at the coffee maker in her kitchen. Each was subdued by dread. They'd spent most of the flight from Atlanta pretending to doze.

"This is it," Zach said.

He pulled the rental car to the curb in front of a brown brick house with cream-colored trim and a green composite roof. He'd told Kate that Mary and Doug Pratt had lived here for the entirety of their married life, and that Rebecca had been loath to claim the humble dwelling as where she'd spent her first eighteen years.

They got out of the car and walked toward the front door. Zach asked Kate if she knew what she was going to say.

"Generally," she replied, "but not specifically. Anything prepared would sound like a speech. I want him to see me as a person, not as a spokesperson."

"Let's hope. Here goes." He pressed the doorbell.

Doug answered the door dressed in khaki pants and a golf shirt left untucked. Kate noted now, as she had at their initial meeting, that the only remarkable thing about him was that he'd fathered someone with Rebecca's exotic beauty and vitality. In every respect, Doug was average: height, weight, mien.

However, when he saw Zach, his bland features turned hostile. He scowled at Kate. "When you called and asked to see me, you failed to mention that he was coming, too."

"I was afraid you wouldn't agree to see us."

"You were right about that."

Before he could shut the door, she said, "Mr. Pratt, Zach needs to be in on this discussion. You are intelligent and reasonable enough to understand why."

"I understand, all right. You two are ganging up on me in the hope of bringing me around to your way of thinking."

"You're mistaken," she said. "Zach continues to honor your wishes."

He moved his gaze from her to Zach. "Are you going to beat me up, too?"

"Beat you up? What are you talking about?"

"That deputy sheriff, Dave Morris, called me this morning, said you busted him up good."

"He threw the first punch, *after* he almost caused me to skid off the cliff. I don't apologize for defending myself."

"He told me you weaseled my name out of him."

"If you wanted to know my frame of mind now that Clarke is free, why didn't you ask me man-to-man? A phone call? An email? Instead you hired a spy."

Pratt set his jaw and didn't respond.

Zach made a sound of disgust. "Grow up, Doug. This issue is a hell of a lot more critical than your pissing contest against me."

Before the interview could unravel further, Kate said, "Mr. Pratt, Rebecca's fate still lies with you."

"Then what is there to talk about?"

"Eban Clarke's fate. Which also lies with you." She let that sink in, then said, "May we come in?"

Looking sour, he unhooked the latch on the screen door and pushed it open. "Hurry, or the cat will get out."

Inside, the atmosphere was stuffy. Dust motes danced in the streaks of sunlight allowed in through slits between partially closed Venetian blinds. Kate was glad when Doug led them through the house onto a screened-in back porch.

"It's not too humid out here today." He sat down in a wicker rocking chair with a faded cushion. A tabby cat—who looked too old and infirm to escape through an open door—came over to the chair. Doug bent down and picked him up, laid him in his lap, and began stroking him.

Kate sat in a matching chair that she figured had probably been the late Mary's customary seat. Zach had a settee all to himself.

Once he was seated, he said, "Doug, my condolences on Mary's passing. I didn't know until Kate told me."

"Didn't see any cause to tell you."

"I was her son-in-law."

"Not for long." He scratched the cat between its rheumy eyes, then gestured over his shoulder. "I can't manage the housekeeping the way she did. Not and still go to the hospital every day."

Kate said, "We stopped there before coming here."

His eyes narrowed with suspicion, and he darted a resentful glance toward Zach before coming back to her. "What for?"

Kate saw that as an opening. "Based on what I'd been told and had read, I had a general knowledge of Rebecca's condition, but thought I needed to see her for myself in order to fully appreciate both Zach's dilemma and the heartache you've endured for the past four years. Your continual care for her is commendable, Mr. Pratt."

"Do you have children?"

"No."

"Then you wouldn't get it. Even being like she is now, Rebecca is still my little girl. Her spirit is in there somewhere. I won't give up on her." He looked at Zach as though expecting him to throw down a gauntlet, but Zach remained silent and stoic.

Kate said, "You demonstrate your love and devotion to Rebecca daily."

"I don't see it as a duty, if that's what you're driving at."

"No, that wasn't what I was driving at," she said with

more patience than she was feeling. "What I was driving at is that, in contrast to your self-sacrifice, the person who did this to her is now free to go about his life without any sense of obligation or responsibility." She reached into her bag for a folder and passed it to him. "I'll leave this with you. You can read it or not."

"What is it?"

"Do you remember Dr. Hawkins, who testified at the release hearing?"

"Yes. He shilly-shallied."

"Who's Dr. Hawkins?" Zach asked.

"The psychologist who was assigned to Eban Clarke while he was in prison."

"What do you mean he shilly-shallied?" Zach asked, addressing the question to Doug.

"On the witness stand, he rambled about Clarke's delusions of grandeur, his sense of entitlement, lofty ego, so on."

Kate picked up. "But when cross-examined, Dr. Hawkins was ground to dust by Clarke's ruthless defense lawyer. He got the doctor to concede that most young men, especially those from prominent families, have inflated egos and feel entitled.

"But the most damaging part of the testimony was when the lawyer finagled the doctor into acknowledging that in some of his sessions with Clarke, he had humbly expressed remorse for his recklessness that night, and said that he would forever regret the tragic result. Words to that effect."

"Was Hawkins lying?"

"No," she said. "Clarke had counted on Dr. Hawkins being subpoenaed to testify, so during their sessions leading up to the hearing he convincingly playacted being repentant."

"My ass," Zach scoffed. "He manipulated that doctor."

"He tried," she said. "Dr. Hawkins is a pro. He saw straight through Clarke's pretending. But on the witness stand, when hammered to answer with either a yes or no, he was under oath to admit that Clarke had, on more than one occasion, shown contrition."

"So what's this?" Doug indicated the folder which he'd set down on top of a thick, well-worn, leather-bound Bible on the table at his elbow.

Kate said, "Dr. Hawkins had a final session with Clarke just before his release. His notes are in that folder. To summarize, Clarke thanked him for his testimony at the hearing. He crowed over having beat the justice system. In reference to Rebecca, he was blasé, even callous. No remorse whatsoever."

Kate heard Zach mutter an obscenity, but she kept her gaze fixed on Doug Pratt, whose hand now lay still on the cat. "Mr. Pratt, Eban Clarke is a sociopath. An extremely clever and cruel trickster. An individual without a conscience. He has an insatiable appetite for every form of self-indulgence. He doesn't care whom he hurts in pursuit of anything he wants, whether it's a fast car, the blind obedience of his so-called friends, or sexual gratification."

Doug winced.

Kate felt compassion for him, but she didn't back down. She was getting to the heart of the matter. This was why she had come. "Do you remember the testimonies of the other two men involved?"

"At Clarke's trial? Of course. How could I forget?"

"Then you'll recall their admissions that, prior to the night with Rebecca, they'd had similar 'sex parties' with scores of women. Every one of those occasions had been orchestrated by Eban Clarke."

She paused. "I fear that other women will be victimized. Different circumstances, different outcomes than Rebecca's, please God. But whether or not Clarke ever goes near another woman again, on that particular night, he stole your daughter's life from her. He stole her life from you and Mary. To the fullest extent of the law, he should be brought to justice for it." Sensing that she'd said enough, she eased back in her chair.

Pratt stared through the screen at the cracked concrete birdbath in his backyard. The standing water in it was stagnant. Ponderous moments ticked by, then he looked over at Zach. "You're ready to do it, aren't you?"

Zach closed his eyes briefly, then opened them and said, "I'll never be ready to do it, Doug."

"But it's as plain as day that you're leaning that way."

Zach took another moment before speaking. "Putting aside your religious convictions, and my moral and ethical ambiguities, and even disregarding the privileged sociopath who's responsible, I've started focusing on *Rebecca*. I think about the indignity that she is subjected to twenty-four seven, three hundred and sixty-five. If we were able to ask her, don't you think she would beg us to end it without delay?"

Pratt inhaled several times through his nostrils. "You know what I think? I think you want payback for her committing adultery."

"Doug—"

"You're tired of paying the bills for her keep at that special hospital. I didn't ask you to, you know. You volunteered, and now you're regretting a bad investment."

"Don't you see what you're doing?" Zach said. "You're angry with me, but you're taking it out on Rebecca."

"You were just itching to kill her four years ago, weren't you?"

Zach ran his fingers through his hair. "Christ." He looked at Kate with asperity and futility.

Seeing that he was getting to him, Doug picked up steam. "What stopped you from doing it then?"

"My personal conflict. Your feelings. Mary's."

"Aw, you didn't give a crap about *our* feelings. It was the bad publicity you'd get for snuffing your ex. Come on now. Admit it here in front of Ms. Lennon. The only reason you spared Rebecca's life then was because you didn't want to look bad to your adoring fans."

"Not true," Zach said softly.

"What's changed your mind? Huh? What's different this time around? I don't think you give a flip about Eban Clarke getting justly punished. I think it's because you're a washup and have less to lose now."

By the time he'd finished, Zach was already on his feet. He said to Kate, "I'll be outside." His footsteps thumped over creaking floor planks as he made his way through the house. They heard the front screen door slap shut.

Kate's cheeks were hot with indignation. She picked up her bag and stood. "That was uncalled for, Mr. Pratt. And beneath you. You have my contact information."

She started for the door, but then turned back. "Why didn't you see to it that Zach resign as her agent four years ago?"

"Wasn't necessary. He cut and ran. Big number twelve turned Rebecca over to Mary and me because he didn't want a media smear if he told the doctors to let her die."

"That's not at all fair, Mr. Pratt. You know that."

"I was there, you weren't."

He bobbed his head as though he'd had his say, and that was all there was to it. But she wasn't ready to let him get away with denouncing Zach. "What about since then? Why haven't you insisted on making your guardianship legal?"

"Haven't needed to. He's left us alone."

"I don't think that's the reason at all. I think you relish keeping him tethered and miserable."

He batted the air with his hand. "Think what you want. But the fact is that as long as he stayed up there on his mountain, fine. But now he's back. He's meddling. I'm going to talk to my lawyer and see what I have to do. In the meantime, Bridger better not try and get the jump on me."

"You mean regarding Rebecca? He wouldn't do that."

"He sneaked down here to see her, didn't he? He had a private meeting with Dr. Gilbreath. He tagged along with you."

Her patience wearing thin, she said, "No, I tagged along with him. He hoped to discuss with you, calmly and reasonably, Eban Clarke's release and how it might change your perspective."

"I think you've changed his perspective, is what I think."

"I've explained the legal ramifications to him just as I did to you."

"You've twisted his thinking, though. He's waffling. I can tell. He could go behind my back and take my girl off the feeding tube before I knew about it."

She could tell that arguing was futile. She pulled her bag onto her shoulder. "Zach told you four years ago that he wouldn't take any action without your knowledge and consent. He's kept that promise. Much to his detriment, Mr. Pratt. And to yours. But, mostly, to Rebecca's."

Kate left him there sitting in his rocker with his mangy cat and made her way quickly through the house. Zach was sitting in the car, his elbows propped on the lowest arc of the steering wheel, his hands clasped above it. The double fist was pressed against his chin and mouth. He was staring through the windshield and seemed not to notice her until she opened the passenger door and got in.

"I should pity him," she said. "He's pathetic. But I can't feel anything except contempt for an individual who claims to be so grounded in religion, but holds you, anybody, in such rank contempt."

"Don't waste your energy being angry with him. I've learned the hard way that it only wears you to a nub, not him."

"No, I'm going to continue being angry. For a while, at least. It made me furious the way he kept goading you about why you didn't take Rebecca off life support before. When all along it was to spare him and Mary. Questioning your motive is so unfair."

"Not really, Kate. My motive wasn't just to spare their feelings. And it wasn't to avoid bad publicity." Still without looking at her, he punched the ignition button and put the car in gear. As he pulled away from the curb, he said, "Rebecca was pregnant."

Chapter 22

Eban!"

Hearing his father's shout, Eban surfaced, shook water off his face, and pushed his swim goggles up onto his forehead. "What?"

"Get out. Come into the study."

"I'm in the middle of my swim."

"Get out and come into the study." Without further ado, Sid pivoted and entered the house through a pair of French doors that opened onto the terrace. Windowpanes rattled when he pushed them shut.

His mental cursing keeping time with his strokes, Eban swam to the pool's edge and hoisted himself out. The pool was heated, but the air was chilly. Goose bumps broke out on his skin. He wrapped himself in the beach towel he'd brought out with him, slid his feet into pool shoes, and flapped toward the French doors.

As he walked into the study, he said, "I had ten laps to go. This had better be important." Spotting Upton, he said, "But it can't be good."

His father said, "Sit down."

"I'm wet. I'll stand."

"Fine." His father also remained standing. In fact, he was prowling the room like a caged lion sorely pissed off at his cub. "Tell him," he said to Up.

Upton cleared his throat. "I just heard from my snitch in New Orleans. Kate Lennon and Zach Bridger visited the facility today."

"*Today?*"

"Around lunchtime."

"Together?"

"Indeed."

Although Eban didn't want to show it, this came as a disturbing news flash. Late last night, those two had been tucked in at Lennon's house. By lunchtime today they'd been in New Orleans, meaning they'd wasted no time beating it down there. They were moving more quickly than he had anticipated. More quickly than he was. Being outmaneuvered bothered him more than anything.

"They stayed less than an hour," Sid said, obviously relating what Up had already told him. "The administrator personally escorted them into Rebecca's room. They spent only a few minutes there before retreating to the doctor's office."

Eban looked down at Upton, who resembled a troll sitting hunched in one of the deep leather chairs. "Did your snitch overhear any of their conversation?"

"No."

"Maybe you're not paying her enough. Offer her more money, and I'll bet she'll grow bigger ears."

"I believe we can assume what the topic of discussion was, Eban."

"Yes, I think that's a safe assumption. What the hell are you going to do about it?"

"Nothing."

Eban was taken aback by the blunt reply, then became awash with fury. He bore down on his godfather. "What do you mean *nothing*?"

"I mean not a damn thing."

Sid had stopped pacing. "He's right, son. Up has taken this as far as he can alone." With obvious distaste, he added, "It's time we got your outrageously expensive and self-aggrandizing defense attorney back in the loop."

"There is no loop," Up said. "Not with me anyway." Reaching into his breast pocket, he withdrew a letter-size envelope and laid in on the cocktail table beside the chair. Ignoring Eban, he addressed Sid. "I'm tendering my resignation."

Sid fell back a step. "What?"

"It's spelled out in the letter." He nodded down at the envelope. "I've made provisions. You won't be without representation. Several qualified attorneys who meet your job requirements will be on hand to assist you immediately. It'll be up to you whether or not you take them on full-time."

"Up, surely you're not serious."

"Let him go, Dad," Eban said. "Good riddance. The Angel of Death has more spunk than him."

Upton smiled and used the armrests to assist himself out of the chair. "He's right, Sid. I'm dying."

"*Dying?*"

"What I initially thought was chronic heartburn is stomach cancer. I'm not valiant enough to take the grueling treatments which, in the long run, would buy me only a few more months of misery." He looked over at Eban before coming back around to Sid. "But even if I weren't about to die, I would stop facilitating Eban's iniquities."

Eban, who'd poured himself a straight vodka while Upton had been talking, said, "Clearing your guilty conscience before meeting your maker?"

"Clearing it would be impossible," Upton said, looking Eban square in the eye. "But I won't contribute to it by advocating on your behalf one moment longer."

"Up, you can't do this."

He gave Sid a rueful smile. "In fact, I can, Sid. I am. I've loved you like a brother, but I'm done." He held Sid's gaze for a moment, then, without even another glance toward Eban, turned and left the room.

Eban shot his vodka. "Well, it wasn't Shakespeare, but that was a moving farewell speech."

"Shut up, Eban."

"Aw, I know how you must feel. Your best friend has walked out on you. That's gotta hurt. But he was old, tired, and terminal. We're better off without him and his sad-sack attitude." He set down his glass and wrapped the beach towel more securely around himself. "I'm chilled. I'm going upstairs to get in the sauna."

"You're going upstairs to pack."

Eban stopped so suddenly he almost slid out of his pool shoes. "Pack? Where am I going?"

"Up told me that he had advised you to go abroad to live for a while. I think that's your best option."

"Well, I think that option sucks."

"I'll make the jet available."

"You're not listening, *Dad*. I'm not leaving the country. If I run off, I'll look guilty."

Sid became perfectly still and locked gazes with him. Eban had never seen him direct this particular level of wrath toward anyone before, not his fiercest business competitor or an insubordinate employee, and certainly not toward him. It gave him pause, but rather than desist, he changed his tactic.

Flashing his most disarming smile, he spread his arms out at his sides. "Who am I to turn down the Gulfstream? Maybe a few days away wouldn't be a bad idea."

"You'll stay indefinitely. Until I call you back."

So much for playing nice. "The fuck I will."

Sid took several steps toward him. "Do not talk to me like that, Eban."

"What is the matter with you these days? You're not yourself. I blame Up. His pessimism has rubbed off on you."

Sid appeared unfazed. "Years ago, when you were in grade school and held that kid's head in the toilet and nearly drowned him, Up was reluctant to pay off the parents and the school superintendent so you wouldn't be expelled. He did as I ordered, but he told me then that you should be taught a stern lesson about accountability for one's actions.

"To my everlasting regret, I didn't listen or heed his advice. Worse, I continued to bail you out, time and time again. Look where my indulgence has brought us. Your mother died a pill junkie because of you and your shenanigans. You were convicted of a felony. Now you've cost me my best friend."

Eban saw red. *"I'm your son!"*

"A fact that does not do me proud."

Eban growled, made fists of his hands, and socked one into the palm of the other. "Why are you blaming me for everything? None of this is my fault. It's that Lennon woman's. All this is her doing."

With that, the fight went out of Sid. His bearing became one of defeat. He regarded Eban with sorrow, perplexity, and—what really disconcerted Eban—pity.

"No, Eban, all this is *your* doing. Furthermore, the consequences of your actions seem not to have sunk in yet."

He assumed an arrogant stance. "So, enlighten me of these consequences, Father dear."

"What you seem not to have grasped is that whenever Rebecca Pratt dies, whether she's taken off life support or dies of natural causes, you will always be liable for her death."

Chapter 23

———◆◆◆———

Rebecca was pregnant.

Zach realized it had been unfair of him to drop that on Kate and then clam up about it. He'd never intended to tell anyone. The only reason he'd told her was so she would know that when he'd had to make the decision between prolonging Rebecca's life or ending it, there had been a consideration that surpassed the Pratts' dogma and the fear of his fans' reaction, as Doug had alleged.

Kate had stared at him, dumbfounded, finally finding enough voice to say, "Why didn't you tell me?"

"I just did. And that's all I'm saying about it."

After that, they'd spoken little on the drive from Doug's house to the airport to catch an Atlanta-bound flight, on which he'd been lucky enough to book two first-class seats.

While waiting for its departure, they'd eaten a late lunch at one of the airport's restaurants. He'd been recognized several times, had signed a couple of autographs, and had his picture taken, but he'd welcomed those short-term breaks from the strain between Kate and him, which his brusqueness had caused.

Now, she sat turned away from him, staring out the airplane window. He'd created the tension. It was up to him to smooth things out. "Kate?" She turned her head away from the window and looked at him. "Have you ever been to Mardi Gras?"

Seeming surprised by the innocuous question, she didn't answer at first, then, "A couple of times. You?"

"Several. One year the Bacchus krewe invited me to ride in their parade. That was an experience."

"You threw beads?"

"By the handful."

"To everyone? Or just to the women who flashed their breasts?"

He looked at her with feigned bafflement. "They're supposed to flash their breasts?"

That coaxed a soft laugh out of her. "I'd wager you saw more than your share. Who on that float ran out of beads first?"

"You've seen one pair..." He yawned. "It almost got boring."

"Oh, right."

She laughed again, and he joined in, but when it languished, he said, "Mad at me?"

"No, not mad. Just trying to think things through."

"Like what?"

"Do you want the topics in any particular order?"

"Make it random."

"Well,"—she sighed—"for one, I was wondering why a man who claims to love his daughter, who demonstrates his love every day, would choose to keep her as she is rather than to let her go. Why not release her and himself from this purgatory they're in? Neither of them is *living*."

"I think it's like he said. In order to understand, it would have to be your child."

"No doubt that's true. He's not a likable person, but my heart aches for him."

"I suffer the same mixed emotions. When he's hurling insults, it's a bitch to take it and keep my temper under control."

"But you do."

"Nothing to gain by lashing back," he said and shrugged. "What else were you thinking about?"

"I was thinking that Eban Clarke will probably get away with it. I'm afraid he will."

Zach let a moment pass, then said, "Are you ready to tell me yet?"

She brought her head farther around so that they were fully facing, but she didn't ask what he'd meant by the question. He figured she knew.

"The matter of the *State versus Eban Clarke* isn't just any ol' legal battle for you, is it, Kate? It's a personal campaign. Or else I'm way off base and you can tell me to mind my own business."

Her gaze faltered, and she said huskily, "You're not off base."

He said nothing more. He'd opened the door. She could go through it or not.

Turning to look straight into the seat back in front of her, she began speaking in a low voice. "Fall semester of my junior year in college. It was a Saturday night. One of my housemates—I lived with three other girls off campus—talked me into going to a party with her. After weeks of non-stop study, I felt I'd earned a night of festivity.

"The party was at a private residence, and the place was rocking when my friend and I got there. Blaring music, lots of people, lots of alcohol, pot was available. You know the scene."

"Too well."

"My friends and I had made a pact not to go to a free-for-all like that alone, and always to look out for each other while there. You know, monitor each other, make sure that no one got too far gone to realize that she was placing herself in a risky situation.

"Shortly after our arrival, I met this guy. Premed. Good looking. Humorous. We hit it off. One thing led to another. By the time the party began to wind down, we were smoochy. My friend sought me out, said she was ready to leave. He stepped in and offered to drive me home later. Moony over this guy, I told my friend that I was pleasantly buzzed but still had my wits about me. She left."

She paused to clear her throat. "He and I found a sofa in a game room and started making out. Everything was dreamy. Until it became a nightmare. Like that," she said, snapping her fingers, "I was being held facedown, and he was on top of me, wrestling with my skirt, then my underwear."

She stopped speaking altogether. Zach wanted to say

something, to touch her hand or her cheek, but he was afraid she might misinterpret the gesture, so he sat still and waited.

"I struggled, but he outweighed me by a hundred pounds. I tried screaming, but he was smothering me in the sofa cushion. He was being rough, calling me awful names, saying all the vile things that women hear when they say *no*. He was intent on raping me.

"But while he was, uh, better positioning himself, his knee slipped off the edge of the sofa. He lost his balance and rolled onto the floor. I sprang up and hurdled the armrest. He was trying to get himself off the floor and out from between the sofa and the coffee table. There was this big, brass bowl of potpourri on the table. I picked it up and banged it against the top of his head with all my might. I don't think I knocked him out, but it dazed him.

"I dropped the bowl and ran like hell. I ran all the way home. I sneaked in, threw up my rum and Coke, which I haven't drunk since. I sat in the shower until the water ran cold, crying, shuddering. I couldn't believe it had happened. Not to *me*. Never to *me*.

"The next morning, my roommate was eager to hear all about this hot med student. I told her he'd turned out to be a dud, that soon after she'd left, I'd hitched a ride home with another girl.

"I saw him only twice after that. Once at a sandwich shop near campus. He looked at me quizzically, like he couldn't quite place me. I hoped he couldn't and pretended not to recognize him."

She turned toward Zach. "The second time I saw him, it

was his mug shot on TV. He'd been arrested for serial rape. Three separate battery assaults. The MO of each matched my experience. Charm and sweetness, and then *wham*. He was tried and convicted and to this day is serving his sentence.

"But because I felt like such a colossal fool, because I was embarrassed by my own culpability, because I was afraid that going public would sully me and negatively affect the law degree I was working so hard for, I never told a single soul. Not my parents or my closest friends, no one."

"Till now?"

"Yes."

"Why me, Kate?"

"Because as the individual who must make the ultimate decision regarding Rebecca, you deserve to know why I'm so passionate about putting Eban Clarke away.

"I don't know where I fell in the order of my attacker's victims, but if I hadn't remained silent, other women might not have suffered his abuse." She took a deep breath. "That's why Eban Clarke's case is personal. I'm trying to atone for my cowardice."

"God, Kate." He reached across the armrest to take her hand, then pulled his back.

She gave him a wan smile. "He didn't leave me sexually scarred. It's all right to touch me, Zach. As you should know by now." She reached over, clasped their hands, and placed them on the armrest. "I like men a lot. But for anyone, of either sex, by force or guile, to claim an unbestowed right to another person's body is a crime."

"Kate, I swear to you, going back to the first time I had

sex, and for all the raucous parties, and the countless one-night stands, I never—"

"Shh. Zach. Don't feel compelled to defend yourself. God help the Dave Morrises of this world who throw the first punch at you, but to force yourself on a woman? No. You were under my roof last night and never laid a hand on me."

"I thought about it, though. Plenty."

Softly, she confessed, "So did I."

Each was so focused on the other, they both flinched when the captain's voice came in over the PA system to announce that they were twenty minutes from landing.

As they were adjusting their seats, Zach asked, "Regarding the case, what's your next move?"

"I'm not sure I have one. If Doug makes his guardianship legal, it's over. He will never concede. And by the time Rebecca dies of natural causes, Eban could have disappeared to God knows where." She hesitated before adding, "But Doug can't become her guardian unless you're willing to resign as her agent."

"I will, Kate. I promised I would never go against his and Mary's wishes or religious convictions."

"I know."

"I'm sorry."

"I know that, too. The hellish irony of it is that I admire you for upholding your promise."

"Well, thanks. But that leaves me useless to you. Even if I was willing to approach Doug and try again, he'll shoot down anything I say."

Thoughtfully, she tugged at the corner of her lower lip with her teeth.

"What?" he said.

"Nothing *you* say will alter his thinking. But what if… what if he heard a truthful account of that night from Cal Parsons and Theo Simpson? What if I could get them to retract their original testimony and admit that Rebecca had said the safe word, or at least had tried to but was past the point of no return?"

"I'm all for it, but why would they be willing to do that? They'd be admitting to lying on the witness stand at Clarke's trial."

"Yes, but what if they were granted clemency for the perjury, and their probation was lifted?"

"In exchange for telling what actually went down?"

"Exactly. Hearing directly from the two of them what Rebecca suffered might weaken Doug's resolve, make him want to see Clarke justly punished."

"Even though it would require taking Rebecca off life support."

"Even though."

In doubt, Zach frowned. "I don't know, Kate. You saw him, heard him. It's going to be a tough sell. And, from a legal standpoint, can you swing getting them clemency, all that?"

"I don't know," she admitted. "The AG may say absolutely not, and that'll be the end of it. But it's my last play."

"Fourth down and fifty, two seconds on the game clock. You gotta take your shot."

"It's my Hail Mary."

He grinned. "When's kickoff?"

"As soon as we land."

A few minutes later, they touched down. During the long taxi to the terminal, Zach checked his phone. "I've got two texts and three voice mails from Bing."

"What does he say?"

"Not much. I think this says it all." He turned his phone so Kate could read the latest text.

Shit show!

Chapter 24

Melinda and Cal Parsons were in a shimmery haze of happiness as they pulled into the driveway of their home. After cutting the car engine, they smiled across at each other, and then both burst into spontaneous laughter.

While out, she'd received a call from a local medical clinic. The home pregnancy test she had taken two days earlier had been confirmed positive by a blood test. Made giddy by the news, they couldn't wait to get home and celebrate.

Cal leaned across the car's console and curved his hand around the back of her neck, drawing her closer. "I love you."

"I love you, too. So much."

They kissed sweetly. He pressed his left hand on her flat belly. "Hard to believe my kid's in there."

She combed her fingers through his thick blond hair. "It

won't be long before we'll be able to listen to the heartbeat. We'll get one of those Doppler ultrasound kits."

"You can do that?"

"Um-huh."

He gave her another quick kiss, then got out and came around to hug her as she alighted. With her arm around his waist, and his draped over her shoulders, they walked toward the house.

They'd leased it with an option to buy. He was hoping he would be able to manage a mortgage after his probation period was over. Melinda's father, also his employer, had offered to make the down payment, but Cal had declined his generosity. He wanted to buy the house on his own merit, not only out of pride, but because he still felt the need to prove to everyone, including himself, that he was worthy of redemption.

Besides, he'd never lived in a house that was owned. His dad had been a gambler, and the family's income had depended on his luck, which had been equivalent to a roller coaster. As a kid, Cal had accepted the instability because he hadn't known any different. But now he did, causing him to mistrust a vertex, because he'd learned early in life that what came after a high point was the inevitable steep plunge.

He experienced a twinge of that familiar sense of breath-grabbing inevitability now as he heard the growl of a motor and felt its throb through the soles of his shoes.

He turned in time to see Eban wheeling his new Porsche into the driveway and pulling it to within inches of Cal's car, blocking it in.

Theo would cite that as a metaphor: Eban was inescapable.

Melinda had never met Eban, but she recognized him from photographs. Upon seeing him, her immediate reaction was apprehension. "Cal?"

"Don't worry. I'll get rid of him."

She hadn't wanted him to accept Eban's dinner invitation and had anxiously waited up for him to get home, her relief evident when he came in sober and none the worse for wear. He'd described the reunion as awkward and had told her that Eban's incarceration hadn't humbled him.

"Not one whit. He was his same, obnoxious self. Acting like a superstar, throwing money around. He likes nothing better than to hold court. Theo and I listened to his bull-shit stories about prison life, but we're not the appreciative audience we used to be. I figure he'll find—more like hire—a livelier set of friends. That's probably the last I'll see of him."

But now, only three days later, here he was, wearing a wide grin as he climbed out of his low-slung car and swaggered toward them. "Swear to God, all this picture needs to make it perfect is a white picket fence."

He formed a frame with his hands and looked at the house through it. "And maybe some climbing roses." He lowered his hands and walked over to them. "You must be Melissa."

"Melinda," she said.

"Oops, sorry. I always had a devil of a time keeping up with Cal's gals. They were legion, you know."

Cal said, "What are you doing here, Eban?"

"Why, I came to meet your lovely bride." He gave her a once-over, then winked at Cal. "Congratulations. She is a looker, but then you have a great eye for quality, uh, female flesh."

Cal wanted to smash his fist into Eban's face, but that was likely the reason for his goading. He was testing the strength of his control over Cal's behavior. Cal refused to give him the satisfaction of becoming riled. To Melinda, he said, "Go on inside. I'll be there in a sec."

She looked ready to refuse, but then Cal gave her a soft look and a confident hitch of his chin. She turned to go, but not before saying to Eban, "You're every bit as obnoxious as Cal has told me." She walked to the front door and let herself in.

Eban whistled low and long. "Saucy. I like her." He slapped Cal on the shoulder.

Cal threw off his touch as he would a wasp about to light. "What do you want?"

"Well…" Eban walked over to a support post for the porch's overhang and leaned back against it. "We have a problem. It's not insurmountable. More like a toenail becoming ingrown, or a toothache you feel coming on, but you can't quite—"

"The state prosecutor."

Eban showed his surprise.

"Theo called me last night," Cal said.

"Ah. Wringing his clammy hands, I'll bet."

"How clammy are yours, Eban? Maybe getting released early wasn't such a good move after all. It caused quite a stir in the attorney general's office. They're not done with you."

"*They* think. But they've got another think coming."

"Oh, yeah? Then why'd you order Theo to research this

Kathryn Lennon? How come you have such an excessive interest in her?"

"Excessive? That's not the word I would use to describe my interest in her. I would use judicious, sensible, rational. *Sane*, maybe. In other words, I'd be fucking crazy not to have an interest in her. And so would you."

"No, Eban, associating myself with you was crazy. I can't change history, although God knows I wish I could. But I did learn from it. I want nothing, I repeat, *nothing* to do with you."

Undaunted, Eban said, "Tonight. Eight o'clock. Theo's place. Be there."

"In case I haven't made it plain enough, Eban, fuck off." Cal turned away and stalked toward the front door.

"Oh, Cal?" Eban called in a singsong. "I have another word for you."

"Leave now, and don't come back. Ever."

"Perjury."

Cal stopped and turned quickly.

Eban smiled as he pushed himself away from the post and ambled in the direction of the driveway. "In case I haven't made it plain enough, I repeat. *Perjury.*"

He got into his car. As he started it, he said above the revving engine, "See you at eight." He backed out. Cal stood in the yard looking after him until Melinda pushed open the front door. "Cal?"

He turned away from the street and walked toward her. When he reached her, she hugged him tightly around his waist and laid her cheek against his chest. "I overheard what he said. He's loathsome. I hate him."

He rubbed her back. "I apologize. He burst our happy bubble over the baby."

She pushed away from him, looked into his face, and said adamantly, "He affects us only as much as we let him." She reached up and smoothed out the frown line between his eyebrows. "Cal, ignore everything he said. He's your past. The baby and I are your future."

He drew her close again and wrapped her in a strong embrace. He didn't deserve this woman who, despite his wayward past, loved him. He didn't deserve the child they'd made, or this house that he'd been fixing up on weekends in the hope of making it permanently theirs.

He'd known the sheer drop was there on the other side of the peak. Fool that he was, he had thought he was braced for it.

Eban wasn't his past. He was very much his present.

Chapter 25

———◆———

Zach didn't know how Bing had managed it, but when he and Kate emerged from the jetway, there was an attractive and mannerly young woman there to greet them. "Mr. Bridger, my name is Leanne. I'm your escort. Do you have all your belongings?"

They hadn't checked bags, so they replied yes, and Leanne said, "Lovely. Follow me, please."

They walked along the concourse, trying to stay out of the way of the poor slobs who didn't have an "escort." In the midst of the hustle, Leanne was an oasis of calm, asking them polite questions about their flight and the weather in New Orleans.

All was fine, well and good, until they passed a sports café, where patrons were seated along the bar with their beers and margaritas, watching TVs...on which was a close-up picture of Zach.

It was eerily reminiscent of the pool bar on Grand Cayman the morning his life had become a living hell. He broke a cold sweat.

"Through here, please." Leanne motioned them out of the flow of foot traffic to a door that read "Authorized Persons Only." She used a keypad to unlock it.

Beyond that door was a sterile tunnel at the end of which was another door with a keypad, and on the other side of it was Bing. He was in conversation with Leanne's male counterpart. The young man was well turned out and emanating courtesy.

Bing, however, wasn't so well turned out, and he certainly wasn't being courteous. As Kate and Zach preceded Leanne into the posh lounge that most travelers would never know existed, Bing stopped what he had been saying and put his hands on his hips. "About fuckin' time. Your flight was forty-three minutes late."

It was an effort for Zach to stay composed in the face of a new and as yet unspecified crisis, but he remembered to thank Leanne. He gave the young man a sympathetic smile as he took Bing by the elbow and propelled him toward a corner that would afford them a modicum of privacy.

"I saw the TVs in a sports bar. What's happened?"

Ignoring the question, Bing glared at Kate, who had accompanied them over. "Who's she? Or dare I guess?"

"This is Kate Lennon. Kate, this rude bastard is Bing Bingham. I've mentioned him to you."

"Mr. Bingham," she said coolly.

Bing gave her a thorough once-over, then shot Zach a sardonic look. "Not exactly the word picture you painted of the 'state prosecutor.'"

Zach didn't address the implication. Impatiently, he repeated, "*What's happened?*"

"You're all over the cable sports networks. Pat called me early afternoon, asked if I had my TV on. No, I said. But when I tuned in, there you were. Old footage, but you're the feature of the day."

"Shit!"

"Yeah. Pat said you weren't returning his calls."

"Who's Pat?" Kate asked.

"My agent," Zach replied. "I didn't answer because I thought he was calling about the mouthwash thing."

"Mouthwash thing?" Bing said.

"He's been trying to talk me into doing a commercial."

Bing grunted with contempt. "I hope you told him to go fuck himself."

"If I was returning his calls, I would."

"I think he's secretly doing handsprings over the free publicity you're suddenly getting, but you're gonna hate it like hell, Zach."

"It's about Rebecca?"

"A replay of four years ago."

Zach dropped his head forward and cursed under his breath. When he looked up again, he could tell that Kate was as distressed as he.

"I came to warn you," Bing said. "Drove hellbent from Greenville to get here in time to meet your flight."

"How did you know we were flying in?" Kate asked.

"Zach always texts me his itinerary. 'Course he failed to mention that he had a traveling companion."

Zach let that dart whiz past without comment, but he said

to Kate, "This isn't the first time Bing has headed me off to avoid media."

"I see."

"I didn't want you stepping off the plane and into a pile of shit," Bing said. "So far, I think you're okay, but my guess is it won't take long for the bloodhounds to pick up your trail."

"Thanks for the escort service," Zach said.

"Don't thank me. I charged it to your credit card. It ain't cheap."

Zach waved that off. "What are they reporting?"

"On TV? Well, let's see. You've made two visits this week to the place in New Orleans where Rebecca is at. This according to a reliable source who chose not to be identified. Speculation is . . . well, you know. Will he or won't he pull the plug this go-round? Million-dollar question. Wouldn't surprise me if bookies are overwhelmed. Sad to say, Zach, but the whole damn thing has mushroomed again."

Zach, sickened by everything Bing had said, walked away and went to stand in front of a darkly tinted window overlooking intersecting runways. No one could see him behind the glass, yet his face was appearing on jumbo screens across the country. By tomorrow it would be on the front page of tabloids. Again, his *life* was being laid bare and dissected for its entertainment value.

Jesus. He was living out the nightmare all over again.

He'd overheard the ebb and flow of Bing's murmured conversation with Kate, although their words were indistinct. Now, feeling a light touch on his arm, he turned to find Kate beside him, Bing lurking behind her, his hands stuffed into the pockets of his wrinkled, baggy trousers, his brow beetled.

She said, "Bing says my name hasn't been mentioned yet."

"No offense, but Rebecca and I will sell more Nikes and Coors."

"No offense taken," she said with a wry smile. "Someone wanted to place you in the hot seat again."

"The unidentified source," Bing said with disgust. "You told me you were going to see Rebecca's daddy. You think it was him?"

"Doug is a candidate," Zach said. "Four years ago, the brouhaha was unavoidable, and he took advantage of it to disparage me. But I can't see him raining this down on himself or Rebecca now."

Kate said, "Nor can I."

"But he's the only one outside Dr. Gilbreath's staff who knew we were there today," Zach said.

"You mistrusted her ability to keep the privacy policy airtight if enough money was offered, remember?" Kate arched an eyebrow. "Who do we know who has both unlimited funds and a stake in this?"

Zach swore softly but elaborately. "I think you're right."

Exasperated, Bing divided a look between them. "Right about what? I'm not following."

"Eban Clarke may be the anonymous source," Zach said. "He's thumbing his nose at us. You mess with me, I'll mess with you, and see how you like it."

He bridged his forehead with his hand and pressed his fingers against his temples in the hope of clarifying his thinking, but he didn't like the track his thoughts took.

He lowered his hand and looked at Kate. "For now, the story is a rehash of four years ago. But if it is Clarke who masterminded this, when the flurry begins to wind down, he'll want to fan the fire with something new. He's whetted everyone's appetite; he'll feed them the next course."

"Me," she said.

"I'm afraid it's only a matter of time, Kate."

She thought about it but looked dubious. "I don't think so, Zach. He can't bring me into the open without revealing my role in all this. If he does that, his legal vulnerability will be exposed. The focus of the story would shift to him, and in a very unfavorable way."

"Unless he's got juicy goods on you," Bing said. "How ugly are the skeletons in your closet?"

Zach snapped, "Lay off her, Bing, all right?"

Bing held up his hands in surrender. "Just sayin'. If there's something you thought was dead and buried, that little shithead has the resources to unearth it. Better to be forewarned and armed to fight off the backlash."

Zach noticed that several people had filtered into the lounge and were casting curious glances at them. "We can't stay huddled in here indefinitely."

"I've booked you and me rooms at a hotel on the north side of the city," Bing said. "We can branch off from there in the morning, me back to Greenville, you to your mountain hideaway."

"Can't," Zach said. "My truck is at Kate's. This morning we came to the airport in her car."

Bing regarded them sourly. "Well, that gums up that plan."

"And anyway," Zach said, "Kate won't be safe alone in her house." He explained to Bing about the suspected intruder.

Bing rubbed his chin, looking doubtful. "Nothing taken, no sign of a break-in? You don't even know there was an intruder. It's quite a leap to think it was Clarke."

"I'm taking no chances," Zach said.

"So then, what?" Bing asked.

"Follow me home," Kate said. "You're both welcome to stay there tonight."

"Thanks," Zach said. "But what if we get there and there's a mob of media camped in your yard?"

"Not a problem," Bing said. "I've got a scattergun in my trunk."

All things considered, especially Bing's scattergun, Zach and Kate decided that the hotel was a better, safer option for where they would pass the night.

The escorts provided them discreet passage out of the airport and delivered them to their respective vehicles. Before leaving Bing at his car, Zach told him to add a room for Kate to their reservation.

"Use Kate Cartwright," she suggested. "Just in case."

When Leanne dropped them at Kate's car, Zach offered to drive. Although rush hour had come and gone, traffic bottlenecked on the downtown portion of the freeway.

While stalled, he looked over at her and asked, "What about the guy?"

"What guy?"

"The one you told me about on the plane. Could he be one of the ugly skeletons Clarke unearths?"

"Highly unlikely. We never got past first names. The one time I saw him again, he didn't recognize me. If he didn't then, when I still had long, brown hair, he surely wouldn't now. He's way down on the list of concerns."

"Well, if he ever does reappear, I get first crack at him."

———

It took almost an hour for them to reach the hotel. By then the day had seemed endless. They were all exhausted, but they convened in Zach's room long enough to share a pizza from the hotel's kitchen.

While eating, Zach flipped through television channels and caught occasional snippets of stories about himself and Rebecca, but already they'd been usurped as the lead story by an NBA superstar arrested on drug charges.

Zach turned off the TV and tossed the remote on the bed. "Maybe by tomorrow, it'll have blown over." But his tone wasn't optimistic, and he could tell that although Bing and Kate gave him hopeful nods, they didn't believe it would.

His and Kate's rooms had side-by-side doors in the hallway. Bing's was across from theirs. The three said their good nights at Zach's door. He took a hot shower. As he came out of the bathroom, there was rapid knocking on his door.

Chapter 26

Thinking it might be Kate trying to beat his door down, his heart gave a little jump of hope and expectation.

But when he opened the door, there stood Bing in only his under drawers. "You gotta see this." He pushed Zach aside and stamped in. "Where's the remote?"

"Now what?"

Bing picked up the remote, but the various steps on the hotel's programming menu were too much for him in his present state of mind.

Over his swearing, Zach said, "Just tell me."

"Kate was wrong to think she was safe. A picture's worth a thousand words."

He finally landed on the channel he sought, and it didn't take but a second or two for Zach to understand why Bing was upset. "Where'd they get these?"

"Someone on your flight leaked them. The station has got

them on a loop, showing them over and over. If Clarke is the culprit, he didn't have to dig for a juicy tidbit, you two served it up on a silver platter."

The pictures being flashed on the TV screen were of Kate and him. They'd obviously been taken in the first-class cabin on a cell phone and shot from the prospective of a row back and across the aisle from their seats.

"There's nothing to them," Zach said. "We're only talking."

"Um-huh. Heads together. Shoulders rubbing. Eyes only for each other. Keep watching. It gets better."

Now on the screen was shaky video. The person with the camera must have been following them a few yards back as they'd made their way down the concourse under Leanne's guidance.

At one point, Kate had turned to say something to him. He'd placed his hand between her shoulder blades and bent his head down low in order to hear her. Her lips were almost touching his ear as she spoke directly into it.

He barely remembered it. His movements had been reflexive. "I couldn't hear her. I—" Bing's glare shut him off, but being put on the defensive also made him mad as hell. "Is that the worst of it?"

"Isn't that bad enough?"

"Have they identified Kate?"

"Only as a state prosecutor. But you know that won't last."

Zach did know that. He yanked the remote out of Bing's hand and switched off the TV. "That wasn't what it looks like."

"Really? I think it's exactly what it looks like. 'All business.

Articulate. Smart.' That was the description you gave me. How come you didn't add that she's cute and has blue eyes as big as china plates? And let's not shortchange the great legs."

Zach fumed. "I'm a grown-up, Bing. I don't have to defend myself to you, especially in this department."

"Correct. But don't you have enough trouble right now? Wise up, for crissake." He hitched his chin toward Zach's middle. "Your pecker's doing your thinking for you? It's an easy fix. Get dressed, go out, find a woman. You'll be back in an hour, and nobody will care, especially the woman. She'll be thrilled. She'll tell all her friends, who will swear she's lying. She'll sell t-shirts that read 'I rode Zach Bridger.'"

Zach brought his anger under control, then said in a quiet voice, "That wouldn't fix it."

Bing gaped at him and must have seen in his expression what he was trying to convey, because the older man groaned and dragged his hand down his face. "Oh Jesus. It's like that?"

"I know. Bad timing."

"Oh, ya think? You go for years screwing indiscriminately, and you pick now to—"

"Stop there, Bing." Zach pulled a clean t-shirt from his duffel bag and worked it over his head, then picked up his key card, went over to the door, and opened it. "Go back to your room before you get arrested for indecent exposure. I'll warn Kate to expect fallout tomorrow."

They stepped into the hallway. Zach tapped on Kate's door. She opened it and poked her head out. Seeing the two of them, she said, "What?"

"Are you watching TV?"

"I've seen all I want or need to."

"That's what you think," Bing muttered as he went into his room and shut the door.

Kate looked at Zack. "That had an ominous ring to it."

He walked into the room, backing her up until he was fully inside and the heavy door had swung shut behind him. "Someone on our flight took pictures and videos of us together, then leaked them to the media."

She deflated. "Oh. He did bring me into it."

"Not by name."

"Yet."

"Yet." He described what was being broadcast. "There's nothing there we have to be ashamed of. But we do appear to be, uh…familiar. Holding hands on the armrest and… so forth."

He made a helpless gesture. "Looking back, I should have booked us on separate flights. Something. If Clarke is the one behind this exposure, we played right into his hands. I'm sorry as hell, Kate."

"I'm the one who should be apologizing. Less than a week ago, you were living privately and peacefully, which is what you craved. You were doing fine until I came barging into your life."

She was wearing her red eyeglasses, a long, sloppy t-shirt, and white socks, the toes of which peeked out from beneath baggy pajama bottoms. The outfit was a far cry from her snug-fitting pencil skirt and stilettos. Her remorse made her look like a waif whose puppy had escaped through a gate she'd left unlocked.

In that moment, in spite of the hell raining down on him again, a warm tide of emotion filled his chest and spread down into his belly. It was gratitude and gladness. He was damn glad that she had busted up his private, peaceful life.

Quietly, he said, "I wasn't doing all that fine, Kate."

He went to her, took off the red glasses, and set them on the dresser. Then he kissed her lips with tenderness. She made a faint whimpering sound. He eased back and saw in her incredible eyes a yearning that matched his.

He wrapped his arms around her, lifted her off her feet, and carried her over to the bed. He eased her back onto it, pulled his shirt over his head and tossed it aside, then followed her down, his knee nudging hers apart.

With their legs interlaced, he hovered above her. "Are we gonna do this?"

She nodded and placed her hands on either side of his face. "Yes. But please be careful with me, Zach."

He lightly ran the backs of his fingers along the slender curve of her collarbone. "I would never hurt you."

She gave him a wicked grin. "The warning was for you."

Then she angled herself up and nipped his lower lip with her teeth. Before he had time to laugh, their mouths were fused. She lay back and took him down with her, twining her fingers up through his hair while she lent herself entirely to their kiss.

God, she was good at it, shifting between seductress and supplicant, and expert at both. When they had to pause for breath, their lips remained touching, flirting with feints and parries meant to entice. He touched the tip of his tongue to the bow of her upper lip where she'd licked off the vanilla-flavored foam. "I've wanted to do that ever since Wholly Ground."

She pushed him up to better see him. "What?"

He snuffled. "Nothing. I'm just happy to be here doing this."

"Me too."

Again, he dabbed that alluring spot with his tongue before they settled into another long, deep, blood-drugging, mind-blowing, cock-killing kiss. He slid his hand beneath the hem of her t-shirt and settled it on her stomach. When she sighed and made a belly dance move of encouragement, he reached higher to caress her breast.

Her nipple was firm against the center of his palm. He ground it lightly, and as it grew harder, he buried his face in her neck and breathed hotly against silky skin that smelled like dessert.

He left an open-mouthed kiss there before inching down, planting damp kisses through the soft cloth of her t-shirt even as he gathered it up from the hem. By the time he reached her breasts, they were uncovered, beautiful and ripe with arousal. He kissed them in turn, nuzzled, then drew the tip of one into his mouth.

Kate moaned his name and began to move restlessly against him. He continued to play his mouth over her breasts as he pushed his hand into the waistband at the back of her pajamas and splayed it over her ass, that adorable ass that had captured his interest right off. He palmed it to draw her up and over until she was making those evocative, undulating motions against his erection.

He growled swear words initiated by pleasure.

She tugged loose the drawstring tie of his sweatpants. Her thumb skimmed the damp tip of his penis.

And her phone dinged the notification of a text.

They froze and held their breath. Only after the second ping did they resume their foreplay.

And then another text message came in.

"Fuck!" He pulled his hand from her pajama bottoms, flopped back onto the bed, and laid his arm across his feverish forehead. "Can you silence it? Can you ignore it?"

She rolled onto her side, reached for her phone on the nightstand, and squinted in order to read the text. "It's the boss." Then she made an inarticulate but mournful sound. "He's seen us on TV."

"Dammit! What's he say?"

She lowered the phone and turned her head to look at him. "For me to call him without delay."

Their gazes held for a moment before she scooted off the bed. "Excuse me." She went into the bathroom and closed the door.

Zach got up and retied the drawstring. He went over to the sliding glass door that accessed a shallow terrace. The temperature was in the forties, but he stepped out barefoot and shirtless and breathed deeply to cool down his enraged cock—if that were possible—and clear his head.

He was out there for five minutes before he heard Kate coming out of the bathroom. He went back inside and slid the door closed. He only had to look at her to know that the conversation with the attorney general hadn't gone well. "How angry was he?" he asked.

"Angry."

"Like pissed, really pissed, or ranting and raving mental?"

She swallowed hard. "He was actually very controlled. He didn't raise his voice once, not even when he told me that I would no longer be working on the Eban Clarke case. Indeed, there no longer *is* an Eban Clarke case."

Chapter 27

It was Theo's front door, but Eban answered the knock on it and greeted Cal with a grin of phony bonhomie. "Hey! I was beginning to think you'd be a no-show."

Saying nothing in response, Cal looked past Eban at Theo, who was standing in the center of his living room, secreting distress from every pore. His smile was tentative. "Hi, Cal. You're just in time for a beer." He went around the eating bar into his kitchen and opened the refrigerator.

Cal stepped past Eban and went inside. "Thanks, but no beer for me. I won't be staying long enough to drink it."

Eban shut the front door. "This from the guy who used to chug one in thirty seconds. Back when he was unmarried and fun."

He plopped down into an easy chair. "But just because Cal is a killjoy doesn't mean we have to be, huh, Theo?

Thanks," he said as he took a cold longneck from him. "Sit, you two."

Theo motioned for Cal to take the second easy chair, which left him with a straight-back. Cal felt for Theo, who was clearly out of his depth. More than likely, he hadn't entertained a guest since the last time Cal himself had been here, which had been a week before his wedding.

Theo had hosted the quasi–bachelor party for just the two of them. He had served spaghetti and meatballs. They'd split a bottle of cheap champagne, and Theo had joshed with him about the entrapments of matrimony. They'd pretended to be sharing a good time between good buddies.

But after spending that awkward few hours together, Cal realized that they'd been going through the motions, each for the other's benefit. He'd predicted that their visits and phone calls to each other would become more infrequent, and they had.

The Rebecca Pratt incident loomed large, an invisible but impenetrable obstacle that prevented them from reestablishing the friendship they'd had prior to it. Its impact on them had been equally profound.

It had made Theo even more timid and insecure than he'd been before being taken under Eban's wing and subjected to his corrosive tutelage. While functioning in Eban's autocratic shadow, Theo had developed a tentative self-confidence. But it had been dashed by the tragedy of Rebecca Pratt.

Following it and its punitive aftermath, Cal had become so steeped in guilt that if not for Melinda's acceptance and love, he would have drowned in it.

Eban, however, seemed only to have been emboldened by the calamity. Having slithered through it with little more than a slap on the hand, he now behaved as though he were untouchable, immune to penalty. Sprawled in the chair, head tipped back to guzzle his beer, one would think he didn't have a care in the world.

The troubling truth was, he didn't. *He. Didn't. Care.* And his utter indifference to decency made him not only despicable, but dangerous.

Melinda had met him only briefly, but long enough for her to be repulsed by his arrogance. She also had sensed his boundless capacity for treachery, and it had frightened her.

Tonight, she'd prepared a special dinner and had planned to follow it with an evening of cuddly celebration over the baby. So after their meal when Cal had announced that he was meeting with Eban and Theo, she'd been struck dumb.

Her silence didn't last long, however. For the next hour, she'd argued, then pleaded with him not to go. She'd calmed down only when he'd held her tightly. "I love you. I love our baby. I love my life now. Which is why I must go, Melinda. If I don't, Eban will keep coming here to pester us, or worse. I've got to sever all ties with him once and for all."

Now, addressing his nemesis, Cal said, "You got me here, Eban, what do you want?"

Eban drained his beer, then looked around for a place to set the empty bottle and settled on the floor beside his chair. He clasped his hands and held them beneath his chin, smiling beatifically. "What do I want? Your loyalty, of course. You know, blood oath. All for one, one for all. Band of brothers."

He smiled at them in turn. When neither responded, he said, "Okay, I can see you're not sold on the idea. Soooo," he said, "I suppose now would be an ideal time to remind you that the tie that binds us is the night our boisterous three-on-one left that whore without a brainwave."

Cal clenched his teeth as well as his fists.

Theo blurted, "She tried to say the safe word, Eban!"

"Did she?" Eban scratched his cheek as though searching his memory. "That's not what you testified to on the witness stand, Theo." He sucked in a sharp breath and looked aghast. "Don't tell me you *lied* under oath. To the jury, the judge, your own attorney?"

"Our attorney never asked us if we were lying or not."

Eban laughed loudly. "He didn't want to know, you dimwit! He'd negotiated a plea bargain that got you probation if, at my trial, you swore on the Bible that Rebecca didn't utter a peep, or make a motion, or signal in any way, shape, or form of communication that she was running out of air. Am I right?"

Theo looked over at Cal, who said, "Theo and I perjured ourselves, yes."

Eban winked. "I'll bet not solely out of the goodness of your heart or affection for me. Be honest now."

"That lackey of your dad's showed up at my house," Cal said. "He had a handful of canceled IOUs that he'd paid off for my old man."

Eban grinned. "Nobody greases the skids more efficiently than sweet, corrupt Uncle Up."

"He paid off my sister's student loan," Theo mumbled.

"To the tune of eighty grand or thereabouts," Eban said.

"See how well that all worked out? Well, except for the fact that I spent over two years in an orange jumpsuit. Let's not forget that." Then he waved his hands in front of his face. "No, let's do. Let's forget about the past and focus on the present."

He got up and began pacing as he stroked his chin, much like a calculus professor trying to decide how best to explain a maximum value to a classroom of numbskulls.

"For instance," he said, "if—and it's a big if—Zach Bridger pulls the plug and sends Rebecca to the great beyond, and if—an even bigger one—this Lennon chick constructs a case for murder that actually goes to trial, you two couldn't recant your previous testimonies without admitting to perjury."

He stopped pacing and faced them, arms spread from his sides, palms up. "Unless I'm missing something?" He waited; neither Cal nor Theo spoke.

"No? Good. We agree on that point of law."

He left them with that thought as he went into the kitchen and helped himself to another beer. After uncapping it and taking a long swig, he belched. Laughing, he said, "Mine still aren't as loud or fragrant as yours, Cal."

Cal didn't react.

"But we're getting ahead of ourselves," Eban said, "because it would be damn near impossible for Kathryn Lennon to build a case without eyewitnesses, i.e., you two. Her only legal maneuver would be to try to strike some kind of deal with you.

"For instance, she might approach you with an offer of clemency, to which you'll say, 'No fucking way, bitch,' or something as emphatic. 'We wouldn't throw our blood brother Eban to the sharks. No, ma'am. Not us.'

"See? All this unpleasantness can be avoided if you simply stick to your original story. You remember the one. The one about the hot piece of ass who had a lively spirit of adventure. If ever asked, you give your account of what happened in that bedroom from beginning to end exactly as you did before, and all this will—" He fluttered his fingers up into the air. "Go away."

Campaign speech completed, he returned to his chair and sat.

Theo cleared his throat. "I think you might be underestimating Kathryn Lennon. The research I did for you? Everything I read made her sound like a go-getter. I don't think she'll back down."

"Excellent point, Theo. Flip on the TV, please."

Theo darted a confused look toward Cal before going back to Eban. "What for?"

"Because I asked you so nicely." He batted his eyelashes.

Cal wondered if he should simply get up and walk out now. Why give Eban another single moment of his time? But he stayed because he didn't trust Eban's complacency. If he was doing the Devil's work, Cal was better off knowing so he would be prepared for its sting, which one could count on being vicious and painful.

While Theo fumbled with the TV remote, Eban checked his wristwatch. "Eleven o'clock. Perfect timing. Tune in to one of those sports networks. They'll be doing a recap of the day's events for your viewing pleasure."

In silence, they watched the news about a basketball

player's drug issues, then, when up popped a video of Zach Bridger in close company with a hip-looking, attractive young woman, Cal knew this was what Eban had wanted them to see.

Cal didn't remark on any of the images, but Theo leaned toward him and, speaking in a low voice, confirmed what he'd already surmised. "That's Kathryn Lennon."

"No need to whisper," Eban said. "In fact, you can mute it. I think you get the gist."

Theo did as told and killed the sound.

Eban linked his hands and turned them inside out as he raised his arms high above his head and stretched. When he relaxed again, he said, "I hope you enjoyed the feature. I gave it a working title. *Phase One of the Dismantling of the Homicide Case against Eban Clarke*. What do you think?"

"How did you manage it?" Cal asked.

"To get the pictures of them?" He winked. "A little birdie told me that the two of them were in New Orleans this morning. They went to the special care facility, saw Rebecca and the administrator, then capped off their excursion with a visit to Mr. Pratt, her daddy. This raised my eyebrows. Also my hackles.

"I placed anonymous calls to a few media outlets beginning with our hometown's CNN, and in no time at all, newsrooms across the nation started humming. Getting a spy on their return flight was a challenge, but money talks, let me tell ya."

Cal scoffed and gestured toward the television. "What have you got, Eban? They were walking through the airport."

"True. They weren't caught *in flagrante delicto*. But you can't deny the goo-goo eyes. You'd expect it from him. When he was playing football, he exploited his super-stud status. Or maybe he was trying to earn it. Who cares? Doesn't matter," he said.

"But for someone in Kate Lennon's position, representing jurisprudence and all, anything less than a nun's scruples makes for a situation that's...hmm...sticky." He grinned. "It hints that something unethical is afoot. It leads one to suspect that when they're not simply walking through the airport they're being naughty-naughty-naughty.

"What I anticipate?" he continued. "By dawn tomorrow, she's going to be busy explaining those moonstruck gazes, defending herself against allegations of professional misconduct, stamping out this flare-up of salacious conjecture before it becomes a wildfire.

"At the very least, her integrity has been brought into question, and that's all it takes, really. Once doubt is cast, we three know how quick Joe Public is to cry foul. The attorney general is up for reelection. Last thing he'll want is a scandal. Bye-bye, Kathryn. Don't let the door hit you in the ass on your way out."

He happily slapped the tops of his thighs. "It's almost too rich. Their churning hormones made my job of discrediting her easy. We've dodged a bullet, boys. For the time being."

During the silence that ensued, Cal watched Eban closely, then softly asked, "What's phase two?"

Eban played dumb. "Hmm?"

"You said that was phase one. What's phase two?"

Eban chuckled and fired a fake pistol at him. "I never

could pull anything over on you. Actually phase two is where you and Theo come into play."

"Us?" Theo squeaked.

At the same time, Cal said, "Like hell."

Eban said, "Hey, y'all, I can't be the only one working on this. Think of what's at stake for you two. If my prediction is wrong, and Lennon still has a job tomorrow, odds are good she'll come gunning for you. At the risk of repeating myself, *you can't change your story without admitting to perjury.*

"In which case, you're both fucked. Probation will end. Off to jail you'll be marched." Looking at Theo, he said, "No more library full of books, no more of this swell little made-over abode you have here all to yourself, just the way you like it. See, Theo, in the Big House, you take a shit, somebody's watching. They really go after scared little rabbits like you.

"And you," he said, turning to Cal. "You'll have to leave your cozy cottage and your pretty wife, who may decide you don't deserve redemption after all and move on to the next sinner who needs the saving grace found between her legs." He barked a laugh. "Your Melinda has got a great thing going. She's got you believing that she fucks you because she wants to save your soul."

Cal lunged from his chair toward Eban, but Eban was ready for him. He kicked Cal hard in the stomach. Cal fell back, landing on his butt. He was so furious, he didn't even feel the pain. Through gritted teeth, he said, "If you come near me or my family again, I will kill you."

Eban said, "Cross my heart and hope to die I won't, *after* you implement phase two."

"Which is what?" Theo asked in a thready voice.

"Well, Theo, the three of us need to put our heads together and figure something out. I'm relying on your egghead noggin to devise a fail-safe plan."

"For Ms. Lennon?"

Eban's joviality vanished. His saccharine mien turned malicious. "For Bridger. He's the one who has the authority to pull the plug. Without him, *nothing* happens. Therefore, phase two is to knock the former quarterback out of his jockstrap."

Chapter 28

———◆———

You know how it's always been between your ex and me. The man and I never could have a conversation without crossing swords. Yesterday was no different."

Doug Pratt gently pulled the brush through Rebecca's hair. Ever since she was old enough to be aware of her beauty, her dark hair had been one of her vanities. She'd always worn it long, never allowing anyone to trim off more than an inch at a time.

Now Rebecca's hair was kept closely cropped, but Doug still brushed it every day. It had broken Mary's heart the first time nursing staff had sheared it. She'd salvaged the long locks, placed them in a shoe box, and tied a ribbon around it. That shoe box with its treasure inside remained on the shelf in the top of Mary's closet.

"Even before I met him, I didn't like Zach Bridger," he said. "I made no secret of it. He led you astray. Him and his flashy, celebrity lifestyle was too much temptation for you to resist.

"Oh, you took to it, all right. Can't argue that. But if it hadn't been for him appealing to your wild streak and introducing you to all that immorality, you wouldn't have met a deviant like Eban Clarke. You wouldn't have been at that orgy, and your life wouldn't have come to this. See? It all goes back to Bridger luring you into his freewheeling way of life."

He gently turned her head to give him access to the other side. "Your mother thought it was unfair of me to blame him."

Mary had said that by the time Zach Bridger had entered Rebecca's life, she had already veered far off the path of the righteous. Until the day she died, Mary had refuted his condemnation of their ex-son-in-law.

What he hadn't confessed to Mary, or acknowledged to himself, was that his anger toward Bridger had long been surpassed by fear of him. He woke up every morning afraid that it would be the day when Bridger said *enough*.

He placed the hairbrush in the nightstand drawer. "I'll water your ivy in a minute." He sat down in the chair beside the bed, slumping, reluctant to broach this subject with her.

"Bridger came to the house yesterday with that Ms. Lennon I told you about. She's pleasant. Polite. Soft-spoken. Not abrasive like you'd think she might be."

He stared at the speckled vinyl flooring between his well-worn trainers. "At Eban Clarke's release hearing, this prison psychologist testified for our side." In layman's language, he explained the thrashing Dr. Hawkins had taken from Clarke's defense attorney.

"Anyhow, what I'm getting to, Ms. Lennon left me with that psychologist's final analysis of Clarke. I read it last night." He raised his head and looked into his daughter's sleeping face. "It's like he doesn't give a damn about what he did to you, Rebecca. Not a speck of repentance. Ms. Lennon says he'll escape the punishment he deserves unless we..."

He cleared his throat as he stood. He went over to the sink, filled a glass of water, drank part of it, then emptied the remainder of it into the flowerpot on the window-sill where the young ivy he'd brought her last week was struggling.

"What got me angry yesterday was that it looked to me like Ms. Lennon's arguments are chipping away at Bridger's promise to stay out of our business." He kept his back to the room, his stare fixed on the parking lot beyond the window. "But don't worry, sweetheart. I'm looking out for you."

He pinched off a leaf that had turned yellow. "There's something else. Bridger's got himself mired in another mess. This time with Kate Lennon. When they were at the house, I sensed undercurrents. You know the kind I mean. It appears that I wasn't the only one who noticed. Last night they were being shown on TV.

"This upsets me, because whenever he's in the news, you're in the news. It's not just his scandal, it's ours. The media is having a field day with our tragedy. Like a rerun. It would tear Mary apart. I never thought I'd say this, but I'm glad she's not here to see it.

"Aside from that, Kate Lennon is the last woman in the world I'd want him to go near, much less become romantically involved with." He turned away from the window and walked back over to the bed.

"What scares me? I could tell that Bridger is on the fence. That has to be Kate Lennon's doing. She's got a sweet face and sincere eyes, she represents the law, but her agenda goes against *God's* law. If Bridger—"

"Mr. Pratt?" He turned to find that Dr. Gilbreath had entered the room. She said, "Sorry to interrupt."

"No problem. We were just chatting."

"Could I please have a word with you?"

"Of course."

"In my office."

It wasn't unprecedented that Dr. Gilbreath sought him out to discuss something regarding Rebecca, but considering that Bridger and Kate Lennon had had a conference with her yesterday, and that she had asked for privacy, his guard went up. Her wistful smile also made him uneasy.

She must have sensed his hesitancy, because she said, "I promise not to keep you long."

"All right." He murmured to Rebecca, "I'll be right back," and followed the doctor from the room.

Bing and Kate joined Zach in his hotel room, where, over coffee, Bing was told about the cancellation of Kate's case against Eban Clarke.

"The AG was ambivalent from the start," she said. "This gave him a good excuse to nix it."

"Just like a goddamn politician," Bing said.

"Yes, well..." Kate said, "it's done."

The solemn group left the hotel. Zach and Kate walked Bing to his car. "Sure you don't want me to stick around, run interference for you, knock heads with any paparazzi who don't understand 'No comment'?"

He included both of them in the offer. Kate gave him a pallid smile. "Thanks all the same, but I don't think knocking heads would work to my advantage."

"Go home, Bing," Zach said. "You've earned some rest. Thanks for getting us out of the airport last night."

"It feels cowardly to tuck tail, hide out, and *rest*. Goes against my grain."

"Mine, too," Zach said, "but this is the time to punt."

"What about you, Kate?" Bing asked. "Eban Clarke must be doing cartwheels. He's off the hook, but you're not. Are you going into your office today, face the music?"

"Absolutely. As soon as I go home and change. Other cases need my attention. Besides, if the case against Clarke is dead, then the AG can't point a finger at me for breaching ethics. Or, to quote precisely, 'fraternizing with a principal.'"

Bing harrumphed and said drolly, "If it had been fraternal, you wouldn't be in Dutch."

He told them to call if he was needed again. As they waved him off and started across the parking lot to Kate's car, Zach said, "He's as down as I've ever seen him."

"I know how he feels," Kate said. "It's going to take me more than a minute to get over this disappointment. You know how important nailing Eban Clarke was to me, and why."

"In time, Rebecca will likely die of natural causes. You

could pursue the case then, and it wouldn't be quite so controversial."

"But in the meantime, Clarke could put another woman in the hospital. Short of that, traumatize her and then terrify her into keeping silent, which would cause her to suffer emotionally for the rest of her life. There's no limit to the damage he could do. And not just to one. To many."

They stowed their overnight bags in the back of her SUV and headed in the direction of her house, where Zach would retrieve his pickup. He drove. Kate used the drive time to call her assistant, Ava. Kate gave her a list of tasks to do ahead of her return to the office. "Just pile everything on my desk in descending order of importance. I should in by ten o'clock."

When she clicked off, Zach said, "Everyone would understand if you took a day or two off."

"I wouldn't give Eban Clarke the satisfaction of seeing me cowed."

"Nobody would see you at all if you came home with me."

She looked across at him. "Zach—"

"No, go. I get it. I'm just doing some wishful thinking here. My jets haven't quite cooled from last night."

She gave him a weak smile. "I hated calling a halt, too."

"In that case, I'll try again. Think about all that's going to waste up there at my place. Crisp mountain air. The waterfall. Wine. Whirlpool tub."

"Tempting, but you know I don't dare."

"I don't want to leave you alone. Your intruder could come back."

"I'm more afraid of a snoopy reporter. We'd be sniffed out in no time. You know I'm right."

"Yes. Dammit. But how long does this distance from each other have to last? When do we see each other again?"

"Give me time to smooth things over."

"How much time?"

"I wasn't fired, but I'm on thin ice."

"A week?"

"Two. At least. Then…"

"Then?"

"We'll see."

He cursed. "When I was playing ball, I was a fairly good sport. Even if the ref was blind and made a bad call, I let it go and concentrated on the next snap. Not this time. This time I'm a sore loser."

"You're not losing. You're punting."

"I hate to punt. It's giving in."

"But sometimes you have to. You told Bing."

He frowned. She could tell he didn't like his own words being thrown at him. "Can I at least buy your breakfast before taking you home?"

Breakfast seemed harmless enough. "I know a hole-in-the-wall," she said. "It's on the way, and the ma and pa who own it pamper me. They won't notify the media."

By an hour later they had demolished their breakfasts. As the waitress came to remove the platters, Zach asked for a coffee refill.

Kate checked her watch. "I told Ava I'd be in the office by ten. You're dawdling."

She'd said it teasingly, but he didn't smile back. "Yesterday, I dropped a bomb on you then left you with no explanation. You're owed one."

Their outlooks this morning had been glum, but his tone and demeanor had turned particularly somber, leading her to intuit what the explanation related to. "Take your time. I'm listening."

He looked beyond her shoulder as though reading from a cue card. "The pregnancy was the one thing I managed to keep secret and out of the media. When I arrived at the hospital, after my encounter with Doug at the elevator, all the doctors who'd examined Rebecca called me into a conference room to give me the lowdown. None of it was good. In fact, her condition seemed so hopeless that I came this close to overriding Doug's objections and asking that all life-sustaining measures be suspended right then."

He exhaled a soft gust of air through his lips. His gaze came back to hers. "Then they told me. They estimated that she was seven or eight weeks along."

"Did the Pratts know?"

"No. I was her agent, so I was the one told. I doubt Rebecca even knew."

Kate was quick to grasp how the pregnancy would have compounded his dilemma. "On top of everything else, you got snarled in the legality."

"You know about that?" he said.

"There have been well-documented challenges to state laws on the matter. In numerous states, including Georgia, law stipulates that life-sustaining procedures cannot be withdrawn from a pregnant woman unless—"

"Unless the fetus is too damaged to develop, and a live birth is unlikely. That's how they spelled it out to me. *Or* if the woman has expressly stated in a directive that she wishes not to be kept alive under such circumstances."

"Which Rebecca hadn't done."

"Correct," he said. "The judgment call from the medical team was that the embryo had suffered the same lack of oxygen as Rebecca. They gave it very low odds of surviving. If by a miracle it did, the child wouldn't have been…"

With a sympathetic nod, Kate indicated that she understood.

"I was encouraged to take into consideration the quality of life that such a child would have," he said. "I was told that neither Rebecca nor the child would have a viable life. I asked for a couple of days to think about it."

He sighed. "There was a lot to think about. There was a father somewhere, but I had no idea who. Chances are excellent that he didn't know he was a father. But I thought that maybe some man, hearing about what had happened to Rebecca, would come forward. No one did.

"A day went by. Two. The picketers outside the hospital grew more aggressive. The media were like hyenas. There were desperate transplant patients waiting for her organs. Doug was scorning me to anyone who would listen. Mary was begging me with tears rolling down her face not to end her daughter's life."

He dug into his eye sockets with his thumb and finger. After a time, he lowered his hand and looked at her. "I couldn't bring myself to do it, Kate. Ending not just one life, but two? I couldn't do it."

She reached across the table and took his hand in hers but didn't say anything. Anything she said would sound paltry.

"I went to the Pratts and told them that I was resigning as Rebecca's agent, that I would leave her fate with them. I knew how they would feel about the child."

"They would want it."

"I'm ninety-nine percent certain. Either way, the decision belonged to them. I left. I locked myself in a hotel room and emptied the mini bar. I got very drunk and passed out.

"The following day, I woke up to my phone ringing. I figured it was Bing. I'd ignored all his calls the night before. I answered. It was one of the doctors. He said I could eliminate the pregnancy as a factor in my decision. Rebecca had miscarried during the night. It looked like a heavy period, but the embryo had been passed.

"I looked on it as a blessing. I asked if her parents had been told. They hadn't because I was still the agent of record. The transference of guardianship hadn't been made official yet. I asked that they not be told. I saw no need for them ever to know. It would only have caused them more heartbreak."

"Doug might feel differently toward you if he knew about that kindness."

"I doubt it," he said wryly. "I should have insisted that he get the legal work done to make him Rebecca's guardian, but I had abdicated, and I didn't want to go back into the fray.

"Already, it had been broadcast that I was not going to take Rebecca off life support. I didn't want to rescind that decision and start the whole goddamn circus over again, with everyone asking for details and demanding an explanation for the reversal. I couldn't explain it without disclosing the pregnancy, and that would have ignited another wildfire."

He dropped his head forward for a moment. When he looked up, he said, "You've asked why I didn't insist on resigning. That's why."

She squeezed his hand. He squeezed back.

Just then her phone jingled. She looked at the readout. "My assistant. Probably calling to see what's keeping me." She put the phone to her ear. "Hello, Ava. I know I said ten, but I got unavoidably held up."

"I'm sorry to rush you, Kate, but this won't keep." Always steady under even the most hectic circumstances, her assistant now sounded breathless. "Did you know Upton Franklin?"

"Sid Clarke's attorney? *Did* I know him?"

"His body was discovered this morning by the man who services his lawn. He died by his own hand."

Zach had obviously been able to hear through her phone's speaker and shared her shocked reaction.

"That's awful," she said. "Are they sure it was a suicide?"

"According to the coroner and the detectives at the scene, every indication is that it was. Besides, he left a note."

Eyes locked with Zach's, Kate asked, "What does it say?"

"You can read it for yourself. It's addressed to you."

Chapter 29

When Zach and Kate arrived at the police station, cursory introductions were made to the two detectives, one male, one female, who were investigating Upton Franklin's suicide. After a round of handshakes, they whisked Kate away.

Zach had been left to wait on an uncomfortable bench in a hallway. Word must have gotten around that he was there, because a continual stream of officers and civilians paraded past. Someone would walk by, then turn their head to take another gander at him. He felt like a zoo animal confined to a small space, stared at and remarked upon.

He kept his feet tucked beneath the bench and his arms folded over his chest. The body language, along with his intimidating game face, must have worked, because no one had dared to speak to him.

He'd been there for forty-two minutes and counting when Kate emerged from a room midway down the hall. She was followed out by the two detectives. Both they and Kate were unsmiling as they came toward him.

He stood up, and when Kate reached him, she said, "Thank you for waiting."

"Like I would leave." He turned to the two detectives and asked if she was free to go.

The man bobbed his chin. "We know how to reach her if the need arises."

"Thank you for your cooperation, Ms. Lennon," said the female.

"Of course." Kate shook hands with them. Each nodded a goodbye to Zach, then, after the man said, "I miss watching you play ball," they turned and walked back down the hallway.

Zach cupped Kate's elbow. "Ready?"

"More than."

On their way downstairs to the ground floor neither said anything, but he sensed her dejection. Once outside the building, she took a deep, cleansing breath. When they reached her car, he said, "I'll drive."

"I'll let you."

They got in, but he didn't start the motor. "You want to talk about it, or not?" He wanted to know the contents of the suicide note, but he wouldn't prod her if she was still trying to assimilate it herself.

She rested her head on the seat back. "The detectives gave me a basic description of the scene. The pistol was lying on the terrace inches from the chaise lounge where the lawn man discovered him. The clip was empty, so apparently Mr. Franklin had loaded only one bullet. It was sufficient."

She swallowed, then waited a few seconds before continuing. "After laying that groundwork, the detectives got both of Franklin's daughters on speakerphone. They'd been notified of his death already, and had been sent a copy of the note, but since it was addressed to me, they wanted to know if I could provide a clearer explanation. Both confirmed that the note was in their father's handwriting and didn't believe it could have been forged." She looked over at Zach. "What it says is evidence enough of a suicide.

"He informed his daughters that he'd been diagnosed with terminal stomach cancer. He chose this easier way out. But beyond the illness, he said, he could no longer live with himself. With his dishonor and dishonesty."

"He wanted to come clean before dying."

"In effect. He implored his family to absolve themselves of any guilt or responsibility for what he was about to do. He apologized for his many failings as a husband and father." She paused and took a breath. "He also apologized to me. He saved me for last."

"Out of importance?"

"I don't know. I suppose. He expressed remorse for tipping off Eban Clarke about me and the case I had hoped to build against him. He admitted that he was violating professional privilege by discussing the Clarkes, but said that it was a minor infraction compared to his countless others."

"What, specifically, about you?"

"When he saw you and me under the glare of public scrutiny last night, he realized that Eban had exploited information he'd given him yesterday morning. In the note, he confessed to having had a staff member at the special care facility reporting to him on an as-needed basis, such as your trip down there earlier this week, and then our visit yesterday. That's how Eban knew we were in New Orleans."

"Did he name the informer?"

"Yes, I put her name in my phone."

"Dr. Gilbreath will want to know."

She gave an absent nod. Zach sensed that she was withholding something, saving it for last as Upton Franklin had done with his apology to her. If it was that important, he decided that a little prodding might be excusable. Softly, he said, "That's not all, is it?"

"No." Hesitantly, she said, "The last part of the note was a warning."

"Meant for you?"

"Yes. He wrote that Eban perceives people in absolutes. One is either his subservient friend, or a bitter foe. There's no in between. So in Eban's mind, I wasn't regarded merely as a threat, but as an enemy. Mr. Franklin emphasized that Eban seeks vengeance on anyone who gets the better of him, even if it's a minor, unintentional slight. And he's relentless. Creating that smear campaign about us last night was only the beginning of what I should expect, he said."

"Did he say what you should expect?"

"What he feared, what he most regretted being responsible for, was Eban's inevitable reprisal against me. 'Inevitable' was underlined."

"In other words, you're in danger from Eban Clarke."

"That was the implication, but—"

"No buts, Kate. What's being done about it? Will Clarke be arrested?"

"For what? He hasn't broken a law. Even if he did create that hubbub over us last night, it was mean but not criminal."

"You're telling me those two detectives just dismissed Franklin's note, the warning? Do they think he wrote all that out of spite against the Clarkes?"

"That was one hypothesis. But in any case, they think Franklin was disturbed, not thinking rationally. Otherwise he wouldn't have taken his own life. Even so, they sent the AG a copy of the note."

"And?"

"He took the warnings more seriously because he's better acquainted with Eban Clarke's case and knows how cunning and manipulative he is."

"Glad to hear that, at least." He staved off her next comment by raising his hand. "I've got a call." He pulled his vibrating phone from the pocket of his jacket. The name in the readout gave him pause. "It's Dr. Gilbreath." He clicked on. "Hi, it's Zach."

"Hello, Mr. Bridger. I need—"

"Hold on. Kate's with me. Let me put you on speaker."

"Is this a bad time?"

"Actually it is," he said. "But one of us would have called you soon anyway. Your strict privacy policy hasn't stopped someone on staff from leaking information. She was being bankrolled by the Clarkes' family lawyer. Most recently she reported that I'd been down there twice this week. Hold on. Kate's pulling up her name."

When he passed it along, the administrator apologized profusely and assured them that within the hour the employee would be dismissed and escorted from the building.

"Thank you. That will send a strong message to everybody else." Zach then asked why she was calling.

"There's been a change in Rebecca's condition."

His stomach dropped. He looked at Kate, whose apprehension matched his. "Changed how?"

"She's developed a kidney infection."

He remembered Dr. Gilbreath telling him at their first meeting that infection was a perpetual concern. "How bad is it?"

"It was detected this morning. She had a low-grade fever, so we did lab work. It's a bacterial infection. Standard treatment would be to start her on an IV antibiotic."

All that was solid information, but none of it had answered his question about how bad it was. "Has Doug been told?"

"He was here when I got the lab results, so, yes, he's aware. He's with her now. Very concerned, of course."

"Yeah, me too. Maybe a renal specialist should see her."

"I've already consulted one. He thinks the antibiotic I recommended is as aggressive as her system can tolerate without incurring damaging side effects."

"I see." As he contemplated what to ask next, Kate reached over and placed her hand on his shoulder, a consoling gesture he appreciated. "Dr. Gilbreath, best-case scenario?"

"The antibiotic will arrest it early."

"And without it? Worst case? Is this serious enough to kill her?"

"With a patient like Rebecca, every infection has the potential of being fatal, even with medication. I tried to convey that to Mr. Pratt, who became extremely upset, not only because of the infection itself, but also because he's afraid that you may choose to withhold treatment and let nature takes its course. He tried to persuade me not even to tell you, but of course I'm under obligation to do so."

"Yeah." Zach massaged his forehead, which had begun to throb. "Yesterday, Doug told Kate that he was going to file the petition that would transfer the say-so from me to him. Do you know if he did?"

"I didn't know to ask, and he didn't say, but I believe that if he had, he wouldn't be in such distress now."

"Right." Which left Zach with an obligation to make a decision. *Now.*

"I take it your meeting with him didn't go well," the doctor ventured.

"No. I'd hoped it would help patch things up, but the rift only got wider."

"I'm sorry. Then this development—"

"Doesn't help."

His bluntness caused her to hesitate before saying in her forthright bedside manner, "It's your call, Mr. Bridger. Do you authorize us to start the IV?"

"Yes."

"I'll do so immediately."

After an exchange of terse goodbyes, Zach disconnected. He dropped his phone into his lap and turned his head to look out the car window. He watched two squirrels chase each other round and round the trunk of a tree and wondered why they would waste so much energy on such a futile pursuit.

After a full minute, Kate softly spoke his name as a question.

"The hell of it?" he said. "My first reaction was to safeguard her life." He snuffled a humorless laugh and came back around to Kate. "How crazy is that?"

She leaned across the console and brought her face close to his. "Not crazy at all, and I'm not the least bit surprised that was your reaction. Especially not after what you told me earlier."

She pressed her lips to his, but briefly. When she would have pulled away, he hooked his hand around her nape and drew her back. He kissed her madly, hungrily. He kissed her like he was as stupidly carefree as those damn squirrels, like a woman's life wasn't hanging in the balance and it was up to him which way to tip the scales, like there wasn't a sociopath of Eban Clarke's caliber making a man so miserable with guilt that he would kill himself.

And Clarke was wreaking all that havoc with impunity.

He broke the kiss suddenly, his breaths coming as hard and fast as when he crested the mountain after his workouts. "What if your boss hadn't called off the case?"

Kate blinked the amorous cloudiness from her eyes. "What?"

"What would you be doing right now if the AG hadn't deep-sixed the case against Eban Clarke?"

"But he did."

"But if he hadn't," he said, giving a stubborn shake of his head. "Last night on the plane, just before we landed, you told me you had only one play left. Remember?"

"Yes, but I can't play it. I'm hamstrung."

He grinned. "I'm not."

Chapter 30

Sid walked into the kitchen where Frida was sectioning an avocado for a lunch he would never eat. He interrupted her tuneless humming. "Frida, please go upstairs and wake Eban. Tell him to get up and join me out on the terrace. It's not optional. I want to see him in ten minutes. Max."

"Is something wrong, Mr. Clarke?"

"Yes, very."

He could tell that his brusque tone and manner took her aback, but before she could question him, he left through the door that accessed the covered outdoor living area. It had a fireplace and was expensively furnished with tables and chairs that he now realized he utilized only a handful of times during the year.

He sat down and stared out across the expanse of his two-acre property. It looked as it always did: stately trees, seasonal color in every flower bed, borders trimmed to the nth degree, everything immaculately maintained. All this he took for granted, never crediting the laborers who kept it this pristine, never allotting himself time to enjoy it, or even pausing to appreciate how beautiful it was. How odd that he would do so today.

But nothing was the same today, nor would life ever be the same.

Up was dead.

His death had hit Sid much harder than had that of his wife. He'd known Up longer, better, more intimately than the woman who'd shared his name and bed. If he added up the hours, those spent with Up would outnumber a thousand times over those he'd spent with her. Her passing had been respectfully observed, but he'd hardly noticed her absence from his daily life, whereas the loss of his longstanding friendship with Up would leave a vacancy he could never fill.

Up was dead.

No sooner had he processed that Up was terminally ill than he'd resolved to convince him to undergo treatments. He'd made a vow to himself that he would be there at Up's side every step of the way until together, the invincible team they'd always been, they beat the odious cancer.

While he'd been strategizing an assault, Up had planned his retreat.

Just like that, he was gone. It was inconceivable.

Eban intruded on his thoughts. "Frida wants to know if you want her to serve lunch out here."

"No. Sit down."

Eban looked back toward the kitchen and sliced his finger across his throat, signaling to Frida that lunch on the terrace was out. He sat in a chair across from Sid's, took one look at him, and said, "What's the matter?"

"Up is dead. Sometime last night, he shot himself in the head."

Eban didn't immediately register a reaction, then he leaned back in his chair, saying softly, "Whoa. That's heavy."

Sid wanted to reach across and slap him. "Is that all you have to say?"

"What am I supposed to say? That I'm sorry? That goes without saying, doesn't it? Was it because of the cancer?"

"I'm certain that contributed."

"He'd been melancholy," Eban said, giving a sage nod. "Not his old self at all. I could tell that during the so-called happy hour the day I got home."

When the elder of Up's daughters had called Sid to notify him of the suicide, she'd barely been able to speak the words. But once she'd gotten her emotions under control, she'd told him about the note. "You should hear it," she'd said. "He mentions Eban."

As she'd read it to him, it had become clear that Up's standpoint on Eban's early release went beyond the misgivings he had diplomatically conveyed. He hadn't confessed all his transgressions, but Sid knew that covering for Eban had figured largely in many of them. Before signing off on the note, he had issued a warning to Kathryn Lennon.

A man minutes away from blowing his brains out wouldn't have written such a ponderous message without having a solid basis for it.

Eban said now, "You know how much Uncle Up meant to

me, so I can only imagine how bad you must feel. Resigning was one thing, but who could've seen this coming? I mean, Jesus. I'm really sorry, Dad." He stood. "I'll leave you to reminisce on all the good times y'all had together. I'm gonna grab some grub."

"Eban, was it you who blew the whistle on Kathryn Lennon and Zach Bridger?"

In all innocence, he said, "Come again?"

"There's a scandal brewing about the two of them."

"Huh. What do you know? A sex scandal?"

"Did you start the rumor?"

"Me? Why would I go to the trouble of doing that? I don't care if they fuck each other blind."

Sid knew he was lying. Up had recognized the unconstrained malice in Eban's character. For years, he'd tried to open Sid's eyes to it, advising him to exercise some discipline over his son. In all else, Sid had heeded Up's counsel, but he had dismissed the admonishments regarding Eban. But, jarred by Up's death, he stopped deceiving himself. His son didn't possess a conscience.

Sid spoke slowly and deliberately. "The last piece of advice Up gave us was that you leave the country. I believe that was sound advice. In any case, it's no longer your choice. I'm mandating it, Eban. I want you to go upstairs, pack, and leave. Today."

Eban gaped at him and then began to laugh.

Sid shot out of his chair and squared off with him. "You find this amusing?"

"Well, it is kind of funny, because I'm way ahead of you, Dad. My bags are already packed. I'm headed to Belize later today. Cal and Theo are tagging along. We got together last night and decided it was time we had a getaway. It's going to be just like old times."

"Not quite. What about their probations?"

"That's why we chose Belize." He winked. "They're lax about checking the passports of people flying in on private jets. I'll send the two of them home in a few days. They'll be back in the States before anybody in authority has missed them."

"What about Cal's missus?"

"She's not invited."

"I mean, how does she feel about his going on this getaway?"

He chortled. "She doesn't get a vote. Of the three of us, Cal's the most excited. If ever a guy needed a getaway... Oh, listen, I've booked the company jet. I hope that's okay."

"When are you leaving?"

"Six o'clock this evening. Theo insisted on finishing his shift at the library." He rolled his eyes. Then he snapped his fingers. "Oh, damn. When is Uncle Up's funeral?"

"It hasn't been arranged yet, but I'll make your excuses. You don't need to come back for it."

"Well, Up won't miss me, that's for sure." He flashed a grin, but dropped it just as quickly. "Sorry. Gallows humor. Now, I'll let you get back to your grieving. I've got a shitload of stuff to do before I leave."

He was about to turn away when he hesitated and looked at Sid with pity. "I really am sorry about Up. Like losing your right arm, I'll bet." He turned, jogged across the terrace, and reentered the house.

Sid sat back down, and for several minutes stared thoughtfully into a concrete planter overflowing with ivy and white chrysanthemums, then took his phone from his pocket. He thumbed to a number in his contacts and placed the call.

The pilot he kept on retainer answered on the first ring. "Yes, sir, Mr. Clarke."

"I was just checking to see if Eban had ordered catering for his flight to Belize this evening."

The pilot chuckled. "Fried chicken and all the fixin's."

"Ah, good. He usually forgets to order until the last minute. And he does love fried chicken. Did he order enough for the two of them?"

"He told me there would be three passengers. Him and two friends. Did someone cancel?"

"Theo Simpson was questionable, but I guess he managed to get off work after all." Checking up on Eban had felt sneaky, but Sid forgave himself for doing it. Eban had given him little reason to trust him.

The pilot was saying, "My copilot and I and the best flight attendant available will be expecting them at the FBO at five-thirty. We'll be good to go at six."

"Thank you. Have a safe flight."

"Sure you won't come along with them, Mr. Clarke?"

"No, unfortunately I'll be attending the funeral of a good friend."

Sid ended the call, but couldn't work up the will to do more than that. He remained for the longest time, phone in hand, staring into the near distance and pondering how he—a man who had accumulated so much wealth—could feel this bankrupt.

Chapter 31

———◆———

Kate had told Zach that the only play she had left was to approach Cal Parsons and Theo Simpson with an offer of clemency in exchange for their eyewitness testimony, this time for the prosecution.

So when he pointed out that the AG couldn't hamstring him as he had her, he'd thought she would jump on the idea of his talking to the two men in her stead. He was mystified and frustrated by her reluctance to act on the suggestion.

"Why not?" he asked. "After reading Franklin's suicide note, your boss backed down from his stand last night."

"To a degree, yes, but he didn't give me the green light to take up the case again. On the chance that he will at some point in the future, I don't want to do anything now that might provoke him, like talking to Parsons and Simpson without first consulting him."

"You wouldn't be talking to them, I would. If you just happen to be along, what can he do?"

"Fire me."

"He won't. He'd be shooting himself in the foot. Firing an ambitious female prosecutor who's seeking justice for a sex offender? Un-huh. Women's rights groups would be all over that, and there go their votes come election day."

"Valid point." But she remained unconvinced. "Let me ease into it with him."

"There's no time for easing, Kate. You heard Dr. Gilbreath say that even with medication Rebecca's condition is precarious. It could quickly go south, and once again I'll be faced with an impossible decision. It might be less conflicting for me, and for Doug, too, if we knew ahead of time that you were ready-set-go to bust Clarke's ass the instant Rebecca's heart stops."

She thought about it for a moment longer then took her phone from her bag and went into her contacts. "That's the number I have on file for Calvin Parsons. But you have to promise me that you won't try to coerce him into seeing us."

"I promise." He placed the call. A woman answered. Zach asked who he was speaking to, and she said, "Melinda Parsons."

"Hello, Mrs. Parsons. This is Zach Bridger."

He got the usual reaction: a pause followed by a stunned "Oh."

"I'd like to speak with your husband, please."

"About what?"

"About the night that changed both our lives for the worse."

There was a hesitation, then, "I don't think his attorney would agree to that."

"Neither would mine. I was hoping to keep the conversation just between us."

"I don't see that happening," she said. "Not without attorneys present."

"There will be an attorney present. Her name is Kate Lennon."

"Kathryn Lennon? She represents the other side," she exclaimed. "Cal shouldn't talk with you. Goodbye."

"Wait. Please." Zach looked over at Kate, who gave a stern shake of her head and made a motion for him to end the call. Which he ignored. "Mrs. Parsons, you don't know me, and most of what you think you know is horseshit dreamed up by people who are paid to shred reputations in a public, global forum. But I'll swear on anything you hold sacred that it will benefit your husband to meet with us."

After a considerably long silence, she said, "Cal isn't here, but I'm available to talk to you."

Zach's breath whooshed out. "That's great. What would be a good time?"

"How soon can you be here?"

"On our way."

After confirming the street address, they lost no time driving halfway across Atlanta to take advantage of her willingness before something occurred that would prevent the interview. Even as Zach pressed the doorbell, he feared Parsons's wife would have changed her mind, or that Parsons had changed it for her.

As they waited for her to answer the door, Kate whispered, "Remember, I'm not here in any official capacity."

"Right. You're arm candy."

The young woman who opened the door was strikingly pretty in a natural and wholesome way. She had long, curly blond hair and a sprinkling of amber freckles across her cheeks and nose. Her girl-next-door attractiveness was marred only by her red-rimmed, watery eyes.

"Mrs. Parsons? I'm Zach Bridger. This is Kate Lennon."

"I'm Melinda." She shook hands with them.

Kate, who also must've noticed her weepy eyes, said, "Are you sure this is a good time?"

"Yes. Please come in."

Kate looked at Zach, who raised his eyebrows. He was as puzzled by the tearfulness as Kate obviously was. Placing his hand on the small of her back, he nudged her across the threshold. Once inside, he thanked Melinda for seeing them.

She gave him a feeble smile. "I certainly wasn't expecting a telephone call from Zach Bridger today, but I'm glad you sought me out. I didn't know who to talk to about this."

"About what?" Kate said.

"Let's sit down." She led them into a sunny, homey living room and motioned them onto the couch. "Would you like something to drink?"

Both thanked her but declined.

Melinda sat down in a chair facing them and addressed Zach. "Let me start by saying how sorry I am about what happened to your wife. Your ex-wife, that is. I'm sorry for how the whole thing also affected you."

"Thank you."

"How is she doing?"

"Not good, I'm afraid."

She shook her head sadly. "Cal will carry his guilt over it to his grave."

Zach held nothing against this young woman, who seemed genuinely regretful over Rebecca's fate and the negative impact it had had on him. However, he didn't feel that charitable toward her husband, and questioned the sincerity of the guilt he carried.

Sensing his reservation, Melinda divided a look between him and Kate, landing on Kate. "Do you think justice was served?"

Kate didn't blink. "No, I don't. I came to the case after Eban Clarke's trial, but I've read the transcript of it. I believe that Theo Simpson and your husband perjured themselves."

"Oh, I know they did." Their astonishment over the declaration didn't escape her. "That surprises you." She gave them a gentle smile. "Before I married Cal, he admitted how out of control and sordid his life had become while in Eban's orbit. It culminated that night with Rebecca Pratt. Cal confessed that he lied on the witness stand about her attempt to say the safe word."

"They lied for Eban's sake?" Zach asked.

"Out of loyalty, yes. Probably intimidation, too. But Cal and Theo were also well compensated. They were bribed."

"By how much?"

"Tens of thousands of dollars each. Of course, lying also worked to their advantage," she said. "Neither served time. But the thing is..." She had to stop and tamp down a swell of emotion. "The thing is, even knowing how deviant and manipulative Eban is, Cal is still under his thumb."

"How's that?" Zach asked.

Melinda looked at Kate. "Will telling you this help Cal?"

"It *could*," Kate said softly, but with emphasis on the qualifier. "All I can commit to is the possibility."

"You're not recording this, are you?"

"No," Zach and Kate replied in unison.

"What if I said something you could later use against Cal?"

"It would be tossed out because it would have been obtained without counsel present."

Melinda looked at Zach, who said, "We're not trying to pull a fast one on you. If you send us away, things stay as they are. If we talk openly, it could work to our mutual benefit."

"You'd swear to that?"

"As I said, I'll swear it on whatever you hold sacred."

"What do you hold sacred? How about your Super Bowl ring?"

He smiled, but without mirth. "I'd have to get it back from my former coach, Bing. After the network canned me, in the heat of the moment, I threw it at him. I guess he still has it."

The young woman nodded pensively, then took a deep breath and told them about Eban's surprise visit of the day before. "We'd just had it confirmed that we're going to have a baby."

After they had congratulated her, she continued. "We were elated. But Eban showed up and ruined the occasion." She looked down into her lap where her hands were clasped so tightly, the tips of her fingers were white. "Last night, rather than celebrate with me, Cal left to meet up with Eban and Theo. I begged him not to go, but he said he must, that if he didn't sever all ties with Eban once and for all, he would continue to hound us.

"But he didn't sever ties." She tilted her head up and sniffed back tears. "Eban has always been the host and paid the others' way. But he's the parasite, and he's feeding on my husband." Her voice cracked, and she began to cry.

Before Zach could react, Kate left the couch, went to kneel beside Melinda's chair, and placed her hands on the young woman's knees.

"I'm sorry." Melinda produced a tissue from the pocket of her shirt and blotted her nose.

"Don't be sorry," Kate said. "You have a good reason to cry."

"Cal told me that you've got Eban worried, Ms. Lennon." She added with heat, "Please, please put him away for good."

"I would love nothing better," Kate said, "but he can't be retried for the same crime."

She patted Melinda's knee then returned to her seat beside Zach on the couch. He could tell that Melinda's plea had sparked Kate's fighting spirit. Her blue eyes were alight, and she was gnawing the inside of her cheek as though trying to contain the things she wanted so badly to say.

"Lay it out for her," he said in a confidential tone. "I won't tattle on you."

Melinda swiped tears off her cheeks. "Lay what out?"

Kate was poised like a sprinter in the blocks seconds before the pistol, but her voice was calm. "For the present, further prosecution of Eban Clarke is a nonissue because Rebecca Pratt is still alive. But upon her death, whenever it occurs and under whatever circumstances, the status would change. At that point in time, the attorney general might be persuaded to pursue a murder case against Eban. If tried and convicted, he could be put away. Maybe not for good, but for a long time."

Melinda wet her lips. "Those are a lot of conditions to be met, though."

"I'm aware," Kate said with a rueful smile.

"Would you be prosecuting the case?"

"I don't know. However, whoever did, before going to trial, should be holding a silver bullet."

"Like what?"

"Like your husband's eyewitness testimony."

"The truth this time," Zach said.

Warmed up now, Kate continued. "For years, Cal was Eban's like-minded sidekick. He knows firsthand how destructive Eban can be, and one of his pet projects now seems to be the destruction of your marriage."

"Because he's jealous of Cal."

"Very insightful, Melinda," Kate said. "I believe you're right."

"Eban recruited Cal as his friend because of his looks, his way with women." With a shy smile, she added, "He's sexy."

Kate smiled, then took a second before saying, "This is an important question, Melinda, so please think carefully before you answer. If everything else fell into place, and Eban Clarke was about to stand trial, do you think Cal would turn state's witness? He would be offered inducements."

In an unconscious gesture of protection for her child, Melinda ran her hand over her lower abdomen. "He loves me. I know that absolutely. He loves our baby already. I would like to think he would testify against Eban even without inducements."

"Forgive me," Kate said, "but I sense some uncertainty in your voice."

Melinda nodded. "Eban is like one of those petty gods in Greek mythology. He plays with people. He wrecks lives for no other reason than his own amusement. Cal sees that, he knows that, but he seems incapable of escaping Eban, even though he wants to."

Her despair was so evident that neither Zach nor Kate spoke. Eventually, he said, "What happened last night when Cal got home after being with Eban and Theo?"

"Nothing. I was hurt and angry. When he came to bed, I pretended to be asleep. This morning, he left the house with a roll-aboard suitcase." Tears once again filled her eyes. "He didn't have breakfast. He didn't say goodbye, or tell me where he was going, or when I could expect him back. He simply walked out. I'll admit I panicked. I forgot how angry I was and tried to call him, but his phone went straight to voice mail and continues to.

"He works for my father's electrical company. I don't know if he reported to work this morning, but I didn't want to call and ask, because I don't want to alarm my parents. They have faith in the Cal they know. They love him. But when Eban was released, they privately expressed their concern that Cal would fall back in with him."

"What about Theo Simpson?" Kate asked. "Could you reach out to him?"

"I tried. I don't know him well. We've only met twice, and the last time was at my wedding. I know that he works in the main library downtown. When I called, I got a menu of options. Theo had a dedicated extension. I punched it, but got his voice mail. I identified myself and left my number. So far he hasn't called me back, and I don't think he will.

"Cal says he's as loyal as a puppy, eager to please. I doubt he would betray either Cal or Eban." She clamped her lower lip between her teeth. "I'm so worried. I'm afraid Eban is luring Cal into something."

"What kind of something?" Kate said.

"I wish I knew. When he was here yesterday, he taunted Cal about perjuring himself. He dangled that like a threat."

"Like, don't you dare think of turning on me and changing your testimony?" Zach asked.

"Exactly like that," Melinda said. "Then he insisted that Cal join him and Theo last night. As mad as I was at Cal for going, I was beside myself with worry, and so relieved when he returned home."

Zach inched forward on his seat cushion and leaned toward her. "Were you afraid that Eban might do something to him?"

"Yes," she said in a rasp. "To shut him up, to ensure that Cal never changes his story about that night."

Zach looked over his shoulder at Kate, knowing that, like him, she was remembering Upton Franklin's note. One was either Eban's subservient friend, or bitter foe.

"But that's not all," Melinda said, drawing Zach's attention back to her. "Eban is shrewd. He may act devil-may-care, but he realizes how rocky his situation will be when Rebecca dies. I believe he wants to solve that problem before it has time to develop. I fear for my husband's life. And yours," she said, including both of them. "I'm afraid Eban will make a preemptive strike against all of you."

Chapter 32

Cal easily found Theo's car in the library's employee parking lot. The slot next to it was empty; Cal pulled in. At five o'clock sharp, Theo exited the building through an employee door. He flipped up the hood of his jacket and cut across the parking lot in a jog.

When he reached his car, he opened the trunk and lifted out a duffel bag. After securing his car again, he stashed his duffel in the back seat of Cal's car and got in on the passenger side. "Hi."

"Hi."

Theo buckled up. "Been here long?"

"Only a few minutes."

"I could do without the rain."

Cal drove them out of the parking lot. "We've got more to talk about than the weather, Theo."

"Yeah, I guess we do. You first."

"Did Eban call you and offer to send a limo?"

"Yes, but I told him to never mind, that we were riding together so we'd have a car at the FBO when we got back."

"What time did he call you?"

"A little after three, I think."

"Huh. He called me at two-thirty," Cal said. "I told him the same as you."

"Then why'd he call me after?"

"To check up on us."

Theo began rocking forward and back in his seat as far as his seat belt would allow. "Why would he feel the need to do that?"

"Because he's Eban. He thinks like a fox. Always calculating. Thinking ahead. Like flying us down to Belize to devise a fail-safe plan for taking out Zach Bridger."

Theo bobbed his head. "That's what he said."

"I don't think that's it, Theo. I think he's got another purpose in mind."

By now they were on the freeway, where traffic had slowed to a crawl due to the inclement weather and rush hour. The stop-and-go seemed to make Theo even edgier. In addition to the rocking, he was cracking his knuckles. "Cal, Melinda called me."

At the mention of his sweet, loving, trusting, pregnant wife, Cal's fingers contracted around the steering wheel. "When?"

"Around noon. I'd gone down to the break room to get my lunch out of the community fridge. When I got back to my desk, the light on my phone was blinking. She'd left a message for me to call her." When Cal glanced over at Theo, he blurted,

"I didn't, though. I was afraid if she started asking questions, I'd say something that would give us away." He waited a beat, then added, "Her voice sounded like maybe she was upset."

"She is. She's been calling me all day, but I haven't answered or called her back."

"Is that fair to her? Keeping her in the dark? How much does she know?"

"Nothing. Nothing except that I left the house this morning with a suitcase."

"Did she ask where you were going?"

"I didn't give her a chance."

"Afraid she would talk you out of it?"

"Afraid she would *try*. But nothing she'd have said would change my mind, and I didn't want to leave with a fight between us."

"Yeah, but, Cal, she's your *wife*. She—"

"Drop it, Theo. It's hard enough as it is, okay?"

Theo mumbled an okay. Neither spoke for a time, then Theo cleared his throat. "All I'm saying is, maybe you should have included Melinda in this decision. Maybe rethinking it wouldn't be a bad idea for us, either. Maybe we should stop and re—"

"I'm not stopping. I want Eban off my back for good. I won't go one day more letting him run my life, *ruin* my life. I just won't."

Immediately Cal felt bad for berating Theo, whose intentions were so well meant. "Look, Theo, you don't have to go along with this. You're under no obligation to me. This is my choice. I won't think less of you if you've had a change of heart. Say the word, I'll take you back to the library."

Theo looked straight ahead, staring through the rain-streaked windshield at the three lanes of red taillights that stretched to the horizon. "No, we decided this together. I'm with you. I won't back out."

"You're sure?"

"Yes, I'm sure."

He'd stopped cracking his knuckles. He was no longer rocking. His jiggling leg had fallen still. For the first time in Cal's memory, Theo wasn't fidgeting.

"I'm long overdue getting that bastard off my back, too, Cal. All these years, he's pretended to be my friend. But I've been like one of those fools in a king's court. Eban's kept me around solely for his entertainment. Someone to poke fun at. Indirectly. Subtly. Tongue-in-cheek." He looked over at Cal. "I don't think he realizes that, all along, I've gotten the joke. It's time he learned."

Cal nodded. Theo was more discerning than any of them. He had Eban pegged. "Okay then, brother. We're a go."

Theo turned his head and looked out the windshield again. "Did you have any trouble getting a gun?"

Cal replied with dead calm. "None at all. While my father-in-law was consulting with a client, I sneaked out with the pistol he keeps in his desk drawer."

———

After leaving Melinda Parsons, Zach and Kate were at loose ends. Also at odds. He couldn't put his finger on why.

As he drove out of the residential neighborhood into a more commercial area, he said, "I could use a cup of coffee."

"Fine."

"Did you know, the last ten words you've said have had only one syllable?"

"You've been counting my words?"

"I can count to ten. Hut hut."

"Very funny."

"You want my opinion?"

"Have I asked for it?"

"No, but you're asking—begging—for a fight," he said. "Why?"

She ran her fingers through her hair, which left it sticking up in spikes like the Statue of Liberty. Taking into account her fractious mood, he had the good sense not to comment on it.

She said, "I don't know what to do with Melinda's warning."

"Well, here comes that opinion you didn't ask for. What you do with it is, you report it to your boss, then you and I head for the hills."

She gaped at him. "Pardon me? I've already told you no."

"You said you didn't dare, but that was before we knew about Franklin's suicide note and what Melinda told us."

Her brows were drawn together. He took that as a sign that she was seeing reason, so he continued.

"We go to my place. The bags we packed for our indefinite stay in New Orleans are still back there." He tipped his head toward the cargo space. "You don't even have to go home first. For now, my truck is fine in your garage. We go to my place, where we can regroup and FIO. That stands for figure it—"

"I know what it stands for."

She was still testy, but he was making progress. "So, do we head for North Carolina?"

"I suppose."

He wheeled into the parking lot of a coffee franchise. "Going inside will take less time than waiting in the drive-through line. Make your call to the AG."

He got out. The line at the counter was long, too. While waiting his turn, he called Bing. "Hey, what are you doing?"

"Watching the replay of a basketball game."

"Who's winning?"

"The team with the most tattoos. What do you want?"

"Did you get home all right?"

"I'm not at home."

"What?"

"You staged that sweet goodbye, but I wasn't about to leave you to your own devices. Soon as you and Kate drove off the hotel parking lot, I circled around and checked back into the room I'd just checked out of."

Zach laughed softly. "Cagey. But thanks, Bing."

"What do you need me to do?"

Zach briefed him on the interview with Melinda Parsons. "She didn't want to alarm her parents, so she's home alone and weepy with worry. It's plain that she loves this guy. They're expecting."

"A baby?"

"Yes, a baby. Until her husband reappears, she shouldn't be by herself."

"I ain't a midwife."

"Just keep an eye on her, okay? At least overnight. You've slept in your car before."

"Am I supposed to let her know I'm there?"

Zach thought it over. Melinda's nerves were already shot. A strange car parked on her block might frighten her. "I'll tell her you're coming," he said. "It'll be up to her whether or not she invites you inside. She's fragile, so be nice."

"Aren't I always nice?"

"Right. And for godsake, wear pants."

Bing heaved one of his put-upon sighs. "Text me her address."

By the time he returned to the car with two coffees, Kate was just saying goodbye to the attorney general. Zach passed her a cup. "Your brew. Foamy. Vanilla flavoring. Watch it, it's hot."

"Thank you." She placed it in the cup holder without uncapping it.

"While your phone is still handy," he said, "please send Melinda a text."

"And say what?"

He told her about Bing. "Emphasize that I vouch for him. She can trust him."

"He isn't my idea of a nursemaid."

"Then think of him as a bodyguard."

He knew that Kate agreed with this move; she just didn't want to credit him with thinking of it. She sent the text.

"How'd your conversation with the top dog go?" he asked.

"He wasn't at all happy with me for speaking to Melinda without counsel."

"You should have put the blame on me."

"Oh, I did. He said that you had overstepped, that you weren't calling the shots on his playing field. You're no longer a superstar quarterback, or hadn't anyone informed you of that?"

He gave her a sardonic smile. "Only every sportswriter in the country." He started the car and got them back onto the thoroughfare before asking if the AG had addressed Melinda's concerns.

"As displeased with us as he was," Kate said, "he couldn't easily dismiss what Melinda told us. Husbands habitually duck their wives. By itself, Cal's failure to answer her calls isn't alarming. However, coupled with the warning in the suicide note, the AG believes her concern has merit." After a short pause, she added, "He also agreed that I should make myself scarce for a few days."

"He's no dummy. He's worried about your welfare."

"He's no dummy. He's worried about his."

"His? What's he got to be scared of?"

"Reelection. So far, Upton Franklin's note has been kept under lock and key, but if what it says about Eban gets out, Sid Clarke could create a hue and cry, and the fallout from it would land in the AG's lap. If that happens, it'll be better if I'm unavailable for comment, since I'm the one who created the ruckus in the first place."

"You didn't create the ruckus. Eban Clarke did."

"I cited that. He gave a grunt of concession. For the present, I'm still on the payroll, and, as soon as it can be arranged, he's going to put an investigator back on Eban."

"*Back* on?"

"He denied my request of two nights ago."

"You didn't tell me."

"Because I knew you'd give me an argument."

She was still trying him, but he let that one slide. "How soon before the surveillance kicks back in?"

"It depends on personnel availability."

"Somebody should be on Eban's tail right now. I might hire my own damn investigator."

"Zach, he can't be apprehended unless and until he does something *criminal*. The attorney general reminded me of that caveat."

"If somebody winds up bleeding because of Clarke, I'm gonna shove that caveat up the AG's ass," he said, raising his voice for the first time. "And while I'm no longer a superstar quarterback, if I start talking, every-fucking-body wants to hear what I have to say and take pictures of me saying it. If he's no dummy, your boss ought to be scared of *me* and what I have to say to the media about *him*."

He ran out of air and had to pause to suck in some. In a mollified tone, he added, "At least he's smart enough to tell you to lay low. Did you tell him where you're going?"

"And make things worse for myself? No."

Hot, rampant anger surged through him. He used the turn signal only a second before swerving into the right lane, then pulled into the parking lot of a big box store, braked hard, and put the car in park.

"I resent being linked to what's *worse* for you, Kate. What you and I do is none of that guy's business."

"He's not a guy, Zach, he's the most senior law officer of this state. He's my boss. As such, he considers that you and

I as a pair *are* his business, and he's right. If it's unethical by an eyelash, it's unethical, period." She made a gesture of impatience aimed at herself. "How did I let you talk me into coming with you?"

"I didn't talk you into a damn thing. The way I remember it, I said, 'So, do we head for my place?' and you said, 'I suppose.'"

"Which implies uncertainty. What I was thinking was that we should put distance between us."

"Then that's what you should have said. I'm not a frickin' mind reader."

"What I'm saying *now* is, if I need to lay low, I should be going to Hilton Head and staying with my parents."

"There's weather in Hilton Head."

"There's weather in North Carolina."

"Yes, but no high surf warnings have been issued for the mountains."

His quip fell flat. He cursed under his breath, which had fogged up the windows. He fumed for another moment or two, then broke the strained silence. "From here to my house is a two-hour and forty-five-minute drive. Are we going to argue for the whole trip?"

"I just feel like we should be doing something."

"We are doing something, Kate. We're getting the hell out of Dodge. What Melinda told us was an echo of Upton Franklin's warning."

"Melinda's concern for her husband is understandable. In her shoes, I'd feel the same. I'd be frantic. But not even Eban Clarke can go around maiming or killing everybody."

"No, but you can be damn sure he's plotting something,

and neither Melinda, nor Upton Franklin, nor you, nor I know *what*. And, in case it hasn't occurred to you, whatever reprisal he's planning will be accelerated if he learns about Rebecca's downturn as of this morning. If he thinks she's about to die—"

"He'll hop on his daddy's jet and leave the country. We'd be safe."

"Possibly. Or, believing she might soon die, he may become desperate, and desperate equals dangerous. When you've got an opposing defense on your two-yard line desperate to make a turnover, you don't give them an opportunity. You don't do dumb shit like throwing deep from your own end zone. Instead, you play it safe and use your running game to gain some yardage."

"Another football analogy?" she said archly. "Really?"

"Sorry. That's all I've got."

She sat silent for a moment, covered a snicker with her hand, then gave up and laughed outright. "Did Bing teach you that?"

"Yeah, and a lot of other stuff, too. Like not to take out your sexual frustration on the very woman you want to bone!" After that near shout, he added in a grumble, "It lessens your chances."

Following a taut and interminable silence, he attempted to restore his dignity. Setting aside his indignation, he looked across at her. "You want to stay with your folks? I'll drive you home, get my truck, and we'll go our separate ways."

As she contemplated, she rolled her lips inward. "If Mom and Dad found out that Eban Clarke had harmful intentions toward me, they'd lock me in my room."

"They'd think you're better off being in the mountains with me."

She looked over at him. "If they thought I was going to the mountains with you, they'd put a double lock on my room."

He smiled. "Was that our first fight? Are we done?"

"As long as we're on the road and you're behind the wheel, yes."

"Which way, Kate? North or south?"

She sighed. "North." However, being Kate, she added, "But this argument isn't over. We'll resume when we get there."

"That gives me something to look forward to." He winked, and that pissed her off, but he laughed.

It had begun to drizzle. As he drove onto the heavily trafficked interstate, he turned on the headlights and set the windshield wipers on low. Keeping his eyes on the road, he asked Siri to call John Meeker, who was in his contacts. He noticed that Kate raised an eyebrow when she heard the individual who answered the call say, "Sheriff's office."

He was put through to Meeker, and after swapping hellos, the sheriff said, "You're back on TV, Mr. Bridger. My wife told me it's all the ladies at the beauty parlor were talking about this morning. They all wanted their hair like Ms. Lennon's."

"That's why I'm calling. I'm on my way home. When I get there, am I going to be ambushed by media?"

"Nah, you're the town's best-kept secret."

"Maybe until a week ago," he said. "Life hasn't been the same since," he added, sliding an accusatory look toward Kate. "What about the ladies at the beauty parlor?"

"They only gossip among themselves. They respect your privacy."

Zach was less confident of that. "Would it be possible to string a chain across the cutoff that goes to my house? You'll get my vote next election."

"How about an autograph?"

"That, too."

"Happy to oblige. I'll put a padlock on it and text you the combination."

"Thank you, Sheriff Meeker. Sorry to bother you with this. I realize you have more important things to do."

"Actually, you're on my to-do list."

"Yeah? How come?"

"I've been needing to talk to you about Dave Morris. His face is busted all to hell. What can you tell me about that?"

"The grille on my pickup did a number on his face."

"Huh. The rumor's true then. Y'all had a set-to. Who started it?"

"What does Morris say?"

"Not much."

Zach gave the sheriff a watered-down version of his fight with the deputy. He didn't tell him about Morris taking bribes from Doug Pratt to spy on him, or of his jealousy over Kate, only about his being angry over his suspension, which he blamed on Zach rather than the general manager of GreenRidge.

"I was on my way home. Morris pulled out in front of me on that narrow road. Barely avoided crashing into him. Words were exchanged. Tempers flared. You know how it goes."

"Hmm. He came in today asking can he come back to work. But if you intend to press charges—"

"No. Hell no. We got crosswise. We worked it out."

"All right. But it's also a departmental issue."

"I don't have any say over how you run your department."

"With discipline. If I keep Dave off duty without pay for another day or two, it'll set an example."

"Sounds good," Zach said.

"What's your ETA?"

"A couple of hours."

"I'll get on that chain right now. Be careful on your way up. It's foggy and rainy."

"Noted. Thanks. Don't forget to text me the combination."

"Don't forget that autograph you owe me."

Chapter 33

———◆———

The sheriff had been as good as his word. When they reached the turnoff to Zach's house, they found a no-nonsense chain strung across the road. He got out and opened the padlock, drove through, then relocked it.

"Nobody's going to get past that," he said to Kate as he got back in. "The chain is as thick as my wrist, and the lock requires six digits to open."

"How can you see anything in this fog?"

He smiled across at her. "Practice."

She didn't smile back. Because of her innate fear of heights, the last fifty miles had been sheer torture. The higher the elevation, the thicker the fog. Since they'd been climbing since crossing the state line, they'd become swathed in a meteorological cotton ball.

On the tight curve of every switchback, all she'd been able to see ahead of them were the fuzzy beams of the headlights, illuminating nothing except fog. She'd gripped the safety strap above the car window with one hand and Zach's thigh with the other.

At one point, she'd said, "There are guardrails, right?"

"Not on this stretch, but we're good."

Zach had laid his right hand over hers and smoothed out the death grip she had on his leg. While she'd wanted to admonish him to keep both hands on the steering wheel, she hadn't. The strength of his wide hand had felt too reassuring.

Once past the chain, Zach's private road leveled out. There were no cliffs on either side, only dense forest. With a short distance to go, he used an app on his phone to turn on exterior house lights. When their halos appeared through the fog, and his house took shape, the tightness in her chest began to loosen. As soon as the car rolled to a stop, she pushed open the passenger door and got out, thankful to be planting her feet on solid, flat ground.

Afraid she'd lose him if he got too far away, she followed him closely as he went up onto the porch, opened the house, and disengaged the alarm. "Go on in. I'll get the bags."

She went inside and tapped the wall switch she'd seen him use to turn on lamps. Their glow felt like a welcoming embrace. She located the thermostat and bumped up the heat.

Zach came in and set their bags inside the door, pushing it closed with his heel. "I exchanged texts with Bing. Melinda welcomed him into the house. He said she's 'in a state,' but he's giving her pep talks and lending a sympathetic ear."

"No word from Cal?"

"Nothing."

"Is he being a jackass of a husband, or has something terrible happened to him?"

"Could be either. That's what's got her in a state. Bing suggested that she report him missing, but she's reluctant to because of his probation. I asked Bing to keep us posted." He motioned toward the hearth. "Fire?"

"Yes, please."

"Wine?"

"Yes, *please.*"

He grinned. "You know where it is."

He removed his leather jacket on his way over to the fireplace. At the bar, she found the bottle of red wine he'd opened for her—how many days ago? Only that many?

She carried her wine and a bourbon on the rocks over to the hearth where Zach was squatted, arranging kindling beneath firewood he'd stacked on the grate. She extended the glass of whiskey down to him, they clinked, then sipped.

"Thanks," he said.

"You're welcome." She shrugged off her jacket and laid it on the sofa alongside his. "Is there any food in the house?"

"Go check it out while I get this going."

"Shooing the little woman off to the kitchen while you do the manly stuff?"

He looked up at her from over his shoulder. One of his eyebrows was raised. "Stuff like delivering you safely after a perilous drive through the foggy mountains while you were cringing in terror and gouging bruises into my thigh? I didn't hear any snarky comments about that manly stuff."

He rose slowly out of his crouch until he was standing at

his full height, which gave him a foot and a half advantage over her. Nevertheless, she held her ground. Watching her from over the rim of the glass, he took a drink of bourbon, then, slowly and with precision, set it on the coffee table.

He moved in close and lowered his head until his lips were within a hairsbreadth of hers. "Still spoiling for a fight, aren't you?" He whisked her lower lip with his tongue. "I'll give you a fight, Kate."

He set his hands on her hips and pulled her against him. He was hard, solid, large, strong, *manly*, and she wanted it. All of it. All of him. "My fight hasn't been with you. It's been with myself. I give." She threw her arms around his neck and hooked her leg around the thigh that no doubt did bear bruises where her fingers had dug into it.

He reached down and cupped the back of her knee to lift and secure her leg around his. The kiss attending that move was purposeful, wicked, and deliciously carnal. He tasted of whiskey, he tasted of Zach, and she became instantly intoxicated by both. She delighted in the rasp of his scruff. His tongue was sleek and deft, and a growl emanated from deep inside his chest when she drew it into her mouth.

The angles changed, they made head adjustments, but their mouths never broke contact, until eventually they had to breathe. His open mouth scaled down her neck, supping on it with gentle fervor. He nuzzled the hollow between her throat and collarbone.

Speaking in a rumble, he said, "Kate, if you don't want this to go any further—"

"I do."

"Thank God."

He swooped in for another kiss, which wound up being awkwardly interrupted when he tried using his shin to push the coffee table against the sofa and create a wider space in front of the hearth. Her leg that was hooked on his slid off.

Cursing their imbalance, he released her to reposition the coffee table. He lifted a folded throw off the back of the sofa and unfurled it onto the rug. It had cost him only seconds to accomplish the rearrangement, but when he came back to her, his caresses were more urgent than before.

He undid the placket on the front of her slacks and she wiggled out of them and her underwear. Her long, slouchy sweater dropped back into place, providing modest coverage as she lay down on the pallet he'd made.

He unbuttoned his shirt only halfway before impatiently clawing it up from his back and over his head. He tugged off his boots and pitched them away, then dropped to his knees, bridging her legs with his. She reached for the top button on the fly of his jeans. Her fingers fumbled to undo it, her knuckles bumping against his erection, causing his breath to burst from his mouth along with an expletive.

"Are you shy?" she teased.

Impatiently, he moved her hands aside and skillfully undid the metal buttons himself, then shoved his jeans below his hips. "I'm shy," he said huskily. "It's not."

Voice faint, she said, "So I see."

He pushed her top above her waist and paused for a heartbeat, maybe two, to gaze at her. Then he parted her thighs, moved between them, and lowered himself until the pressure and weight and substance of him settled into her cleft.

But now wasn't the time for settling. They began feverishly rubbing against each other. He thrust. And again. The imperative prods seeking entrance. When he found her, she was open and giving and glazed with want. Intent and possessive, he penetrated, grafting himself to her completely.

Braced above her, he looked into her face. His was flushed and taut. His eyes glinted with firelight and lust. His body radiated more heat than the flames licking at the logs.

Beneath him, she stirred. A slight lifting of her hips. A subtle grind. He hissed, "Christ, Kate."

He pressed deeper and, lowering himself, took her mouth in a passionate kiss as he began to move. Her body fell into a rhythm of expansion and contraction. She wanted to clench him tightly and hold him deep, but his slow withdrawals and rapid stroking felt so good that she gladly gave herself over to the tempo he set.

As it escalated, he nestled his face against her ear and spoke in a rushed litany. The words ranged from romantic to earthy, sometimes profane, and often unintelligible.

But when an orgasm seized her, he also came, and his gruff whisper was clear, dear, and unmistakable. "It's you, Kate."

Gazing into Zach's face, she knew that her smile must look very sappy. He lay on his back, eyes closed, lips slightly parted, limbs loose and still, a study in lassitude. Just when she was about to ask if he was awake, he emitted a soft snore. She felt her smile becoming even dopier.

Before she'd met him, she'd known what he looked like, of course. But she hadn't been prepared for him to be *quite* this appealing. Every time she looked at him, she was struck anew by his appeal. Little wonder that people stopped and stared when he walked by. His chiseled visage and amber eyes, the mussed, burnished hair he seemed never to pay attention to, and his athletic physique were the attributes of someone favored, graced by a deity, genetically star-kissed, not those of a real-life, ordinary human being.

But what she really hadn't been prepared for was the man inside the incredible packaging. She hadn't thought she would like him at all, handsome or not. She'd figured him for a jerk, but, with the exception of their first couple of hostile meetings, he'd turned out to be gentlemanly. He was good company.

He could be arrogant, yes, but his record-holding statistics on the gridiron had earned him the right to be. He downplayed his fame, but whenever one of his admirers had the temerity to approach him, he always asked their name. He always repeated it as though committing it to memory. His warm smile said *You're that special fan I've always hoped to meet*, and the individual went away believing it. Despite his disclaimers, he wasn't all that opposed to being recognized, but primarily because it made the fan's day, not his.

Above all her other misconceptions, she'd assumed that he'd washed his hands of Rebecca's ill fate four years ago. Because he'd failed to attend Clarke's trial and release hearing, she'd reasoned that he'd become uninterested in Rebecca's current circumstances.

On that score, she had misjudged him. Mightily. That torment was Zach's constant companion. It was as ever-present as his palm print. It accompanied him like a shadow. It mastered him, governing every decision and deed.

Which made her heart ache for him.

She would think about all that later, though. For now, she wanted to be selfish with this slice of time and take in the view. Her eyes tracked the yummy trail that had sold tens of thousands of posters to women who didn't give a flip about football. She tested the satiny strip with her fingertip, which caused his breath to catch, although his eyes remained closed.

"About time you woke up," she said.

"Wasn't asleep."

"Yes you were."

"Un-huh."

"You were snoring."

"I was breathing."

Laughing, she bent over him and ran her tongue along the yummy trail until the sleek hair turned to rough. She nuzzled the thick column and licked at the saltiness on the smooth tip.

His eyes sprang open. "I'm awake."

Indeed he was. Very.

<hr />

Exerting minimum effort, he lifted her over to straddle him, then angled himself up, held her face between his hands, and kissed her hotly and at length.

When done, she slumped against his chest, saying breathlessly, "You're forgiven for conking out on me."

"I was dreaming."

"Really?"

"Um-huh."

"About?"

"This really amazing, otherworldly fuck."

She laughed and sighed against his mouth, "We had the same dream."

"It ain't over yet." Giving her his best devilish grin, he fiddled with the hem of her sweater, then slipped his hands beneath it and ran them up her bare thighs to where they met. He feathered his fingertips over the damp flesh and soft hair. "I like this outfit."

She rocked against his questing fingers. "Do you?"

"A lot. I was going to ask you to lose the sweater, but…" Hands still underneath it, he reached around and unhooked her bra. "I'm kinda liking it." Moving his hands to her front, he pushed them into the bra cups and gently squeezed her breasts, teased her nipples. Lifting sweater and bra out of the way, he rubbed his lips against them, dabbed them with his tongue. "It makes me feel like I'm getting away with something dirty." He sucked a nipple into his mouth.

She clutched handfuls of his hair. "You are getting away with something. But don't stop."

He placed his hands high on her thighs again, fitting them into the shallow channels at the top, and used his thumbs to draw lazy spirals against the heart of her sensitivity. The caresses caused her whole body to quicken and her breath to puff against his face, until she threw her head back and keened his name.

He lifted her and guided himself inside in time to experience her orgasm, this one more sustained than the previous one, and it milked from him a wrenching climax.

They clung to each other until the aftershocks had finally subsided, then he lay back, bringing her down with him. They disengaged, replete but still throbbing, and neither was willing to leave the other entirely. Her sex created a snug cove for his as she stretched out along his torso and rested her cheek on his pec.

For a long time, neither moved nor said anything. He welcomed the quiet. He wanted to savor this, because since that first day when she'd told him off and then sashayed back to her mean-looking SUV, he'd fantasized a moment like this with her. Not just for the sex.

Although . . . goddamn.

But for this closeness with a woman. One who counted.

He'd never attached a name to that *something* that had been absent from his life. Even at the pinnacle of his fame, amid all the ado, and glamour, and headiness of it, he'd felt an emptiness he couldn't identify. He'd missed his parents, then and now, and he always would. But this hollowness was apart from that.

The crisis with Rebecca had dilated it and had continued to scoop it out incrementally over the past four years, until it had become an aloneness that went soul-deep.

He knew now that what had been missing wasn't an abstract. It was a person. A woman. No, not *a* woman. *The* woman. And she had a name.

"Kate." He didn't realize he'd spoken aloud until she responded with a muffled, "Hmm?"

He didn't tell her what he'd been thinking. A declaration this soon and that serious might scare her off.

And he couldn't rightly make any sort of profession because of the *issue*, and all its tentacles that kept him entrapped. Until he was free of it, he couldn't invite Kate or anyone to join him in that snare of moral ambiguity.

Instead he said, "I was just wondering why both of us are still half-clothed?"

"Because you were impatient. Primitive. Practically an animal."

"Animals mate naked."

She raised her head and stacked her hands on his sternum. "Excellent point. Do you actually have a whirlpool bath, or was that an empty boast?"

"It's big enough for two."

"In order to avail ourselves, we'd have to get unclothed."

Seconds later they were on their way upstairs, the throw from the sofa bundled up along with their boots and the garments they had discarded in haste. He hustled her through his spacious bedroom, promising to let her explore it to her heart's content. But later. He rushed her into the bathroom and turned on the tub's faucet.

"Temperature is preset," he told her as he shucked his jeans. Turning to face her, he pulled her sweater over her head. Her bra was barely hanging on; he freed her of it. His hands went directly to her breasts, supporting them in his palms. There was a whisker burn on the slope of one. He stroked it tenderly. "Sorry about that."

"Not me."

He smiled, but only partially. He looked up from her beautiful breasts into her so-blue eyes. "What's your dad like?"

"My *dad*?" she repeated, laughing. "He looks nothing like me."

"Does he own a shotgun?"

She looked at him like he'd lost his mind. "We're naked, at last, and this is what you choose to talk about?"

He took a deep breath and exhaled, saying quietly, "I might have gotten his daughter in trouble tonight."

When comprehension dawned, her cheeks turned pink. "Oh. No. You're safe."

"Wasn't me I was worried about. I'm okay if you are."

"I'm okay." She looped her arms around his neck. "Actually a lot better than okay."

He pulled her to him and held her, his chin resting on the top of her head. He ran his hands down her back, over her smooth, shapely bottom. He couldn't get enough of touching her, but eventually, he eased back and checked the water level in the tub. "If it fills up any more, it'll be over your head."

She took his hand and raised it to her lips. She kissed the bumpy knuckle of the index finger that had been broken three separate times by big-footed linemen. Tilting her head back to look into his face, she said softly, "I'm already in over my head."

They languished in the bubbly hot water, hands and lips idly exploring terrain previously undiscovered. They frequently changed positions, each indulging the other's curiosity. While not canoodling, they talked, but about nothing of consequence. Eban Clarke wasn't mentioned. Nor was Rebecca. They took a time-out from the crisis that had brought them together, and which could well keep them apart.

When they got out of the tub, they were weak from the extended time they'd spent in the hot water. After drying off, he led her into the bedroom, where he lit the gas fireplace while she turned down the bed.

Under the covers, they kissed and petted until he turned her to face away from him, and they spooned. As he nuzzled the back of her neck, he mumbled, "Be sure to wake me up when you want to do it again."

"You'll be the first to know."

They slept. But it wasn't a pang of sexual desire that woke her an hour later. It was her noisily growling stomach. They hadn't eaten since breakfast that morning, roughly fifteen hours earlier. Surely she could scrounge up something. If nothing else, she knew he had energy bars.

She slipped from the bed without disturbing him and retrieved her slacks from the pile of clothing he'd dumped on the floor when they'd entered the bedroom. She pulled them on along with her sweater, which was anything but sexy…unless Zach's hands and mouth were marauding underneath it.

She couldn't find her socks without turning on the light, so she left the bedroom in bare feet and started downstairs. The lamps were still on. The fire had burned down to embers. She padded into the kitchen and flipped on the light.

And came face-to-face with the muzzle of a pistol.

Her eyes tracked the barrel of the gun past the hand holding the grip and up to the handsome face of Cal Parsons.

"Don't move," he said. "Don't say a word."

She did neither.

She screamed bloody murder.

Chapter 34

———◦◦———

Bing had married young because that's what people did back then. His bride had been pretty in her way. She knew southern etiquette forward and backward. Her family's reputation was free of scandal except for an uncle who was a drunkard and had been banished from the bosom of the family years before. She was a good cook who kept a spotless house and an even temperament.

He'd never been so bored.

The only ever Mrs. Ned Bingham had tolerated him for three years before he put her out of her misery and asked for a divorce. She'd accused him of loving coaching more than he loved her, and she'd been right. She'd predicted that one day he would regret giving her up for football, but she'd been wrong.

"I've steered clear of the altar ever since." He'd related his sketchy marital history at Melinda Parsons's request while they sat at her kitchen table nursing mugs of herbal tea.

"No children?" she said.

"A few hundred." When she looked at him quizzically, he said, "All the boys I coached. Some of the names I don't remember, but I can see all their faces. They cycled in and out along with the football seasons, but I recall every player I ever blew a whistle at."

"I bet they remember you, too."

He hacked a laugh. "Oh, I made sure they would. I was rough on a good number of them who had potential, but lost opportunities because they didn't apply themselves. I couldn't stand to see bright possibilities going to waste. So I was even rougher on the ones who had real talent."

"Like Zach Bridger."

He chuckled. "No, none of them came close to being like Zach. He was one of a kind. In my book he *is* one of a kind." He gazed down into the steeped brew that smelled like dead flowers and tasted like the stagnant water they'd died in. Out of politeness, he'd managed to swallow a couple of sips.

"Zach's the best player I ever saw," he said. "He played with heart, with everything in him. Over the length of a coaching career, you only get one like Zach, and only if you're lucky. Lucky like winning the Powerball when it's up above five hundred mil."

"Then what went wrong there at the end?"

"He never lost his skill or drive. He lost the *mind* game. That woman was the death of it."

"Rebecca."

"Hate to talk bad about her, considering, but she was ruination personified."

Melinda stared pensively into the near distance. "We

don't get to choose who we love. We simply do, and we can't help ourselves."

"But see, that's the real tragedy of it. Rebecca didn't love anybody but herself, and Zach didn't love her. Like near everybody else, he became enamored with the *idea* of them as a couple.

"He got caught up in all the hype, which she stoked. She dressed the part, acted the part. She was drop-dead gorgeous. Sexy, and knew how to use it. What guy in his right mind would stop to think long-range about the substance and true nature of this hot romance? Anyway, he didn't.

"Paparazzi started trying to catch a photo of an engagement ring on her finger, and one day she was wearing eight carats." He raised his shoulders. "It was like that. She knew a good thing when she saw it. She laid claim."

He pondered the contents of his mug again, adding, "What I hate? She has a much more binding claim on him now than she did before."

Melinda didn't have to ask *Before what?* Neither mentioned that night at the Clarke mansion and her husband's involvement, but it hovered between them like the unsavory aroma of the tea.

After a brief silence, she said, "Neither he nor Ms. Lennon had reason to be kind to me, but they were."

"Honey, they don't hold anything against you. Else why would Zach have asked me to come over here and keep you company?"

"It was very thoughtful of him, in light of what they're going through. Who do you think is behind leaking the videos and pictures?"

"They think Eban Clarke."

"So do I," she said. "It's sly. Like something he would do." She hesitated, then said, "Is there anything to the implication about them?"

"I can't say."

She smiled. "That means yes."

Just then her cell phone rang. She nearly knocked over her tea mug in her eagerness to snatch it up. When she looked at the readout, her hopeful expression collapsed. "It's my dad." She answered. "Hi, Daddy. Fine. No, Cal's not here right now."

She pushed her chair back and left the kitchen table, moving into the other room for privacy. Bing got up and busied himself at the sink, placing their supper dishes in the dishwasher.

He'd resented Zach's asking him to babysit her, but now he was glad he'd been here today for this young woman when she'd needed a shoulder. Bing figured a stranger's was easier to cry on than that of someone who knew her well and had probably warned her not to marry a man with a background as sullied as Cal's.

Soon after he'd arrived, she'd had one long crying jag while wringing the life out of a tissue, asking repeatedly, "Why doesn't he call me? Where is he? What's happening?"

Now, she reentered the kitchen looking stricken and pale. Whatever her daddy had told her, it wasn't good. "What is it, honey?"

"Cal was at work this morning, but he left early."

"Did he tell anybody why, where he was going?"

She shook her head. "He left without saying a word to anyone. No one saw him leave. They just noticed him gone."

"Has he ever just walked out like that?"

"Not since I've known him. Not since he went to work for Daddy. Daddy didn't think much of it. He figured something had come up, that I needed Cal at home, or that he wasn't feeling well. But then…" She stopped, swallowed with difficulty. "But then he discovered that the gun he always keeps in his desk drawer is missing."

The scream brought Zach bolt upright.

"What the—" In less than a split second he realized that Kate was no longer beside him. "Kate!" He threw off the bedcovers, his feet hit the floor, he made it to the open doorway in three strides and charged out onto the gallery. He was about to shout her name again when it died on his lips.

The tableau below made his heart stutter. Cal Parsons was holding a pistol to Kate's right temple. Theo Simpson was standing on her left, both his hands wrapped around her upper arm, securing her in place.

Of the three, Simpson seemed to be the most rattled. He stammered, "Do you know who we are?"

"By photos. By reputation. You two get off by mistreating women."

"S…she had no reason to scream."

Parsons said nothing, but his eyes were fixed on Zach; his left arm was around Kate's waist holding her against him, and his right index finger was crooked around the goddamn trigger of what looked like a Saturday night special.

Nothing fancy, but lethal.

Zach gripped the gallery railing with enough strength to uproot it from the floor. "No reason to scream except for the gun being held to her head."

Theo looked abashed.

Cal displayed no emotion.

"They haven't harmed me." Kate sounded remarkably calm, although she might have been faking it, maybe for his benefit.

"This isn't going to sit well with your probation officers," Zach said, addressing Parsons, who replied, "I'm way past caring about that."

"Obviously," Zach said. "Going for broke?"

"You could say."

Theo looked past Kate toward his partner. "Cal, maybe—"

"Shut up, Theo," he snapped. "Get down here, Bridger."

Zach stared directly into Kate's eyes. She could die. Right here in front of him. His heart was thudding, his thoughts spinning erratically. He needed a weapon. *Jesus!* He needed a plan.

One thing was certain: He couldn't do anything bare-ass naked and with Kate so far out of his reach. He shifted his gaze back to Parsons. "Let me get some pants on."

He turned toward the door to the bedroom, but Parsons barked, "Hold it! Theo, make sure he doesn't get a phone, or anything else." He hitched his chin up toward the gallery.

"What about her?" Theo asked.

"She's not going anywhere." Cal tightened his hold around Kate's waist. Theo let go of her arm and, with obvious hesitation, walked toward the staircase.

Parsons said, "We don't have all night, Theo."

Theo climbed the stairs. When he reached the landing, Zach turned to face him down the length of the gallery. Zach had spent the better part of his life in a locker room. He was indifferent to his nudity, but Theo seemed embarrassed for him.

He averted his eyes. "Where are your pants?"

"You'll find a pair of jeans on the bathroom floor."

"I'll get them, but no funny stuff."

It was a ludicrous line because Zach had absolutely no fear of Theo Simpson. Based on everything he'd read or heard about the trio, he knew that Theo was the tagalong who took his courage and cues from the other two.

Eban, the undisputed leader, wasn't here to orchestrate, which left Cal in charge. He was the threat. Maybe he was trying to earn his spurs, or to usurp the leadership role from Eban. Whatever, for as long as he held that gun to Kate's head, Zach would cooperate.

He raised his hands in surrender and said, "Fine.

From below, Cal said, "Bridger, put your hands on the top of your head and back away clear of the bedroom door. Theo, hurry up."

Zach did as he was told. Theo scuttled past him and into the bedroom. Zach held Kate's gaze, not taking his eyes off her once. He wished he could tell her how awesome he thought she was, how brave and smart and beautiful, how incredible making love to her had been.

All this, plus the memory of every second he'd spent with her, flashed through his mind in the time it took Theo to return with his jeans. "Did you check the pockets?" Cal asked.

"Only a key fob. No phone."

"Wallet?"

"It's in my duffel bag." Zach nodded toward where he'd left it on the floor just inside the front door. "I don't like sitting on my wallet while I'm driving."

Cal thought it over, then gave Theo the okay. He tossed the jeans to Zach, and he pulled them on.

"All right, Bridger," Cal said, "hands on your head again, and you lead the way."

Zach moved past Theo and started down the staircase as directed. Theo clumped along behind him. When they reached the bottom, Cal asked, "Does the fob belong to the car out front?"

That was too easy to check, so Zach didn't lie. "Yes. It's Kate's. My pickup is in her garage in Atlanta. What about your car? How'd you get past the chain?"

"We pulled our car off the road into some underbrush and came on foot."

"Huh. How'd you get into the house?"

"I jimmied the lock on a side door off the kitchen."

So much for his forethought to have his private road blocked. It hadn't occurred to him that anyone would brave the unfamiliar and hazardous terrain on foot during a dense fog.

And, *dammit*, the one time he'd failed to set his house alarm. He'd been so wrapped up with Kate...Seeming to read the silent apology in his expression, she gave him a tiny smile and an almost imperceptible shake of her head.

"Bridger," Parsons said, "you must have a phone. Where is it?"

Zack nodded toward the sofa. "Side pocket of my jacket."

Theo responded to another signal from Cal and went in search of Zach's phone. When he produced it, Cal said, "What about yours?" He squeezed Kate's waist.

"In my shoulder bag on the console table by the front door."

When Theo had both phones in hand, Cal said, "Pitch them into the fireplace. The key fob, too."

Theo looked conflicted, but he moved aside the fire screen and did as he'd been told.

As the items landed on the embers, the four of them watched them flare. Sparks flew up the chimney. One of the smoldering logs reignited with a loud pop.

Zach didn't know until that instant what he was going to do, but he'd built a career relying on gut instinct and lightning-quick reflexes. He flung his arms out to his sides, giving Parsons a clear shot at his bare chest.

"Hey!" Parsons swung the pistol away from Kate and aimed it at Zach.

Theo cried out, "Cal!"

Kate shouted, "No!"

And Zach said, "Everybody, calm the fuck down."

He'd said that a thousand times in huddles after a play had gone terribly wrong and hotheaded team members began blaming one another for the blunder that had cost them yardage. With the right intonation, it had never failed to get attention, and it didn't now.

The other three had frozen in place, but all were poised for action, watching him, waiting to see what he would do next and act accordingly. "Let Kate go," he said to Parsons, keeping his arms extended. "I'm an open target. Shoot me."

"No!" Kate said in an adamant whisper.

"Eban wants you dead," Theo blurted. "Because only you can pull the plug on your ex." He was swaying from side to side, his eyes darting from Cal, to the pistol, to Zach, in a manic circuit.

Cal growled, "Quiet, Theo."

"So this is Eban's idea?" Zach said. "You kill us, and all his problems will go away? I seriously doubt that, guys, but I guess it's possible. On the other hand, your problems will have just started. Eban puts Kate and me on TV, makes us big news, and twenty-four hours later, you knock us off." He smacked his lips. "For you two, that plan blows."

Zach prayed to God that his hunch was right and that what he was about to do wouldn't get Kate killed. In which case, he would have to kill Parsons. Not that he would mind that all that much, but he would hate it for Melinda and her unborn child.

Looking directly at Parsons, he said, "Congratulations on your baby."

Theo squeaked, "Baby?"

"Hasn't he told you yet, Theo? He and Melinda are pregnant with their firstborn."

Cal's stern expression showed signs of weakening. "How do you know about the baby?"

"We visited with Melinda today," Kate said.

Parsons took his eyes off Zach long enough to glance at her. "What the hell for?"

"I'll be happy to tell you all about it, but not while you're threatening our lives."

Zach's mention of his wife and expected child had the desired effect. Cal's gun hand wasn't as steady as it had been. "You had no right to bother my wife."

"Actually, as an officer of the court, I did have a right," Kate continued in that same measured voice. "But Melinda was already bothered when Zach and I got to your house. She'd been unable to reach you. She was crying because Eban Clarke is back in your life, and she despises him."

Zach said, "She hates even more that you ask how high every time Eban says jump."

"Shut up, Bridger. You don't know anything about me."

Zach started walking toward them in an unhurried tread. "I know you'd like hearing what Kate has to say. Why don't you stop this craziness and listen? Melinda did. She listened hard. It beats me why she loves you so much, but the poor lady does and—"

"I said to shut up!"

"—you're dogshit for making her worry herself sick, especially now that she's having your kid."

Cal's chest was heaving with agitation. Zach feared he might have pushed him too far, so he stopped several feet short of them. "Kate's barefooted. Her feet must be cold. I know mine are. But I think you're the one with cold feet, Cal."

He allowed the other man time to answer, but when Parsons just chewed the inside of his cheek and didn't say anything, Zach continued. "See, what you've done makes no sense. It's like you're going for two when you've already got the game won with the touchdown."

"What the hell are you talking about?"

"It's a football analogy," Kate said. "He uses them a lot."

Zach said, "I figure that if you had really and truly come all this way with the intention of killing Kate and me on

Eban's behalf, you would've just shot her, then me, and been done with it.

"You wouldn't have bothered with this B-movie stand-off. You wouldn't have taken the trouble to destroy our cell phones. What would have been the point? We'd be dead. No, if you'd come to kill us, you'd have already done it and would be halfway back to Atlanta by now."

"He's right, Cal," Theo said.

Zach and the other two looked over at him. He was no longer swaying. His voice wasn't quavering, and his eyes weren't darting around as though afraid to light. "Why drag this out? Enough with the intimidation. Let's just get it over with, okay?"

"Okay." Parsons tightened his grip on the revolver.

Zach thought, *Fuck me, wrong call.* He locked eyes with Kate.

Then Parsons dropped his gun hand to his side and said, "We confess."

Chapter 35

———◦◉◦———

Kate was too stunned to move or speak. She'd been certain that the last thing she would see was Zach, looking at her with desperation.

Cal withdrew his arm from her waist and walked over to an end table, where he set the pistol down.

Having regained her breath, Kate asked, "How did you know we were here?"

"Didn't. But after seeing the stories on TV, you two together, the innuendos being bandied about, we figured you might have gone into hiding, and this was the logical place to look first."

"But how'd you find my house?" Zach asked.

"I work in a library," Theo said and gave an apologetic shrug. "County records. Process of elimination. And then for five bucks a guy at a filling station on the edge of town told us which road to take off the highway. He said your private drive wasn't marked, but to go until we couldn't go any farther and there it would be."

"Did Eban provide the pistol?" Zach asked Cal.

"It belongs to my father-in-law. Eban hasn't plotted your demise yet. He was counting on us to help with that. We wanted no part of it, of him."

"If you didn't come to kill us, why did you think a gun would be necessary?" Zach asked. "Why all this tough-guy crap?"

Theo muttered, "Told ya, Cal."

Which he ignored. "Would you have greeted us like long-lost friends?" Cal asked Zach. "I couldn't be certain of your reaction to seeing us and wanted protection, just in case. That chain across the road seemed like a warning for intruders to keep out."

"It was a warning for—"

"All right," Kate interrupted. "Let's not dwell on the past ten minutes. I'm more interested in the next ten, or twenty, or however long it takes to talk this through. But before we begin, I'd like to get my boots. Zach is right. My feet are cold."

Zach and she went upstairs and finished dressing. They were back down in under five minutes. Theo was seated on the hearth. Cal had taken Zach's favorite chair. The coffee table had been moved back to its rightful place. Kate wondered if they'd guessed why it had been pushed up against the sofa. Worse, did they know? That prospect made her queasy.

To put her mind at ease, she asked how long they'd been inside the house before she'd walked into the kitchen.

"Only a few minutes," Cal replied. "We thought maybe you'd heard us come through the side door and were coming down to check."

"Maybe I did hear you on a subconscious level and just didn't realize what had awoken me." Self-consciously she glanced at Zach, where he had sat down beside her on the sofa.

He wasn't looking at her, however. He had a bead on Cal. He said, "Well, you're here and we're listening. Where's the confession?"

Cal took a deep breath and began by saying, "I'm sorry, Bridger." There was humility in his posture as well as in his voice. "The apology is long overdue. I should have contacted you years ago and told you how sorry I was—am—for what happened to your wife."

"She wasn't my wife at the time, but she was a person with years left to live, and those years were taken from her."

"They were, yeah." He lowered his head. "I'm sorrier than I can say."

"That goes for me, too," Theo said. "But nothing we say will offset what we did, or didn't do, that night. Speaking for Cal and me, we wish we could rewind, erase it. We'd do anything to make up for what happened."

"Anything except tell the truth about it at Eban's trial," Zach said. "You could have done that."

Kate placed her hand on his knee, a silent signal for him to exercise restraint. His antagonism toward them was understandable. It wasn't only Rebecca's life they'd destroyed; they'd also derailed his. But they were talking. She wanted to keep them talking.

Turning her attention to Theo, she said, "Is that what you came here to confess? You lied on the witness stand?"

Theo looked at Cal, who said, "Yes."

"You understand that you've just admitted to perjury," Kate said.

"Yes."

"Your lawyer won't be happy with you."

"*I'm* not happy with me. I've got to own up to my part in this or I'll never be happy. Neither will Melinda." Looking tortured, he added, "I could lose her over it."

Kate said, "Did you seek me out with the expectation of being granted clemency, or to try and strike some other deal? Because I can't guarantee that will come about, Cal. I made sure that Melinda understood that."

"We came with only one expectation," he said, "and that's of seeing Eban put away."

"He was put away," Kate gently reminded him.

"Not for long enough," he said. "He all but killed that girl."

She looked at Theo, who confirmed Cal's incriminating statement with a nod.

Without having realized that she'd been holding her breath, Kate now exhaled slowly. "Are you waiving your right to have counsel present? Please respond audibly."

Both said yes.

From a personal standpoint, she was exultant.She'd been given an opportunity to atone for her cowardice, her silence and failure to act after she'd been attacked, which had enabled a sexual predator to victimize other women. The personal aspect notwithstanding, it was vital that she make the most of this chance to shut down Eban Clarke.

She took a deep breath and said, "Theo, why did you lie to cover for Eban?"

"Well, first off, we didn't want to go to jail. But we also owed Eban and his dad."

"Explain that to me."

Between them, they confirmed what Melinda had said about the Clarkes' hefty bribes.

Theo said, "Eban rarely comes right out and says what he wants you to do. It's always implied, but clearly understood. In exchange for those financial favors, Cal and I knew what was expected of us when we testified. We went along. Like always."

"Like you did the night of the party," Kate said.

The two men looked at each other, then both looked uneasily at Zach. He gave them an opening by asking, "Who suggested the experiment?"

They answered simultaneously. "Eban."

"Was Rebecca coerced, cajoled, forced?" Zach asked.

"No. *No*. I swear it," Cal said. "You gotta imagine the scene. It was one of Eban's typical orgies. Open house to anyone who drove an expensive car and was wearing designer labels."

"Even Cal and me," Theo said. "Eban bought us new clothes for that night."

Cal continued. "He hired bouncers to pick and choose who got inside the gate. Unlimited food, drink, sex, and drugs. Name your preference, your poison, it was there, readily available."

"Was Rebecca Eban's date for the night?" Zach asked.

"No, she just showed up," Theo said, "like most everybody. But she stood out. She was a stunner."

"Not anymore." Zach's sharp retort caused both men to cast their eyes downward. He waited a beat, then continued. "Had you ever seen her with Eban before that night?"

"No," Theo said. "I didn't even learn her name until the next day when the police questioned me. That's when I found out she was your ex."

"I was with Eban when he spotted her," Cal said. "He made a crude remark, guy talk, you know, then he homed in on her. Later, I saw them doing lines of cocaine together. They were drinking vodka from the bottle."

With a trace of impatience, Kate stopped them there. "This much you testified to in court. Zach and I have read the transcript. It's from this point forward that your story turned murky. You claimed to be hazy on the details because you were so stoned that night. But you remember more than you told the court and more than you're telling us now."

"Get to the part that you lied about," Zach said.

The two men remained silent. Kate had to bite her tongue, but she wanted to wait them out and give them no prompts. She could tell that Zach was on the verge of saying more. She subtly squeezed his knee.

Cal spoke up first. "The party got wilder. Louder. More…" When he paused to find the right word, Theo said, "Orgiastic."

"Right," Cal said. "Eban and Rebecca came over to Theo and me and suggested that the four of us go to one of the guest bedrooms upstairs for 'some grown-up fun and games.'"

Theo nodded. "His words exactly."

"You testified that this invitation was nothing remark-able," Kate said.

"It wasn't. We'd had group sex before," Cal said.

"To each his own," Zach said. "I don't care about that. How did Rebecca come to be oxygen deprived?"

Theo looked pained. He hunched forward and hugged his elbows, leaving Cal to be the narrator. Kate looked at him inquiringly. He said, "Eban likes to watch. He likes to call the shots, direct the action. Like a play."

"For his gratification," Zach said.

Cal shrugged. "A warm-up anyway."

"What happened when you got to the bedroom?" Kate asked.

"She let her dress drop. There was nothing underneath. Then Eban and the two of us stripped. Eban told us we could go first."

"You had sex with Rebecca," Kate said.

Cal cut a look toward Zach before coming back to her. "Yes. Together. We admitted that at the trial."

Zach said, "You testified that she was conscious. True or false?"

"Yes, she was conscious," he said, testiness creeping into his voice. "Hell, yes. She was stoned, but willing. No, make that *eager*. She was giggly, flirty, inviting. Uninhibited," he said with emphasis and defiance.

Going back to Kate, he said, "She was conscious enough to support herself on her hands and knees, okay? Eban staged it. Theo in front of her, me behind. He told us not to let up and not to finish until after she'd had an orgasm."

Kate said, "Was Rebecca all right with the 'play'? With having an audience?"

"Yes," Cal said tightly. "I swear to God. I swear on my baby's life, she was into it."

"It's not easy to talk about," Theo said thinly, looking warily at Zach.

Zach swore under his breath. "Look, you can take off the filters about the sex, all right? I don't care about that. What I care about, what I want to know is why Rebecca gets fed through a goddamn rubber hose."

In obvious distress, Theo cupped his hand over his mouth.

Kate gave them all time to settle down, then asked, "What happened after the ménage?"

Cal resumed. "Theo and I sort of crashed. Theo collapsed onto the floor. I stretched out on a lounger across the room. Rebecca stayed on the bed, lying on her back.

"Eban carried over the bottle of vodka they'd been sharing and told her to open her mouth. When she did, he poured vodka into it. Or tried. His aim was off. They made a game of the splashing. And then some spilled into her mouth. She strangled on it. Maybe that's what sparked the idea for Eban. Or maybe that was what he wanted to do all along. I don't know."

He stopped and looked over at Theo, who was fiddling with the zipper tab on his rain jacket, still leaving the narrative to Cal. He picked up. "Anyway, at first we didn't understand what he was talking about. We'd done some wild things, but never anything like that. He hadn't even mentioned such a thing."

"What did he say?" Kate asked.

"He told Rebecca he'd like to try something really exotic. It would give her an orgasm like none other. She would erupt. She would see God."

Zach said, "Did he tell her that, in order for this miracle to take place, he would choke her?"

"Yes, but he was tender about it. Sweet. He sat down on the bed and stroked her hair. 'Only if you're game,' he said. And she pumped her fist and said, 'Fuck yes.'"

Theo spoke up. "That's right. Eban looked over at Cal and me and, one at a time, asked us, 'You heard me ask her, right? And you heard her say yes?' We both nodded yes. We'd heard."

"But Rebecca wanted a safe word," Zach said.

"No," Theo said. "*Eban* said they needed a safe word."

"Eban?" Kate said. "Are you sure?"

Cal gave a definitive nod. "Yes. He said if you do kinky, you must have a safe word. Theirs would be Porsche. He had a hankering for one, he said. If Rebecca said Porsche, it would get his attention, and he'd be sure to stop. She laughed and said, 'Don't count on me saying it.'" As though he feared that Zach would challenge that claim, he looked straight at him. "That's what she said. Clear as day."

Zach cut him no slack. "But she did say the safe word, didn't she?"

"She tried." Cal shifted his gaze from Zach to Kate. "That's what we lied about. Eban was on top of her, missionary position," he said, giving an ironic snort. "Since then, I've learned that people who're into this asphyxiation thing usually use a garrote from behind. But Eban was facing her, and he had both hands on her throat, pressing down, right on her windpipe. She was..." He looked to Theo for help.

"At first everything appeared normal," Theo said. "They were going hard at it, but that wasn't anything different. Then Eban started up this weird chant. 'You like it. You love it. You love it, don't you?' Other things. Vulgar things. I noticed that her movements changed. They became frantic. She was twisting underneath him, digging her heels into the mattress, thumping his back with her fists, and not like in ecstacy. In panic.

"I was still on the floor, out of it, but I had enough of my faculties to recognize that she was struggling to breathe. I crawled over to the bed." He paused, swallowed. "Her eyes were this big." He made twin circles with his fingers. "Terrified. Like a trapped animal. Her mouth was open. She was trying to say something, but couldn't. Trying to breathe, but couldn't.

"I yelled at Eban, told him to stop. But he was past hearing. It was like he was possessed. Demonic. And he kept up that creepy chant. Scared the hell out of me. I shouted at Cal."

Cal said, "I was almost too stoned to move. I'd been watching them. But detached, you know? Like watching porn on TV. When Theo started shouting and punching Eban's shoulder and trying to drag him off of her, I realized something bad was going on. I couldn't even stand up straight, but I made it over to the bed.

"I took one look and knew that she was past being able to say anything, so I screamed 'Porsche, Porsche,' directly into

Eban's ear, and tried to pull him away. But, like Theo said, he was in another zone. Unlike I'd ever seen him, and I'd seen him wacked out completely. This was different. He seemed not to hear or feel or see us. He just kept pounding into her."

He had been talking rapidly, as though feeling the same surge of adrenaline, the same urgency he had in those moments when he'd tried in vain to prevent the tragedy. Now, he sagged weakly back into the chair and took several deep breaths. He ran his hand over his face, as if in an attempt to rub away the memory. Dully, he said, "Eban pulled out and came on her stomach. Then he flopped onto his back beside her and said, 'Man, that was fucking fantastic. Who's next?'"

The ponderous silence that followed seemed to have a heartbeat.

When Kate finally spoke, she asked quietly, "Who called 911?"

Theo cleared his throat, but his voice was still a croak. "I did."

"That pissed Eban off," Cal said. "He kept saying that she was fine, that she would come around. But anybody could tell that she hadn't merely passed out. Theo and I tried CPR, but it didn't do any good. We were so wasted, we probably didn't do it right. While we were frantically trying to get her to breathe, Eban repeated over and over that she had never said the safe word. How was he to know that he was taking it too far? He kept spewing stuff like that, right up till the EMTs got there. They worked on her. They rushed her out. But too much time had passed. I knew she was as good as dead."

All four of them started when a voice came from the direction of the kitchen. "That was quite a story."

There stood Eban, smiling like he'd arrived late to a party.

"And you two told it with such passion," he said. "Y'all kept me on the edge of my seat. Truly. I'd applaud you, but..." He raised the evil-looking pistol attached to his right arm with a brace. "...my hands are full."

Zach lurched toward the end table where Cal had set his father-in-law's gun.

"Don't!" Eban aimed toward Zach. "I'd really hate having to shoot you first, Bridger. If I did, you'd miss out on all the fun. No, I'm saving you for last." Then he swung the weapon in the direction of Theo. "But you outlived your usefulness ages ago."

Three shots *pop-pop-pop*ped. Theo opened his mouth but didn't utter a sound. He slowly crumpled forward off the hearth and onto the floor.

Eban said, "Well, that was easy."

Chapter 36

———◆———

Doug Pratt came awake abruptly and righted his head, which had been lolling to one side and giving him a crick in his neck. Dr. Gilbreath had come into Rebecca's room accompanied by a nurse, who went to the far side of the bed and went about checking her vitals and IV.

Embarrassed for having been caught sleeping, he started to stand, but decided he didn't have the energy, so he remained seated as he said to Dr. Gilbreath, "I thought you'd left for the day."

"I only went home for dinner. Have you eaten anything?"

"I will later."

"That's what you said hours ago, Mr. Pratt. You really should eat."

He glanced at Rebecca. "I'm not very hungry."

The doctor was holding a manila folder against her chest, obviously waiting for the nurse to finish her routine so she could speak to him alone. It was unusual for her to return to the facility after regular hours. She only did so if a patient was in crisis. He braced himself for what was coming.

Discreetly the nurse finished her tasks and left the room. Dr. Gilbreath closed the door behind her. "I have the results of the most recent lab work."

He'd been afraid of that.

"It's not what we had hoped for," Dr. Gilbreath said.

"The antibiotic isn't working?"

"Indications are that the infection is intensifying, not abating."

He drew in a breath so deep it made his breastbone hurt. "So, what now? A stronger antibiotic?"

The doctor pulled over the extra chair and sat down facing him. "I was duty-bound to notify Mr. Bridger of any change in her condition."

"I guess he's winging his way down here then."

"Actually, I've been unable to reach him. His cell phone is going directly to voice mail. I've left two messages, but he hasn't called back. The alternate number he gave me is for a Mr. Bingham."

"His old coach. They're real close."

"Yes, I spoke with him. He said Mr. Bridger is at home in North Carolina."

"Cell service may not be that reliable in the mountains."

"That's a problem, because, according to Mr. Bingham, Mr. Bridger doesn't have a land line. I was wondering if you know how I might go about contacting him up there?"

Doug looked at his daughter. He reached out and stroked her cheek with the backs of his fingers. He could tell her fever was high, higher than it had been this morning. "Is the infection serious enough that you have to talk to Zach tonight? The antibiotic hasn't had much time. Maybe by tomorrow morning it will have kicked in." He pointed to the folder containing the condemning lab report. "You could check things out again and, if called for, up the dosage."

"That would require Mr. Bridger's authorization."

This created a quandary. He could buy time by pleading ignorance and making it difficult for Dr. Gilbreath to reach Zach. But in the meanwhile, Rebecca's condition could worsen to the point where no amount of antibiotic would save her. If the doctor wasn't going to increase her medication before getting Zach's okay, then he was left with only one choice.

He said, "There's a deputy sheriff up there who's familiar with Zach. His name is Dave Morris. I have his cell number."

"Still going to voice mail," Bing reported to Melinda with disgust. "Zach hates phones. Has a bad habit of ignoring calls. No luck with Kate?"

Melinda held up her phone so Bing could hear Kate's request that the caller leave a name and number. She clicked off.

Querulous, Bing said, "Why'd she give you her cell number if she didn't plan on answering calls?"

"I'm sure there's an explanation."

"I'm sure there is, too." Bing figured he knew what Zach and Kate were doing that made them unavailable at the same time. He scowled and said under his breath, "Hope they're enjoying themselves."

"Did the doctor in New Orleans say that it was an emergency?" Melinda asked.

"Not in so many words, but that's the feeling I got. I don't think she would have resorted to calling me in search of Zach if it weren't."

"Lord." Melinda pressed her hands against her face. "If she dies, and Eban learns of it, he's liable to do anything."

Acting like an exclamation point, her doorbell rang.

She and Bing sprang from their chairs and headed for the front of the house. His tricky LCL chose then to act up. By the time he'd popped his knee back into place and caught up to Melinda, she had answered the door.

The man said, "Mrs. Parsons? My name is Sid Clarke."

Bing recognized him from having seen pictures. Melinda bristled. "I know who you are."

"May I come in?"

"No." She was about to close the door in his face, when he raised a hand.

"Please. I'm here to see Cal."

Bing stepped up. "What do you want with him?"

"And you are?"

"What do you want with her husband?"

Clarke frowned over Bing's rudeness, but he said tightly, "I can't locate Eban. I'm hoping that Cal knows where he is."

Melinda looked at Bing with apprehension, like he was supposed to know what to do in this situation. Hell, he didn't even know these people. He didn't know why Zach chose now not to answer his goddamn phone. He didn't know shit. What business was this of his, anyway? Why wasn't he at home relaxing in his chair with a cold beer and watching knights in armor chop each other's heads off?

In a guttural voice, he said to Melinda, "You'd better let him in," and moved aside to allow Clarke into the foyer.

But that's as far as he got. Melinda blocked him from advancing any farther. "Cal isn't here. He hasn't been at home since early this morning, and he hasn't answered his phone all day. I assume he's with Eban."

"Why do you assume that?"

She gave a bitter laugh and rolled her eyes. "I don't know where they are, Mr. Clarke. If I did, I would go there and pull Cal back by the hair of his head if that's what it took to get him away from your son. He's poisonous."

Despite the insult, Clarke's expression remained impassive. "Did Cal mention going to Belize?"

"Belize?"

"That's what Eban told me this morning. A getaway. The three of them."

"Theo, too?"

"Yes. Just like old times, he said."

He told them about Eban's scheduling the private jet and his own confirmation with the pilot. "I believe Eban covered his bases on the outside chance that I would check. But even after the pilot confirmed the flight, I was suspicious of this sudden getaway plan and thought it might be a decoy. So I went to the FBO on the pretext of seeing them off.

"The plane was on the tarmac, fueled and ready to go. Red carpet rolled out. Catering onboard and champagne chilling. The two pilots, the flight attendant, the traffic controllers in the tower, we all waited for the arrival of the three passengers, none of whom showed up."

Melinda backed into the wall and leaned against it for support. She looked done in. Bing wondered how many more hammer blows she could take.

Sid Clarke continued. "Over the course of that two-hour wait, I spoke to Eban three times by cell phone. He was as chipper as always. He apologized for the delay in their getting to the airfield. He said they'd been held up. First the rain, then the traffic, then a necessary return to the house to pick up something he'd forgotten to pack. A lie soon debunked by our housekeeper."

He gave a rueful smile. "My son obviously has no scruples about lying to his own father. Ultimately, I canceled the flight and began searching for him. I started with Theo. According to his coworkers, he put in a full day at the library and left at five o'clock, his normal quitting time. But his car is still in the employee parking lot." He let that sink in, then said, "I ask you again, Mrs. Parsons, do you know where Cal is?"

"What, are you deaf?" Bing had taken an instant dislike to Sid Clarke. He'd never trusted men who were smooth-talking during a crisis, or who wore shoes with tassels. "She already told you she didn't know."

"It's all right, Bing," Melinda said. She told Clarke what she knew about Cal's reporting to work but leaving early. "He didn't tell anyone. That isn't like him. It's not like him to leave the house with a suitcase and ignore my calls, either."

Clarke took a moment to absorb all that, then said, "My oldest and best friend killed himself last night."

The statement had come from out of nowhere and was apropos of nothing that Bing could tell. Melinda seemed just as taken aback.

"His daughter informed me of it this morning," Clarke said. "It was shocking news. Even more disturbing is that in Up's suicide note—"

"Up?" Melinda said. "Uncle Up, the lawyer?"

"Yes. How do you know him?"

She wetted her lips. "I know about him from Cal. On your behalf, he bribed Cal and Theo to give false testimony at Eban's trial."

Clarke didn't admit it aloud, but he looked resigned over their knowing and continued what he'd been saying before Melinda's interruption. "In his note, Up held Eban largely responsible for the unbearable guilt that had driven him to take his life." He paused and breathed deeply. "He closed the note with a warning for Ms. Lennon."

Bing reacted with a start. *"What?"*

"I warned her, too," Melinda said. "And I didn't even know about this suicide note."

"When was this?" Clarke asked.

Melinda told him about Kate and Zach's visit. "I told them I was afraid that Eban would make a preemptive strike."

Sid Clarke had begun to look a little green around the gills. "This is troubling. Eban's clever. He's conniving. He cooked up this Belize trip to throw us off track. I'm afraid to surmise why he went to all that bother."

Bing fisted a handful of Clarke's expensive lapel. "You're afraid to surmise that your psycho son is going after Kate and Zach?"

"I don't want to hazard a—"

"Fuck you." Bing let go of Clarke's lapel, reached past him, and snatched his jacket off the hall tree, then poked his index finger at the tip of Clarke's aristocratic nose. "If he harms either of them, you won't have clever, conniving Eban to worry about anymore because he'll be dead. I'll kill the little shit myself."

Melinda grabbed his arm. "Bing, wait! Cal's got the pistol, remember."

"Pistol?" Clarke said.

Ignoring him, Melinda wailed, "Bing, Cal will do whatever Eban tells him to."

"I'm bettin' he won't, honey," Bing said. "I'm bettin' he won't. You're welcome to come along."

She grabbed her handbag, pushed past Sid Clarke, and ran after Bing.

Chapter 37

———◆———

The gunfire was still reverberating off the high ceiling of Zach's living room when he disregarded Eban's warning and lunged from his chair toward the table where Cal's pistol lay. Another shot halted him, inertia rocking him forward as he regained his balance.

"You're just asking for it, aren't you, Bridger?" Eban said. "Touch that gun, and your new girlfriend dies. Or you can *sit the fuck down!*"

Zach raised his hands and began backing toward the seat beside Kate that he'd just left.

"No. Over there." Eban motioned with the braced pistol toward a tall-backed armchair, one of a matching pair that sat on either side of the wide stone chimney.

Zach calculated the distance between the chair and Kate. No. He'd be too far away from her. He stayed where he was.

Eban snickered. "Oh, I see your dilemma. How about I just solve it for you?" He aimed the pistol at Kate.

"I'm going!" Zach backed over to the specified chair and sat.

Kate had cupped both hands over her mouth in horror as she'd witnessed Theo's execution. She lowered her hands now and curled her fingers over the edge of the sofa cushion as though holding onto it for dear life.

Her eyes met Zach's, communicating to him that she understood the peril they were in, that she was mindful of Eban's derangement and their need to go along with him for as long as possible until an opportunity to escape presented itself. If ever.

Eban came farther into the room. When he reached the end table, he used his left hand to heave up the edge of it until it fell over. The ceramic lamp crashed. The glass shattered in the frame holding the picture of Zach and his parents. The pistol that Cal had brought landed beyond the edge of the rug and went sliding across the hardwood floor, but in the opposite direction of Zach's chair. He couldn't hope to reach it before Eban shot him, which would leave Kate at this maniac's mercy.

Eban walked over to the pistol on the floor and nudged it with the toe of his shoe, chuckling with derision. "Mine's a whole lot bigger than yours, Bridger."

Zach wasn't bothered by the phallic innuendo, but the comparison of the two firearms was worrisome. Zach was no expert, but he recognized the difference between a small, five-shot revolver like Cal's, and Eban's fully automatic .45. The brace was secured to his forearm by sturdy straps, which made the weapon an extension of his hand. He could kill all of them in a blink.

"You're supposed to be in Belize." That from Cal, who was staring at Theo's unmoving body.

"Well, hello, Cal," Eban said. "I thought you'd nodded off. Good of you to rejoin us."

Eban's cavalier tone jolted the other man. He jerked his head around toward Eban. No longer in a stupor of disbelief, his eyes blazed hatred and contempt.

"Surprised to see me?" Eban laughed and gave an exaggerated wink. "I thought you and Theo had agreed a little too quickly to the getaway idea. I had an inkling that you might conspire to turn on me, try to strike a deal with the state prosecutor over there." He pointed the pistol at Kate again, and Zach's gut clenched.

But Eban's attention immediately reverted to Cal. "I took the precautionary measure of going to your workplaces today and putting a transmitter—courtesy of Simply Simon, who keeps a warehouse stocked with toys like that—on each of your cars. What's funny..." He stopped to laugh. "I was doing that during our phone call when I offered to send a limo for you. You declined so graciously, Cal."

His voice changed to one of feminine sweetness. 'Thanks all the same, Eban, but Theo and I can handle our own transportation.' You were downright syrupy. But you were lying through your teeth. You never intended to fly to Belize with me."

"Not a chance in hell," Cal said.

Eban snapped his fingers. "I bet you feared that you wouldn't come back from that trip. You were afraid that you and Theo would fall victim to a violent crime, or get eaten by a jaguar in the jungle, or drown in the Caribbean. Did the thought cross your mind that the two of you might never return from one of our jaunts?"

Cal only glared.

"After all we've meant to each other, Cal, how could you think that I might arrange a fatality? Although," Eban said, dragging out the word, "your demises would have been convenient because, let's face it, you do—did—pose a threat to the quality of my future."

Cal still said nothing.

"Anyhow," Eban continued, "you picked up Theo right on schedule. So far, so good. But you didn't steer toward the airfield. No, you sped off in the opposition direction. I can't tell you how much that disappointed me. My two best friends, cutting out on me."

He shook his head in sadness, then shrugged. "The transmitter led me right to you. I parked my car next to yours there among the trees at the turnoff. Hell of a trek to this house, though, what with the fog and all. But I've got excellent night vision."

Suddenly, his affable posturing vanished. His eyes narrowed on Cal with malice. "You fucking traitor. Did your Pollyanna wife talk you into betraying me? Hasn't she realized yet that behind your sexy smile and bedroom eyes you're nothing but white trash? She—"

"Shut up about my wife."

"Or what? You're gonna engage me in fisticuffs?"

"You're going to burn, Eban."

"Oh, I don't think so. Dollface there thought she had it all figured out. Didn't you, Ms. Lennon?" He looked at Kate. "State prosecutor," he scoffed.

With his free hand, he reached into the pocket of his trousers and pulled out what appeared to Zach be a scrap of black cloth. But then Eban dangled it, and Zach realized it was a thong panty.

"You're nothing but pussy," Eban said to Kate. "Strutting through the halls of justice in your stilettos, trying to do a man's job. Sorry, baby, your little project failed. You underestimated me." He balled up the thong and threw it at her, striking her in the face with it.

She didn't flinch. She let the thong drop into her lap. Looking him squarely in the eye, she said, "Yes, Mr. Clarke, I egregiously underestimated you."

"She speaks!" he chortled. "Using big words, too."

"I underestimated your depravity," she said. "However, I do understand why you exploit it with such enthusiasm. It's all you've got. Without it, you'd be a waste of the space you occupy. You'd be a speck."

Zach wanted to cheer her. Without a qualm, she was facing down a monster. Inside, she might have been quaking in terror, but outwardly her demeanor remained cool. Her voice was low-pitched, definitive, tinged with scorn.

However this ended, she had achieved her goal. She might never prosecute Eban Clarke in court, but, by showing no fear of him, she had reduced him to insignificance. It was the best offensive play she could have devised.

The affront wasn't lost on Eban. His face had turned florid.

"She's right," Cal said. "You're a waste of space. All

posturing and guff. I can't believe I ever bought into your bullshit."

"You never *bought* a goddamn thing," Eban sneered. "I paid your way, and I don't remember you ever griping about my generosity."

"Generosity? That's a laugh. Anything you ever did, you did for *you*."

Eban pretended to ponder that, then sighed theatrically. "Too true."

"What thrill did you get out of killing Theo?" Cal said, his voice cracking. "Harmless *Theo*? For years he licked your boots. He tried so hard to please you, to get one kind word from you, and you killed him! *How could you do it?*"

"Well, I pulled the trigger. Like this."

Zach saw it coming but was helpless to prevent it. Eban couldn't have missed if he'd tried. Cal was too close, his torso too large a target. His arms flailed as the bullet struck, and he dropped.

Kate shouted in outrage and horror, *"No!"*

Eban swung the pistol toward her, but Zach was already on him, having lurched from the chair just as he'd fired on Cal. He grabbed Eban's right arm and redirected the lethal apparatus away from Kate and toward the ceiling. The next burst of gunfire shattered the globes of the chandelier. Glass rained down.

Eban caught a shard. He yelped and raised his left hand to his cheek. Zach wrapped both hands around the encased barrel of the pistol and angled it away from himself, away from Kate, as he rammed his shoulder into Eban's middle like he would a tackling dummy. Digging in, he pushed and kept going until Eban lost his footing and fell backward. His head banged hard against the granite of the wet bar.

Zach spun away. "Kate! The lamps."

She was already off the sofa. She ran over and slapped the wall switch. It plunged the room into total darkness, but Zach had a clear path to the front door. He bolted toward it, reflexively ducking his head as Eban, screaming in fury, released another barrage of bullets.

Kate already had the door opened. Zach shoved her out onto the porch, then grabbed her hand and ran like hell.

———

Dave Morris had replaced the Glock that that asshole Bridger had thrown into the woods the night of their fight. He'd gone searching for it in daylight, but it had been hopeless. A buddy who ran a pawn shop had sold him one under the counter.

Most of the swelling in his face had gone down, but the bruises were still evident. Everybody in town knew who was responsible for the whipping he'd taken, and that was the most galling thing of all, to have been bested by that has-been.

And even after he'd done the bastard a favor and told him about his ex-father-in-law's spying scheme, Bridger had won the ear of Sheriff Meeker, who, with Bridger's urging, was keeping him on unpaid suspension indefinitely.

After all the hardship he continued to suffer on Bridger's account, he questioned why in hell he was risking his neck to make this drive up the mountain in pea soup conditions to deliver a message.

However, the request had come from a doctor—Gilbreath, he thought she'd said—and it was more about Bridger's ex-wife than it was about the asshole himself, and Morris wasn't completely immune to compassion.

He was doing his good deed for the day. For the year, maybe.

But when he reached the turnoff to Bridger's place and discovered a chain across it, his altruism receded. *Who the hell and what the fuck?* He drummed his fingers on the steering wheel, considering his options. He wasn't an errand boy. He wasn't Bridger's private secretary, and sure as hell wasn't his buddy.

But he remembered his ex-wife as being a hot ticket. Face a ten, figure an eleven, and now she was on life support, for crissake.

In the trunk of his car was a pair of bolt cutters. He'd used them to carve that gash down the side of Bridger's pickup. To make up for that, he would deliver this damn message, and then they'd be square. He'd be done with Mr. MVP once and for all.

Cursing himself for being a soft-hearted sucker, he got out and took a Maglite and the bolt cutters from his trunk, then sauntered over and bent down to inspect the chain.

When he saw its heft and the quality of the lock, he muttered, "No way." Biting through those links was going to require more effort than he was willing to exert, and his bolt cutters would probably break before the chain did.

And this really wasn't Dave Morris's problem, was it? In order to drive up here, he'd left a cozy bar, a cold longneck, and a ten-dollar wager riding on a pool tourney. No, that doctor down in New Orleans would have to find another way to contact Bridger. He had tried.

He was walking back to his car when gunshots stopped him in his tracks.

Having lived in the area all his life, he knew that fog was deceptive. It could muffle sound or magnify it. It fooled you about the direction of its origin, and from how far away it had traveled. Even on clear days, sound waves ricocheted off the mountains in ways that defied physics.

But hell if he didn't think those shots had come from Bridger's place.

When he heard another spate of gunfire, he was certain of it.

He dropped the bolt cutters but kept his Maglite. He chambered a round in his new Glock, jumped the chain across the turnoff, and started up Bridger's private road, plowing through the fog.

———

Zach was so familiar with the trail he'd charted, he could run it in the dark, in the fog. He knew where there were boulders to dodge, low limbs to duck, fallen tree trunks to hurdle. He knew where runoffs, no more than mere trickles, could make rocks and forest debris hazardously slippery.

"How can you see where you're going?" Kate was panting, but she kept her voice at a whisper.

Zach had cautioned her to be as quiet as possible because he hadn't wanted to make it any easier for Eban to follow them. He hoped that whatever inevitable sounds they made would be overridden by the thrum of the waterfall.

"Just step where I step," he said.

"How do you know where to step?"

"I hike this trail several times a week."

"This is your hike?"

"This is it."

"This is a *trail*?"

"Low branch coming up on your right."

She cleared the branch without breaking stride. "Do you think Eban is coming after us?"

"What do you think?"

"Murderers don't leave eyewitnesses."

Zach guided her around a flat rock where he sometimes stopped to drink from his water bottle.

"But unlike you," she huffed, "Eban won't know where he's going. He won't be able to follow this trail. He'll turn back. He probably already has." When Zach didn't respond, she said, "You don't think so, do you?"

"I think we need to keep running."

"So do I. How far to the turnaround?"

He didn't have the heart to tell her that the turnaround was the white-water river at the bottom of the gorge. "Just stay right behind me and don't let go of my hand."

"Is it downhill all the way?"

"That's in our favor."

"But it's steep."

"If you lose your footing, I've got you."

Thank God they'd put their boots back on. Doing this barefoot would have been impossible. But their outerwear had been left behind, and the air was cold and laden with mist. Their labored exhales vaporized, swirling the fog in front of their faces before becoming one with it.

He wished for their cell phones, for the key fob to Kate's car. He wished for the pistol that had been of no use to Cal. He wished Kate didn't appear so small and easily breakable in contrast to the rugged, unforgiving terrain.

He hoped she was right and that Eban wouldn't risk coming after them. He hoped that Eban had emptied the clip and wouldn't have another. But he reasoned that those hopes were probably in vain. Eban believed himself to be invincible. He would stop at nothing.

And then, although he'd done everything he could to avoid stumbling blocks, an exposed tree root caught the toe of Kate's boot, and she fell. Her knee landed hard. Reflexively she cried out.

Zach came to a dead stop.

She stayed as she was on the ground until he gave her a hand up. "Oh, God," she mouthed. "I'm sorry."

"Are you all right?"

She nodded.

"Hurt?"

She shook her head and then would have said something, but he placed his index finger vertically against her lips. Cocking his head, he listened.

"Yoo-hoo."

The eerie, high-pitched call came from above and behind them, dashing their faint hope that Eban had given up the chase. Although it was difficult to tell how far back he trailed them, he was close enough to have discerned that they'd stopped.

"Giving up?" he called. "You must be getting winded. I know I am. Who made this damn trail, anyway? Must've been you, Bridger." He fired four rounds.

The loud report of the four shots caused both of them to cringe. But they also caused a thought to flit through Zach's mind. Before it left him, he snagged it with a whispered, "Fourth and short."

"What?" Kate mimed.

He reviewed the idea for all of a second and a half, then said to Kate, "Don't worry anymore about making noise. Let's haul."

With no more explanation than that, he grabbed her hand and took off again, going faster than before, trying to make up for the gain they'd lost when they'd paused. His long strides ate up distance. Without complaint, Kate kept pace. Whenever he felt her about to tumble, he drew hard on her hand to keep her upright.

They'd been moving so rapidly, she sensed immediately when he began to let up. Her breaths were coming from between her lips in ghostly puffs. "Why are we slowing down?"

He towed her forward until they came to the brink of a chasm. At some point in time, it had been caused by a geological calamity. To Zach's reckoning, it cut across the entire width of the mountain face like a crooked smile. The course of his trail had been predicated on it, because the crevice was narrower here than at any other place he'd found, and he'd explored it extensively.

When Kate realized she was overlooking a void, she immediately tensed and tried to back away. Zach held fast to her hand. Because of her fear of heights, he'd known she would balk. But she had to jump it. Blindly.

He placed his hands on her shoulders. "It's not that wide. I can practically step across it. Not that deep, either."

"I can't see the bottom."

"Because of the fog. I'll go first. Move back three steps to give yourself a running start, then jump. I'll be there to catch you."

"I can't."

"No way in hell would I let you fall."

"I can't do it."

"You can, Kate. You have to. You have to now."

He didn't have time to cajole her. He kissed her hard and quick, then released her abruptly and leaped across, landing easily. Although he had to admit that being unable to see the other side would have terrified him if he hadn't known that it was closer than one's imagination might make it.

"Stopped again?" Eban called. "Ready to cry uncle?"

"Kate!" Zach hissed.

"I can't see you!"

"I'm here. Do it. *Now*."

He heard her take the backward steps, then her running footsteps. He knew the instant she launched herself. He reached out. She actually overshot and landed against his chest like a fluttering bird who'd flown into a windowpane.

He wrapped his arms around her, hugged her tight, and drew her behind the trunk of a stout tree. He bent his head down low and burrowed into her neck where he could feel her pounding pulse.

"Perfect jump. Perfect. Now, don't move a muscle or make a sound."

"What?"

"Stay behind this tree."

"*What?*"

"Trust me, Kate. No matter what happens, do not move and *not a single sound*. Got it?"

She clutched at the sleeve of his shirt, but he pulled away and dashed across the path. As he'd anticipated, the sound of him smashing into undergrowth drew Eban's gunfire toward him and away from Kate. Bullets whizzed through the fog. One smacked into a nearby tree trunk; another struck the rock formation Zach had crouched behind.

When the fusillade stopped, Zach howled Kate's name. "No!"

Out of the fog came Eban's evil cackle. "Uh-oh."

"Kate? Kate? Oh, Jesus." Zach gave a tortured shout. "Clarke, you murdering son of a bitch!"

Zach could hear tree branches snapping and rocks scattering underfoot as Eban made his way down the path.

"Kate, talk to me," Zach crooned.

"You're breaking my heart, Bridger."

Eban was breathing so heavily now, Zach heard every labored inhale and exhale. He was picking up speed, coming on fast.

Zach moaned Kate's name. "Please."

"Aw, is she dead?" Eban taunted.

A thud. He'd run into something. He stopped, cursed a blue streak, fired several rounds. Then he began moving again, huffing breaths, rapidly stumbling along. "That's too bad, Bridger. Y'all looked so cute together."

"Where are you, Clarke?" Zach shouted. "I'm going to kill you."

"Oh, I don't think so. I—"

When the ground suddenly dropped out from under Eban, he uttered an exclamation of shock. As he fell, the pistol attached to his hand clattered against the sheer rock walls of the chasm, which tapered to a jagged floor much farther down than Zach had intimated to Kate.

In the last split second, Eban must have realized his doom. One sharp scream erupted from the crevice, but it was soon absorbed by the opaque, silent fog.

Zach waited. When no other sound was forthcoming, he came out from behind the boulder, walked over to the edge of the fissure, looked down, and said, "I doubt you saw God."

Chapter 38

—◆—

"Zach?"

"Here."

He drew Kate from behind the tree where she'd waited silently and motionlessly. Neither said anything, just clung to each other. Eventually, he ran his hand over her head, where her hair was damp and plastered to her skull. "Are you all right?"

"Basically."

She was holding it together, but her teeth were chattering, probably more from the aftereffects of the trauma than from the chill. He stroked her cheek. "For right now, basically is pretty damn good."

She glanced in the direction of the chasm and shuddered. "What do we do now?"

"Go back to the house. Notify the authorities. I don't have a land line. We'll have to use either Cal or Theo's phone to call in their murders."

"Oh, Zach."

"I know. They didn't stand a chance. There was nothing we could do. Still—"

Suddenly the fog became a winding sheet of glaring light, blinding them.

"Freeze!"

Neither did. Both raised a hand to shield their eyes. Zach made out the shape of the man. In his left hand he held a powerful flashlight. In his right, a pistol.

"Morris?" Zach said. "Turn off that damn light."

"Throw down your weapon."

"I don't have a weapon." Zach stepped away from Kate and slowly raised his hands.

Kate said, "Can you direct the light down, please? It's blinding us."

"And let Bridger slip away in this fog? I don't think so."

"I have no intention of slipping away."

"You were running from a crime scene. I heard gunshots. There are two dead guys inside your house."

"Which is why I was running away." Zach was about to lower his hands when the deputy brandished the pistol.

"Keep your hands where they are!"

"You can't think that Zach killed those men," Kate exclaimed. "Eban Clarke did."

"Clarke? What would he be doing up here? You know what? Save it. I'm taking you both in. Maybe the sheriff will give me my job back." He took a step toward them.

"Stay back!"

"Don't move!"

Responding to their simultaneous alarm, he stopped.

Kate said, "There's a crevice."

"Crevice?"

"A deep one," Zach said. "Directly in front of you."

The deputy pointed his flashlight downward and moved the beam along the ground until it shone on the brink of the drop-off. The emptiness below was layered over by a thick blanket of fog.

Zack said, "Eban Clarke is at the bottom of it."

"Holy shit. How deep is it?"

"Deep enough, and he took a hard fall."

"Dead?"

"That would be my guess."

Morris inched forward and called down several times. He got no response, not a moan, not a stir, not a breath. "Jesus. What happened? And I want to hear it from Kate, not you, Bridger."

"Eban Clarke tracked his two friends here." She told him their names and their reason for seeking her out. "Then Eban surprised us all." She described his arrival and the brutality of the murders. "He had this…" She looked to Zach for help.

"Clarke had a braced automatic forty-five."

"Zach and I managed to get away," she went on, "but Eban came after us. Heckling. Shooting sporadically. He had almost caught up." She paused, then said, "He didn't see the cranny."

Still holding his pistol aimed at Zach, Morris leaned forward slightly and again peered over the edge into the crevice. "He fell?"

"Yes," Kate replied.

"He wasn't pushed if that's what you're implying," Zach said.

"Cool it, Bridger. How'd you two get across?"

"We jumped," Kate said.

Morris snorted. "You expect me to believe that?"

Before Zach realized what she was going to do, Kate moved back several feet, got a running start, and leaped. She made a sure-footed landing, but Zach's heart almost burst from his chest. He hadn't been there to catch her. Morris held something in each hand. He'd been too astonished to have grabbed her if she'd faltered, and he was too much of a lummox to have done so even if he had been prepared. *Christ!*

"Everything I've told you is the truth," she was saying to the deputy. "Eban Clarke would have killed us."

"Are you going to shoot me if I come across?" Zach asked. Without waiting for Morris's permission, he jumped. Ignoring Morris's bluster, he said, "Put the pistol away. Kate and I don't pose a threat to you."

"No, just to my job. You're keeping me off the payroll."

"That was the sheriff's decision, not mine."

"But you—"

"Do your job now, and he won't have an excuse to keep you on suspension. Have you called in what you discovered at my house?"

Morris, still looking hacked, slid the firearm somewhere inside his jacket. "Yeah. They'll beat us there. But I need to let the sheriff know to dispatch Rescue and Recovery for

Clarke. Helicopter's out of the question," he said, looking through the fog toward the sky. "Cell signal is weak, but it might work."

Morris got the call through and soon was speaking to the sheriff in stops and starts, frequently asking, "Can you hear me?"

Kate placed her hand in the crook of Zach's elbow and turned him to face her. Speaking softly, she said, "Fourth and short. I get what you meant now. You faked Eban out to draw him offsides."

"That's what you try to do when you only need inches for a first down. Most of the time the ploy doesn't work. It did this time."

She placed her hand on his chest. "Thank you for saving my life."

"Thank you for coming into mine."

Whatever else might have been said went unspoken. Morris rejoined them. "Service was spotty, but we were able to communicate the main stuff. Sheriff's assembling the rescue squad. Wants to hustle them down here in case Clarke's alive. But they won't know where to find him. Says if I lead them down here, I'll get my job back."

"Let's not waste any time then. Stick close." Zach claimed Morris's flashlight and held it pointed down at the ground as he started up the trail in the lead, Kate's hand in his as she followed. Morris brought up the rear.

Speaking over his shoulder, Zach said, "Morris? What were you doing up here tonight, anyway?"

"Oh, Jeez. I forgot. I had an important message for you."

They made their way uphill as quickly as they safely could. Knowing Dr. Gilbreath must have an update on Rebecca's condition, Zach postponed calling her until he could get a clearer cell signal. He told Kate he didn't want their conversation to be fragmented.

After that, he said very little except to warn her and Morris of obstacles along the trail. The flashlight was of some help, but by the time they reached the plateau at the top, every muscle in her body felt like jelly, and her lungs were on fire.

In the cul-de-sac, her SUV was the only vehicle that didn't have multicolored flashers. Fog created halos around them and limned everything with a pulsating aura that made the scene appear even more surreal.

Uniformed emergency personnel wearing reflective vests were milling about, conferring with one another. Some were stringing crime scene tape from tree to tree.

Zach approached one of the officers and asked to borrow his phone, then went over and sat down on the stump where he'd set his coffee mug the morning she'd disrupted his peaceful existence.

Sheriff Meeker had been alerted to their arrival. He jogged over and met her and Morris at the twin stone pillars flanking the walkway. He introduced himself to her. An accompanying deputy passed her a bottle of water, which she gratefully accepted. Another draped a Mylar blanket over her shoulders. She clutched it closed against her chest.

The R and R team were geared up and standing by. Morris gulped a bottle of water, took another with him, and struck off down the path with the crew following. She actually felt sorry for him. She would hate having to make that trek again, especially knowing the difficult task awaiting them at the crevasse, even if Eban were still alive.

"Over here, Ms. Lennon." The sheriff indicated an ambulance where a paramedic stood waiting in the open doors.

"I'm fine."

He pointed down at her knee. The fabric of her slacks had split open. The blood was fresh. "I fell down and scraped my knee. It's nothing."

"Let's take a look."

She got the feeling he wasn't giving her a choice. Under the sheriff's guidance, she walked over to the ambulance but insisted on sitting down in the opening, not being lifted inside.

She peered around the sheriff in order to keep Zach in sight. He was still on the phone, pinching the bridge of his nose as he concentrated on what he was being told. When the sheriff turned to see what she was looking at, she said, "He had an emergency call."

"Morris told me."

The paramedic was swabbing her knee with antiseptic that stung. "Do you need oxygen?" the young woman asked.

"No. I'll catch my breath in a minute or two."

Her blood pressure was taken. When satisfied that she wasn't suffering from anything except fatigue, the young woman left her alone with Sheriff Meeker. "I've heard a lot about you, Ms. Lennon," he said. "All good. I regret we're meeting under these circumstances."

She nodded absently, her attention focused on Zach, who was now walking toward them. Looking at Kate, he gave a solemn shake of his head. "The infection has ramped up. Doug wants to keep her on the antibiotics. Wait and see. Maybe increase the dosage. Dr. Gilbreath needed my input."

Kate reached for his hand. "What did you tell her?"

"To hold steady until I can get down there. I need to go first thing tomorrow."

The sheriff said, "If that's the case, I'll free you up from here as soon as I can. Morris briefed me on what you told him happened. Crime scene unit is still in there conducting their investigation. They'll be questioning y'all separately." He looked down at their clasped hands. "I'm sure you appreciate why procedure is important, Ms. Lennon."

"Of course."

"Using their driver's licenses, we identified the casualties as Theodore Simpson and Calvin Parsons. Whose twenty-two pistol?"

"Parsons brought it," Zach said.

"Figured it belonged to one of them. I sort of pieced together why they wouldn't take kindly to you," he said to Kate. "But Morris said you told him they'd come up here to confess."

"To perjury. They lied at Eban Clarke's trial. Since then, both had undergone a change of heart."

"Clarke killed them before they could recant their story."

Answering with a soft yes, Kate hugged her elbows and glanced toward the house. "Are they still in there?"

"The coroner is examining the one," Meeker said. "The other, we got down the mountain as quickly as we could. Still don't know if he'll make it. It'll be touch and go."

———

Neither Bing nor Melinda had said much during the long drive from Atlanta. Bing had to concentrate on navigating, while she sat tensely in the passenger seat, staring through the windshield as though the force of her will would get them to their destination faster.

Bing couldn't wait to be at the end of this trip. On the other hand, he didn't know what was awaiting them. His conjectures on what they might find made his palms damp and his stomach queasy. He repeatedly told himself not to imagine the worst. Nevertheless, that's what he was imagining.

They had just reached the outskirts of town when his phone rang. He plucked it out of the cup holder where it had been charging. When he saw the unfamiliar number in the readout, he grumbled, "Don't those damn telemarketers ever sleep?"

"Maybe you should answer," Melinda said.

He harrumphed but clicked on. "Who's this?"

"Me."

"Zach!" Bing swiveled his head toward Melinda, who was biting her lip and looking at him with expectation. "Whose phone is this?" Bing asked.

"Are you still with Melinda?"

"Yeah, yeah, she's right here beside me."

"You need to drive her up here. Leave right now. Don't pack, don't do anything. Come immediately."

"We're already here."

"What?"

"We couldn't reach y'all. Sid Clarke showed up at her place and—"

"Sid Clarke?"

"Long story. We'll tell you when we get there."

"You can't get to the house. They've got the road blocked."

"Who's they?"

"Take Melinda to the county hospital. Cal's been shot, but he's still alive."

Chapter 39

The fog lifted, leaving only tendrils that looked like wraiths moving through the forest. The improving atmosphere made the recovery of Eban Clarke's body easier. Once it was pulled from the crevasse, it was evacuated off the mountain by helicopter.

Zach and Kate were separately questioned by Sheriff Meeker's homicide investigators. Their accounts matched to the letter, but they talked their throats raw before being given clearance to leave.

The sky had turned predawn gray by the time they wound their way down the mountain in her SUV and drove to the county hospital where, for hours, Cal Parsons had been stubbornly refusing to die.

Sheriff Meeker had provided Zach with a burner phone, so, throughout the wee hours, he and Bing had been in periodic contact. Their conversations had been brief, but each had kept the other abreast of developments. The most recent had been that Cal had survived the intricate abdominal surgery.

Now as Zach and Kate stepped off the elevator on the surgical floor, they found Bing and Melinda seated in side-by-side chairs in a compact waiting area. Both looked ravaged by exhaustion and mental anguish. Bing was patting her back and holding her hand, but he stood when he saw Zach and Kate.

Kate took his place next to Melinda and began talking to her in soothing tones.

Zach asked Bing, "Anything new?"

"He's still in recovery ICU. Surgeon said he had to stitch a lot of gut back together."

"How'd he keep from bleeding out?"

"One of two ways. It was either a miracle or a God thing."

"That's the same thing."

Bing shrugged. "You asked."

"What are his chances?"

Bing flipped his hand back and forth. "The surgeon served two tours in Afghanistan. Said he'd seen men die of less and others survive with worse."

Zach looked over to where Melinda was crying softly on Kate's shoulder. "How's she holding up?"

"Poor little thing is completely tuckered out, but she's as stubborn as a damn mule. Refused to let me get her a motel room. No rest, no food. Says she won't leave until she's seen her husband. Her folks are on their way here. Maybe she'll listen to them." He paused and gave Zach a once-over. "When's the last time you had a meal or looked in a mirror?"

He and Kate were wearing the same clothing they'd had on during their chase down the mountain and back up. Her bandaged knee could be seen through the tear in her slacks. Their boots were caked with mud. Exposed skin bore scratches and scrapes.

"As soon as the sheriff finished with us, we came straight here," Zach said. "We didn't even want to take the time to clean up. Besides, there was no privacy to be had. The house was full of personnel. Our bags are still packed. We brought them with us."

He watched Kate and Melinda for a moment, then remembered something Bing had told him earlier. "You said Sid Clarke showed up at their house?"

"From out of nowhere. He was looking for Eban. Admitted he'd been hoodwinked and had a bad feeling that his nutcase son was up to something."

"He called it right." Zach rubbed his forehead. "Eban shot those men in cold blood, Bing. Right in front of Kate and me. He would have killed us, too, if we hadn't managed to get away."

Bing laid his hand on Zach's shoulder and squeezed it hard. He didn't get sloppily emotional, but there were tears in his eyes that attested to how relieved he was to see Zach intact and unharmed. Gruffly, he said, "The one time I wasn't there to cover your ass, and look what happened."

"Thanks for being here now."

"Where else would I be?"

Zach pulled him forward and gave him a man hug, then walked over to where Kate sat with Melinda. He crouched down to be on eye level with them. Kate's solacing had helped Melinda collect herself, but she still appeared on the verge of collapse.

He said, "Listen, you're going to make yourself sick, and that's going to piss off your husband. Kate knows of a nice bed-and-breakfast here in town. Why don't you let us take you there and get you a room, get you fed—"

"No thank you," she said before he'd even finished.

He pressed. "Kate will stay with you till your folks arrive. I've got to head to New Orleans, but—"

"New Orleans?" Bing said. "What for?"

Zach ignored him. "Melinda, you need to rest."

She gave a firm shake of her head. "I'm not leaving until I at least see Cal, even if I can't talk to him."

"When will that be?" Zach asked.

"They're gonna let her know." Bing cast a sour look down the hallway toward the nurses' station.

Zach looked at Kate, then at Melinda, then without a word stood up and headed down the corridor. Within minutes, he returned with a nurse, who said to Melinda, "I'll escort you to Mr. Parsons's unit, but you'll have to put on a sterile gown and mask."

"Gladly." Melinda tearfully thanked Zach and Kate, gave Bing an extra-tight hug, then hastened down the hallway with the nurse.

As the three watched them go, the elevator doors behind them opened. They turned just as Sid Clarke stepped out.

He didn't look like the man always featured in photographs, standing tall, emanating self-confidence and arrogance. As he came toward them, he looked vanquished, his bearing drained of all pride and hauteur.

He made fleeting eye contact with Bing but didn't acknowledge his scowl. He addressed Zach and Kate. "I'm Sid Clarke."

Neither said anything, but Zach bobbed his chin.

"The morgue is in the hospital basement. I accompanied my son's body here." He stated it quietly and without rancor. "Theo had been brought earlier. I confirmed his identity. I asked the staff about Cal's condition and was told he was undergoing surgery. So…" He raised his hand in a gesture of helplessness. "I came to inquire."

After a lengthy and solemn silence, Zach said, "Cal has made it so far, but he's not out of the woods. It could go either way."

Looking pained, Sid gave a slow nod. "His wife?"

"She's with him now."

Clarke's gaze moved to Kate. "Kathryn Lennon?"

"Yes."

He looked her over, noticed the tear in her pants leg, the bandage, her dishevelment. "Are you all right?"

"I'll be fine."

"Good. That's good." His voice had thickened, and he seemed at a loss as to what to say next. He heaved a deep breath. "I spoiled Eban rotten. I also refused to acknowledge his all too apparent predisposition for cruelty, his tendency toward violence. Consequently, I must assume responsibility for the destruction he caused, in particular your former wife's unspeakable tragedy, Mr. Bridger. You also suffered greatly from that. An apology is insufficient. In your place, I would rebuke it. But I *am* sorry. If ever there's anything I can do for you, I—"

"Actually, there is," Zach said, surprising them all, especially Sid Clarke himself.

He looked at Zach with a ray of hopefulness. "Name it."

"You have a jet. Rebecca Pratt is in crisis. I have a duty to her. I need to get to New Orleans."

"When?"

"Yesterday."

Without a moment's hesitation, Sid Clarke pressed the down button on the elevator. "I'll make the calls. Meet me in the entrance lobby in ten minutes."

Once he left them, Bing rounded on Zach. "Why the hell would you ask a favor of him?"

"He's not doing me a favor, Bing. I'm doing him one."

Later, Zach recalled only snatches of the hours between leaving the county hospital in North Carolina and arriving in New Orleans.

Bing had excused himself on some pretext, allowing him and Kate to have a private goodbye, which had been abbreviated but emotional. "I'm leaving you here to face this mess by yourself when it was my house, my property, my mountain," he'd told her. "I won't be here to help you fend off the media jackals."

"I'm not afraid of them."

"You've proved your mettle." He chucked her under her chin. "Jumper of chasms. When you jumped it without warning, I nearly had a heart attack."

"You lied about how deep it was."

"It was the only way to get you across it."

They'd smiled at each other, but their smiles had been bittersweet because of the reason for his rushed departure. She'd said, "Without Eban as a factor, there's no longer any pressure on you to make a decision about Rebecca."

"No legal pressure, Kate, but pressure of a different kind."

"Do you know what you're going to do?"

"I swear I don't. I'm hoping that once I get there, I'll have some clarity." After a long, lingering kiss, he'd left her under Bing's watch.

He'd expected Sid Clarke to drive him back to Atlanta, but they only had to travel one county over to a private airfield that had a landing strip long enough to accommodate Clarke's jet.

While they'd waited for its arrival from Atlanta, which was barely a half-hour flight, Zach had availed himself of the FBO's shower room to clean himself up and change into clothes packed in the duffel bag he'd retrieved from Kate's car.

By the time he'd emerged, the jet had landed and was waiting for him on the tarmac. Clarke had walked him out to the plane. "Thanks for this," Zach said.

Sid, still looking humbled, said, "It's the very least I could do. I'll send it down for your return."

"That's unnecessary. Besides, I don't know when that will be."

"I only need a couple hours' notification."

Realizing that Clarke's generosity was his way of trying to make recompense, Zach had left it alone and graciously accepted. They'd shaken hands; Zach had climbed aboard.

The flight attendant had served him a hot breakfast, which he'd eaten ravenously, then he'd reclined his seat and slept. He hadn't awakened until the attendant had tapped him on the shoulder and politely asked him to fasten his seat belt for landing. A chauffeur-driven car arranged by Sid had been waiting to transport him directly to the special care facility.

Now, here he was.

He stood on the sidewalk looking at the facade of the building, reconciling himself to the obligation that Rebecca had taxed him with, bolstering himself for the inevitable turmoil that awaited him.

This morning, people were waking up to the news about Eban Clarke's death and the bizarre circumstances of it. Whatever Zach did in the next few hours would create a national groundswell of interest. What should be an intensely private resolution to his soul-searing dilemma would once again become a public debate.

The only way to get through it was to get through it.

Dr. Gilbreath was waiting for him in her office. She'd been fully apprised of last night's events. As he sat down across the desk from her, she said, "I'm glad you and Ms. Lennon escaped unharmed. This situation with Rebecca couldn't have come at a worse time for you."

"I don't know, Dr, Gilbreath. In a way, with Clarke's death, it seems that everything has come full circle. There's a weird symmetry. Karma. Cosmic intersection. Something."

She nodded with understanding and then began explaining Rebecca's condition, not in medical terms, but in layman's language. She kept it factual. She didn't editorialize, proselytize, or advise.

When she finished, he said, "What you're telling me is that Rebecca could stave off this infection, but the aftereffects of both it and the medications might weaken any or all her systems and leave her susceptible to further complications."

"That's right."

"She won't ever get better and could continue to deteriorate." When she hesitated to reply, he said, "I know. You're not God." He lowered his head and addressed himself more than he did her. "If she survives this round, there will be another. I'll be faced with the decision again. And again. And again."

"Until Rebecca succumbs," she said softly.

"Or Doug agrees to become her guardian."

"Which he remains reluctant to do."

"Because he's not done punishing me."

Dr. Gilbreath didn't say anything, but regarded him with sympathy, then got up and said, "I'll leave you to think over your options."

He remained seated, focusing his eyes on nothing, letting his thoughts take him where they would. They tapered into detailed pinpoints. They ventured onto aimless tangents. He considered various actions and the ripple effects of each. He brooded on inaction and its dreary forecast.

Eventually, all his musings crystallized into a solid resolve: He wouldn't remain fettered by this obligation for one more day.

On the surface, even to his own mind, it seemed so fucking selfish. But he shouldn't be indefinitely consigned to this heartrending treadmill, and neither should Rebecca's father.

He got up and opened the door. Dr. Gilbreath was just outside the office, leaning against the hallway wall, arms folded over her midriff, patiently waiting.

Zach said, "Is he here?"

"In the chapel."

Zach pushed open the door to the dimly lit room. A center aisle divided six rows of cushioned pews. At the front was a small altar, although it wasn't designated for a particular religion. Above it was a faux stained-glass window, lending the space the reverent atmosphere of any house of worship.

The room must also have been soundproofed, because it was perfectly silent, and empty except for Doug Pratt, who sat in the back row with his head bowed. Carpet absorbed Zach's footfalls, but when he reached the end of the pew, Doug turned his head toward him. "I've been expecting you."

"I got here as quickly as I could." Zach sat down in the pew in front of Doug's, placing himself at an angle so they could talk face-to-face.

"I heard about what happened last night up on your mountain. Eban Clarke is dead?"

"Yes."

"And one of the other two?"

"Theodore Simpson. Cal Parsons is hanging on by a thread."

He gave Doug time to comment, but he didn't.

Zach resumed. "Before Eban shot them, they spoke candidly to Kate and me about the night of the party. They owned up to their complicity." He spared Doug the description of his daughter's final minute of sentience.

"They had no part in the asphyxiation except to wait too long to try to stop Eban, and, when they did, their efforts failed. They confessed to perjuring themselves about Rebecca's attempts to say the safe word. They were genuinely remorseful, I think."

"Little good their remorse does Rebecca."

"In so many words, they acknowledged that also. An apology can only go so far. If Cal Parsons lives, he will regret Rebecca's tragedy until his dying day. I'm certain of that."

Doug lowered his head, saying under his breath, "No better than he deserves."

They lapsed into a weighty silence, each realizing that they now had arrived at the crux of the matter. Zach delayed no longer.

"Rebecca is in a bad way, Doug. I know that Dr. Gilbreath has told you how unlikely it is that she'll improve. I'm no longer comfortable with extending her life only to stand by and watch her steadily decline."

Doug raised his head and looked at him directly.

"There are two choices open to you," Zach said. "The first is for you to legally become Rebecca's guardian and release me from this ill-gotten obligation, which both of us resent."

"Let you off the hook."

"Yes."

"No."

That was the reaction Zach had anticipated. Neverthe-less, he hated hearing it, because it forced his hand. "Then I'm going to exercise the authority Rebecca vested in me, do what I believe with all my heart and soul that she would wish, and request that life-sustaining measures be discontinued."

Doug stared at him for at least half a minute. Zach didn't back down, didn't avert his gaze, just stared back.

After a full thirty seconds, Doug stood up and walked to the end of the pew. Zach expected him to turn out of it and head for the exit. Instead he came even with the pew in which Zach sat and reached into the back pocket of his khakis.

He pulled out a folded sheet of paper. "You don't have that authority." Carefully he unfolded the sheet, the creases of which were threadbare and discolored from having been folded and refolded so many times. Doug held the sheet out toward Zach. "*I* do. I have all along."

Chapter 40

———◆———

Zach came to his feet and snatched the sheet of paper from Doug's hand, demanding, "What is this?"

"Rebecca's most recent medical directive. It revokes the one that named you as her agent and assigns me instead."

The typewritten letters on the page seemed to squirm and scramble so that Zach couldn't arrange them long enough to make sense of the words. But snippets finally coalesced.

In the event . . .

. . . a condition determined to be irreversible . . .

. . . I request that all treatments be discontinued or withheld . . .

. . . allow me to die as gently as possible . . .

. . . no life-sustaining measures . . .

. . . no feeding tube or other device . . .

It was dated months after their divorce was finalized. Rebecca had signed it in her flourishing handwriting. It had also been witnessed by two people Zach had never heard of.

He looked at Doug with a mix of fury and incomprehension, shaking the paper in front of his face. *"Why?"*

"Because her choices went against my beliefs."

"Your beliefs? Your *beliefs*! My *life*," Zach shouted. "Rebecca's life. You son of a bitch! You expressly went against what she stipulated. How many times have you gotten in my face, yelling about adhering to Rebecca's wishes? And all along...? God, when I think of the hell you've put me through!"

He was so furious, he could feel the heated blood pulsing through the veins in his temples. He raised both hands, one still fisting the directive, and barely resisted the urge to throttle the man.

"You think having a Bible at your elbow makes you holy? Righteous? That it gives you license to play with other people's lives? You're an unforgiving, lying, vindictive hypocrite."

He looked down at the directive and slapped the back of his hand against it. "These witnesses. Who are they? Do they even exist? If so, where have they been? Why haven't they come forward to expose your deceit? Was this ever filed with an attorney?"

Doug let him smolder for what seemed a very long time. When he did answer, it was in an infuriatingly bland tone. "After your divorce, Rebecca was flitting from here to there, never staying in any one place for long. She used our mailing address as hers, so she wouldn't miss any official or important correspondence.

"Your attorney sent the notification that you'd changed your will and directives. I advised her to do likewise. She planned to come down for Mardi Gras. She said she would take care of it then.

"I printed out the Louisiana state forms off the internet. They were standard, nothing fancy, but officially binding. It was supposed to be easy. But when we got down to it, Rebecca did a one-eighty on the life-sustaining instructions. She said that when y'all drew up the originals, she'd gone against your leanings just to aggravate you."

"That part I believe," Zach said, still seething. "What about the witnesses?"

"Men from my church."

"Like-minded?"

"Yes." Doug puffed his chest up. "Men who believe only God can give or take a life."

"Wrong," Zach fired back. "Unless you believe that Eban Clarke was carrying out God's will last night when he killed Theo Simpson in cold blood."

"The devil does his work, too."

"He sure as hell does. This is the result of it." He raised the directive again. "How did you get away with this?"

Doug's lips formed a stubborn line, and he stayed mute for so long that Zach thought he might have to wring the answer out of him. Eventually he said, "I swore the witnesses to secrecy. Since they shared my beliefs on the matter, they swore an oath never to reveal that this document existed."

"Not even when Rebecca lost all brain function."

"Especially then."

Zach's anger had gradually ebbed into dismay. How could a man who wore religion on his sleeve, who was so proud of his piety, be so deceitful? "You never filed this with a lawyer?"

"No. Only Rebecca's new will and a POA for business matters."

"She didn't follow up?"

"No. She was off in England with a tennis pro."

"I remember. Their affair ran hot and was all the rage."

"Only for the length of the Wimbledon tournament."

Hearing the note of sorrow in Doug's voice, Zach felt a twinge of pity for him. Which the man didn't deserve, he reminded himself. "What did Mary have to say about this new directive?"

"She knew nothing about it. When you showed up at the hospital in Atlanta, she was under the impression that the old one was still valid. She was so afraid that you would side with the doctors' recommendations, exercise that substituted judgment thing they kept harping about, and take Rebecca off life support."

Zach thought about the reason he hadn't followed the doctors' recommendations: Rebecca's unknown pregnancy. Had Mary and Doug known of it, he imagined the additional hysteria it would have caused. Quietly, he asked, "What if I had decided to exercise substituted judgment, Doug? Would you have produced this then?" He slapped at the document again.

"No. Mary and I would have had to let her die."

"Yes, let her die, but let me take the fall for it. For doing precisely what Rebecca had mandated in this new directive."

Doug raised his shoulders in a shrug before letting them slump back into place.

Zach gave a bitter laugh. "You made me out to be the bad guy who sailed in and welcomed the opportunity to kill my cheating ex-wife."

Doug just looked at him from beneath his sagging eyelids.

"You fed me to the cannibals. Why? Was that my punishment for divorcing your daughter?"

"No, for marrying her."

Zach shook his head in bafflement. "You disliked me that much? To that extent? You dismembered my life, Doug. What did I do to deserve that?"

"You corrupted my daughter."

"I did not," Zach said hotly. "Rebecca was well on her way to rack and ruin when we met. We never would have met if she hadn't been out advertising the goods and trolling."

"Oh, I know she was living wild. I got calloused knees from praying for her salvation. I held out hope for it. Then you entered her life. Your fame, your money. Hobnobbing with movie stars and rock bands, giving her access to every kind of vice."

"I can't deny the access," Zach said. "But she indulged on her own, not with me, never with me." Glutted with memories of their angry encounters over Rebecca's substance abuse, he raked his fingers through his hair. "She showed up at one of our home games so stoned and making such a spectacle of herself, the other team wives called security and had her escorted out of the stadium.

"Do you really think I encouraged or nurtured that kind of behavior, Doug? No. It was humiliating. The drugs, the booze, the affairs she flaunted. By the time she and I split, she'd become an embarrassment, not only to me but to herself."

Doug backed across the aisle and sat down on the armrest at the end of the pew. His torso caved in. His head hung heavily between his shoulders. "Mary told me I was wrong to hold you responsible. She and I didn't disagree on much. We sure did about that, though. She said I was wrong to place the blame on you. But I had to blame somebody. Somebody besides myself."

He turned his head aside and looked toward the altar, but Zach got the impression that instead of the colored window behind it, he was seeing years unwinding into the distant past.

"We named her for the Rebecca in the Bible. From her toddler days, I drilled religion into her. It didn't take. She rebelled against it. Mocked it. The more I preached, the more disobedient she became. She defied every form of punishment, became incorrigible. By the time she got to high school, it was like her hobby was to shame us.

"When she flunked out of her first semester of junior college, we had a big blowout. That was the tipping point. She told us she'd had it with us, with our dull and dreary life. She said, 'I'm going to do my own thing, and you can't stop me.' After she slammed out of the house, bags packed, Mary cried for days."

He paused and coughed behind his fist to cover his emotion. "I loved her from the day she was born. I still do. But I . . . I'm not sure if I ever told her that I loved her. Not in so many words." He wiped his nose on his sleeve.

"I've spent many an hour thinking back, asking myself if I shouldn't have lectured her so hard. If I had been a little bit more bending, maybe she wouldn't have been at that party in Atlanta, wouldn't have been seeking a new thrill. Wouldn't have . . . wouldn't have have gotten herself choked."

Zach waited in silence for half a minute before crossing the aisle and handing the directive down to Doug. "I won't be sworn to secrecy about this, Doug."

Doug took the sheet of paper and smoothed it out against his thigh, as was obvious he had many times before, fermenting in his guilt for keeping its edict to himself. "I'll hand it over to Dr. Gilbreath."

"You realize what that will mean?"

"Means you'll finally be off the hook, Zach." With his fingertip, he traced the swirly signature at the bottom of the document. "And Rebecca will do her own thing."

Epilogue

———◆———

I missed you, but it was very decent of you to stay with Doug," Kate said as she snuggled closer to Zach. She was curled up in his lap, in his favorite chair, in front of the fireplace where a low fire burned.

"He needed a lot of help dealing with it. Dr. Gilbreath was a godsend."

"I'm sure her compassion was genuine, but it's also her job to render comfort. For you to stay was a kindness Doug didn't deserve, but it was the sort of thoughtfulness I've come to expect from you. That is, since I've gotten to know you."

"Since you've gotten to know me?" he said.

"Well, that first morning, I thought you were—"

"A complete ass."

"As I had always assumed you would be."

"What changed your mind?"

"Our first French kiss."

He laughed, hugged her closer, and tipped her face up for a repeat of that first kiss.

During his three-week stay in New Orleans, the entire main room of his house had undergone a restoration. He'd assigned the overhaul to the original designer-decorator, who'd temporarily abandoned his current project in order to restore Zach's home to its pre-catastrophe state.

The hardwood floor had been taken up and replaced with new, as had all the rugs. A new chandelier had been installed. Everything that hadn't been replaced had been thoroughly cleaned.

Even so, Zach had wondered how he would feel when he returned to it. Had the events of that terrible night left a permanent taint? Would the main room forever evoke memories of what had taken place there?

But this afternoon when he'd stepped inside for the first time since his absence, sunlight was pouring in through the two-story wall of windows at the far end. Kate had been attending a flourishing orchid on the new end table. The photo of him and his parents had been reframed. Bing had been arguing with an electrician who was perfecting the range of a dimmer switch on a replacement lamp.

The domestic sight had wiped clean all the bad memories. The only sensation he'd experienced was one of eager anticipation. He wanted to make new memories in this house he loved, with the woman he loved.

Yes, he'd reached that conclusion. He loved Kathryn Cartwright Lennon and couldn't foresee his future without her at the heart of it. The kiss they were now engaged in demonstrated just how much he desired that life with her and how soon he wanted it to start.

After they broke apart, he stretched out his legs toward the new coffee table, intending to place his feet on it. But a fruit basket was taking up almost every square inch of the surface. "Who sent that monstrosity, and what for?"

"Mr. Mackey Parks."

"The general manager of GreenRidge?"

"He delivered it himself this morning."

"You're kidding."

"During the restoration, he sent some of his contractors up here to help so the work could be accomplished in a timely manner. He asked me to tell you that he was sorry for all that you'd endured at the hands of Eban Clarke, and that you will no longer be pestered by delegates from his sales team. He said that you've more than earned your side of the mountain."

"Decent of him."

"And he'd love to treat you to eighteen holes whenever you want to play."

"I'll see."

"It might be good for you to come down from the mountain every now and then," she said. "Get acquainted with some local men, hang out, knock back a couple of beers, swap dirty jokes, belch, scratch your privates."

"How do you know what men do when they hang out?"

"Don't try to get me off track." She ran her finger down his cheek. "You've been a hermit for a long time. Too long."

"You're beginning to sound like Bing. God help me."

She didn't let him tease her out of acknowledging the elephant in the room. She reached up and smoothed a strand of his hair back off his forehead. "You don't have to live in seclusion anymore, Zach. It's done. Over. Are you ready to talk about it?"

"To you, yes. Not to anyone else."

"You have my sacred trust."

He stared into the flickering fire. "After Doug signed off, it took a long three days. Rebecca wasn't suffering, but he was. It was agonizing for him. He stayed in the room with her most of that time. I left him to himself.

"After she passed, he just seemed lost. That's why I stayed for so long. He couldn't hold a thought, couldn't complete a task. I intervened. People still respond to a request from *the* Zach Bridger. I played the celebrity card to make things go as smoothly as possible."

"He did you a terrible wrong, Zach. You went beyond forgiving him. How did you do that?"

He thought on it, then said, "If it had been my child? My only child?" He stared deeply into her eyes. "If it had been you? I think I might have killed anyone who tried to coerce me into letting you go."

Her eyes filled. "You're going to make me love you, aren't you?"

"I'm working on it."

They held each other's gaze for the longest time. There was still a tremor in her voice when she said, "You never told him about Rebecca being pregnant, the lost child?"

"No. He and Mary were spared that."

She nodded slowly, then, "What about Rebecca's funeral?"

"Wasn't typical of New Orleans. No jazz band. It was sedate, private, with only Dr. Gilbreath, me, a few of the facility's staff, and a handful of Doug and Mary's friends from their church."

"Media?"

"None."

"You shamed them into staying away."

After Rebecca died, he'd gone outside the facility to address the crowd of reporters and photographers who'd been assembled for days on the lawn and in the street, awaiting word. He'd figured the longer he dodged them and refused to comment, the longer they would hound Doug and him, becoming increasingly persistent. In the hope of avoiding that, he'd met them head-on.

He'd waited mutely until the throng had stopped hurling questions at him and then he'd announced that Rebecca had died peacefully and that he wouldn't answer any questions about it.

His remarks had been televised on national newscasts. So he'd been told. He hadn't watched.

"It was a brilliant statement, Zach," Kate said. "It struck just the right chord. The line about the gladiator was inspired."

"Gladiator?"

"You said that communications technology and social media have changed the world in positive ways. But that they've also created a public arena in which anyone, not only celebrities, but anyone, could find themself defending their privacy, their integrity, even their life, for the amusement of a universal, bloodthirsty audience."

"I didn't say gladiator."

"But that's what you meant."

"Whatever I said, it thinned out that crowd at the facility, and they stayed away from the funeral."

"Because of the circumstances of his death, Upton Franklin's funeral was also understated," she said. "The AG attended. He told me that Sid Clarke sat alone and wept quietly throughout the service."

"What about Eban's?"

"No observance, private burial in the family plot. Rumor is that Sid has left the running of his conglomerate to chief executives and has gone abroad for an unspecified length of time. He's been disgraced, and he had a long way to fall. He's rather pathetic, isn't he?"

With Doug's profound grief fresh on his mind, Zach wasn't ready to be quite as merciful as Kate, but he didn't envy Sid Clarke the years he would spend trying to live down the tragedies wrought by his son.

"Theo?" he asked.

"Another quiet service. I was unable to attend, but I sent something and signed it from both of us."

"Thank you. You're back in the AG's good graces?"

"Oh, my, yes," she said with a wry smile. "Secretly, I think he's relieved that it ended the way it did."

"He can tick the Eban Clarke box."

"Correct. Problem solved. He didn't have to publicly address a muddy issue, and his hands stayed clean. At a press conference, he publicly commended my courage to tackle the tough cases."

"Did the son of a bitch mention that you narrowly escaped with your life?"

"As a footnote."

"Bastard," Zach muttered.

"Doesn't matter. I know he'll always be a politician first."

After more muttering, Zach said, "Cal is still on the mend?" He'd been released from the local hospital and taken back to Atlanta.

"He's expected to make a full recovery, hopefully before the baby arrives. Bing was going to return to Greenville via Atlanta so he could stop and check in with them. He and Melinda have formed quite a bond."

"Should I be jealous?" Zach asked.

She laughed. "I don't think so. He's devoted to you, Zach. He loves you."

"Both a curse and a blessing."

"You don't fool me. You love him back. In any case, before he left today he invited himself to spend Thanksgiving up here with us."

He gave her a dubious look. "Can you cook?"

"Hmm, basics. But a Thanksgiving dinner is beyond my skills, so Bing offered to bake the turkey."

"Be afraid."

Again she laughed. "He'll have help. Mother will make the side dishes."

He raised an eyebrow.

Sheepishly, she said, "I included my parents. I hope that's all right."

"Sure. As long as they like football."

"Not to worry. They're big fans. Fair warning, Daddy will be starstruck."

"Even though I'm sleeping with his daughter?"

"Just that once."

He growled, "More than once."

"We only slept for an hour, though."

"But I had carnal knowledge of you three times."

"Three if you're counting...*that*."

"Oh, I'm counting *that*." He ran his thumb along her lower lip, pressing down the center of it with the pad and pushing it between her teeth to touch her tongue. "Before *that*, I thought you licking off that coffee foam was the sexiest thing I'd ever watched."

Her cheeks flooded with color, and she made a breathless little sound as she moved his hand away from her mouth. "You got us off track again."

"Not me. I stay on this track." He slipped his hand under her top and into her bra cup. "Which is good, because it seems like you're planning to spend a lot of time here."

"Well," she said, removing his hand from her breast and assuming her firm prosecutor's voice, "there are a few logistics to be worked out first, Mr. Bridger."

"Like what?"

"Like an invitation from you."

"You're invited. What else?"

"I have a job. I'm good at that job. I want to keep that job."

"So keep it. I have a job that I'm good at, too, and I plan on keeping it."

"But I want you, too. So much."

"That's the only thing I needed to hear, Kate. It's the only thing that counts. We'll work out the logistics as we go along. One day at a time. Okay?"

"Okay. But—"

"But?"

"I am a planner."

"I have a few plans myself." He looked around. "This is a big place. We should fill it up."

"Your decorator has done a more than adequate job of furnishing it."

"Yeah, but I was thinking more along the lines of a boy to teach to throw a spiral. I don't know much about little girls, but no reason for them not to toss footballs around, too, is there?"

Kate pushed away from him and sat up straight. "You're skipping about five steps."

He scooped her up into his arms and headed for the staircase. "There's one step we're skipping that I'm going to fix right now."

Even carrying her, he climbed two stairs at a time. In the bedroom, he set her down and cupped her head between his hands. "Do you want to lie down?"

"Not necessarily."

Mouths fused, he backed her against the wall. After a fierce kiss, he began undressing her, tugging at articles of clothing—cursing the uncooperative ones and tossing them aside when they came free—until he knelt and peeled off her slacks. He kissed her through a pair of underwear so small and sheer as to be token. They didn't last long.

And then his mouth was on her, sipping at her, seeking

with his tongue that pleasure point that soon had her clutching at his hair and repeating his name in gasps and groans. He continued to press and stroke until her climax subsided and she wilted over him.

He stood, bringing her limp form with him, and carried her to the bed, where he laid her down. She watched with drowsy but lustful eyes as he hurriedly undressed. "You're gorgeous, and I love you." She reached for him. "Come here."

He stretched out over her and, in a fever to possess her, penetrated the soft, giving femininity with a primal mating urge that stole their breath.

Number twelve, who had saved hard-fought, bone-breaking, bloodletting championship games with a final-second touchdown pass, had been saved from himself by this beautiful, dainty creature with hair the color of a rising full moon and eyes like blue topaz.

With every thrust, he spoke her name in a whisper of fervent thankfulness for the day she'd trespassed onto his property and into his heart.

When he came deep inside her, his soul didn't shatter.

It broke free.

THRILLINGLY GOOD BOOKS FROM CRIMINALLY GOOD WRITERS

CRIME FILES BRINGS YOU THE LATEST RELEASES FROM TOP CRIME AND THRILLER AUTHORS.

SIGN UP ONLINE FOR OUR MONTHLY NEWSLETTER AND BE THE FIRST TO KNOW ABOUT OUR COMPETITIONS, NEW BOOKS AND MORE.